Praise for the Mindspace Investigations Novel
Clean

"Hughes's world is an intriguing one, a world of flying cars and noirish, steamy streets that are a fun blend of *Chinatown* and *Blade Runner*. The cat-and-mouse murder investigation between those who can both kill and hunt with the power of the mind is fascinating. . . . Hughes knows how to unfold a mystery to be sure she never loses sight of her characters' humanity. She understands the nature of addiction, and has a keen understanding of the human condition, with all of its desires, fears, and frailties. I look forward to jumping back into Mindspace again."

—James Knapp, author of
State of Decay

"A solid, tightly written story." —*Publishers Weekly*

"I am addicted to this world, this character, and this writer. Alex Hughes spins stories like wizards spin spells . . . a stellar debut!"

—James R. Tuck, author of the
Deacon Chalk series

CLEAN

A MINDSPACE INVESTIGATIONS NOVEL

Alex Hughes

A ROC BOOK

ROC
Published by New American Library, a division of
Penguin Group (USA) Inc., 375 Hudson Street,
New York, New York 10014, USA
Penguin Group (Canada), 90 Eglinton Avenue East, Suite 700, Toronto,
Ontario M4P 2Y3, Canada (a division of Pearson Penguin Canada Inc.)
Penguin Books Ltd., 80 Strand, London WC2R 0RL, England
Penguin Ireland, 25 St. Stephen's Green, Dublin 2,
Ireland (a division of Penguin Books Ltd.)
Penguin Group (Australia), 250 Camberwell Road, Camberwell, Victoria 3124,
Australia (a division of Pearson Australia Group Pty. Ltd.)
Penguin Books India Pvt. Ltd., 11 Community Centre, Panchsheel Park,
New Delhi - 110 017, India
Penguin Group (NZ), 67 Apollo Drive, Rosedale, Auckland 0632,
New Zealand (a division of Pearson New Zealand Ltd.)
Penguin Books (South Africa) (Pty.) Ltd., 24 Sturdee Avenue,
Rosebank, Johannesburg 2196, South Africa

Penguin Books Ltd., Registered Offices:
80 Strand, London WC2R 0RL, England

First published by Roc, an imprint of New American Library,
a division of Penguin Group (USA) Inc.

First Printing, September 2012
10 9 8 7 6 5 4 3 2 1

 REGISTERED TRADEMARK—MARCA REGISTRADA

Printed in the United States of America

PUBLISHER'S NOTE
This is a work of fiction. Names, characters, places, and incidents either are
the product of the author's imagination or are used fictitiously, and any
resemblance to actual persons, living or dead, business establishments,
events, or locales is entirely coincidental.

The publisher does not have any control over and does not assume any
responsibility for author or third-party Web sites or their content.

ALWAYS LEARNING   PEARSON

To Paula Gillispie and Julie Gray, because I promised.
To Dan Marshall, because he deserves it.

CHAPTER 1

My first interview of the night was Esperanza Mensalez-Már, a thirty-something woman dressed in a pink-pressed suit I suspected cost more than my last paycheck. Not that I'd seen the paycheck, but that was the kind of impression she gave off, like she had too much money to cope. She was here as a suspect in the death of her husband.

A uniformed officer escorted me, today's babysitter to make sure I didn't break any laws while interrogating. He took a menacing position at the back of the room and glared at the woman like she was his worst enemy— exactly what I wanted.

I entered, carrying my props: an old-fashioned ream of paper and two sharpened pencils. From the tape they'd given me, I'd pegged Esperanza as a control freak. So I threw the paper down crooked, spilling it everywhere, adding the pencils so they rolled along the table, then slouched back in the chair. I grabbed one of the pencils just before it hit the floor and started tapping it on the table. *Tap, tappity-tap. Tappity-tap, tap, tap.* Just for fun, I altered the pattern every now and then to keep it grating on her nerves.

I stared at Esperanza for a long time while the pencil tapped against the table. Since Lieutenant Paulsen had exiled me to the interview rooms again, I'd be here three hours or more with nowhere else to go; I thought about that hard, knowing some of it would leak into my face.

After ten minutes, her hand shot out and flattened mine against the table, stopping the pencil. "Stop," she said. "Just stop."

Once her hand touched mine, I had what I needed. "I'm required by law in this situation to tell you I'm a Level Eight telepath."

Her hand shot back immediately. She wiped it against her skirt by reflex, as if she'd touched something slimy. The cold mask she'd worn had transformed into a look of abject horror. "You—"

"I'm also required by law to tell you that skin-to-skin physical contact increases my ability to read your mind. Under certain conditions, it can be hazardous to your health and mental well-being, so for most people it's considered wise to avoid all physical contact with telepaths." I quoted the standard write-up the Guild gave the public. In reality, touch was only dangerous when the telepath wasn't expecting it, and I'd figured her to do just what she had. So I'd blocked as a precaution. Any normal could have told you all she was thinking about was the tapping anyway.

She started to say something, but I cut her off. "I'm very impressed, Esperanza."

"It's Mrs. Mensalez-Már," she said evenly, steel in her voice. I'd hit a nerve.

I slouched back in the chair and started tapping the pencil again, staring at her patiently. I'd noticed in the previous interviewer's tape that the more he attacked her on a point of her story, the more she'd get cold and professional. So I'd back up, let her own fears work on her a bit. See what would happen.

She couldn't take the silence long. "You can't possibly—"

"I can feel how much you hated him," I stated calmly, in the tone of voice you'd use to start a long story. "But the hyphen on your name was worth, what, four hundred thousand ROCs?"

"Eighteen million," Esperanza corrected, her eyes narrowing.

"The house alone was worth, what? Maybe two?"

"Three point eight." She preened.

"It was a masterful plan. You must have set it up two years in advance. More maybe." My tone was admiring, flattering.

"Four," she sniffed. "The idiot never even saw it coming."

I got in three more questions—with answers— before her brain caught up.

Suddenly, her eyes widened as she realized what she'd said, and the ugliness in her soul came out like a plague. "I want a lawyer," Mrs. Mensalez-Már said. "Now."

I pulled out a pack of blue cigarettes and lit up, breathing in the nicotine a little desperately. I was on the smoking porch, an old slab of cracked concrete with a little awning behind the main bulk of DeKalb County Police Department Headquarters, where the shadow of the four-story building cooled down the air a few degrees at this time of day. In August in Atlanta, when the heat flattened you like the arms of a heavyweight boxer, you'd take whatever relief you could get.

As I stood, sweat already beginning to gather in a pool at the top of my shoulder blades, I tried to retrieve my sanity from wherever I'd left it last. I wanted Satin, a drug, a habit, a poison—the fantasy I'd denied myself for three long years. It would have been six if I hadn't fallen off the wagon twice. If it had been six, would this be easier? As my hands shook with a need for something I couldn't have, I thought, It has to get easier. I couldn't have that rush, that stark perfection, not today. Not today.

My hands shook and my brain cramped while I took another desperate drag of nicotine, looking out over the grimy courtyard and the old steel building behind it, watching the drizzly rain migrate more pollution into the soil. I struggled to focus, to remember the cops behind me. There was a reason I worked for them. On my better days, I knew they'd keep me on the wagon or die trying. Never mind the hostility. Never mind that I had to keep up a steady supply of rabbits to pull out of the hat just to earn my place.

When the Telepaths' Guild kicked me out, I had all the tests, all the ratings, all the gold stars a man could get. Level Eight, seventy-eight-P, I was a stronger telepath than most of the elite, and could predict the future correctly better than three times out of four. Still could, at least when the precog felt like working, but it hadn't in months. Lately I was starting to run out of rabbits, not good for my relationship with the cops. Speaking of . . .

Behind me, the heavy door creaked open, and I greeted the mind behind me. "Cherabino."

Detective Isabella Cherabino was a thirty-something brunette, stacked, pretty, a workaholic, and perpetually in a bad mood. We would have been partners if we had been equals, but we weren't. I was her pet cobra, maybe, or the monkey with the cymbals that followed her around. If a monkey could solve crimes in Mindspace, or pull rabbits out of hats and interview suspects, if the monkey was a dumb guy who annoyed her at regular intervals, that's maybe what I was to her. Maybe. On a good day.

On the porch, her nose wrinkled at the smell of the cigarettes.

"I don't understand why you like it out here. It's miserable."

I shrugged. "It's scenic." It was also deserted, at least ten feet from anybody's thoughts in Mindspace. Stressed-out cops, suspects freaking out about inter-rogations, hostile criminals . . . Let's just say the men-tal surroundings reeked. Even the heat was a break.

"I heard about the confession. Do too many of those and they won't ever let you out of the interview room again." She looked at me critically. "If you're feeling twitchy again, I can wait while you call Swartz."

I snuffed out the cigarette under my shoe, ignoring the comment. I didn't want to talk about my craving to my sponsor right now. I could feel Cherabino's tension and a hint of purpose—probably a new case—but she got testy when I jumped ahead. "What can I do for you?" I asked her.

"You've heard about the murders?"

"The serial thing, right?"

Her jaw tightened. "Captain says we don't say serial. Try to keep it quiet. Hope the papers don't put it together." She was obviously not a fan of this plan, but Cherabino could toe the line when she had to.

She was thinking loudly, and I didn't bother shut-ting her out. Six bodies? Really? "Six bodies in two months, it's a serial. Doesn't matter what they call it."

"*If* they can link them," she returned. "We aren't pub-licizing cause of death, and the victims aren't related any way I can see. Might take them some time, and in the meantime we have a shot at solving it." Her "we" meant her, the team, and me . . . specifically.

"Why me?" I asked.

She frowned at me. Oops, jumping ahead again—have to watch that.

"We're stuck. As I suppose you already know. I was

hoping you'd do the Mindspace thing and get me a lead. Or two. Two would be nice."

I thought about another cigarette and gave it up as a lost cause. She was going to ask me to leave now. I didn't think I had any other priority interviews scheduled this afternoon. I rubbed my jaw, thinking, and along the way realized I hadn't shaved . . . since yesterday morning, felt like. Maybe a little longer. Have to take care of that soon.

"You listening?" she spat.

I blinked. "Yeah, just let me get my stuff and check in with Paulsen."

It took her a minute to realize she hadn't asked me to leave yet and that I'd read it straight off her mind. She stared and seriously considered slapping the hell out of me. "Stay out of my head, damn it! I've told you before."

I stepped back, and she stalked off. Great, now I'd made Cherabino mad at me, and I knew better.

I sighed, wishing for another cigarette, and fought down guilt. At least now I wasn't craving my poison so bad. Distraction was a great trick, one of the first ones they teach you in the program. If I was going to see a crime scene, there would be plenty more distraction— even if it was stuff I'd rather not see.

I patted down my pockets, made sure I had everything, the lighter and pack where they were supposed to be, and rolled my sleeves back down. I didn't advertise the scars on my arms, not for any reason, and if long sleeves in August were the price I had to pay, so be it.

I held on to the car door with a white-knuckled grip, and took deep breaths. Cherabino had hit the flyer anti-grav in the middle of the groundstreet—highly illegal—risen up two stories within the span of a second with no warning, and was now flipping off the BMW who'd had the temerity to get in her way. She merged into the correct sky lane, narrowly missing the floating marker.

Below, a police-sponsored sign on the old Decatur train station's roof reminded commuters: fly safe and in your lane. Not that there was irony or anything.

Cherabino turned on the siren for no good reason and forced herself into the air traffic over East College Avenue. She got too close to the air stream from the bullet train on the railroad tracks below and the flyer dipped alarmingly—I swallowed bile—but she recovered, muttering obscenities.

I thought about reminding her about the new fuel/flight restrictions for the department, but her mental cursing got louder. I took a breath and blocked her out, giving her the privacy she'd demanded. It was a lot harder than it should have been.

Her driving regained a measure of sanity as she leveled off and set the altimeter to auto. I looked down as the shadow of the police cruiser fell on the dirty redbrick buildings and the stream of groundcars below. It was lunchtime congestion, the yuppies out for quick carnivorous lunches fighting with the second-shift blue collars already late for work in the factories to the east.

I decided to risk talking. "You said there were six victims?"

"That's right." She adjusted a mirror, gave a suspicious look to the driver minding his own business behind her, then glanced back at me. "In order: thirty-something male Hispanic, an old white woman, a young black one, Indian scientist forty-something, and the two Asian teenagers from last week. I can't see they have anything in common other than the way they were dumped—and trust me, we've looked."

"You look worried," I said.

She sighed. "He's escalating, to have another this quickly. And I need a break in the case. Badly."

"You don't know it's a he," I said. "Do you?"

"You kidding? It's always a man with a group like this. Women take murder a lot more personally."

She had a point, but I replied, "Nobody says it can't be a group."

"Don't be a smartass," Cherabino said without malice. Garden roofs and skyboard advertisements dotted the tops of the otherwise-grimy ancient buildings below as we crossed west into the East Atlanta borough. "God knows we need a break in this case, yesterday. Captain got a phone call from the mayor Tuesday. He wants this solved, *before* the papers start splashing 'serial' across the front page."

"Something like that could be bad for business. Not like a normal murder or anything."

"Yeah." She blew out a long line of air. "These are anything but normal."

I could feel a line of worry coming from her, and I blocked harder. A flash of an upcoming date next week came through—I frowned. What were we talking about again? Oh yeah. "What's so different about these?" I asked. "Other than the hodgepodge of victims."

Her lips pursed. "Everything. There's no obvious cause of death. No weapon marks, no fresh wounds, tox screens clean. If the bodies hadn't been dumped, we probably would have assumed stroke, maybe even for the teenagers. There's just no reason why they should—"

I suppressed a yell as Cherabino grounded too quickly on Hosea Williams Street—not dangerous, not illegal, but scary as hell without a warning.

She glanced back over at me disapprovingly as if her driving was my fault. "The fact I can't connect the victims is starting to piss me off. No serial I've ever heard about picks random victims off the street this different—they always have a type. They work the type. Every briefing in the world says they work a type."

"I thought we weren't saying serial."

"Multiple, then. Whatever." Cherabino took a turn. Now the buildings on either side were three stories tall with cracking facades and battered brick, making the small street claustrophobic.

She pulled into a weed-grown rocks-and-grass field labeled parking and cut off the car. I let go of my grip on the handle.

Cherabino turned to look at me, tension in her brown eyes. "You okay?" I knew she was referring to earlier, on the porch, the craving that still sat in the back of my head like an unwelcome neighbor. She could smell it when I got twitchy, after five years of working together on and off, and she'd taken the last dive off the wagon very personally.

I looked at her, backlit by the sun like an angel, a grumpy beautiful angel. A lock of hair had escaped from her bun and lay across the soft curve of her cheek. I suppressed a sudden urge to tuck it behind her ear. I was supposed to keep my hands and mind to myself. Even if I wanted more sometimes.

"Okay?" Her voice cracked like a whip, bringing me back.

I coughed and sat back. "I'm fine." Probably I'd say that if I was lit on fire and covered in supercancer, but that was beside the point. "Um, crime scene?"

"Yeah." She opened the car door and let the heat in. "Time to go to work."

I got out of the car, the strength of the heat and the sun nearly knocking me over. I put on a pair of cheap sunglasses and hurried after Cherabino, who was moving toward a nearby alley. Judging by the wind blowing a certain smell our way, our body was in that direction.

Something she'd said earlier was bothering me, and I fished it out of memory. "Why a stroke?" I asked. "I thought you said they had nothing in common."

She glanced back, nose scrunched up against the smell. "They don't. Just the brain damage."

"That's what a stroke is, Cherabino."

She shook her head, her face growing cold as she prepared herself for the scene ahead. "Not if it's specific. All the victims have damage in exactly the same spot."

I stopped walking. It took her a minute to realize I'd fallen behind—a minute before she was yelling at me to hurry the hell up.

This was not good, I thought, as I complied. This was very not good.

The alley was long and skinny, two painfully hot brick walls behind the abandoned shell of a Thai restaurant. There was an empty dumpster at one end, coated with the smell of old garbage, a smell that mixed in bad ways with the reek of three-day-old decaying body in the heat. I told myself I never had to eat Thai again if I didn't throw up. No vomiting in front of the cops. I was a consultant, not a cop, and they'd never let me live it down.

Three forensic techs filled the alley with careful thoughts while they took samples of every conceivable surface and mark. Two more detectives and a couple of beat cops were here, murmuring among themselves, angry at their helplessness to catch this guy. They deferred to Cherabino but gave me hostile looks.

Myself, I was standing maybe six feet away, near the mouth of the alley, trying to take in the scene.

Cherabino came up behind me with an electronic notebook. She was one of maybe six detectives in the department authorized to carry them, since she helped out with Electronic Crimes. She had to pass a background check to do it, and the notebook didn't even have a transmitter. Police data within spitting distance of a transmitter was just asking for trouble—even those of us too young to remember the Tech Wars could agree to that.

"You about ready?" Cherabino asked.

I noted the lab techs. "Any physical evidence to link the cases to this point?"

She sighed. "Not yet. We're waiting on the lab for a few generic fibers, a couple of footprints, piddly stuff. I'm not holding my breath."

"The labs backed up again, huh?"

"Yeah. Since the mayor called, maybe we'll get bumped up in the queue. But I don't think there's anything there to find."

I took a moment to dip my toe into Mindspace, see what I was facing. "We need to clear out the alley," I told her.

"Why?" She looked up from her notes.

"Because."

Cherabino sighed and tucked her notebook under her arm. She moved away from the wall, took a deep breath—somehow, without gagging—and yelled at the crime-scene techs. "Everybody out!"

She dealt with the murmuring, the threats, and the

complaining without batting an eye. I stayed against the wall, out of the way, until she gestured me forward. Impatiently.

I moved to the center of the scene, six inches from the dead body. The smell was almost overwhelming; the only reason anyone had found the body, after all, was the smell leaking into a shop three doors down.

I fought down bile at my first look; the face was swollen horribly and covered in maggots. The thing had emptied its bowels, as dead bodies tend to do, which only made the smell—and the insect issue—worse. I made myself change my pronoun, after taking a closer look at the clothes. He. *He* had been out three days in the worst of the heat and pollution, at the height of the summer, I told myself. He couldn't help this.

His clothes had originally been clean, well kept; he'd been wearing pricey workout gear, new shoes, with a short haircut. Probably athletic, considering the attire, but hard to tell for sure. His dark complexion was still obvious if you could get your brain to focus past the flies. Black man, like one of the others, I thought. Couldn't tell the age, but not a kid and not old.

I wanted my poison, but my mind wasn't kaleidoscoping, my hands weren't shaking, and I had control over my stomach—mostly. I had to hold back a gag as the wind changed. I was okay. Time to work.

"May I?" I asked Cherabino. She allowed me—reluctantly—to use her as an anchor when I went deep enough into Mindspace to need one.

"I guess," she said, and braced herself, holding out the "hand" I needed as the anchor. She blanked her mind so forcefully I knew she was hiding something. It took a real effort not to find out what it was, not to pull it from her mind. I didn't *need* her cooperation. I was strong enough—and well trained enough—that she probably wouldn't even know. But she was off-limits, and doing me a favor. I'd respect her and leave it alone.

She made some scathing comment I ignored as I eased all the way down into Mindspace, until I felt the vibration of the minds of the forensic techs who had just left. I should have had her clear them out earlier; two of the men had been excited about a strip club they'd seen last night, and ethereal images of the dancers marred the surface of the space, mixed with the intense anger and frustration coming from the cops.

The rest of my senses faded away, grayed out until Mindspace was all I could perceive. My link with Cherabino trailed up into reality behind me like a long, flat, yellow extension cord—yellow where no yellow should ever be. I could not see in this space, but I knew its depths and its shallows in the back of my head, a picture made by vibrations like a bat echoing through the night, a world complete without light.

The alley was full of emotion-ghosts, layer upon layer of shifting vapors left by excited minds on their way to something else. The walls were porous here, and I could feel the very faint ghosts of harried restaurant workers through the bricks, while outside insects swarmed with flittery hive minds over the rotting food in the dumpster. The dancers the techs had created leaped around imaginary poles, fading already.

A few old junkie-spikes dotted the walls, most from cigarettes or heroin, the occasional street cocktail. None were very recent, and none had the cloud-cut feel of a high-grade Satin boost.

In the center of the alley there was a cold void, both expected and unusual. From the body itself I felt only absence, something I expected since his mind would have gone on to . . . wherever minds went when they died. But the void was still there. Three days after the death, it was still there. Something was off.

"The victim died here, in the alley," I said, and in the back of my mind felt Cherabino making note of it.

Most of the other bodies were killed off-site, she said, as if from a hundred miles away. *Any idea how it was done?*

I walked out carefully and tested the area around the void. Fear permeated the space, and with it the stench of death so terrifying, anyone with any trace of Ability would know something bad happened here. I gulped down bile. This was probably why the victim hadn't been robbed; no one with any Ability or any sense at all was going to get this close. The techs all had to be deaf as doornails.

I tried to put it into words: "He knew he was going to die, was dying already, no details on how. He was terrified—it's pretty bad. Very bad. But . . ." I took a closer look. Something was wrong, the ghost of his mind almost . . . patchy. Disappearing in places, strong in others. "His ghost is wavering in and out like a bad radio station, even now. I've never seen anything like this before."

I combed the area carefully, looking for the traces of the killer. I found him, his mind separate from the victim's. He was worried, scared, disgusted . . . but not angry. He also felt familiar, like a song just out of reach. I had no idea where I knew him from.

There was also another man, farther down the alley, this presence so faint it could mean nothing at all. Both men were telepaths, I thought, which was bad news. Anyone who could feel a man's mind die while he killed him went at least a little insane. To do it outside a war or a threat to your family, to do it without any pressing reason at all . . . A chill came over me. I didn't think I'd like these guys. Not at all.

One last look at the void, running my not-there fingers around the cold edge, trying to see if I could get any more information about cause of death, about the killer's intentions or how he did it. I tried to pick that vaguely familiar trace out of the middle of a haystack of violence, sharp fear and urgent, dull pain, desperation—

Decade-old instincts were all that saved me, and I pulled back desperately. The world stopped. Then I was back in the alley, heart pounding a million miles per hour. Cherabino looked at me quizzically, as if she'd felt the edges of my panic.

"I'm okay," I told her, trying to be convincing, working on breathing deeply to slow down my heart. What had just happened? The back of my head said . . . something bad.

I thought through it. That feeling, like I'd just escaped Falling In. Which was impossible. Nobody Fell In three days after a death.

Telepaths died occasionally from that sort of thing; there'd been cases where, if you knew a dying person well, if you were connected to him at the time, you could be pulled in after him. Almost happened to me once, when my then-girlfriend's mother had died faster than anyone expected. We'd both almost been sucked in to . . . wherever minds went when you died. We'd barely pulled each other out. But even then, death was gone from the room a few seconds later. I wouldn't have been able to Fall In if I'd tried.

I needed another look—dumb as hell, but what I needed. I opened myself back up to Mindspace, slowly, slowly, sinking back in all the way, to the depths, too deep to see anything but vibrations.

I approached the edges of the void, slowly, slowly, so carefully it hurt to move. There, overlapping the edge of the void, was something, like the tiny chip in a wine-glass you noticed more with your fingers than with your eyes—an aberration. Small, not exciting. But it could crack our case.

If the killer or killers had really used Ability, there should have been, well, a smear, where they'd walked away, taking the edges of the death with them for a few steps before it dissipated. But the smear wasn't there.

Instead, the Mindspace puckered. Just a little pucker. And it was *good* to have a certified Guild education, because I knew what that meant.

Now I only had to explain it to Cherabino.

CHAPTER 2

Sergeant Branen was the head of Homicide and Cherabino's boss, a short forty-something man with overstyled hair and an air of confidence that made you want to trust him immediately. This made me dislike him on principle. He didn't understand what I did and didn't feel he needed to—but he did believe in results, and the conflict made for interesting meetings.

Branen was also one of only three people in the department who could get me fired at any time. It was my goal in life—at least in front of him—to be twice as useful as annoying.

"So," he said after the second time I'd gone through what I'd found in the scene. "There was a . . . pucker in . . . Mindspace. What exactly does that mean?" He smiled his habitual smile, his eyes tired. His tiny beige office was almost too neat, his battered desk and guest chairs scrupulously clean.

"It's very rare," I said, carefully neutral. "Like I said, it's a small aberration in the fabric of Mindspace, a hiccup in the ghost, if you want to put it that way."

Branen looked pained. It wasn't a good look on him. "You want to fight the Guild for jurisdiction and data . . . because you found a hiccup?"

"Not exactly." Although let's be honest; I'd fight the Guild for a lot less. In this case, though, I just wanted some information from them. Nothing for Branen to get so worked up over. Just information.

Cherabino noticed my attention flagging. "Does it work with the fish-tank analogy?"

"Um, maybe?" The downside to Cherabino's sharp mind was that she got insufferably grumpy until she understood what was going on. Back in the beginning, she'd pumped me for weeks about the telepathy before I'd given her a good-enough analogy to get her off my case. She just didn't understand Mindspace—no matter how eloquently I tried to explain it—so I'd had to get creative. Don't ask me why the fish tank made her happy; it just did, so I used it a lot.

"I'm waiting," Branen said.

"Okay," I began. "Imagine the world is a fish tank. One of those huge, multigallon monstrous fish tanks they have in ritzy offices. Better yet, picture the alley as a fish tank. You have sand on the bottom, and a definite ceiling, maybe even a sand castle or two, some coral. It's a nice place. There's all sorts of fish in it—you and Cherabino and half the world are shiny orange goldfish, Guild telepaths are those monster Japanese goldfish— what do you call them?—and you have a couple rogue bottom-feeders. So you're going along, doing your goldfish thing, until one of the goldfish discovers an Ability."

Branen sighed. "How is this helping me?"

"I'm getting to it. Now, what happens if one of the goldfish goes quantum and pops over to the other side of the tank?" I stopped, then explained, "He teleports." Cherabino seemed to be following okay; she wasn't asking her usual slew of questions. "Two things happen. The water's going to shoot out in a little explosion where he pops in, because now you have, say, an inch cubed of goldfish mass where there didn't used to be any, and the water has to move out of the way very suddenly. It's kinda messy, though, and it's hard to identify that's what it was if you weren't there at the time. But the other thing that's going to happen is on the other side, where he started out. Suddenly, the water has the same-sized hole where the goldfish used to be, right? So it rushes in. But the water thing's only an analogy—the way it works in Mindspace, the water moves weird, slow like honey, and what you're left with is a little area where the water is less dense, and comes to a weird little pucker to show you where the fish used to be. At least for a few minutes."

"A few minutes?" Branen echoed, struggling with the concept. "So, what you're saying is, our suspect teleported out of the area slightly before the police arrived. He was visiting the body?"

"Not exactly," I said, a little defensively. "It was a hot spot, and he was pulling along more than his own metaphysical weight, so it was like two of the monster Japanese pond-rats popped out together. The hole takes longer to fill in."

Branen sighed. "So we're talking teleporter. Which means Guild." He rubbed his head. "And the victims? They're not Guild, correct?"

"Correct, sir. They're not in the Registry." Cherabino sat back in her chair comfortably, but then again she and Branen got along great. Me, on the other hand . . .

Well, I had to say it. "They could be low-level, normal jobs, normal lives."

They both turned to me. "What?" Cherabino said.

"You know the Guild's Registry is only a partial list of members, right?" Their shocked looks told me obviously not. "It's an industry list. If you want to hang a shingle and make money off your Ability—and you're legit—you go through the Guild process, you get trained and certified, pay the money, and you get registered. They get dues every year; you get the resources of a large organization and sometimes a job." For the low-level guys, it wasn't a bad deal. You kept your nose clean, you showed up at the mixers, you went home every night, and you raked in the money.

"So it's like the Bar Association?" Cherabino leaned forward.

I shrugged, stretched out in the chair. "I don't know much about them."

"Organization for lawyers? Total control over your professional future, takes money from you and you have to be a member?"

I blinked. "Actually, that's not too far off. But the Guild's only like that if you're powerful enough. On the low end of the scale, it's optional. If you don't want to work for them, if you want to be an accountant, or a lawyer, or a bricklayer, you can. Keep your nose clean, you'll never hear from them. But there's a point— usually a heavy five in telepathy—where it's not a choice anymore. At that point you work for the Guild directly, you do what they say, and you're registered in the lists the Guild provides the public." Well, most of them. The Guild held back a lot of information from the cops. A lot. Which was why I got paid my consultant fee, to tell them at least what they didn't know.

"What happens if someone wants to quit?" Cherabino asked, curious.

I suppose it was an obvious question, but the truth was . . . "That's not really something we talk about."

Both cops stared at me. I looked at my shoes, set on worn industrial carpet at least a decade old. When I looked up again, I stared past Cherabino at the speckled walls. Even in my situation—unusual, to say the least—I had certain obligations, and I did *not* want Guild Enforcement coming after me, not for something stupid like this.

"The point is," I changed the subject, "somebody at the scene—I'd wager the killer—teleported out of there. Considering there weren't any drag marks on the ground on the way in, I'd wager he teleported in as well, carrying the victim with him. Means he's at least a 3-T, plus a telepath as well—maybe a six or so. We're talking double trouble here."

I rubbed my neck. "There are maybe twelve guys in the whole Solar System who can do both those things that strong, and they'll be on the Spook list. The Guild will know what they're doing at every moment of every day, and we wouldn't be having this conversation, because after one body, the Guild would have taken lethal action."

Branen rubbed his head and picked up the phone on his desk, pushing a speed-dial button. After the call went through, he asked, "Have a minute? I need your expertise."

In the silence after he hung up, I ventured, "Basically the—"

He raised a finger for me to wait.

I thought about attempting small talk, but I was bad at that sort of thing.

A knock came on the partially open door.

"Come," Branen called out.

Lieutenant Marla Paulsen entered the room and gave me a nod. Great, he'd invited my boss.

She glanced at the chairs, and finding them occupied, leaned against the door frame.

Branen inclined his head in my direction, eyes on her. "You know he's assisting with the multiples case, right?" She nodded. "Well, we've got contradicting theories, and they all point to the Guild. You still keep up with the Koshna Treaty law changes?"

"Not too many changes lately, but yes."

Paulsen was a strong woman with a strong face, skin the color of cinnamon sticks, and more than a few old-fashioned wrinkles. At a young sixty-mumble, she was a stickler for Tech Separation (she remembered the aftermath of the Tech Wars) and she wore her uniform like she'd been born to it. Paulsen had high standards, and as she'd told me more than once, she expected those standards to be met.

Branen caught her up on the discussion and my Guild ramble in about three sentences, then said, "So with a perp who shouldn't exist and victims who aren't registered, can we ignore Koshna?"

Paulsen frowned. "Well, technically the treaty says we're supposed to call the Guild at first suspicion of anything, but the courts have been siding with the cops lately. Koshna Accords are there mostly to let the Guild police their own. Clearly they're not policing themselves in this case." She looked at me. "You sure this guy is a—what do you call it?"

"Double trouble," Cherabino offered.

"Thank you. Double trouble. You sure he's Guild?"

I straightened in my chair reflexively under her look. "I know a teleport when I see one. I know a telepath. But there were two guys there. I think it's one guy who's the telepath and teleporter, I'm almost sure. We're not guaranteed, though. They could be different guys."

Branen leaned back in his chair. "Worst-case scenario," he addressed Paulsen. "We don't report it. We track it down to its conclusion, capture the perp, submit the findings in triplicate to the political guys to fight out with the Guild directly. What are we looking at?"

She shook her head. "Won't get that far. Besides the legal red tape, we can't hold him without Guild support."

I nodded reluctantly and confirmed. "He'll Jump out of the cell. Or convince the guard's mind he wanted to let him out in the first place. The strong guys are hell to hold if you don't know what you're doing."

Branen sighed. "Let's say we put boy wonder here on guard. What's worst case?"

Hold on now. "I'm not nearly—"

Cherabino waved me down, and I seethed.

Paulsen frowned slightly. "It's a high-profile case, or could be made one with a hint to the right reporter. They'd have to fight it in the courts."

Branen glanced at Cherabino, then back at her. "We still have friends in the DA's office who'd be glad to take something like that on, for publicity if nothing else. Meanwhile the killer's off the streets, and the captain doesn't have to field a phone call from the mayor asking why we're not doing anything about the East Atlanta murders. I say we do it."

"Do what?" I asked. I was shielding hard enough to give myself a headache, and I was definitely not tracking as well as I could have been.

"Work the case without the Guild," Cherabino said. "You might want to try to keep up."

I admit that the Guild weren't my favorite people since they'd kicked me out, but . . . "Can you do that?" More important, could I do that? As bad as things were for me right now, they'd be a lot worse if I got the attention of their Enforcement unit. Still, it would twist the Guild's tail, to have one of their people held responsible to the real world.

"We're going to," Branen said, then addressed Paulsen. "Unless you have an objection?" They were technically equals, but Paulsen's department was much larger, handling anything the other three didn't. She was also more senior than he was, so while he didn't have to defer, it was a good idea.

She shook her head. "I'll clear it with the captain, but it's our case. In our jurisdiction."

After four hours of interviews, I was bone tired. The ancient elevator seemed to crawl. I mashed the third button twice to get it to engage, the buttons so old their imprinted numbers were worn away by a hundred years of fingerprints.

Working for the Guild had given me a lot of numbers behind my name. Other than the eight and the seventy-eight percent, my next big number was one-ninety. That's base valence; it means I can flex to read maybe ninety-five minds out of a hundred. A big number for anybody; for a guy, it's impressive. Or was.

Unfortunately, it meant I could read almost everyone in the station, four floors of constant disturbance like ripples on a very windy lake. When I was this tired, the ripples came through my shields in waves, half-heard and insistent.

I only got the hard interviews, the ones that had stumped some detective, some beat cop to the point where he'd passed it up the line. I got the guilty, the difficult, the ones who cried heartbreaking manipulative tears, the angry men with something to hide and the women who thought they could sleep their way out of anything and didn't realize a telepath couldn't do casual sex even if he wanted to. In those times I was glad for Bellury, or McDonnell, or anyone else there.

If the interviewee made it through me, he got a

round with Paulsen, and she didn't like to be disturbed for anything short of an asteroid barreling toward the Earth. I'd gotten real good, real quick, as a result—it helped that I could spot a lie at twenty paces. I also said right off I was a telepath, which sometimes made a gullible perp confess for no good reason. But no-holds-barred crazy people gave me nausea or worse, and some really annoying perps actually paid attention to the Guild's service announcements.

A bit of advice: if you must throw a telepath off your trail, be nice and recite multiplication tables or something. Concentrating on an out-of-tune rock song like the last suspect had just makes me want to hit you.

I still had the ear-wrenching, repetitive song stuck in my head from the last suspect. The low-level cacophony of the station was rubbing at me like sandpaper. I was exhausted. And I wanted a hit with every fiber of my being. I thought about my tiny holdout stash in my apartment, the two little vials I'd put in a hole in the wall. I thought, Tonight might be the night to take them out again.

The elevator attempted to ding when it hit the floor, instead managing only a tiny metallic thud. I struggled to focus, bracing myself before walking out into the cubicle farm that was the third floor, detective alley. This was my least favorite part of the day.

Cherabino's cubicle was all the way at the other end of the building, past at least thirty cubicles full of thinking minds—row after row of forgettable boxes and claustrophobically crowded detectives, none of which said hello.

I walked past their silent eyes, unable to completely block the mixed-bag observations on everything from my hairstyle to my history, the tightness of my butt to my latest successful interview. Also complete indifference and a lot of thinking on actual cases. They did actually do work here, some of them.

The last two lines of cubicles were larger and had more space between them, with real windows on this side of the building. Over here it was quieter in Mind-space, the detectives here and bigwigs upstairs all calmly efficient, the secretaries below happy with their gossip. Some part of me calmed, knowing no one was paying any attention. I managed to put the shields back up, slowly, with a lot of effort.

I passed Cherabino's cubicle neighbor, and I said hello to Andrew. I think he was an accountant; he thought about numbers a lot, was always in the cubi-cle, and had gourmet coffee. The real stuff, from beans. He shared the coffee cheerfully, and never once labeled me felon in his head.

Andrew was on the phone, but he went ahead and waved me toward the coffee set up in the back of his cubicle. He hit mute briefly, and told me, "Get Cher-abino some too—she's been in there since noon."

"Thanks," I said, and went to get the coffee. The first for me, black with sugar. Cherabino liked hers with one liquid creamer, half of one of the blue not-sugar packets, and about three spoons of water. Andrew was already back to his phone call when I left, carrying two cups in my hands.

She was hunched over, her face in her hands as she shook her head back and forth.

"Cherabino?"

She shot up, narrowly missed hitting her head on the desk lamp in the process. "What?" After blinking a few times, she said, "Oh, it's you."

"I have coffee," I said, unnecessarily, and put her cup next to her hand on the only free spot on the desk.

The rest was covered in paper and objects in a messy smorgasbord.

I moved a pile of printouts off the cubicle's second chair, placing the papers carefully on the floor separate from the other piles. For all the apparent mess around here, Cherabino claimed there was a pattern to the madness. That being said, the second chair and the counter next to it were sort of mine.

I sat down. There was a scarf in a plain plastic bag on the desk, which was weird since Cherabino didn't wear scarves. I picked it up and paused—the thing had a very clear effect on Mindspace. I could feel the kindly old woman who'd worn the scarf almost every day. Another presence, hanging over the thing like a faint perfume. Was that the presence from the crime scene? It felt familiar somehow.

"Where is this from?" I asked Cherabino. I didn't get impressions from objects often—they had to be in very close proximity to a person for a long time to pick up Mindspace—but it looked like I was just tired enough to notice. Maybe we could identify the guy from this.

She turned around to face me, rubbing her eyes. They were bloodshot, with deep circles, and the rest of her face didn't look much better. She looked . . . wilted, almost—but when I checked, no migraine. She sighed. "It's from the second crime scene. It's a reminder."

I studied the scarf again, but there were no blood spots. "I thought you weren't supposed to take evidence from the file room."

She grabbed the scarf. "I'll give it back when the case is over." She pulled out a drawer, deposited the scarf, and shut it firmly. "Is there a reason you're here?"

I pointed to the cup I'd just given her. "Coffee, remember?"

She turned around as if just now remembering, and took a sip. A pleasant warm feeling spread through her, the taste comforting.

I sighed and worked a little harder to shut her out. "How's the work coming?"

She sighed and took another long sip of coffee, frowning. "Who battled the Hydra?"

"What's a Hydra?"

She blinked. "I thought you were proud of your Guild education. Maybe it was Jason. This big, huge monster—you cut off one head and two more grow up in its place. That's what I'm doing, chasing illicit net porn. No matter how many perverts we shut down, you turn your back and there's six more just waiting for you to find them."

"I thought you weren't working Electronic Crimes anymore," I said.

"They're understaffed," she said. "Two more rounds of job interviews, a little training, and God willing I'm off for good. Two weeks, three maybe. But I'm waiting for some tests on the multiples case." She took another sip of coffee, then looked at me again. "How are you?"

"Other than feeling like someone has beat me with sticks, I'm fine." She looked at me strangely, and I clarified, "Too many interviews, and the last guy was difficult. Really difficult. Any news on the case?"

She sighed. "We've got several local cops going door to door tomorrow and Saturday, guys who've done patrol in the area and know what they're looking for. Paulsen's handling details since they're her guys, so if there's anybody good, you'll probably get them in the interview room. Just keep me in the loop, okay? I'd like to sit in if it's possible."

"Possible?"

She sighed, pointing to a loose stack of three files

next to the computer that had previously blended into the mess. "Three new cases today, and only one's Electronic Crimes. Branen's going ape-shit because the county turned down his request for more personnel. If Paulsen didn't share, we'd all be underwater by now."

"Any city funds?" I asked her. The City of Decatur usually preferred to help fund the DeKalb County homicide and drug divisions rather than tackle it on their own. They did their own patrols, but that was about it.

"Not so far." She rubbed her head. Wasn't a migraine, not yet. "Though knowing them, they'll slip them in right before elections. Listen, I'm going down to the morgue tomorrow morning to see if they've got anything on the latest multiples victim. You should come."

"I'm allowed at the morgue?"

"You are if you behave yourself." She frowned. "Why, weren't you going to?"

I ignored the sidebar and reiterated. "I'm not usually invited."

"Well, you are if I say so. With the Guild connection, people are going to talk. I want you there to debunk the myths before the rumors turn into anything. The last thing we need is a mass panic against the telepaths again."

"Again?"

She shook her head. "Don't be a moron. The last time, they called them witch hunts, and honestly, I don't have time for that kind of foolishness."

She wasn't quite right about the history. Most of the witches at Salem weren't telepaths, just old women herbalists. Well, except the one, and she was famous in Guild circles; she projected a lot of the fear on the townsfolk. Perfect example of what not to do as a telepath.

Still, what Cherabino meant by it was good. Kind, even. Fighting the prejudices against the telepaths; she didn't have to do that. I looked at the circles under her eyes again and asked the question quickly, before I could think better of it. "You got anything I can do to help with the caseload?"

She shook her head. "Not at the moment, unless you've got new skills with the computer you've never told me about. I'm trying to finish up the Net porn case today, and it's not minor-level coding. Advanced polygon cipher, at the very least, maybe worse."

"Um . . . is that good?"

Cherabino laughed. It was a small laugh, more shocked than anything, but it counted. "Probably. We're maybe halfway done."

"Congratulations," I said, with as much cheer as I could muster past my general exhaustion.

After just a little more small talk, we settled down to work in companionable silence, her on her cases, me on paperwork.

In the quiet fifteen minutes later, I found the pencil she'd been looking for and handed it to her. In Mindspace, Cherabino's presence was shocked, but I kept working, chewing on an antacid for my stomach as I filled out paperwork I'd rather not do. Whatever she was shocked at was probably something I didn't want to see anyway.

That night, I went home and slept, unaided. The vials stayed in the wall, and I stayed on the wagon. I was tired.

CHAPTER 3

I tapped my fingers against the wood grain of the table. Swartz was late. And by late, I meant, not early. Swartz was one of those spry sleepless old men who showed up to everything at least a half hour early. So it was unthinkable, with me arriving a whole minute and a half before the agreed time, that he wasn't here yet.

Here being an out-of-the-way corner of a faded old coffee shop, what had once been a pub before the owner's mother joined AA more than thirty years ago. A long wooden bar still dominated the space, beat up with coffee stains and long scratches. Pub tables lined the walls with chairs and carefully repaired leather booths. Behind the bar, the owner nodded at me and turned around to brew a pot of dark licorice coffee.

That black licorice-flavored liquid was a taste I'd never known existed until I met Swartz. It was too strong a flavor for me to say I liked it, exactly, but the pungent taste and Swartz's abrupt truth mixed together in my mind over and over until the tradition of both became a stalwart against weakness, until the black licorice clung and clung and made me want to be a better man. Or spit it all back up again, all at once. I had days of both.

There was Swartz—the whole dark room flashed with the outside sun as he entered; then the room dimmed again as the door swung closed. He made his way toward me, his slate gray hair slicked back in a style that had been old when his grandfather was alive. The pronounced wrinkles on his thin face in no way took away from his air of authority. He wore a pair of beat-up khakis and a textured golf shirt.

Swartz sat down, the leather on the seat creaking, and nodded a greeting. Then he waved to the owner, who held up a finger to let us know it would be another moment.

I nodded in return. He made me come up with a list of three things I was grateful for every week—I had to tell him three brand-new things at our usual weekly meeting, or he'd give me this look, all disappointed. And the feeling I got from his mind was worse, like "ungrateful" was an insult of the worst order. So, I studied. I thought. And for six years running now—not counting the two weeks I'd missed the last time off the wagon—every week I had three new things. This week I was having trouble.

"How are you?" I asked, hoping to delay the inevitable question for another few minutes.

"I'm okay," he said. "School starts in a couple of weeks and we go back a week before the kids do. I'm putting together some lesson plans, looking for some new stories to get their attention." Swartz taught history at a poor high school south of Decatur, and spent the summers reading. I'd heard some of his stories—all based in real history, apparently—and wished I'd had him as a teacher at some point.

"Think I might quit smoking," he added.

"That's crazy talk," I told him. "What will you do when you get a craving?"

His bushy gray eyebrows went up a little. "Pray. Go to a meeting. Call and talk to someone who understands—same thing we do now. You are still doing those things." He made it a statement, looking directly at me.

I sighed. "Maybe not the praying so much." I also hadn't called Swartz yesterday, which he wasn't mentioning but I knew he'd noted. I was supposed to call him every day. Twice a day, four times a day, more, if needed. The only time I couldn't get him was when he was at school, and he'd call me back at the very next class break. It was a rule.

He sat back as the owner arrived with an ugly squat brown coffeepot and two uglier cups. The man set both cups down then filled them with the coffee. "Be careful; it's hot," he said, and went back to the bar.

I was antsy today, ready to jump out of my skin, but I pulled the coffee cup over to my side of the table. I'd get through this, and then go to work. I would.

Swartz took a sip of his coffee. "You're letting Step Seven go, son. Asking God to remove your shortcomings is the only way this is going to work long-term. We're coming up on three years now, that's good, that's wonderful. But you let the humility go, you let it all go. You can't handle this by yourself. If we could, we wouldn't be sitting here." His mind echoed a weak picture of me at that first meeting, then the knowledge of his own struggle. "We need the system, we need God, we need each other."

"The Higher Power," I corrected.

He pierced me with those sharp eyes. "Is calling him some vague title going to change anything for you? He's God either way."

"Aren't we going to talk about my three things for the week?" I asked him, to change the subject.

"We can," he said, but I knew he wasn't done. I'd get an earful of the God-talk later.

"Air conditioning, good coffee, and . . ." I made something up on the spot. "The fact that Cherabino called me out on a case again. One I can actually help with."

"You've used coffee before. Twice."

"This is good Jamaican coffee, not the swill at the police station but the good blue stuff Cherabino's neighbor brings in."

He let me get away with it. "Okay. Tell me about Cherabino, then."

"She's okay. Overloaded. Deep in the case, worried, angry, not happy at me, but—other than a migraine Tuesday—okay."

"You said she invited you to a case?" Swartz put his hand on the back of the leather booth.

I told him the nonclassified parts, holding back the number of victims and the cause of death, and finished with the probable connection to the Guild. "That's the thing, though. I'm not sure I can ethically not tell them. I mean, delay, yeah, everybody delays, but if we get to the end of this thing and I haven't told them, it's going to be bad for me." I hated the Guild sometimes, for what they'd done to me. But I couldn't rip out their training so easily.

He took another swallow. "You've been blacklisted for years. What else can they do?"

The Koshna Accords didn't mean a thing to the normals, except for the occasional political power play like the cops were planning. A play I wasn't entirely certain I should support.

"Well, they could rescind my employment papers, for one. They can lock me up in Guild holding indefinitely. I'm still a telepath, a Level Eight. All they have to do is declare me a danger to myself or to society and that's it." My worst nightmare was waking up in a Guild facility scheduled for a mindwipe. And the thing was, it was all too possible. To someone like me, the treaty was a red line in the sand that gave the Guild any power they wanted.

When the Tech Wars ripped the world apart, the Guild stepped up to save it. But they had to get scary to do it—real scary. They'd won the right to govern themselves, to have political independence, sure. But they'd lost the casual trust of most of the normals along the way. When your pit bull saves you from the robber about to kill you, you're grateful. But when the pit bull tears the guy apart in little bloody ribbons, you never look at the thing the same way again.

"I'm a telepath, Swartz. A Level Eight. For all intents and purposes that means the Guild owns me, even now. No normal court of law in the world is going to stand up to the Guild, to the treaty. Not for me."

"I just don't believe that, kid," Swartz said. "Think about it. You really think Paulsen and Cherabino will let you disappear without a fight? You've earned yourself friends in the system, kid."

"Maybe, maybe not," I said. "People are different under pressure, especially around telepaths. Plus I cause them a lot of headaches."

"You're selling yourself short. The department kept you on after the last fall off the wagon. That means quite a bit." Swartz shrugged. "They're not exactly helpless. I wouldn't worry about the Guild too much."

"Sure," I said, to stop the conversation. I didn't really want to have the cheer-me-up moment right now. But the Guild did mostly keep to its own ethics. Mostly. If I kept to the same I might have a chance. And that old lady's scarf was bothering me.

"You're awfully quiet."

"Just thinking." I shrugged. We sipped our too-hot coffee, enjoyed the air conditioning.

"How are you?" Swartz prompted.

I stared at my hands, decided what to say. Maybe the truth this time. "A tough week, a very tough week."

"Why is that?"

"The interview room has been hell. Two crazies yesterday, in a bad way. I've wanted Satin pretty much every day. As great as another case is, this one's a lot of pressure—the case is weird, I know too much, and there's a lot of pressure. I'm ex-Guild, not a detective. That's Cherabino's job. . . ." After a pause, I looked up. "But everybody's looking at me for that rabbit, that sudden push out of the hat, and the precog's not cooperating. It's a lot of pressure. Screwing up. Coming up with the rabbit. A *lot* of pressure. Plus whatever I end up having to do with the Guild."

Swartz sipped his coffee. "How are you handling it?"

I sighed. He wasn't going to take less than the truth. "Not great. Want to fall off the world for a while. I've thought about the craving way too much today, thinking, what if I gave in?" It would be the easy way out.

Swartz gave me the most disapproving look I had ever received, and that—considering he'd been my sponsor for six years—was really saying something. "That's dangerous. You can't afford to think like that, ever. And even if you do, *not* out loud. I'll say it again, kid. Satin is your *enemy*. Your poison. Your worst enemy. Responsibility is something you need to be embracing, not running from. I'll tell you as many times as I need to."

I set my jaw. "You want truth, you get it."

Swartz let the statement hang, and I sipped the cooling coffee. The taste of the licorice filled my whole mouth, my nose, my throat. I wanted to spit it up, have done with it, but instead I choked the taste down. I was going to do it today, I thought. Today I was going to choke it up and stay on the wagon, let the vials stay where they were. Today I was going to try.

"Now," Swartz said, pulling out the Big Book. "Let's take a look at the steps again."

CHAPTER 4

At the station, Cherabino led the way back through the sea of open desks downstairs, nodding to junior cops as she went. Damn it. We were going to walk, weren't we? Ninety-two degrees in the shade at eleven o'clock in the morning, and we were going to walk.

"How far to the morgue?" I asked her, hustling to keep up.

"Just three blocks down West Ponce," she said cheerily, and didn't even pause as she headed out the back door and into the punishing heat. I followed, cursing under my breath while I still could, sweat already breaking out on my neck.

I had my department ID on with the jeans and the button-up shirt. Cherabino's white shirt, black slacks was the same standard cop-wear as anyone else's in the department. Same as she'd been wearing for days.

We crossed over the office building's courtyard and through a walkway to the street. West Ponce was a windy road in spots, but here it was three-story buildings on either side, mostly government buildings. We'd probably end up in one of those if I didn't pass out from the heat first.

Our shoes padded silently, and the portable radio on Cherabino's hip sputtered occasionally. I was breathing heavy from the cigarettes and the pollution. Not so bad as it used to be, though; she'd been dragging me walking enough that my wind was starting to come back. Even if I did feel like I was melting. Above us, cars and the occasional city bus whisked by in the sky lanes. I carefully did not look at Cherabino walking briskly down the street.

"So," I started. "How does this morgue thing work?"

She slowed down, a graceful change. "You know, dead bodies in drawers, quantum stasis, autopsies, lots of chemicals. Weird smells. Don't you watch television?"

"Don't own one," I told her. "Waste of time." The truth was, I'd sold it my second time off the wagon for drug money and had never been able to replace it. The only way the department would take me back afterward—even with Cherabino putting her job on the line—was if I didn't handle my own paycheck, and if I didn't keep anything worth anything in trade. But if my rent was paid on time, groceries appeared every week, and Bellury took me out for clothes occasionally, I figured that was good enough. I had four pairs of shoes, none of them with any holes. It wasn't too long ago I couldn't say that.

Cherabino climbed the worn, chipping steps of a particularly boxy building and led the way inside. Blessed air conditioning, I thought, as I followed her down an old hallway and into a large, smelly freight elevator. She hit the worn button for the basement. After making sure she wasn't looking, I fanned my shirt surreptitiously, trying to get as much air conditioning in the thing as possible.

"Why is the morgue in the tax office?" I asked Cherabino, having noted the signs on the way in.

She shrugged. "Decatur Hospital's basement kept flooding, and the city had the extra room."

The freight elevator moved very, very slowly, with creaking sounds I'd rather not have heard.

She took pity on me and started explaining. "They're understaffed, just like everybody else these days, so be nice because we jumped the line to get here. They'll have cleaned up the guy since the crime scene and done an autopsy—so he'll be without clothes with a Y cut, cooled down some, and they'll have taken care of the bugs. If you can't handle what you're looking at, stare at the floor on the other side of the gurney and try to breathe through your mouth, shallowly. You're here because the bodies are the only real clues we have right now, and I want you to hear what the coroner has to say about cause of death."

I thought about protesting that of course I could handle it—handle what exactly?—but the freight elevator chose that moment to come to a screeching stop.

The stainless steel doors opened up to a concrete-floored hallway with doorways on either side. Cherabino led the way to the first one on the left and I followed, nervous. What could be so much worse than the crime scene that she felt she had to warn me?

The first thing I noticed was the smell: decay and formaldehyde and metal. It was cold in here, even for me, and the faint Mindspace buzzing on the far wall was distracting.

The large room was painfully bright with fluorescent bulbs, the old-style artificial light combining with cold steel tables to assault the eyes. After I forced myself to focus, I wished I hadn't. The three bodies out in the open lacked even the dignity of a towel, their splotched forms too still, too . . . absent. They lacked any form in

Mindspace, even the decaying ghost of a last emotion, now well gone. The rows of steel drawers lining the back wall only made it seem more inhuman. I was betting the buzzing came from there, probably an activated quantum stasis generator disrupting the flow of Mindspace, but it didn't help that the drawers looked like what they were—steel boxes to store corpses.

"Cherabino," a woman's voice greeted her from the far side of the room. "Thanks for coming." Her accent had a hint of a lilt to it, maybe Jamaican.

Cherabino made her way past the bodies on the tables as if they meant nothing. I breathed shallowly, through my mouth, and followed her.

"Where's Petie?" she asked the woman.

"Out sick. It's just me as usual." The coroner was dark skinned with her hair done in many tiny long braids, and had a beautiful smile which somehow seemed inappropriate while standing over a fourth body, this one from the crime scene, or so I thought. I didn't look closely.

She gave me a bright smile. "I see you brought a friend."

I thought about objecting to the title, but I didn't have a better one. "You have information on the case?"

The coroner led the way to the far side of the table and picked up a clipboard. "Black male, thirty-five, identified via AO serial number as Tom Turner, a businessman from the west side." I carefully didn't look at the body, sliced up and empty.

"Reported missing?" Cherabino asked. The coroner must have called down to the county records office, or have a copy of the database or something, but wasn't it Cherabino's job to do that? Seemed odd, but what did I know?

"Yes, the wife reported it Tuesday morning after he didn't come home Monday night."

"I'll see if the uniforms have talked to her yet," Cherabino said, making herself a note.

The coroner waited for her to finish, then continued. "I'm putting time of death as Monday between eleven a.m. and three p.m. He didn't have anything in his stomach and the heat accelerated decay, so that time is approximate. Hopefully when the entomology tests come back we'll have a precise window." She pointed out a few of the more disturbing features of decay, including the insect damage on the man's face. At that, I had to look away or throw up. I took Cherabino's advice and stared at the floor on the other side of the steel table, shielding against empty Mindspace.

The coroner's cheerful voice kept talking, my mind freaking out as I accidentally took a far-too-deep breath through my nose and smelled a scent I hoped to never smell again—a more concentrated, alcoholed version of the decay I'd experienced at the crime scene. In triplicate. I took a step back and fought down bile.

Cherabino put her hand on my shoulder—I was shielding too hard to read her—but I remembered suddenly I was here to hear what the coroner had to say. I started to pay attention again.

"This one like the others?" Cherabino asked.

"Yes. A few defensive wounds." The coroner pointed to scrapes on the man's knuckles, bruises on his forearms. "The scrapes are clotted well enough I'm putting them several hours before death. He didn't fight right before, unless the bruises on his back are from more than falling down on concrete. Same damage to the brain, but something new . . ." She pulled the man's head to the side slightly, displaying a discolored stripe with more insect damage I had to look away from. "Bleeding from the ears."

"What's the cut on the neck?" Cherabino leaned forward, clearly a lot more comfortable in this situation than I was. I didn't look.

"That? Oh, that's the incision for me to take out the artificial organ—a thyroid gland, in this case. I made it right over the old scar."

"Didn't we identify the last few bodies from AOs?" Cherabino asked.

"They're more common than transplants now and most of them are traceable, especially the glands to administer drugs. It's usually the easiest way to identify someone," the coroner said. "Sometimes a person will request his name be kept out of the database. But usually it's straightforward, and they send me a new version every year, so it's not too far out of date. I'd say half of the bodies I get these days are identified through that database."

"That many?" Cherabino asked. "What happened to dental records?"

The coroner laughed. "With the insurance companies pushing the new glands over med regimens? We'll all have AOs before the decade is up. Dental records are going the way of the dinosaurs."

Artificial organs were old news to me, since they had to be tuned to the body's neural net by a telepath to ensure compatibility. So I changed the subject, back to what had bothered me earlier.

"Do you have a picture of the brain damage?" I asked, interrupting their conversation and not caring. The coroner was grinning merrily, which disturbed me to no end.

"Let me show you the tissue—"

"No, a picture. An HD MRI or something?" I asked a little desperately.

She shrugged and pulled a few films from the bottom of the clipboard. "Couple of cross sections on the scanner, nothing fancy." Turning on the light on a board on the wall, she clipped the film up. "What are you looking for?"

"I don't know, exactly." As I walked closer, I put my hand up to touch the bottom of the third film, the tacky texture of the biofiber sticking to my fingers. I didn't know what I was doing; I was a software guy, not wetware—not the brain tissue itself. But I'd had to study structure in depth as part of my deconstruction training, not just the mind, but the brain. So I did know what I was looking at.

The first slide showed some damage to the hindbrain centered around the pons, likely what had killed him in the end. Intermittent damage across the temporal lobe. But on the third slide a burned-out section as big as my thumb in the lower parietal lobe. I put my thumb over it, thinking.

"It's very odd. That section shouldn't do anything. There's no reason for it to be burned out in every victim," the coroner put in.

I peeled my thumb off the film and backed up, then asked a question about the kind of cross section it was, just to be sure. Then I sighed. "No, it's not. That's a major center for processing Mindspace signals, if the rest of the brain is set up to receive them." I didn't have the right cross section to see if this guy had Ability—though a few extra folds in certain spots weren't guaranteed in even the stronger telepaths. Brain waves were a better indication. But the fact he had damage in that spot really, really wasn't a good sign.

"What does that mean?" the coroner asked.

I sighed, not knowing how much I could safely explain. "It means we have a problem."

As we walked back, Cherabino pestered me until I told her, "Look, I'm not a wetware guy. I could be wrong. But if I have it right, and the damage is—well, somebody's overloading their brains. Through Mindspace." If that didn't point to the Guild, I didn't know what did.

West College Avenue was, if anything, even hotter, with almost no one around. You could fry an egg on the pavement, and I had no idea why we were walking. Even the wilted brown grass was trying to get out of the sun. I was already sweating, already miserable.

Part of me wanted to do a little jig here in the middle of the street, celebrate the Guild screwing up. Get the newspaper to print a huge front-page story: guild screws up, me proved right. Start the media sensation of the century over exactly how and why, rub their noses in it. But the rest of me—well, that athletic guy hadn't asked to be dead. Shouldn't be dead, bug damage or no.

Cherabino pursed her lips. "So?"

I avoided looking her in the eye, but kept my voice even. "I'm only going to say this once, so listen up. I'm in over my head. I need a lot more information and some more resources. Maybe another telepath, a Battle Ops guy. We need to call the Guild."

She stopped walking and stared. "Call the Guild? Seriously? It's our freaking case! And you . . ."

"I'll admit they're not my favorite people," I said. "I'm not talking about Enforcement. I don't want to deal with them right now. I'm talking about help. About information. About getting this guy off the street faster—a couple phone calls and some begging."

"I don't beg," Cherabino said.

I gritted my teeth. "Asking nicely, then. I'll do that much. With this getting so much press, even they have to know they can't drop off the radar at this point. A little help, a few diplomatic channels, that's all I'm asking, Cherabino."

She strode on down the street, her legs stretching at a painfully fast walk. Her annoyance drifted off her in waves. "You were there when the brass decided not to consult the Guild. You can't just go off on your own, you know. The decision's been made. If you have new information, great, but right now the only thing we even have that points to the Guild is your say-so—"

She was cut off by the distinctive whine of a whipcord-thin humblade beginning to vibrate behind us. We turned. Cherabino fell into a defensive crouch and went for her gun.

A light-skinned man so thin his cheeks were gaunt held the highly illegal humblade, brandishing the thin hilt and vibrating cord that would slice through concrete like butter. The bruises along his arms underscored the desperation in his face. A junkie.

"Give me your money," he said, in a voice frighteningly committed.

Cherabino shifted her grip on the gun. "You have *got* to be kidding. We're within sight of the police station. You're holding up a *cop* right next to the *police station*. How stupid can you get?"

Please don't antagonize the junkie with the humblade, I thought as the man tensed to move. His mind was on the sharp edge, coming down off a high. I needed to disable him. . . .

He sprang at me. I snatched at his wrist—not the blade, his wrist—and missed. I dodged to the side—the edge of the blade hummed far, far, too close to my face. The junkie caught his balance again.

Cherabino kicked him, a sweeping roundhouse kick—connected with the wrist I'd missed, her gun somehow now in its holster. I danced back, back, away from the flying humblade, which whooshed past.

The blade embedded itself in the concrete sidewalk two feet behind me. As it vibrated, the hole it made widened with small cracks. A flash of decision from the junkie, and I was moving away again. He swung at me wildly—he had to have the money, he had to have the drug. At any cost he had to have it. I understood, but not now—he couldn't steal from us.

He hit Cherabino and she fell, sweeping his legs out on the way down. I jumped in, trying to pull him off her. He had the strength of the insane, laying blows left and right and hitting my face. I saw stars.

I opened up, my mental training coming into play as I held him desperately with my hands, wrestled him down. His mind was erratic, spotty, hard to hold; whatever he was on changed the shape of it. I paused, trying to find a hold—

Cherabino got the grip she needed and flipped him facedown on the concrete, his arm wrenched behind him. She muttered under her breath about stupid unarmed perps, "Give me an excuse to shoot you, just give me one."

The perp pushed up against her, tried to get away, only hurting himself worse in the process. His high was starting to wear off, his strength gone.

I disengaged. Sat back, panting. She had him. I didn't need to disable him—I didn't have to find a grip on that slippery mind.

Cherabino pulled out her cuffs and forced his other

arm behind him. The alloy strongcuffs *snipped* as they engaged.

The strength slipped out of the junkie, and he collapsed. I got a grip on his mind, but it wasn't a ploy. He was beginning the slide into withdrawal. I held him down, my right knee in his back. I hated everything he stood for, everything I used to be and hoped I wasn't still. I understood his desperation all too well. Impotent anger pushed at me, but I held on. I could do this. I would do this.

"You have the right to remain silent," Cherabino began, continuing to recite his Mirandas. Then straight into the Paglinos, one phrase flowing naturally into the next.

Abruptly, my precognition kicked in. I got a flash, Cherabino putting a hand out to catch her balance, a hand that landed on the still-active humblade. Blood everywhere, pain, pain. Then, a jarring shift, and I was back in the now.

Cherabino shifted in her crouch to keep the man down, but she was losing her balance. . . .

I grabbed the back of her shirt and *yanked* her in my direction.

We both fell, on top of the suspect, who *oofed* and started whining.

"What in the hell was that for?" Cherabino punched me and pushed up. A long, bloody scrape marred one of her cheeks.

I yanked her to the side suddenly, away from where she was stepping. "Humblade."

Understanding hit her like a freight train as she looked over to where she would have put her hand, where she could have stepped. She bent over to turn the blade off. Added the safety.

She met my eyes as she straightened, tucking the now-harmless handle and floppy cord into a pocket.

"Let's go," she said. Fear and anger roiled off her. I hurried to keep up, my own heart beating far too fast.

That had been far too close.

CHAPTER 5

We dragged our prisoner into Booking with full ceremony. Dirty, pissed, and with a loudly mumbling burden, we made quite a sight. Two bored cops followed us in our little parade through the department—it was day shift and lunchtime on a slow day, so any distraction was welcome. We probably weren't as gentle as we could have been with the suspect.

The booking officer looked up. "What'd he do?" she asked, actually interested.

"Tried to mug us within sight of the police station," I said flatly, before Cherabino had a chance to get into it. Judging by her expression—and her treatment of the suspect—she'd happily get into a diatribe if I let her.

The two trailing cops laughed, loudly. The booking officer tried hard, but she also snickered.

"And you ended up looking like *that*?"

The cop behind me guffawed. "Must have been quite a fight!"

"Well," I said with full dignity and no small frustration, "it was."

As soon as Cherabino got the guy booked in, I pushed her back to her cubicle to cool down, telling her I'd finish the paperwork. She left with noises of cleaning up in the ladies' room. The cut on her cheek was still seeping blood, and she looked pissed.

The booking officer scanned in the paper forms as soon as I could fill them out, but we still had to have the original hard copies filed away. It was stupid, mindless work, and exactly what I needed to calm back down. The junkie's face, his desperation, was sticking with me all too clearly.

I focused instead on the stupid hard-copy forms, line after line, box after box filled out in pencil in block caps so the secretaries could read them. Hard copy, for all it was dumb, was necessary. Nobody remembered losing all their records in the Tech Wars the way the cops did. Electronic quarantine and antivirus, separation and security—they were all good to have and the cops were fanatical about them. More important was keeping data and transmissions separate, checking every byte of new data, every new program as if it was the new End of the World. Because once it had been.

No one remembered the war like the government, like the cops, who told one another the stories over and over again. Bombs had split the sky, and worse, the superviruses split our minds from the inside, until the toll of death made people look at computer technology like the Black Plague. Even now, more than a half century later when small computer chips were let out on a leash—small ones barely powerful enough to run an oven timer, and still frightening to the diehards—the real Tech, the sentient computers and the implants and anything *powerful*, was outlawed with terrible penalties.

People were afraid. Still. Terrified of the computers, the data, even the smallest transmission of information over unsecured lines. So if it took three days to send an e-mail through all the layers of Quarantine, if the small Web was regarded with the same respect/fear as a pit viper, if even Cherabino had to have a thorough background check and be monitored constantly in the Electronic Crimes works for fear she'd come across something truly dangerous, well, a lot of people had died in the Tech Wars. A lot of data had been erased beyond retrieval; a lot of holes had been made in the history books. A lot of loss, period. Hard copy? Hard copy was safe. Hard copy was forever. And if India and Mars and Brazil made fun of the West for our caution, well, they hadn't taken the brunt of the Tech Wars, had they? They hadn't died in the millions and rotted on the street and watched while their neighbors died, trapped in their houses while a madman held them captive through their Tech. Never, never again would that be possible, we had sworn. Never.

And so here we were, fear burned in the memory—and schooling—of every American, every European since. Caution was king, even from those like Cherabino who policed the tiny Net that remained. Some things would never happen again. Could never happen again.

It was still a pain in the ass as far as paperwork went. Hard copy was slow, tedious, and had a regrettable tendency toward paper cuts. But even I wasn't stupid enough to suggest a change. Biology, artificial organs, physics, anti-graviton generators for flying cars, drug-assisted telepathy—the world might be perfectly fine with those kinds of technologies. They didn't talk to one another. They didn't grow minds of their own. But computers? Data? Tech? A complete WorldNet with instant e-mail and a phone system connected to the computers? Not in my lifetime. People were just too afraid, with too good a reason. The population might be rebounding, but memory didn't leave that easy. So I filled out paperwork, hard copy, and didn't complain.

I finished checking the last box. I said good-bye to the booking officer and the secretaries and found my way to the men's room to wash the pencil lead off my hands.

In the elevator I ran into Paulsen. Papers and coffee flew everywhere—I managed to grab the cup as it half spilled on my shirt. The stale donut I'd grabbed was a lost cause, now covered in dirt. I sighed and bent over to pick up the papers from the floor. At least Paulsen helped.

"I was looking for you," she said, once I'd regained my mental balance. "We have a hot one in the interview room." She met my eyes. "Wait for me before you start, okay? Recording tech has the brief."

She handed me the last paper and a napkin before getting off at the main floor. I hit the button to the basement, still mourning the lost donut. I'd wanted that donut, damn it.

The doors opened up on a badly lit hall with nine doors—four interview rooms with mirrored walls that let the cops observe while the suspects sat, plus the entrance to the holding cells farther on. All the doors had unnecessary bars on the windows for effect. But only the entrances to the actual interview rooms, the housing for suspects, had double lights above the doors to show when they were in use. The third room was full and interviewing, and the second had a suspect but no interviewer. I was betting that was me.

I opened the second cop's door, nodded hello to the recording tech. The room was long and skinny, filled with boxy recording equipment with built-in self-diagnostics and absolutely no connection to any other equipment. The recording ban in public places had gotten a—carefully controlled—reprieve in police interview rooms, but it was still bound up in a lot of laws and regulations I was glad not to keep track of. The interviews were *always* transcribed, printed in permanent ink, and filed within twenty-four hours. The army of secretaries upstairs wasn't just for show.

I lit up a smoke; the recording tech turned on the air filter without comment. We'd wait however long it took Paulsen to arrive, hopefully a while. It'd give me some time to settle.

Through the glass, the suspect was pacing the room. At the moment, he was facing away from us, head down, looking like any other self-important lowlife. "What's he accused of?" I gestured with the cigarette, the smoke making sinuous trails on its way to the filter.

"Actually, this one's on spec." Paulsen's voice came from behind me.

I turned. "The multiples case?"

She frowned, the wrinkles on her face deepening. "Might be. Department received an anonymous note this morning telling us to talk to the guy. Likely another trafficker trying to improve his own business, but we're going to check it out anyway."

"Trafficker?" I said cautiously. "You mean drugs."

"Yeah. You're interviewing the beta for a ten-block radius in East Atlanta. For the local Darkness ring, apparently, not just drugs, though of course we can't prove anything."

I took a breath. "Anonymous note, huh? Does sound like a local squabble with amateur tactics. Any finger-prints?"

She snorted, as if to say, "Of course." "The thing's sitting in the lab waiting for the techs to get to it. Low priority, but might turn into something. I want you to ask him about the multiples case either way. It's his territory; he probably knows something we don't."

The tech's boredom lightened suddenly, and I turned back to the glass to see what he was reacting to.

It was then I got my first good look at our suspect's face, and my stomach sank. "Joey the Fish? That's your beta? Seriously?"

"Do you know him?"

I ground out the cigarette. "He was muscle for Harry and Marge, maybe part-timer for some other groups. You're serious, he's second in charge?"

"For ten blocks, yeah." Paulsen's nose wrinkled, and she cranked up the air filter to try to clear the air.

"Peachy."

Joey was my fault, and I knew it. When I went clean—and then when I came back on the wagon the second time—I'd helped take out all of the guys who'd ever supplied me with Satin. Vindictive? Not even a little. I'd helped take down all the big fish, the Harries and Juans and Marges; I'd sicced the cops on them in one industrial-strength drug raid after another, until the last guy who'd helped me sell out my soul was off the streets. So the little fish, like Joey, had really risen in the ranks. Unfortunately, he knew me and had access to plenty of info on me I'd rather the cops not remember. Now I was going to interview him, in front of Paulsen. This day just kept getting better and better.

"Is there anything else I need to know about this?" I gestured to the glass.

"Nothing I can tell you right now." Department policy—written by Paulsen herself—was nobody prejudiced my interviews.

Would Joey recognize me? I did look a lot different now, bulked up from regular eating and lifting weights, had even shaved. I'd grown out my hair and lost the half-dead look of desperation. Maybe he wouldn't even question the clean-cut interrogator. It would be a big bet—for high stakes—but a fair one.

"Let me get my files," I told Paulsen, and she nodded.

Assuming he didn't bring up my past, I knew exactly how to deal with Joey. Me and the file clerk had gotten together a nice little collection of repro files, glossy photos of gory crimes solved while my grandparents were still in diapers. I retrieved the smaller set from the file room and started back; they were three files, not real thick, the glossies inside only medium-shocking and unlikely to fall out without my meaning them to.

Joey's room was the worst of the four. It was done for atmosphere. Ancient, beat-up furniture you wouldn't wish on your enemies, so dirty I couldn't sit in there too long before I needed to steam myself clean.

The man himself looked like he hadn't showered in at least a week, and even across the room I could smell rancid sweat and caked-in pollution. He was wearing the latest street fashion, an upscale fan-denim, faux-fur jacket combo, his hair greased from sweat, his face streaked dirty from the air outside. The look in his eyes carried your final impression, though, a look that mixed anger and a subtle intelligence that just wouldn't let you dismiss him.

I slammed the door open with a *bang* against the inside wall. Dirt from the old ceiling fell in a flurry, but I ignored it, doing my best angry-badass walk to the table. I was a good enough telepath to project at low levels even to the "deaf" non-Able like Joey—I did it then, nothing illegal, nothing coercive, just the kind of menacing anger that raised the hairs on your spine.

The other officer in the room—my official observer

this round, though Joey wouldn't know the difference—blinked twice, but then settled back complacently in his chair to the right. Bellury was an old cop, uniformed, had never really risen through the ranks but hadn't wanted to either; he was past retirement but didn't want to quit. We worked well together. He even sometimes gave me some pointers on the best way to legally threaten a suspect.

Joey looked a little disconcerted at the anger in the air. When I slammed the repro files on the table in front of him, he shifted back. I pulled the chair out, hard—it screeched. I reversed it and sat down, my hands crossed over the top. I leaned forward.

"You've been a very bad boy, Joey," I said, with menace. I checked his mind—no recognition. He had no idea who I was. Good.

I opened the top file, the jumbled-up one with ink too light to be read upside down. "Manslaughter, arson, grand theft auto, assault and battery . . ." I went on for another few seconds, making it about halfway down the randomized list of crimes considered felonies in the state of Georgia. I stopped, abruptly, and gave him a look. It was the same look my father had given me over the vidphone when he'd found out about my poison—mingled horror, disappointment, and damning wrath.

Joey sat back in the chair, crossed his arms, tapped his foot. "Didn't do it." I didn't need telepathy to tell he was lying, but it certainly didn't hurt my act to get a confirmation. He was guilty of something on the list—being a beta, probably several somethings—and we both knew it. The trouble was, I had to get him to admit to guilt out loud.

"Didn't do what?" I said. Maybe I'd get lucky; he'd think about something too hard.

He looked at me. "Nothing on that list. I'm a fucking model citizen."

I pretended to study the paper in front of me. "Really? That's not what the file says," I responded. And if he hadn't been caught red-handed on *something*, the cops just weren't doing their jobs.

Silence reigned in the room. I could *feel* him thinking, the wheels turning. A careful assessment of risk and reward. Finally Joey asked, "What do you want?"

"I want you to start talking." With nothing more than a note, I was fishing anyway. I wanted him to dwell on one of the flashes I'd seen in his head—let me see the violence a little closer, let me get him to admit to it. Or something. I was bored, and Paulsen was watching.

I felt a decision and Joey opened his mouth. I thought for a second I had him. But no.

"What am I supposed to talk about, exactly, then? I ain't a mind reader."

"No, that's me, Joey," I said, and his eyebrows drew together. "Level Eight telepath, in case you're wondering. I'm required to tell you if you ask."

"A teep? Silver spoon in your mouth fucking teep. What're you doing at a police station?"

"I'm a consultant," I returned evenly. "I'm consulting."

After a pointless staring contest during which he imagined at least three ways to hurt me, I got bored and decided to switch tactics. Maybe he knew something about the multiples case. He was from the right territory.

"What I'm asking today has to do with the six dead bodies found on your block, not a mark on them. Word on the street is it's your block, that you arranged the hits yourself."

"The ones in the paper?" The side of his mouth crooked. "That's what this is about?"

"Those are the ones. Why? You know anything about them I should know?"

"Sure, there's a lot of things you should know." He crossed his arms. "But I don't have anything to say."

I cranked up the low-level anger projection and smiled my best evil smile. "Oh, you have plenty to say. I'd hate to have to call in an outstanding mind-warrant to pull it out of you myself."

Bellury next to me suppressed a snort. Yeah, I knew, the odds of me getting a warrant of any kind weren't good—ex-felon, after all—and for a mind-warrant, it was just asking for trouble. As ridiculous as saying the pope was my homie. But the suspect didn't know the difference.

Joey frowned. "You wouldn't."

I sat back, still smiling evilly. "I would." Not that I was exactly eager to roll around in the particular pile of waste that was Joey's mind; even across the table, his mental presence felt as sour as his smell. But I would if I had to.

He was looking at the table, at his hands, very intently. He was also thinking, hard, in scattered pieces I couldn't follow without tipping him off to my probe.

Joey, sprawled out in the chair, put a hand on the table. His mental scales of risk and reward had settled on him talking. "Not a single mark on 'em, scared to death like dog-caged rats? Those're the ones?" I nodded, and he continued. "You never found 'em all. 'Bout three? Four? A month since May. Nobody from around here, just turned up dead here."

"Why haven't we found the other dozen bodies? Seems unlikely we'd just suddenly start finding them. Tell me the truth, Joey."

He shrugged. "Maybe. Maybe I heard somebody made a deal with somebody else to hide the bodies, and, say, stopped later when up the line the boss gets angry." Meaning him and his immediate superior Maloy—well, in the beginning anyway. But I had to get him to say it out loud for the recorders.

"Your boss?" I asked to confirm.

"Maybe we're saying farther up," Joey said. "Not sure who exactly. But the word came down. Nobody deals with the Frankies anymore. Frankies can hide their own fucking bodies."

Who the hell were the Frankies? He wasn't even picturing them, but he was sure as hell angry at them. An opportunity. Any time there was a falling-out, there was a weakness to exploit.

"So who do you figure hid the bodies, Joey?" I asked. "You dumped them in the alleys what, early morning?" Behind me I could feel Paulsen get very, very interested.

"Wasn't me, and I don't know nothing," Joey said pointedly. "But maybe we're saying bodies before that."

"Before that?"

"Could be," Joey said.

"Okay, where are the bodies hidden, then?" Was he just making this stuff up? Didn't feel like it from his thoughts, but there was a lot he wasn't thinking about on purpose.

He just looked at me.

Different angle. Pretend to know what's going on even if I don't. "Who are the Frankies, then? Germans?"

His eyes narrowed. "Why would you think that?"

I made myself stop tapping on the table—just in

case—just in case. "Tell me what the Frankies are. Who they are."

He was suspicious of me now, but he had decided to talk and wasn't going to go back on that quickly. "Frankies are guys from the north side, rich guys. Wouldn't give their names. Boss-man says we gotta call them something."

"So why Frankies?" I asked. "Sounds like a stupid name to me."

He shrugged. "Boss-man, he says they're messing in stuff they don't need to be messing in. He's the boss-man, you know? If he calls them the Easter Bunny, I go find eggs."

Okay. I took a moment to get that image out of my head. "Tell me about the Frankies. What do they look like?"

"I told you. White guys, young one, old one—not too old, fifty maybe. The young one talks more, yells a lot. Old one has a purple patch on his jacket he keeps covering up like he thinks we can't see. He's always worried."

A Guild patch—he was picturing something like a Guild patch. I knew they were involved somehow! The brain damage alone . . .

But it wasn't any good if I didn't confirm it for the recorder. I took a second to sketch out the Guild tele-path patch on a piece of paper and do another couple wrong ones, the Ruten space shuttle service patch and one I made up on the spot. I pushed the paper over to Joey. "Anything look like what you saw?"

He pointed to the Guild's, and I handed him the pencil so he could circle it. He did, and I gloated inter-nally for a long second before getting back to work.

"So how do you know so much about the Frankies?"

I asked him after he was done. "You see them kill those people?"

Joey shut down like I'd flipped a switch. "Didn't see anything," he said. Huh. First time he'd shut down. Could mean nothing but . . .

"Your boss dealing with the Frankies directly, Joey, cutting you out of the deal? Must be worth a lot of money, a bit of body disposal like that."

He set his jaw and thought nasty thoughts about me in specific, creatively nasty thoughts. "Didn't see anything."

"How do you know so much about the Frankies, then, Joey, if you didn't see anything?"

He paused, looked at me suspiciously. "I hear plenty. Just about the time they tell you not to ask no more questions, people start asking 'em. I keep my ears open. Keep my eye on the business, you know? A lot of attention on the neighborhood for no reason. I don't like the Frankies, nobody here does."

For the record, I said, "Because they killed a bunch of people and dumped them in your neighborhood after you made a deal to dump them somewhere else."

"Yeah," he said. "It's insulting, you know? And even if I was inclined to look the other way, too much of that, it's bad for business. Too much attention. And they're cutting us out of the game. Bad for business. Somebody should cut them out of the game, you know, all the way out."

I ignored the veiled death threat. I needed more details, some actual hard facts I could use. I started tapping the table. "What kind of game we talking, Joey?"

"The Frankie game," Joey said with a bit of an attitude. "All the Dead, Dead, and the money."

"Where's the money, Joey? What money?"

He looked at me for a long moment. Apparently he was willing to help me only so far. He looked down at the table, at my tapping hand. I stopped as I felt him recognize the gesture and try to place it.

Quickly. "The bodies found in your neighborhood, the ones killed without a mark?"

"Yeah?"

"You're saying the Frankies killed those seven people?"

"You said there were six. Paper said six too."

Bellury gestured significantly. We weren't disclosing the last body. Crap. At least it would give me an excuse to distract Joey.

I backpedaled like a marathon biker. "Six, then. Sorry. I have trouble with numbers sometimes."

"Dyslexia?"

"Yes," I gritted out.

"You should go to some of them classes. Really helped a buddy of mine."

"I'll look into it," I lied. This was good, probably. He'd never believe the guy he'd known then would struggle with the words. Even high as a kite, I'd done crosswords. Well, when I'd been in touch with reality.

Joey shifted in his chair. I think somewhere in his subconscious he did remember me, and that was probably the only reason he was being even this friendly. I hated it. I hated him and the whole former life of mine he stood for, but I couldn't exactly stop him talking to prove it.

Joey sat back in his chair. "You're not really a telepath. You're bluffing with me."

"That so? Well, I know that regardless of what's on the file, you've stolen at least three cars personally.

Before you started muscling for Marge. The first was a"—of course, now he was thinking about it—"bright yellow classic Camaro. Black stripe. Second was a Mercedes A-34400."

He looked very disconcerted. "There's no way you could know that."

"Want me to tell you how you did it?" I asked. Parlor trick, but it would do the job.

"What do you want?" he asked me in a dangerous tone.

"I need to know how all of this relates. Something I can use."

"What can you use?"

My eyes narrowed. "Dead bodies. Frankies. Your neighborhood. Why?"

"Don't talk to me like I'm stupid."

I held his eyes with a small smile. I faced scarier things than him every day in the mirror.

"The boss man doesn't like the Frankies," he said flat out. "He don't care who knows that. They're making a lot of trouble for the neighborhood, bad for business."

"Who's the boss-man?"

He snorted and leaned back. "You think I'm going to tell you that?"

"I need a name."

"Maloy," he spat out, with a good flash of the man's face and the worry that something had happened with the man out of town. I had no idea what to do with the information.

"And proof of the killings," I said. "Something to connect them to the Frankies."

Joey shifted in his chair. He'd made a deal with the guys—or Maloy had anyway—and he was thinking he couldn't break it, couldn't turn the bastards into the cops. Maloy had forbidden it.

I frowned. "I'll get a police sketch artist in here so you at least can give us a picture of the Frankies. How do you know they're the guys we're looking for? I'd be very disappointed if you gave us the wrong ones."

"I'm no good at the sketches," Joey said. "You going to pull stuff out of my brain? Start something here? Or are you going to let me go?" I felt his decision not to buck Maloy no matter what happened—to hang in there until the man got back, even if it was in a holding cell.

He set his mouth. Let me feel his contempt for rich telepaths born with the fuckin' silver spoon. He wasn't going to do anything else today.

Standing up, I grabbed my repro files and waved Bellury with me into the hallway for a chat.

"Can I arrest him? Or at least hold him for a while?"

Bellury lifted an eyebrow. "Can you prove he's committed a crime?"

"Not unless you'll take my word for it."

"Hard evidence. Something on the recorder?"

"Well, no."

"Then you can't arrest him, can you?" He shrugged in a way only old cops can. "Why don't you go on to Paulsen and I'll take care of the guy, huh?"

I sighed. "Okay."

In the interview observation room on the other side of the glass, Paulsen was seated in the only wobbly chair, alone, a paper in front of her. She'd obviously sent the recording tech away already.

"Editor sent over a copy of tomorrow's lead story." She offered it to me. Her voice was more intense, her waves in Mindspace more angry than her actions would suggest.

"'Serial Killer Stalks East Atlanta,'" I read. Crap. "This is what the mayor wanted *not* to happen, right?"

"That's correct." She stood, her hands going to her lower back as she looked at nothing in particular, her anger simmering under the surface. "When the mayor gets his morning coffee, Captain Harris is going to get a very unpleasant phone call. Branen is going to have an unpleasant morning apologizing. And I— well, I had a very long list of meetings before this happened, and I don't imagine the list is getting any shorter." Her eyes focused on me. "Good work in there. It's a whole lot of nothing, but between that and the forensics from the last scene, at least we'll have something to show."

"It's not a whole lot of nothing. Remember the patches Joey identified? I've got his mark on it confirming. No mistaking what it was. Plus he's saying there's more bodies we haven't found."

She shrugged. "Not important. His credibility is nonexistent."

I realized I hadn't identified the patch out loud. Sloppy of me. "That's the Guild patch. The Telepaths' Guild? Remember them?"

"I've had—"

I barreled ahead. "At least one of the Frankies is Guild! I was suspecting two—"

"Do not interrupt me. I have had a hell of a day and am about to have a hell of an evening." She took a deep breath. "Whether Joey's testimony means anything or not is something you and Branen will have to figure out."

"We need to go to the Guild," I insisted. "For information if nothing else. The brain damage . . ."

She stopped, listening now. "What brain damage?"

"I thought you were up on this. The coroner yester-day."

"*Don't* sass. You will treat me with respect. This is not my case. If it weren't for the goodness of my heart, it wouldn't be yours either. Now, tell me what it is you think is so important." She looked at me critically, and I knew what I said in the next few minutes would determine whether she'd ever listen to me again.

I sucked in air. "Every victim has brain damage in the parietal lobe, in the area controlling Mindspace processing. The victim's brains were burned out from within."

"You mean a stroke?" She was listening, arms crossed while I could faintly feel an ache in her back.

"No, a literal burn, an excess of energy. They were killed with the mind. I'd lay good money on it. I'm betting it's those Frankies Joey was talking about—the ones with the Guild patch. Not easy to get if you're not Guild." And though it stuck in my throat to say it, I continued. "We need to call them, Lieutenant. I know we agreed we wouldn't, but I'm finding more and more details that tell me we need to. As much as it's the last thing I want to do. You want this guy—these guys—off the street, you want the murders to stop, we need to contact the Guild." At minimum, I needed a list of names to cross-check with Joey's description. I knew better than to trust the list they gave the cops.

"It's quite a can of jurisdiction worms you're talking about, a can I don't see any reason to open," Paulsen said. "And I don't know why you're the one bringing this up. We've already made the decision."

"I know," I said. "I know. But if Joey's right, and it's two Guild guys killing—at least seven bodies that we know about? Maybe more? That's not an accident.

That's not an oops-I-didn't-mean-to-kill-the-poor-citizen moment. That's somebody with purpose, maybe two guys with purpose. I can't be everywhere. I can't protect everyone. And all it takes is five seconds, five seconds for someone to burn your brain from the inside."

Her eyebrows narrowed. "Why didn't you say this before, when we were talking about the killer in the first place?"

I took a breath. "To be honest, we're not supposed to talk about details. The training is limited to maybe a handful of guys. There's rules, Enforcement. Process. I'd rather not deal with any of that crap, trust me. But I can't be everywhere at once. We need to call them. There's things they can do we can't touch."

She leaned back, keeping a lid on her anger only with difficulty. "I swear, you were put on this earth to make my life difficult." She blew out a line of air. "The Guild's trouble. You yourself have said it a hundred times. And I'm not convinced we need them. Two guys, well, we can track the records, start eliminating suspects. Sounds like something *you* should do. Like something you should have done before this."

"I can try to run down the records, cross-check." I folded my arms. "But half of the guys with that training are off the books on purpose. Black ops."

"Of course they are," Paulsen said. She muttered under her breath for a good long moment, and I did not listen in.

"We need to call the Guild," I repeated, though it burned to say. "They have resources, names, and data that we need. Maybe they'll even share."

She looked up, scrutinizing my face, my body language. "What aren't you telling me?"

Um, what to say? I settled on a version of the truth. "There's a lot I'm not telling you. I *can't* tell you, kicked out or not—there are a lot of Guild secrets I only know of through rumors. I'm not getting my ass in trouble for rumors. But I can tell you this much: At least one of the killers is Guild. Not affiliate, not I-joined-because-you-made-me-and-I'll-just-coast-along, but hard-core, invested, I-know-the-company-secrets kind of Guild. The I'm-not-listed-in-any-public-database kind of Guild. The scary kind. The kind we probably can't touch legally. We need help here, Lieutenant."

She seriously considered it, and a chill ran through me. Was I really asking for this? Killer or no, breaking ethics or no, these were the people who kicked me out. Who humiliated me. And who might easily come after me for telling their secrets. I was not the guy I was ten years ago. I was not the golden boy, the genius professor, the idealist anymore. I was a drug addict, a cynic— a doubter. Pathologically. I knew all the things that could go terribly wrong, and if I reported every little violation of ethics, I'd never stop. People broke the rules. That was life.

I took a breath, clamped down on all of my complex feelings about the Guild. I was probably making myself a bigger target by doing this, but I didn't care. There was part of me that was still that idealist telepath. Part of me that thought killing with the mind was a sin worse than murder with a knife. A part of me that still lived by those ethics, those Guild ethics. I was in trouble, I thought. I was arguing for contacting the very people who made my life living hell. But I couldn't take it back.

Lieutenant Paulsen took a deep breath. "Get out of here. I'll talk to Branen, but I don't see why you can't call them for information if it's so incredibly important to you."

I looked in the face of what I'd asked for, scary as hell. And I didn't run away, not quite. I kept it to a walk. A sedate and dignified walk.

CHAPTER 6

I was sitting on a small chair in the coffee closet, turned sideways to fit in the narrow space. The creaky table, coffeepots, and endemic stale donuts to my left had a comforting smell, the closet light above pleasantly dim. There were no desks for ten feet in any direction, so the minds of those around me receded to a dull whisper and I could think. Well, until Cherabino walked in my direction.

She stuck her head in the door without knocking. "Want to grab some food?"

At least I'd gotten half an hour to stew about the mess I'd somehow gotten myself into. Not long enough to come up with anything useful, but long enough to calm down.

Her gaze flicked around the tiny space. "I don't understand why you like it here. It's like a coffee-scented coffin. Tiny."

"But delicious smelling," I said. I forced myself not to rub my head, not to twitch, not to put any warning signs out for her to pick up. "My turn to buy, right?"

"Guess that means Mexican again," Cherabino said. She didn't really like Mexican.

There were no stars in the sky, but I could see the full moon through the haze of night pollution. The streetlights here were all either burned out or set on low to save the city money. We had another block up the hill and across the train tracks to the restaurant, a trek we'd made a hundred times. I was keeping my ears open in Mindspace, making sure I'd see trouble coming. I didn't want a repeat of the junkie this afternoon. I was also trying *not* to think of the Guild, *not* to consider what I was doing. I would deal with it when it came.

"Any news on the case?" I asked her, in an attempt at distraction.

"Some." She was walking slouched, her hands in her pockets, turned in on herself. "Fingerprints came in from a couple of the early scenes. There are some smears on the bodies, but otherwise no prints but the victim's. He might be using gloves or skin sealant to hide his prints."

"A teleporter with gloves?" Really?

"Lots of people actually watch television," Cherabino said, tired. "Fingerprints have been around so long, the shows actually get that much right. Watch the fibers be generic cotton too. I'm telling you, this case is seriously pissing me off."

"That's why we should call the Guild." At her nasty look, I said, "What? Cause of death and the Mindspace evidence—"

"Which no one can see but you."

"I have a rating of—"

"Blah, blah, your fabulous rating. If we can't put you in front of a jury, it doesn't mean anything."

"Doesn't mean anything? I got a guy to talk today about seeing our killers. On tape. You put a monkey in front of a suspect and get the information on tape, it's admissible. Isn't that what you keep telling me?" I asked her, furious.

She ignored me. "Killers?"

I was overreacting. I put my hands in my pockets. Nodded. "Says there's two."

"And what do these two killers look like?"

At least she was asking. "Two white guys from the north side, rich, no discernible accent, one younger and one older."

"Well, that's only forty percent of the population."

"It's better than we had."

She blew out a breath. "How reliable is the witness?"

"He's a beta for the area surrounding the scenes. Joey the Fish? He claims the murders are bad for business, and he wants the guys to go away."

She stumbled on an uneven sidewalk. In the back of her mind, I got a glimpse of a name connected to Joey, and a worry that the thing he was connected to—and the case—would interfere with her ceremony next week.

"Who's Fiske?" I asked her without thinking. Crap, double crap, I was reading her again without meaning to.

Cherabino stared at me as we passed out of the area of one streetlight and entered another. Her face flashed with surprise, disbelief, irritation, and something that on anyone else I would have called vulnerable. "Keep your mind to yourself! That name—which you should forget—is Joey's connection to Them." She meant the Darkness. What used to be called the Mafia back when it was still a small-time Italian job. That much was obvious. I mean Joey was the beta, right?

"This guy is his boss?"

"I can't talk about an investigation for the Feds," she said firmly. "Try to forget you heard it. And stop snooping! One of these days you're going to end up dead for having the wrong information. That and it's rude. Really rude."

I moved forward at the same time that Cherabino grabbed the restaurant's door, and somehow we ended up nose to nose.

"I've got the door," she said.

I didn't move away and neither did she. Her eyes widened. I looked at her mouth. She couldn't hide the buzz of reluctant interest, but she looked away, a rebuff.

"You go, then." She relinquished the door.

I hesitated before moving inside the restaurant, suddenly confused. I put my name on the list.

Cherabino waved to some of the other cops already seated. This was a popular hangout for the second-shift "lunch." The parking lot had almost as many cop cars as the department parking lot.

The waitress seated us in a booth. We'd been here more times than I could count, but suddenly it felt different.

"Good interviews today?" Cherabino asked. She studied the menu like it was the key to the universe, but this was not new. For a split second I wondered if I'd only imagined the attraction in her mind.

As the waiter arrived, I tried to smile; I'd waited tables for maybe two weeks somewhere in my slide to the streets. I'd been a shitty waiter. It was a hard job, and much harder when you were doped up to your gills. I ordered for us both.

"You know, I might have wanted something different this time," Cherabino said.

"Did you?" I asked her. She always got a plain quesadilla, no meat, no salsa, nothing fun at all. "I can call the guy back."

"That's not the point."

I knew I was stepping in it, but I had to ask. "Well, what's the point, then?"

"The point?" She smiled wryly. "You have heard of feminism, right? Respect? Women making their own choices?"

"Yeah, I've heard of it. The downside is when you get predictable. Efficiency, you know?" I smiled back, unable to help myself, glad for once to see her happy.

"Efficiency is it?"

"Yes," I said solemnly. "Much faster when hungry he-man needs to eat."

"He-man?" She started laughing, and I let her, my tension dissipating as hers did.

The food arrived and I dug in. We talked about inconsequential things while her happiness started to bleed over into me. I basked in it—stood under it joyfully like a warm sunbeam on a chilly day.

I loved this, her happiness, her openness—I couldn't name the last time I'd seen it. Her smile, rare as an old two-dollar bill, made something inside me smile too.

"We should go out more often," I said without thinking.

Her eyes changed. I felt her nervousness.

"Out of the station," I said quickly. "Food's much better here."

We held eye contact for a long moment, and I memorized the blue of her eyes, emphasized by that dark stuff she put on her lashes.

She looked down. Twisted her napkin in her lap. She fought interest and unease, neither feeling easy to ignore.

"Is it just me or is the workload getting heavier for DeKalb?" I asked. Work seemed to put her at ease, and I wanted that happiness back from earlier. I wanted her happiness more than anything else right now.

She glanced at me, a furtive glance from under her eyelashes. She thought my stubble was sexy. Did I really have—oh. Yeah. Hadn't shaved since yesterday. And she thought—

As Cherabino told me crime was up and budgets down, I realized. I shouldn't have been able to read that thought about my face. It had been a quiet, private thought.

I closed her out with a lot of effort. Had I used her for an anchor too much? Concentrated on her mind to shut out the others one too many times? After six years of working with her on and off, had I crossed some vague line and connected us? Even the lightest, most polite Link in the world meant any concept of privacy got real fuzzy real fast.

Personal space and privacy were strange things; some people didn't care at all, some would freak out from the slightest touch, but most people would let you in freely, and then kill to protect those last few inches. Cherabino was one of the last camp, and no matter how forgiving she was on the surface stuff, I knew the whole concept of mind reading bothered her more than she admitted. It was important I didn't ruin whatever trust she had left in me. And the part of me that was still Guild—the part of me that still believed in certain ethics as a telepath—that part was very very disturbed by this . . . connection of ours.

What I'd meant to be a Scotch tape connection was turning into something more—maybe duct tape, maybe stronger still. A connection that, if I was right, could break all the location-based laws of physics and let me find her anywhere, talk to her at any time. Let her do the same to me—if she could. I didn't know what to do about it. I didn't know at all, and that scared me.

A Link—even a light one—was a big deal. There

were rules I was supposed to follow, Guild rules sure, but rules. Ethics I used to buy into wholeheartedly; ethics I'd quoted to myself earlier when I decided to put my hand in the hornet's nest that was the Guild. Ethically, I had to tell her. I had to tell her that we were bound together, by purpose or accident. I had to. But I couldn't picture a version of that conversation in which I would come out unscarred.

I studied her. Straight posture, long brown hair in a ponytail, makeup today and a white shirt that on all the other female cops looked businesslike and on her looked sexy. Truthfully I didn't want to tell her.

She laughed in a small burst. "You weren't checking me out, were you?"

"No, of course not," I lied, and smiled to soften it.

Wrong move. She looked away, like the slamming of a door.

I nodded politely at the waiter as he refilled our waters, but he was in and out too fast to notice.

"Are you okay?" I asked her. I hadn't flirted, not really. I mean, if I had been flirting, it would have been a lot more—

"Fine," she said, and set herself to eating again.

"I didn't mean to—"

"It's fine," she said, and looked me in the eye. "Can we talk about something else?" I had no idea what she was thinking about at that moment.

"Sure," I said. Maybe it wasn't even a Link. Maybe I was overestimating the connection. And if it was, it was only a little, light one. Right? Either way I couldn't tell her about it, not now, not with whatever this was on the table between us. I told the ethical part of me to shut up and go away.

The waiter came back with the check, and I gave him my humiliating cardboard Food Card. It wasn't worth anything, just a handshake agreement with a few local restaurants for the department to pick up the tab. The accountant checked the expenditures every week. I'd complain, but they'd hired me again after I'd betrayed them. It still galled.

"Still got all those extra cases from Electronic Crimes?" I asked Cherabino.

She made a face. "Two more now." She launched into a running commentary on the corrupt budgetary system keeping the cops' hands tied.

I listened with half an ear, paying more attention to her mood, which was stabilizing as she fell back into her passion for justice. I ate my third California-style fish taco and asked the occasional question. Tried to figure out what I was going to do about my own problems.

I had the Guild to face if I was unlucky, Paulsen if I wasn't, the case to solve either way. And I had the feeling that, no matter how good Cherabino was, I was going to be seeing more dead bodies. Hopefully none of them was mine.

On the way out of the restaurant, we ran into Branen. His expression was annoyed, but the feeling from him in Mindspace was tired and full of dread.

He held up a finger to silence the detective beside him. The man frowned.

Branen caught my eye. "If you think the Guild's so important, you call them," he said.

Beside me, Cherabino's anger hit like a nuclear shock wave. She breathed through her teeth. "Calling the Guild, sir? You said we wouldn't."

Branen frowned at her. "Stay on top of your case, Cherabino. Boy wonder here thinks we need the Guild to hold our hands. Paulsen's pushing for it."

"Not hold our hands, give us names and data," I said. Maybe some backup if I needed it.

"Whatever," Branen said. "But if this goes south, you'll be the one telling Captain Harris why the spooks started a fight."

"It's not—"

He cut me off. "Nice to see you, Cherabino."

"Yes, sir," she said. Furious, she grabbed my arm and marched me outside away from the restaurant.

Under the third streetlight, she turned. "How in hell do you get off on steamrolling me?"

Great. Now she was mad at me. "I told you, the—"

"You told me jack shit! I told *you* to follow orders for once in your life. You can't just argue with the brass whenever something doesn't go your way. We were at *dinner. Talking.* And you said *nothing!* If you were going to go over my head, you should *at least* have had the courtesy to tell me!" She took a big step forward.

I saw her seriously consider hitting me. Saw flashes of me on the ground, me hit in the balls, me immobilized in any one of ten judo moves while she broke my arms and called me names no lady should know. And at the end of it, I saw her chest heaving with angry breaths, her sensei's voice giving her a lecture on nonviolence. She controlled herself, her jaw tight.

"There's no need for violence," I started carefully. But honestly I had no idea what else to say.

"You went over my head on *my case.* I brought you in. You talk to me—it's courtesy! If you were a fucking cop, you'd know that."

I held my ground, though she was in my personal space and blazing like a furnace. "I'm sorry, okay?"

Sadness hit her anger like a dampening cloth, but she set her jaw. "First apology you've given me since rehab," she noted.

"It's part of the steps," I said. I hated apologies, steps or no. They were humiliating. But I'd done it then, and I'd do it again now, for her.

"It doesn't mean you're off the hook." In the back of her head, she was already calculating how she was going to clean up my latest mess. Get back in good with Branen. Get her notes from the widow in the case files.

I cast about for some way to make it up to her, if the apology wasn't enough. "I can take the notes to the secretaries tonight."

Before I could duck, she cocked back and punched me.

Pain exploded in my jaw. I staggered backward, clocking my rear against the hard steel streetlight. I literally saw stars.

"Stay out of my head!" she told me.

I held my jaw. Waited for the breath to come back. To the left, her footsteps walked away.

CHAPTER 7

When the lights of Swartz's aircar came over the hill, I was sitting on the worn steps of the police station while a streetlight sputtered above me. My jawbone ached, my whole body ached, and I was begging the Higher Power for another junkie to come along so I could beat him up and steal his stash. I didn't have time for anything more complicated, like a trip to the South DeKalb projects that would still sell me Satin. Assuming they still would; I'd shut down everyone in Decatur who would sell me anything, and dealers talked. Eventually, they talked.

Like the bastard he was, of course, Swartz showed up right on fucking time. I knew he'd tear the city apart if I wasn't here, if I wasn't sitting at the station. With the night shift all on the main floor facing the windows, cops looking on, all gloating as I sat on the steps. Swartz would have known if I wasn't here right on time. And in ten minutes I wouldn't have gotten five blocks. Swartz said God had a sense of humor, and I thought he was probably right.

Time to break out one of the emergency vials at the apartment. Call in sick tomorrow. Fall back down the rabbit hole.

Of course, Swartz chose that moment to settle the air-car near the curb and get out. He waved at the cop on

Reception, and I stood. My hands were shaking with need. I put my hands in my pockets so Swartz wouldn't see.

But he wasn't an easy man to fool. After one look at me, he said mildly, "There's a Friday late-night meeting at the North Decatur Y I've always wanted to try. The leader brings lemon cake, the real kind. There might even be a few ginger cookies." When I said nothing, he said, "You look like you could use a meeting, kid."

I wasn't a kid, but I wasn't going to argue tonight, not when I might give something away. I'd go along with his plan, stay quiet. Knowing the vials were still there, waiting for me at my apartment. That empty gaping hole inside of me subsided a bit, knowing it would get its fix. Just a matter of time.

Swartz put his hand on my shoulder, forced me to look in his eyes. "We're going to the meeting." It wasn't a request.

I picked up my bag from the worn police steps and got into the aircar. Quiet as a church mouse, I buckled my seat belt.

"Lemon cake?" I asked. Lying to Swartz was like sandpaper on my soul, but it was just a little lie, I told myself. More omission than anything.

After the Narcotics Anonymous meeting, the emptiness had settled into patience. Swartz took me back to my apartment, driving me across the city without complaint. The problem was, he wanted to visit the apartment.

"I'm tired tonight," I said.

"You look twitchy," he responded.

Just a matter of time, I told myself again, as we walked up the five front stairs to my building, avoiding the worst of the crumbling steps and the suspicious green spots. Before the Tech Wars, this had been a proud boxy office building, but now it was smudged, cracked, and discolored. Like a very old woman, beauty still there despite the wrinkles.

I nodded to the bored lobby guard as we made our way to the only stairwell of the building. I found my door, letting us in and hitting the light. Behind me, Swartz was calm but worried. He wasn't going to leave until he was sure I was okay. I appreciated the sentiment, but just now, I wanted him to leave. Go away. Let me deal with things on my own. Quiet as a church mouse, I told myself. It would just be a matter of time.

I locked the door, then grabbed a pack of cigarettes and a lighter from the cabinet above the sink. "Want a cigarette?" My tiny apartment was a closet, barely big enough for my beat-up thirdhand couch and half-sized card table. He was in the small living space now, I was in the kitchen, but we were close enough to talk without raising our voices.

He sat on the couch. "I'm trying to quit."

I looked at the small blue nicotine stick, decided the emptiness in me needed a small reward while it waited, and lit up, taking a long drag like it was salvation itself. I retrieved a worn pack of cards from the cabinet and settled in a chair across from Swartz, ready to wait him out. He took the cards from me and dealt a hand of solitaire for himself.

When his hands were busy, he asked, "You ready to talk yet?"

"Not really." I slouched in the chair, my knees sprawled. When that didn't feel right, I leaned forward, taking another drag of the cigarette before snuffing it out in the empty ashtray on the beat-up coffee table.

Swartz played solitaire quietly, his presence in the apartment normally calming, but today, an intrusion. I didn't have to say anything if I didn't want to. The only reason I was willing to talk, normally. But he wouldn't leave any time soon, not without me talking, and I needed him out.

Fine. I'd talk. "Cherabino hit me today," I said. "I sort of deserved it—she's told me again and again to stay out of her head, and I didn't. But she hit me." A betrayal. A stupid sucker punch.

Swartz turned a card over and made a neutral noise.

"It's *Cherabino*."

"So? She pulled the punch, didn't she?"

"Pulled the punch? No way. It hurt like a son of a bitch."

Swartz looked up. "You're still standing, aren't you? Next time she hits you, hit her back. Didn't they teach you anything in that fancy Guild school of yours?"

I set my jaw. "Apparently not."

His grizzled face creased with deeper lines. "What's really bothering you? A little love tap isn't going to put you in this kind of spiral."

"What if it did?"

He looked at me.

I looked at him. I couldn't tell him about the Link any more than I could tell him about the vials in my wall. But he wasn't going to back down, so I had to tell him something. "Fine. It's the Guild, okay?"

He put the deck down and leaned forward. "The Guild? You still obsessing over them?"

"I'm not obsessing. These are the people who kicked me out. Who put me on the streets. Bad people, Swartz—at least to those of us who don't toe the line. So far as I know, I'm the only one they've ever let go, the only one with the temerity to work with the cops—and that without somebody looking over my shoulder."

He nodded. "The watcher issue."

"Just because they haven't set one yet doesn't mean they're not going to. I need somebody dogging my steps like I need a set of blisters on a ten-mile walk. But I can't not tell them. I can't. Legally, they can lock me up any time—I have the numbers. Koshna's clear. Guild stays out of politics, out of the police force, they get to do whatever the fuck they want to the poor idiots with Ability. That's me, Swartz. It's still me. No matter how much I hate them. No matter what they did to me before."

Swartz shrugged. "You're not too afraid of the people if you're pushing the police to contact them."

"It's the right thing to do. It's the only thing to do— I'm sure as hell not going to guard the Guild killer for weeks while the trial gets going. He's powerful. He's possibly more powerful than I am, and I don't have the training to watch him around the clock without slipping somehow. So I've got to do it anyway. But I don't want to turn over this particular rock. I don't want to remind them. I don't really want to face them. Face what happened." I stubbed out the cigarette. I hadn't meant to go on like this. Truth was a dangerous habit— I'd need to be careful I didn't say much else.

"Is it really going to be that bad?" Swartz asked. "They treated you well enough when you worked for them."

I was quiet for a long time, while Swartz picked up the deck and started playing again. He wasn't going to rush me, not on this.

"Black eight on the nine of diamonds," I pointed out.

We sat in silence for a while, until Swartz had to shuffle for a new hand. "Well?" he asked me, making eye contact.

"Yeah." I looked at my hands and decided to lie. "Listen, Swartz, I'm tired. Can you pull this out of me a different day? I have an early interview tomorrow morning."

He frowned at me a minute. "We're doing the service project tomorrow."

"Cherabino called at the last minute," I lied. "I can't make it." I'd be sleeping in, enjoying the high.

Swartz gathered the cards up. "I'll see you Sunday, then."

I shut the door behind Swartz with a sense of relief and anticipation. I lit another cigarette and went back to the bedroom.

Suddenly I was exhausted, so tired my bones hurt. I sat down on the glorified cot that was all they would give me—real beds were still worth something in trade, apparently—and leaned back carefully against the lumpy wall. Was I really going to do this? Three years thrown away? I took a long breath of the smoke, and thought, Maybe. Maybe, just give it a minute. The smoke curled up to the low ceiling above me.

The room was maybe two inches longer than the solid cot beneath me, and maybe twice as wide. Mine was the largest floor plan this building had—central area with a separate bedroom and bathroom, both—and even this one was tiny.

Despite its size, this apartment was worth whatever the department paid for one, impossible feature. The building had been a haven for small technology companies before the Tech Wars, office in a box or some such. A developer had converted it badly when demand froze after the technology companies all went under. What mattered was the "badly" part. The walls were still full of original, inactive Tech.

The lumps behind me were carbon-based microcircuitry, layer upon layer of electric loops, stacked and quiescent. They'd wrenched out the triple central-processing relays in the remodeling—along with every other semisentient computer in the city, all destroyed more than fifty years ago—but the rest was still there, still waiting. I'd had an electrician reconnect the components and put in a couple of "gates." Two weeks of hairsbreadth tuning with a 'scope, but it had been worth it.

I took one long, final breath from the cigarette, then snubbed it out in the ashtray on the floor next to the cot. I braced myself.

Then I reached out my leg and bumped the waist-high switch with my foot. Behind me, the wall hummed to life. The lightbulb above me flickered, but nothing else happened in the realm of the five senses. I was not fooled.

Wrenching pain wrapped around me in Mindspace, like a tidal wave hitting a wall of pines, pressure, pressure in a torrential rush . . . then . . . nothing. Literally nothing. I took a deep breath. Mindspace was gone. Or, more literally, I was gone—from Mindspace. My thoughts slowed down, quietly, like I'd had one too many glasses of alcohol on a calm day, and I took a deep breath.

I could think, finally, but the emptiness was still there. The promise I'd made to myself, to get away, to give in, to have one moment when it all made sense. I got up and ran my hand over the lumpy wall until I found the hidden switch. A circuited panel opened, and the two medicinal vials in the little recess in the wall stood out—two dots of pale color in a gray box. Three small needles.

The vials were old stuff, their bright blue color faded to a dull pastel; it had been six months or more since I'd bought them. But the drug would still work. Not as strong, not as sharp, but it would still work. I could always buy more tomorrow, the good stuff. Leave work a little early, have plenty of time to get to South DeKalb or Fulton by bus, easy peasy.

I took a breath. Okay. I reached into the box, pulled out a needle and a vial, set them on the bed. Rolled back my sleeve, and with the confidence of long-ago practice, measured out a small dose. My tolerance would have gone down, I told myself, watching the blue liquid wander up the glass tube of the needle, climbing up the little marks. I didn't want to overdo it on first go.

I heard a dull thumping from the living room, a knock on the door. I paused. The knocking came again. Whoever it was would have to go away, I thought.

"It's Swartz," I heard muffled through the door. "I'm coming in." The metallic scraping of a key sounded in the lock.

Oh crap! Why did I give Swartz a key?

In a panic, I threw the measured needle under my pillow with shaking hands. Pushed the rest into the alcove. . . .

A hand clamped down on my shoulder. Out of nowhere.

Why didn't I . . . oh. I stared at the lumpy wall, at the fuzzy not-there feeling it was putting off. The machine was on, the illegal machine Dane had designed for me years ago. My stomach sank. I couldn't feel a stampede of minds with the machine on. I'd had no warning Swartz was coming.

I turned, slowly, trying to block the alcove with my body.

He pushed me aside. Stood there, a look of dismay on his face. "I'm getting too old for this," he said, and scooped the entire contents of the alcove in meaty hands, needles and all. "This stuff's poison, boy. I've said it a hundred times."

He advanced to the bathroom with his hands full, refusing to stop, his body like a freight train. I grabbed at his sleeve, his shoulder, but he just kept going. He just kept going, unfeeling, uncaring.

I pleaded, "Don't do this. It's just for emergencies. Don't do it!" I tried to dig in my heels, but he outmassed me and I was too panicked to think of any tricks.

He wrenched open the door of the tiny bathroom, threw the glass down hard into the metal sink. I heard the sound of all my hopes shattering, the glass falling to bits. I slammed my body forward, one last dash—and he blocked me.

He held me back with an arm, with a white-knuckled grip as all my plans seeped in blue droplets down the drain.

Then he turned on the water.

My heart dropped in my chest. It was gone, and Swartz knew. "You didn't have to do that," I muttered.

"You should have done it yourself." He pushed past me, heavy footsteps going back to the bedroom, a death knell.

I slid down the wall to the hard floor, staring out into my bare apartment, the emptiness sweeping over me like white noise, all-consuming. Swartz would find the dose under my pillow; he always found them. I should get up, scream, start swinging, get cruel to keep that last shred of hope. I should.

I was still three years clean. The emptiness mocked me. My own mind mocked me.

Swartz moved past me to the bathroom again, destroyed my escape one more time with the distinctive sound of metal on metal and shattering glass. My last vial.

Then he came out. He loomed over me. I stayed where I was.

"I'm not getting down on the floor, kid."

Too bad, I thought, closing my eyes and leaning my head against the wall. Isn't that too bad for you.

"Is that the last of it?"

I was silent.

He sighed, and I heard his footsteps as he searched the rest of it, systematically. It took a while, even in the little space I had. I wondered what he thought of me.

Finally the footsteps stopped next to my head again.

"Why'd you come back?" I asked, quietly.

He took a breath. "If there really was an interview tomorrow, it wouldn't be Cherabino who'd call. Plus, you just said she's mad enough to hit you. It didn't add up."

"Oh."

I heard the very faint sound of him punching in numbers on his phone.

I looked up then. Crap, he was really going to do it, wasn't he? I stood up, to at least face it like a man.

"This Bellury?" Swartz met my eyes, his mouth set in a deep line. He nodded to the person on the other side of the phone as if he could hear him. "That's right. You might want to sit down. I have some bad news."

At two in the morning, I sat in my bedroom, on my cot. The machine was still on and Swartz was asleep on the sofa in the living room. I'd just gotten two hours of lecture from him—disappointment and understanding and censure—and I didn't really want more from his mind right now. His words were ringing in my ears as it was. He said I should be getting past this by now, I should be starting to make some of my own positive choices. The vial in the apartment was a choice, damn it. It wasn't like he'd never been tempted.

I sat and stewed. Thought of the drug, pleasure/painful memories of the days I'd been lost to it. Thought of the last time I'd fallen off the wagon, how bad it'd been then, for months, for over a year. Thought of my big screwups at the Guild. And, oddly, I remembered Dane, the guy who'd designed this machine behind me, the machine that had saved my sanity more than once, the machine that had gotten me caught tonight.

Dane had been my best friend. He'd sat down in the desk next to me in a Third School history class and introduced himself, and we'd just clicked. For ten years, we were inseparable. Dane was a microkinetic with spiky blond hair and a zest for life that wouldn't quit; you never knew what he would do next. Guild guy to the core, though; his research those last years, into applications of technology in Ability, was illegal in all fifty states and most of Europe. The Guild kept it quiet, and I didn't care. I was Guild then myself.

Hell of a gadget I had behind me; it was probably illegal, against the spirit if not the letter of the Tech laws. But worth it. Technology fields and human-driven Mindspace influenced each other in weird ways; like electricity and magnetism, they were two forms of the same thing. But unlike electro/magnetism, no one yet had a formula to describe the interaction, to even begin. They said math didn't go that far yet. They said you couldn't describe a human mind accurately enough to start.

But Dane could. He'd modeled the shape of my mind, modeled it well enough to echo with Tech. He'd designed a machine to mimic my mind in reverse. Like those headphones you wore to hear nothing, the machine echoed the shape of my mind, and the waves canceled one another out. When I turned it on, I stopped existing in Mindspace, and Mindspace stopped existing for me.

But even Dane wasn't perfect. There was a flaw. The mind was fluid and the Tech was not; if you thought hard enough, differently enough, if you moved far enough away, it would stop working. Your brain waves and the machine's waves would start to clash painfully. Then you turned the Tech off, or you'd end up with rips in your mind. Short-term exposure, you could heal in a week or so—the physical brain slowly overwriting the mind until you were back to normal. Long-term exposure, on the other hand—well, you'd be lucky to be a vegetable. Your physical brain left empty without software to run it.

It was a crazy, bitter thing that I hadn't thought outside the bubble tonight; it hadn't torn my mind. Apparently panic and anger, bitter gall, and helplessness were normal for me. Normal, as depressing a thought as that was.

I saw the breaking glass again, the drops of blue salvation running out, wasted. I saw Swartz turn the faucet handle. . . .

My mind grabbed for something, anything, to not think about it. And I got Swartz's words: "I'm so disappointed."

I shied away from that too, and ended up with Dane's face in my mind, a different kind of older pain. I missed him, still missed him. It wasn't fair. Aneurysm was such a small word for something that destroyed everything. There wasn't even any warning. I couldn't even try to save him. He was dead by the time we got there.

I thought, It's his fault. His fault for dying. If he'd been there, maybe I wouldn't have found the drug. Maybe I wouldn't have gotten hooked. Who knows, maybe Stewart wouldn't have asked me in the first place. He'd been one of Dane's friends, working in the same hush-hush experimental section. He would have kept his stupid drug research to himself. But Stewart was just the kind of bastard to have asked either way.

He was researching drugs to improve telepathy, to bolster Ability long term. Satin had been one of the drugs he was testing; it had a strong effect in Mindspace, and it hadn't been illegal then. Stewart had been looking for some volunteers to try it out. Two days after the funeral, three days after the aneurysm. I hadn't been thinking straight.

The first three doses weren't my fault. They were Stewart's, the Guild's. Given to me, in the lab, like a rat. After that, well, after that there was plenty of fault to go around. Breaking into the lab to steal the drug was the least of what I was guilty of. When it all came out, in the end . . . Well, things fell apart, my bridges burned in slow motion, burned my old life, my good life, to pieces. Sitting in the ashes afterward just reminded me I'd set the match.

I'd lit another match this time, and I could feel the bridges burning again. Swartz might never look at me the same again; the cops either. Cherabino might throw me out like garbage, especially after what I'd done before this. But as I sat in the ashes of the night, as I remembered other nights, as I missed Dane again with a pain that cut at my heart like a knife, my eyes watered. Just when I thought it couldn't get any worse, it did.

I could feel the precog waking up, the crazy, stupid, unreliable precog. I could feel something coming, something bad. Something dangerous.

And I had just done the one thing in the world that would keep anyone from believing me.

CHAPTER 8

Bellury showed up at the door the next morning. I glanced at Swartz—who was still glowering—and let him in. The older cop had a small leather case with him. We both knew why he was here.

Bellury paused in the center of the living room, exchanged an inscrutable old-man look with Swartz.

"Can at least I finish my cereal?" I asked them.

Swartz nodded. I ate slowly.

Finally I did it, peed in the cup when I was told. Bellury watched me do it, like I was a newbie all over again, like all the trust in the world had run out for me. I wasn't stupid enough to protest, but the humiliation of it burned.

I put the cap on the cup, set it in the clear baggie he held out for me, and zipped up.

"Can I at least wash my hands in peace?"

He nodded, tucked the baggie away in his case with a frown, and shut the door. I heard his footsteps as he walked away, across the apartment, and said good-bye to Swartz. The outside door creaked and slammed.

Finally, I turned the water on.

When I emerged, Swartz told me to get ready. "We have a park to clean," he said.

"Give me a minute," I said.

Most of the NA chapter showed up for the cleanup project. We picked up trash, cleared brush, trimmed bushes and branches; we even planted a few flowers that wouldn't mind the heat. I bitched and sweated through two shirts, my muscles getting more and more sore while the back of my neck sunburned bad. It was miserable and hot and unhappy, but I went home with a small and angry sense of satisfaction.

When Swartz signed us up for another Saturday next month, I complained louder than anybody—I hated the heat, we all did—but I didn't take my name off the list.

Swartz sat on my couch while I called the Guild on Sunday. More specifically, their external relations department. It had to be done, and the weekend was already a low point in my life. What was one more humiliation? It wasn't like they were going to call Enforcement on me. Probably not, anyway.

Swartz nodded encouragement, and I picked up the phone, dialing slowly. I watched him play solitaire as the phone rang.

A young-sounding male voice picked up the call, and I relaxed one small degree. It was probably a student, judging from his general lack of confidence. Only six rounds of I-don't-know and let-me-ask-my-supervisor-tomorrow before he'd write down what I wanted. After getting all of my old Guild information and current department contact—good for him—he repeated my request carefully and promised to send it on to the attaché.

"When?" I asked.

"When she gets in tomorrow," the guy replied. "Um, Kara is usually in about eleven."

"Kara?" I repeated with a sinking feeling. The universe could not be so cruel as to make it be . . .

"Yeah, Kara Chenoa. The attaché? That is who you wanted to meet with, right?"

I dropped the phone to my chest. Swartz looked up, frowning, but I waved him back to what he was doing. I picked the phone back up, gritted my teeth, and dealt with it. "If she's the attaché, that's who I need to talk to."

"Do you have another number we can reach you at?" the guy asked.

Lacking anything better, I gave him Cherabino's work number. I probably couldn't use Swartz's for a police investigation.

My head in my hands, I spent the next twenty minutes *not* explaining who Kara Chenoa was to Swartz. Who was Kara? Only the woman who'd betrayed me to the Guild. The woman I thought I'd marry.

I wanted to throw up. But somewhere deep inside, I also relaxed a small, terrified degree. Kara might kill me herself, she might twist the knife on every bad thing I'd ever done, she might humiliate me in a hundred legitimate ways, but—but. She wouldn't string me up for something I didn't do. She wouldn't call Enforcement. Kara had been fair to a fault, political as hell—but she would follow the rules if it killed her.

I could work with her. It would be hell, but I could work with her.

CHAPTER 9

Monday morning, I got a cheese Danish and a cup of café-bought fancy coffee for Cherabino. It had taken a two-block hike in the early-morning heat to get it, but it was a peace offering. It wasn't supposed to be easy. With my stomach in knots, I climbed the stairs to DeKalb County police headquarters with a deep sense of foreboding.

I stared at the main common area, currently crawling with people shouting at the top of their lungs. Looked like a lot of teenagers, sullen and yelling teenagers, while their parents—I assumed the older people were their parents—sobbed and screamed and threatened to hit the cops.

A few fistfights were breaking out in Booking to the left, the secretaries had abandoned ship to the right, and the officer normally on Reception was escorting a very huffy teenage girl to the restroom.

Great. Whatever was going on, I'd see it in the interview rooms soon, which meant a lot more work for me.

I dodged chaos on my way to the elevators, making my way through desks and screaming suspects.

I had screwed up my courage to apologize to Cherabino. I had a peace offering. I thought maybe, if I gritted my teeth, I might even manage to deal with Paulsen. I'd get through this. I had to.

Upstairs, I found Cherabino hunched over her desk, the overhead light off, sunglasses on. I set the Danish and coffee down next to her. Some of the tension went out of me. She wasn't mad; she probably couldn't even start to be mad with a migraine. "Did you take your meds?" I asked, voice pitched quiet and low.

Her shoulders were hunched in, almost collapsed, and she was leaning over the keyboard. In Mindspace, I could see the slow, inexorable pound of pain.

She shifted her head slightly: a no. I sighed and fished out the bottle of pills from her second drawer. Handed them to her. Repressed a lecture. They didn't do her any good if she wouldn't take them, but she knew that.

"You been to the doctor?"

She forced down two of the horse pills, swallowing them with a face, then gulped the fancy coffee. "No," she said, in that telling, raspy whisper. "Nothing they can do if I don't want the surgery."

Obviously she didn't.

I knelt down by the side of the chair, close enough to feel the pounding pain, which suited my mood about now. I met her eyes. "About Friday—"

"I'm sorry I hit you," she said, reaching a hand out toward my still-tender jaw, pulling her hand back before she touched me. She looked away. "Just don't go over my head again, okay?"

"I won't," I said. I hoped it was true.

"*What* are you doing? Three botched interviews in a day, and I had to be called down twice. It's the effing start of the week!" Paulsen pushed her paperwork aside and got to her feet.

I stood at attention—or the best approximation I could get without any formal training—in front of her desk, trying not to cause any more trouble than I already had. If the captain and Branen could fire me just because they felt like it, Lieutenant Paulsen was worse. She could make my life a living hell, and maybe today I would deserve it.

"Got anything to say for yourself?" she asked. "Or are you standing there just to rearrange my neurons?"

"I wouldn't dare," I said truthfully. She'd find out, somehow, and do . . . something very bad. I didn't know what, which made it worse.

"Good." Her wrinkles deepened. "Now. What's going on? You haven't screwed up in months, and now three in a row? Is this about the phone call I got from Bellury this weekend? You're lucky as *hell* your test came back clean." She leaned on the edge of her desk, arms crossed in front of her. "We've been through this one too many times. I've got five cops a quarter in my office wanting me to get rid of you. Your rap sheet, your numbers—half the department's convinced you're playing us all. Taking secrets back to the Guild." She paused, as if waiting for me to respond. "You can't afford another screwup, not like the last time."

I thought about several possible answers, and settled for polite. "No, ma'am."

"I can't afford another screwup like that one. The perp lost the lawsuit by a hair. Five million dollars— that's enough money to shut all of us down. We can't do that again. Not ever, understand? You're making me nervous, and I'm not happy when I'm nervous."

"No, ma'am."

She sighed. "Do you know why I've kept you on?"

"Not really."

"That confession rate of yours is twice my next-best interrogator. Branen says you've upped Cherabino's close rate another fifty percent. We like results. Those kinds of results, they're good for the budget. But they've got to keep going, not like this morning. Not like before. Your results stop now, I'm not sure I can protect you. You understand me? No more leash, no more tolerance."

I swallowed. "Yes, ma'am."

She studied me. I tried to stand motionless, but I don't think I succeeded. Finally she said, "It's not just about you. You screw up an interview, you screw up an investigation. Sometimes it can't be fixed—sometimes the hard cases don't talk at all. It's not about you. It's about the investigation. You need a break, you take a break. You get your head in the game."

I nodded.

Her eyes narrowed. "Don't let me catch you abusing the system. And I've arranged for weekly drug tests until I say different. Am I clear?"

In that moment, her mind was wide open. I couldn't help reading the truth of her words, and a distrust that burned me, that echoed my own. "Understood," I said. "No more screwups. I'm supposed to talk to you the next time something's up."

She blinked. Guess she hadn't said the last out loud. But she continued, "That's right. And the interviews?"

"Take time if I need it. Get my head in the game." I was angry now, but I wasn't going to show it, not here.

"I'd rather a delay than a screwup. We only get one shot at these guys, and you're on the hard cases."

"Understood."

We faced each other for a long moment.

"You can go now."

"Yes, ma'am." I turned around and left, grateful to go. The distrust burned like acid, and the weekly tests were just one more indignity on top of the pile. But I'd done it before. I was not happy, but it could have been so much worse. I'd expected so much worse.

I had just about reached the door when she spoke again.

"Wait," she said.

I turned.

"Make sure you show up early for the case briefing this afternoon."

"What case briefing?" I asked.

"Cherabino's having her team go over the multiples case. Wants you there. *Don't* embarrass me by being late."

I turned to go—but she stopped me again.

"Also." She reached behind her for a plastacard, which she handed to me. "I had Bob run a data search on the Guild in the public records. Any reference to any member with a high rating in either of the two fields you were talking about. See what you can do to narrow it down to the ones with the right skill level, will you? It would be a miracle if something pops, but we're looking for the miracles."

I agreed and took the card.

"Get me something I can use. Now, get out of here."

I got.

CHAPTER 10

The meeting was held in the smaller of the two conference rooms—they called it Holmes, as in Sherlock. With four plain walls, a large bleached-wood table, and old wheeled chairs, the only real color in the place was the name. I was furious, disappointed, the scent of my own failure far too strong. But I had also had a long walk across hostile cubicles—I would keep it together if it killed me.

Finally I reached the conference room. In the back, behind the huge table, one of the junior cops was setting up two rolling bulletin boards. A mountain of papers and a box of pushpins were sitting next to him on the table, ready for him to start affixing clues. He started with a map with seven red X's on it, what looked like the East Atlanta area.

Cherabino came in, her migraine easing but still there. She gave me a funny look, and I read fresh distrust and frustration. "You're early."

Great, now she knew about my slip and wasn't happy. I held my ground. "You asked me to come."

"Yeah." She took a breath. "Find something useful to do."

Branen arrived at the conference room door with a handheld notebook and a cup of coffee. After Cherabino shot him a look, he explained, "I'm just sitting in.

After the papers this weekend, I think it's clear I'll be answering questions from the media." He was also thinking, if Piccanonni showed up, he wanted to be here to run interference. Whoever Piccanonni was.

Cherabino swallowed a protest and gestured for him to take a seat where he could see the board. Impatient, she gestured at me to help the junior cop.

I sighed. The junior cop gave me a stack of pages and pushpins, shooing me over to the board on the left, and I started pinning. We'd just have to put everything back in the murder book later, but maybe they thought it would spark new ideas. I'd do far stupider things to earn my way back to Cherabino's good side.

Picture after picture went up on the board, sad morgue pictures of seven dead faces. One was an old woman who'd owned the scarf in Cherabino's office, her face discolored with a massive bruise. The rest were younger; the teenagers, their faces stuck in sullen despair, broke my heart. They should be irritating their caregivers and getting into trouble, not laid out like carrion on a metal table.

Someone Guild had done this, had taken the information that should have been a sacred trust, and turned it on these people. Had broken them beyond repair, beyond even the hope of repair. The thought made me disgusted all over again. Anyone powerful enough to manage this should have been caught long ago by his handlers, by the Guild, and tried and executed. Murder was a big deal, but the Guild wasn't doing anything. So now the cops had to handle it.

I pinned up footprint pictures and sketches of other physical evidence, and another few people arrived at the conference room. One was a blond woman whose thoughts were curiously ordered, laid out in rows with tags like a dictionary. The other two visitors were a cop and a female tech, respectively. I had no idea what the blond woman was, but when I turned around, I noticed her sitting very straight in her chair, almost too straight, like she wasn't comfortable here.

None of the crowd introduced themselves, as if everyone knew everyone else—except perhaps for the blond woman. Either way, I was the one loser left out of the equation. I stayed very quiet, determined to work, to fit in. I did find a seat, though, at the end near the techs.

Cherabino stood. "Okay, thanks for coming. This case has just jumped four levels in priority, and we're all here to share information and try to figure out what's going on."

"Why the jump?" the tech asked. She was a short twenty-something with pink hair and a wrinkled shirt. "We're backed up in the lab as it is."

Branen leaned forward. "The captain got another call from the mayor over the weekend. He's . . . upset over the story hitting the papers."

Cherabino looked at him cautiously. Then she started again. "Let's go around the table with our information. We'll start with you, Michael." She nodded to the junior cop, a slight Asian guy, and sat down.

He cleared his throat and looked at his notebook. "Um. Yes. Two kids playing in the abandoned store across the street saw a white or gray air sedan fly over the buildings and land in a parking lot two weeks ago. Old white guy who got out was carrying a heavy, long garbage bag. Lumpy, they said."

"How old were the kids?" Cherabino asked.

Michael looked at the notes. "Nine and thirteen."

"Old could be anything over thirty, then," she said. "Only the one guy?" When the man nodded, she told him, "Could be one of the bodies being dumped. Good work."

"Ma'am?" he added. "I'd like to stay on this case if you have the work."

Cherabino glanced at Branen and shrugged. "There's always plenty of work." To Michael, she said, "Could you take a sketch artist to the kids and see if they remember enough to be useful? Two weeks is a long shot. . . ."

"But a picture of the killer would be invaluable," Michael agreed. "I'll take care of it."

Cherabino nodded at the next one along the table, the pink-haired tech.

"Trash bag?" the woman asked Michael, who nodded. "That would match with the bag piece we got from the sixth victim." She straightened and looked at Cherabino: "Like you asked us, the lab reran the clothes from the fourth and fifth victims. In addition to dirt, and normal scene contaminants, we found trace amounts of a processed talc powder mix. No soap this time, though."

"What kind of powder?" Branen asked.

The woman glanced at the notebook. "Manufactured talc. The kind used to coat the inside of latex gloves."

"Like a surgeon?" He frowned.

"Well, yeah." She tilted her head. "But I use latex gloves too. They're not as permanent as skin sealant, less likely to contaminate your sample, and you can take them off if things get icky. They're pretty common." She held out a hand. "And before you ask, no, there's no way to tell brand from the sample. Since they did away with cornstarch, everybody uses the same formula. Now latex, on the other hand . . . If I'd gotten a sample of that, I could tell you anything you wanted. But the gloves *are* kinda designed not to fall apart."

"Anything else?" Branen asked.

By now I was tapping on the table, and Cherabino was crossing her arms, glancing at Branen when she thought he wasn't looking. Just sitting in, huh? I made myself stop tapping.

"A couple of blue poplin fibers, fifty-five/forty-five cotton polyester. Used for a lot of things, most commonly medical scrubs."

"So he's a doctor?"

"Could be." The tech shrugged. "He could also be a guy who bought a pair of slouchy pants at the local thrift shop and doesn't like to get his hands dirty. I don't think it's conclusive."

"What about the soap?" I asked. Everyone looked at me. So much for being quiet, but it was new information. If I was going to pull a rabbit out of the hat any time soon, I needed all the information.

"Where have you been? Liquid Dawn dishwashing detergent, Fresh Spring scent, very diluted traces. We identified it on the first body and all the rest."

"Sadly, you can buy it anywhere in Atlanta," Cherabino told me.

"But not on this victim?" asked the blond woman with the organized thoughts. Maybe forty-five, she spoke with a gravelly voice I'd never heard on a nonsmoker. "What else was different about this scene?" She was looking at me directly. "You're the telepath, aren't you?"

"I am. And you are who exactly?"

Cherabino's hand came down on my arm, a warning to be careful.

"Claudia Piccanonni, the GBI lead profiler. Your department asked me to take a look at this case." Her hard eyes studied me. "I prefer to see a staff meeting than have my own. I repeat, what else was different about this scene?"

"Me, for one. I wasn't at the others. At this one, I found traces of two guys in Mindspace," I told her, uncomfortably. "But the kids saw only one guy. And the second one at the scene seemed pretty angry, like something was different. Maybe he wasn't there at the other scenes."

"These are not where the bodies are being killed," Cherabino put in. "We know they're dump sites. If he set down in a parking lot, we may not have noticed the vehicle marks. I don't think we canvassed that far out."

Michael put his hand on the table. "The kids said the aircar was weaving a little and landed hard. The older one thought the guy might have an issue with one of the anti-grav generators."

"How would the kid know?" I asked.

"His dad's a mechanic and he hangs out in the shop on weekends, he said."

Cherabino blinked. "Was this in the report?"

He shrugged. "Yes, ma'am."

She made a mental note to read reports more carefully.

The tech leaned forward, excited. "A bad anti-grav generator can compress a patch of ground pretty bad. It wouldn't wear away for a couple weeks on soil, longer on pavement—it'd have to wait for the next paving truck to come out." She turned to Branen. "If you'll let me take a couple of guys back to the scenes, I'll see if we can find the impressions."

Branen frowned. "Why wasn't this done already?"

"No reason to canvass that far out," Cherabino returned. "We had more than enough to do in the crime scenes themselves."

"Quite a few man-hours to correct it now," he said. "Would the anti-grav generator make a positive ID on the killer—or killers?" He added the last words with a glance at me.

Cherabino's knuckles got white on the stylus she was holding as she struggled not to contradict her boss. *Sitting in, my ass!* she muttered mentally. *He's trying to take over.* Then, out loud she said, "It would corroborate the kids' stories and help us confirm how the bodies were transferred. Might eventually lead us to confirming the car."

"Go ahead," Branen said with a sigh. "But no more than two techs, hear me?"

The next cop around the table was about to speak when the blonde interrupted him.

"I'm sorry; perhaps I wasn't clear. What changed in the last scene?" She folded her hands. "Change always means something in these cases. Always. If the second man was not at the other scenes, his presence means something. The fact that this body, of all of them, was not washed, tells me something. Was there a difference in position?"

"I'm sorry?" Cherabino asked.

"In how they were found. I can see on the board at least one was left lying horizontally, arms tucked at the sides, legs together. That's rarely a position of death. Were the others the same?"

"The first six were like that," Cherabino said. "The seventh was sprawled as if someone had dumped him."

"And was not washed."

"That's correct."

"I would venture to guess that the second man was *not* at the other scenes, and that the change in disposal was due to his influence."

"They also didn't take an aircar," I put in.

Those cold eyes turned back to me and blinked. "I'm sorry?"

"They teleported into and out of the scene," I said. "Probably the second guy is a teleporter, a really strong one to be able to carry two men besides himself, one of them dead."

"Is it harder when they're dead?" the gravelly voice asked without emotion.

"A lot harder."

"Why?"

I shifted in the chair. I supposed it wasn't a secret. "There's no shape in Mindspace to hold on to—literally, deadweight, and weight no amount of thinking is going to convince you is part of you, like clothes. Anything outside the body is hard to move, but something nonliving and big—that's the hardest."

Cherabino cleared her throat. Looking at nothing in particular, she said, "Actually, the coroner said he was still alive when he arrived at the scene, though probably dying of whatever it was by then. The other victims were dead when they were dumped."

"Oh," I said eloquently. That was right; I'd felt the guy's fear.

"Still alive?" Piccanonni asked. "With different transportation and a new modus operandi? Then for certain the relationship between our two criminals has changed, and changed radically, between the last death and this one. I wouldn't be at all surprised if they begin to escalate their behavior."

"Escalate?" Branen said, going a little pale. "As in more killings? Worse killings?"

"How can it get worse?" I asked.

"We don't know they worked together on any of the other killings," Cherabino put in.

Piccanonni looked at us all calmly. "More killings,

in a faster time frame. Given the facts you've presented, I'd say the first man approached the victims with dignity. He washed the bodies; he laid them out carefully. The second—assuming that's what caused the change—the second man is not so respectful. He's dumping the bodies like garbage, a clear statement he thinks of them as anything *but* human. The fact that the first man was there and didn't stop him suggests that the second is dominant; bad news for us. We're looking at an increased time schedule. More violence. Escalation, and fast. If I'm wrong—and I'm never wrong—we are at least looking at an individual who is growing more unstable and more violent, quick."

Cherabino flagged me down after the rest left, Branen escorting Piccanonni out and trying to convince her to handle any other information she needed by phone.

"Did you call the Guild yet?" she asked me, standing at the end of the table awkwardly. She'd heard about my weekend—and the test coming back clean—and didn't know how to treat me now.

"Sunday," I confirmed. "They're supposed to call me back today—I gave them your number, actually, so you might want to check your messages."

She nodded, looked away. "You said something about specialized Guild training?"

I paused, standing with one hand holding the other wrist, feeling awkward too. "You didn't think just anybody could kill with their mind?"

She shrugged. "Hadn't really thought about it."

"Well, they can't. It takes a certain level of Ability. Plus specialized training. Or, well, at least working in the right kinda field. One where the training already gets you close—most Minders, for example, can probably figure it out. They're not taught it, though."

"Who is taught it, then?"

I supposed it was the logical question. "The answer's a little long."

"I'll listen," she said. "I've got nowhere else to be."

Me, on the other hand . . . I was already late for the interview room, but the perps could wait. They should wait, actually, if they hadn't already. It made for better interviews, and Paulsen said I should take time if I needed it. "Well, the microkinesis guys can kill, the bio-chem medical guys could do it too, but neither one of those would look like this. I suppose an electric-fields guy could do it if he had enough knowledge of the brain, but it would be simpler just to burn out the back brain, not mess around with the higher cortical functions at all. Wouldn't look like this."

She was getting impatient. "What would look like this?"

I breathed, decided I could probably tell her. "Psych, Off, and Construct." When her eyes narrowed, I explained. "Psych is trained in psychology and telepathy; they treat mental illness. If you want somebody to lose their mommy issues for good, you call Psych."

"So schizophrenia and stuff?" she asked.

"No, schizophrenia is actually a brain-chemistry or mind-structure issue—Biochem or Construct. Psych treats the more normal kinds of mental illness, usually the severe ones talk therapy doesn't touch. Off is Offensive Battle, the black ops guys. They're trained to kill, because, well, that's what they do for a living. They're all at least a little crazy by definition, and mostly you hope it's not at you. And Construct—the deconstructionists—well, we're the structure guys. The mind, not the brain, though the two influence each other. If you want a criminal to literally not be able to think about molesting children again, or if you've lost your ability to see color from a brain injury and you want it back, or if you want to literally upgrade your personal memory and remember more of what you see, we're the guys you call."

"You're a . . . ," Cherabino trailed off.

"Deconstructionist, yes. I've told you that before."

"It's weird," she said. I could see the wheels turning; then she glared at me. "You're saying you could have killed those people? You've had the training?"

Of course that's the first thing she was going to think, especially today. "I was in the interview rooms Wednesday afternoon," I said testily. "We have at least ten tapes showing it."

"Oh," she said, but she was going to check. Of course she was going to check.

"Anything else you want to know?" My tone had bite.

"No, I think that's enough for now." She gestured to the door.

I stomped out, watched her leave, went for a cigarette on the back steps. The drizzling rain suited my mood as I told myself I couldn't have Satin and would have to make do with a second cigarette. At least out here no one would bother me.

CHAPTER 11

Two o'clock, and I snuck into the Electronic Crimes section to borrow a computer with decent processing capacity, pulling out the plastacard Paulsen had given me. I wasn't technically supposed to be there, but Cherabino had all the codes in her head and thought them loudly.

I opened up the plastacard, full to the brim with data strings, captured at great trouble and risk from the WorldNet over the weekend. Apparently all the data had passed Quarantine without eating our computers or anything, so I could start sorting through what they'd captured by hand. Fun.

It would take me hours just to skim the hundreds of pages of information the search had turned up. Hours. When somebody with an implant—or even a better computer-assist—could get it done in ten minutes or less.

Paulsen didn't trust me, not now, or she would have taken my lead a lot more seriously. Devoted processing time and resources to the query. I wondered pettily if Cherabino's leads got a plastacard and a pat on the head. Somehow I doubted it. "Get me proof," Paulsen had said.

I sighed, muttered angrily to myself, and started reading. I pulled a notebook over to jot down names.

Maybe I'd find a list of names near the beginning of the stack, labeled neatly with very strong teleporters who are also telepaths, complete system-wide list. Maybe I could teach pigs to fly too.

I was still muttering darkly as I waded through page after page, over an hour of skimming in the hope of finding the right needles in the haystack. It was so bad that I was actually relieved when they called me back to the interview room and chewed me out for using the computer. The public information on the Guild and people with Abilities was terrible! I had a grand total of five names. As rare as the teleporter/telepath combination was, there would be more than five names. Even interviewing was better than this.

On the way to the interview room, Clark held a hand out to block my way. He was a big guy, and normally even tempered. Today, he glowered.

I looked at him, at the hand. "What's going on?"

"In this section, everyone has to pull his own weight," he said with a little too much emphasis. "Don't be thinking I don't know what's going on."

I paused. "And what is that?"

"You're setting up one of those excuse fests where we pull doubles and triples and you sit in a facility somewhere with your feet up on the department's dime. I'm not putting up with it this time," he said, the glower deepening. "And if I have anything to say about it, neither will anyone else."

"I never asked you to cover for me."

"And I didn't. But the work has to get done," he said. He was thinking I hadn't shown up all morning, and if he had to listen to one more rumor . . . "The work has to get done no matter what."

We stood there, him blocking my way, for a long moment.

"Your spot could be filled with a cop."

And there it was. "I tested clean," I said tightly. "One hundred percent clean, yesterday and today both with separate testers. I never asked you to work double shifts for me. I never asked you to . . ." And the elephant in the room was his daughter's fifth birthday, which he missed, and now regretted, furious at me. It stood between us, but I couldn't say anything, not without making things even worse than they were. "Look, I pull my weight. I take the hard cases off your plate, I do the work. Twice the work of anybody else here, and you know it. If you'll move your hand, I'll do it again."

I held his gaze, refused to look away. I'd never apologized for the last time off the wagon, not to him, and Swartz said I had to get in the habit of humility. But today wasn't going to be the day for that apology.

He stood, blocking my way, his brain practically shouting his contempt for me and his plans to go to Paulsen to get a real cop in the spot.

"I do twice the work of anyone here," I repeated. "Now, move your hand or I'll move it for you."

He backed off, slowly, eyes following me down the hall. His mind shouted his intentions to watch me like a hawk.

Go on and watch, I thought, as I kept walking. Go on and watch.

Even with extra interviewers from Vice, the perps from the raid took all morning to process. Clark gave me all his difficult ones, the pushers, the senior guys who knew better than to talk, while he got the kids caught in the wrong place at the wrong time. I managed, head pounding from stress and strain, teeth gritted to get through the junior pushers high on drugs—they made me want my own fix, too much for comfort. Between everything, I got one confession and two solid leads out of the morning's work. Not too bad, considering.

The last interview of the day was a normal case, a standard investigation. But what happened in it was anything but normal.

The suspect was a minor perp, a minor player in a minor crime the detective in charge was investigating more out of sense of fairness than any real caring on her part. I think the man was accused of stealing something. That was not the important part.

What was important happened about the point I'd convinced the guy talking was a better idea than keeping silent.

My sight cut out. I could hear him continue to speak for a moment, but that faded too, as my lately dramatic precognition flared up with a full vision. I had no input over the process—the precog did what it wanted, when it wanted. And this time it wanted three perfect dimensions, full stereotropic sound, and eerily real physical *touch*.

I was caught up in a choke hold against a wall a foot off the ground, staring into my attacker's eyes. He was a skinny guy, really, one of those pasty-geek types complete with old-fashioned glasses, and under normal conditions I would have put money against him being able to lift me even against a wall. Despite this, he was holding me up, all the way off the floor, without apparent effort. That was the first clue. I went to punch him and couldn't move the hand from the wall—and it wasn't tied down—and then I knew. He was a telekinetic, and suddenly I knew he could teleport too, that he was the bad guy I'd told Cherabino we were looking for.

He was strangling me with such heavy force, I couldn't breathe, and my sight was starting to go gray around the edges. He stepped back and removed the hands, but the choke pressure on my neck only got worse. Even though this was a vision—not real, not yet—I was starting to get worried. If my body was convinced enough it couldn't breathe, I could suffocate in the real world—and really die. And frankly, I'd rather the guy actually kill me, face-to-face, you know, so someone, somewhere could prosecute him for it, rather than me just dropping dead in an interview room with no one knowing what had happened. So I started fighting against the vision rather than going with it; sometimes I can "wake myself up."

I was still in it enough to register the angry expression on his face as he backed away. But then I saw in the back corner of the gray warehouse we were in—I saw Cherabino. Tied up, unconscious—but breathing, thank God!—and dirty, like she'd been there for days, collapsed in the corner like a puppet with its strings cut. She was covered in bruises and cuts, one of her legs bent wrong, and her torn clothes said she'd been assaulted. The way she was staring blankly at the wall told me that whatever made her *her* had long since checked out.

I pulled *hard*—against the invisible chains, not the vision, I had to stay in the vision to find out how to save Cherabino, or at least how to kill whoever'd done this to her—but the bonds just stretched and tightened down hard, and the gray was closing off my sight.

The nerdy son of a bitch in front of me was talking. I started listening. Any info I could get to string him up for murder and worse, I'd take, and run with it. He deserved whatever he got, he and whoever'd helped him extinguish the fire from her eyes.

"Thought you were so smart, didn't you?" he said. "Thought you knew what was going on, sending sniffing cops all around my apartment, trying me out, thinking I'd slip and leave some evidence there. Even sending the girl cop, thinking about you like a billboard. Like I'd let that go. But I was smarter than you, stronger than you, took her right out from under your nose. Who's laughing now, Golden Boy? Who's weak now? You're going to die, and I'm going to be rich."

Did I know this guy? He sure seemed to know me. What was going on?

He started watching my face, waiting for me to pass out and then to die. "I told Neil at the beginning this was a messy business, but he couldn't take it. Had to go and clean up the victims—stupid. Stupid. More than stupid. It's his fault the cops are onto us in the first place. Well, he paid for it—paid in full. And I'll be gone before anybody else can find me. And he wanted me to *stop*. They always want me to stop. Well, I won't. And you'll be rotting garbage while I'm rich. Respected. While I have whatever I want. I want you to know that, as you die. I want you to remember."

At that point, my vision contracted all the way and I passed out. But rather than slide into unconsciousness, I dropped right back into my body in the interview room, my lungs expanding desperately for air.

"Whoa," I said, my eyes snapping back into focus, looking straight at the current suspect's face back in the interview room.

I don't know what the suspect saw on my face, but he started backpedaling like a marathon biker. "Get the freak *out*! Out of the room! I'll tell you anything you want to know—just get the freak the *hell* out of my space."

Bellury, frowning at me, still had enough presence of

mind to respond. "You ain't telling us anything, and he's staying."

"No, really! I'll tell you everything! I'll tell you how I killed him! Just get the freak *out* of here!"

Since the guy was wanted for stealing, I hightailed it out of there. Any way we could get a murder charge for free was worth doing. And as he confessed to the murder of his brother right then, right there, I moved even out of the observation room.

I wanted my poison, I wanted Paulsen's trust back, but more than anything, I wanted an explanation—and an identification.

"Hey, Bob," I said with false cheer.

Bob looked up. He was an overweight, balding caricature of a fifty-something cop—he even liked donuts—and he couldn't chase down a suspect on foot if his life depended on it. But he never had to; Bob did something else completely.

He frowned again when he saw me. "Hello." It wasn't a greeting. I must have interrupted something, but I didn't care. The urgency of the vision was still riding me, the pain and the desperate need to head it off, to make it not happen. I wasn't supposed to talk to Bob without authorization—wasn't supposed to be taking up his valuable time, wasn't even supposed to be in the protected section—but right now I didn't care. I'd deal with the consequences later.

I pulled a piece of paper from my back pocket and unfolded it, laying it across the front of his cubicle. There they were, my five names I'd spent an hour pulling out from hundreds of pages of data. All strong telepath/teleporters, all within two hundred miles of Atlanta (the largest range I knew of for a teleporter). I was hoping—*hoping*—by some miracle one of the ones on this list would match the guy in my vision. The odds were against it, but I had to try.

Bob took the paper and smoothed the edges down. I could see his fingers flex absently as he started processing, and the monitor behind him flashed a steady stream of images I couldn't understand. Tower, egg, golden retriever, sixteen houses in a row, then data in long solid lines. After a few seconds, Bob remembered me and looked up again. I could almost see the lines of data swimming behind his eyes.

"Could you get me pictures?" I asked, uncomfortable but determined. I had to have information, and quickly.

Bob nodded, then turned back to the monitor. The next four and a half minutes crept by as he sorted through the entirety of Earth's WorldNet. I'd never seen him take this long before, not for anything. Either what I'd asked for was harder than it sounded, or he was checking Station records too. Not Mars and Calista, not the Belt; those Webs took twelve hours minimum for free access; even I knew that. But the Station was faster.

What Bob was doing now would have taken me three days. Not for the search itself; most of that was automated. But to sort through the three million hits to find the ones I wanted, to chase down a hundred false leads that looked good—it took a while. Or would, with all the Electronic Crimes safeguards. But Bob . . . Bob had an implant, one of those cybernetic wonders that let him sort as fast as he could think. Faster than he could think, if he was good. He was.

Implants were vanishingly rare, since nearly half a million people died with the Wetware Virus in the early two-seventies, right at the beginning of the Tech Wars. No one wants to take the risk of frying the brain—and worse, people are afraid of anyone who does. Bob had gotten his implant late, five years beyond the curve; he was still the youngest person I'd ever met with one, and he'd been ostracized his whole life for it.

But as for me, even if I'd wanted an implant—and been willing to take that kind of risk with my wetware, willing to be different and feared even more than I was—I couldn't get one. Strong Abilities and implants didn't mesh; the competing energy fields tore each other apart, and you were lucky to end up in a coma— lucky. So I was stuck doing a hunt-and-peck with the rest of the world through Quarantined data or asking help from someone like Bob. He wouldn't ask a lot of questions, just get me the information. Even if he didn't like me much.

His body language changed abruptly, and my attention came right back to him. His hands gestured wildly and then settled. The screen came up with seven pictures, arranged in a neat row.

Bob sat back, pleased with himself.

"There are seven pictures there, Bob. The list had five names." I wasn't even looking at the photos, I was so distracted by the long line of people. The last, a random woman with gray hair, looked vaguely familiar.

"You want to tell me how to do my job?" Bob smirked, arrogant. It didn't sit well on his too-friendly face, as if he looked too harmless to ever hold the cards that he did.

"I asked for five pictures," I returned, putting a full hand of fingers up. "Five." It was important that none of this got screwed up, that it all got done right the first time. We didn't have time to make mistakes.

"No, you asked for pictures from the global list of

people with some very odd things in common. All Guild members with high-enough ratings that Guild membership is compulsory—and also on the Guild Spook Watch list. They all have current wills and three traffic tickets or more. Four out of the five had an aunt or great-aunt named Edna . . ."

"It was a popular name." I also had an aunt named Edna, and I didn't see what that had to do with anything.

". . . the last with a second cousin of the same name, all advanced speakers of a second or third language with a current passport and no children. You thought you had me with the Edna thing, didn't you? And leaving the last two names off the list—that was devious. But those many things in common, it wasn't hard to find them." He reached forward and hit the print button. Then he turned back. "Have another puzzle for me?"

"Not right now," I said, all bravado and desperation. "But I'll be back."

"Um-hmm," Bob said, engrossed in the computer again.

I took the printout from the pile next to the printer— Bob had helpfully labeled it with my name and "seven pictures"—and took my first good look at the faces of the people.

The second row, first column, staring out from next to the faces of random strangers. That was him—the perp from the vision—and suddenly the urgency rode me like a horse, spurs against my side, and I knew what I had to do next.

I looked at the line of text underneath the picture. Jason Bradley, age thirty-one, resident of Atlanta, was not going to get away with it. I was going to stop him before he ever got the chance to strangle me, to turn Cherabino into something that stared blankly at a wall. That future couldn't happen. At any cost, it couldn't happen. Especially since the son of a bitch seemed to know me,

I went directly to the captain, straight into his huge corner office—without knocking. He was on the phone. I'm sure the look on my face mirrored my state of mind: I needed to talk right now, and I wasn't taking no for an answer. Even if it got me fired.

"Can I call you back?" the captain said evenly to whoever was on the other side of the phone. He nodded, and then hung up. "What's your problem now? Don't think I won't—"

"I know who it is," I said.

"Who *who* is?" the captain asked. Annoyed was a mild word for the emotion coming off him; he was having to field meetings about me, and now here I was, making his life worse. I didn't care.

"The serial killer responsible for all the deaths in East Atlanta. Remember those?"

"Look, first, we're not using the word 'serial.' Then— boy, you're here on my sufferance, take a hell of a big step—" The captain blinked, and his eyes narrowed. "The 'Mystery Death' killer? You figured this out in, what, a week? Your tea leaves happened to line up?"

"I had a vision," I said through my teeth.

"A vision?" The captain snorted and sat back in his oversized chair. "Well, that makes it so much better. I'll get on the phone and tell the mayor we've solved the case. If God himself is giving you names now, odds are we don't even have to bother with a warrant."

I took a deep breath and refused to back down. "It's not that kind of vision."

"Really? Then what kind is it, genius?" From the

gleam in his eye, the next thing I said would save me or damn me, no waiting.

I shifted my stance. "His name is Jason Bradley—he's going to choke me to death in an abandoned warehouse, choke me to death and attack Cherabino. Soon, before the summer heat is over, probably within the month. And—as you should know by now—my P-factor, when it comes to my personal safety, is *above* ninety-three percent. Whatever we're doing now's going to backfire."

The captain's face sobered. "I will give you a hundred ROCs if you'll tell me who it was I had on the phone when you walked in." A hundred Re-Oriented Currency units were worth quite a bit.

His mind was carefully blank, so there was no reading it off the surface of his mind without tipping him off. So I thought about it. Still far too early for Cherabino to have done anything, Paulsen was busy at the moment, and he was acting very serious all of a sudden. Political?

"The governor," I guessed. "The president?"

A small note of relief entered the air, and his mouth relaxed. "No. Actually, that was my ex-wife. Perhaps you've heard of her—Jamie Skelton."

"No shit! Jamie Skelton is your ex-wife?" I stared at him. No way this old gray man had been married to the woman who'd run the Guild's precog department for more than twenty years. Not him. I mean, she was hot, and he, well . . .

"Yes," the captain said, "And do you know what she told me?" I shook my head. "She told me not to let any of my people go into warehouses alone—or even in pairs—for oh, the next week or so. She said if we didn't listen, a man and a woman from the department were going to die in a warehouse before the month is out."

"I thought you didn't believe in precog," I protested, dazed. Maybe he hadn't heard about this weekend. . . .

"I don't. But I believe in my ex-wife. Jamie's never been wrong about anything she's ever told me. So, what now?"

I rubbed my eyes. "Bradley's registered. So we have to talk the local Guild attaché into a premises warrant. That's not going to be easy. And while we're at it, we're going to need the full list of telepath/teleporters within two hundred miles of them, confirm this the old-fashioned way. Otherwise we don't have much to go on."

"Really?" the captain said drily. "We don't have much to go on now."

I looked at him. "Well, yeah. But a vision should be . . ."

"A vision's not shit," the captain said. "But Jamie's word is. I'll let you play this out with the Guild attaché—if you can get them to listen—and maybe even back you up. But right now the only thing you've got for sure is I've got a couple of people in danger, one of them the cop with the highest close rate in the department. So we'll need to find you a bodyguard. One for Cherabino too. Nip this in the bud."

"I don't do bodyguards."

We stared each other down.

"As I recall, Cherabino feels the same way. Suit yourself," the captain said. "But no fieldwork for you until this is over. That goes double for her—I'll tell Branen. Now go find this guy. Both of you."

I turned around to leave.

"*No* warehouses."

"Yes, sir," I said, not turning around.

"Now get the hell out my office," he said as I was

halfway out the door. "I don't want to hear about you again for at least a week—from anybody, we clear?"

I went for another cigarette, quick, before I saw Cherabino. Somehow I was going to have to convince her to trust me again. Let me keep her safe. I couldn't let this go, not a vision this strong. I couldn't.

CHAPTER 12

"You leaving?" I asked.

Cherabino was in her cubicle, dumping a few paper files into a duffel while her notebook copied files from her unnetworked computer one by one. Scanning each one a hundred ways for electronic protozoa or worse; Electronic Crimes was a stickler, even for unnetworked computers, about anything coming into contact with data that had been on the Net. After the Tech Wars hijacked technology, nobody wanted to risk that kind of destruction again, not for any reason as stupid as a quick e-mail. Data was the enemy, especially the transmission of it to anyone else.

"What?" Cherabino said, not bothering to look up.

"You aren't going home, are you?"

"It's seven o'clock. I can't work late *every* night." She zipped up the duffel and shouldered it. "I need to get to the grocery store before it closes. Don't worry, I'll probably be working from home again in a couple hours. You can call me if there's a problem." She paused. Cautiously, she asked, "Did you need a ride?"

"That would be great. Give me a second. I'll get my bag."

She gave me a funny look. "Okay. But just a second. I want to get to the grocer's early enough to get actual meat and not that processed nonsense."

"I, uh, need a few things too," I lied, "so it works out."

She followed along after me, waiting just on the other side of the men's locker room door. "Paulsen know you're leaving?" she asked.

"Would you tell her?" I called out, loud enough to reach to the other side of the empty locker room. "Please?"

She cursed softly. "What are you hiding?"

"Nothing!" I said.

She cursed at me specifically, louder, and left. I really, really hoped it was to talk to the lieutenant—not leaving, leaving.

I sped up my pace, shoveling my overnight junk into a big shopping bag, the good kind made of actual recycled plastic, and added a whole bunch of stuff I probably didn't need. (Where did that yellow rubber duckie come from? I put it back in my locker.)

Then I sat down on the bench, trying to time it exactly. I went fuzzy, trying to get the precog to cooperate around the edges; it was working today. In exactly fifteen seconds, it felt right. I shouldered the bag and followed Cherabino, just slowly enough so I wouldn't have to talk to Paulsen myself.

With exact timing, I caught Cherabino on her way out of the lieutenant's office. She was frowning.

"What?" I said.

"Come on—you're going to make me late," she said, grabbing my arm. Even through the sleeve, the touch gave me that extra connection, and I got a flash of her strong annoyance with me. The lieutenant had offered her a bodyguard and wouldn't tell her why.

Cherabino was a second-level black belt in American Judo. She didn't need a bodyguard. Unless there was something they weren't telling her. She glared at me. There was something they weren't telling her, wasn't there?

An evening of boring shopping later, Cherabino was driving. The first tinge of dusk colored the air, the sun setting late in the summer. We were on the ground-level Lawrenceville Highway, colorful car dealerships on either side.

Cherabino asked me where I wanted to be dropped off, what with the bag I'd brought along and all. I suggested her place a little too quickly.

She turned, taking her eyes off the road. "What's wrong with your place?"

I thought frantically. Just a little too late I offered, "The exterminators—"

"They were there two weeks ago. Remember, you were whining about it all over the office?" She blinked as the car behind her honked, turning back to the road. She pulled our car forward, into the intersection and through the now-green light. "So why are you lying?"

A dozen explanations filtered through my head, discarded one after another as I tapped my pen against my knee. She wasn't going to like this. She *really* wasn't going to like this.

"Just tell me."

"I—"

"The longer you put it off, the worse it sounds. Though if you're following me home like some dog, it had better be pretty—"

"*Cherabino.*"

"Sorry." She adjusted her grip on the steering wheel and coasted to a stop in front of another light. This time she didn't look at me. "Go ahead."

Cherabino quiet was trouble, and Cherabino apologizing—well, it didn't happen often, and usually someone was dead. I stopped the tapping at once. "What's wrong?"

There was a long, long silence, while the light turned green and she pulled back into the traffic again. Instead of her usual weaving, speeding, anything to get ahead, she drove sedately.

"Isabella," I said softly, looking directly at her face.

She turned her head to look at me. Her knuckles went white on the steering wheel. "You were saying. Your latest crisis."

"Am I not supposed to—?"

"Shut up." She took a deep breath and changed lanes directly in front of another car. "No, talk. Talk, damn it."

After a moment of mental tennis, I won the match with myself. Unfortunately. It had to be the truth. "I had a vision."

Cherabino nodded, narrowly missing a fire hydrant. "Paulsen said. What was this one about?" In the back of her head, she wondered if the bodyguard was related. Her mental state was still more curious than upset, but depending on what I said, that might change fast. She was anticipating something bad.

I shifted the pen from hand to hand a few times. Then I looked back at her. "It was you, actually. After a bad attack."

After a long moment she said, "Okay. What kind of attack?" Her cop voice was back, the competent, good-in-a-crisis voice that let nothing slip.

"A bad one."

"What *kind*?" Her mind was so blank as to be un-readable.

I paused. "It's not going to happen. I won't let it."

At the last possible instant, she screeched the car into the parking lot of the South DeKalb movie theater and cut the engine, ignoring the honks from the surrounding cars. Then she shifted to meet me eye to eye across the car. "*Tell* me."

I stared back, narrowing my eyes. I was not going to lose. Telepaths were *trained* in winning the battle of the will—and this time, I had right on my side. She did *not* need to hear what I'd seen.

After a long moment, she gave up, collapsing all the way back in her seat, her hands out on the wheel to steady herself. "That bad." Her stomach fluttered in reaction, her mind trying not to picture scenarios. . . .

"It's not going to happen," I repeated. "It won't. We won't let it."

She pushed the car into park and put her feet up onto the seat. Then she put her head in her hands, closing her eyes, thinking. Trying to think, to work the problem. "How are we going to avoid this?"

I faced her, turning all the way sideways until my seat belt dug into my hip. "Well, we're not going into any warehouses alone, no matter what they offer us. We got a confirming vision from somebody outside the field, from somebody I respect. And other than that— I'm not leaving you. I'm not letting you out of my sight until all of this has blown over."

Her head turned, her eyes coming open. "What does that do? You're not SWAT. You failed half the entrance tests—and that as a consultant. If you're worried, we'll get you a bodyguard. We'll get me some backup. We'll handle it."

I reached for calm and failed. "Handle it, bullshit! I'm not worried, damn it. I don't need to pass some shit test to watch your back. I'm a telepath—a class *four* defensive-trained telepath. It doesn't matter two shits if I can run, not in a fight." I didn't mention that I hadn't practiced the defensive stuff since college. I was still better than any bodyguard on the force, at least against what these killers could throw at her.

She blew out a breath and turned to face me. "It always matters. What are you going to do if they come at you with a gun?"

I looked at her for a long, long moment. Then, in desperation, I cheated to prove my point—I "leaked" a long line of angry concern into her head. *Are you really asking?* I said, just at the forefront of her thoughts, angry. I made myself very obvious.

Cherabino blinked, frowning. She nodded, her surface thoughts flowed sluggishly by. She didn't like that I was in her head, but she'd asked for a demo, sort of. If I was volunteering to show her exactly why I was so vaulted dangerous, she wasn't going to whine about the methods. She wasn't that dumb.

If you want a demo, this is going to hurt. I released the thought into her mind.

She met my gaze, impatience hitting me like the tip of a boxing glove, tap to get my attention, tap for a beginning to the match. *Just do it.* She was as ready as she was going to get, she thought.

I sighed, braced myself hard, and visualized sharp pain—pain like an iron to the skin—like an ice pick on fire—settling in on her shoulder, trailing in a long red-hot brand down her back. Then I hit her with the pain of a crushed nerve, suddenly, strongly, until her whole right arm fell down, unusable, until her teeth—

Then I stopped it. Cold.

The first tears had gathered in her eyes, and her face

was torn open, completely open with the pain. And she blinked, and she breathed; she took a whole minute to come back to being Cherabino.

"That hurt like hell," she said finally.

"Yes."

Her whole mind closed. "That doesn't mean you're a bodyguard." With that, she put the car back in gear. She left the theater's parking lot and pulled back into traffic, her driving even worse than usual as she took the left turn to North Druid Hills. She seemed to be thinking. Thinking far too hard. But the thoughts were too disorganized—and her too wary—for me to follow without breaking her trust. Not with her shut down.

I breathed myself, recovering slowly as we drove past endless fast-food joints and a lot of old trees. What I'd shown her was actually pretty mild. They trained us in far worse at the Guild. Repeatedly. But I was out of practice, and the major limitation with that sort of stunt was how much pain you could tolerate. There were no free rides in life. For every brand, every shooting pain I inflicted on her, I endured the same and worse.

Back at the Guild, I had had a real reputation for being a badass—a little shock like this wouldn't have even phased me back in those days. But I'd gone through a lot since then, seen a lot, and Ability didn't work when you were strung out on Satin—not in any way where you could control it.

The next ten minutes of the ride were spent in silence, while my white-knuckled grip on the door relaxed slowly and the sides of the road opened up into larger neighborhoods. Her driving didn't get better, but my distraction did. I was worried. Real worried, about the vision.

"Why you?" she asked, finally. "We've got officers *trained* for this situation."

"Cherabino, our perp is double trouble, with maybe another telepath for backup. You're no lightweight, but either one could knock you out in nothing flat. Same for anybody we could pull—you don't know how to defend what this guy'll throw. I do. There isn't anybody here trained for what you need. Nobody but me."

We turned right onto a smaller street, and she looked over at me. "Helluva ego you have there."

"Yeah, well. It's called Ability."

She took a few turns and pulled into the driveway of her small brick house. She turned off the car and stared at the wheel for a very long time. There were town houses to the left of her single-family, and a monstrosity of a mansion to the right, but her small green lot held on to the original brick building.

I waited. And waited. Finally I asked, "Are we going in?"

"I'd rather we didn't." Her body language was slumped but tense, as if she were bracing herself against some unnamed fear. The discomfort was coming off her in small waves, but with her this intentionally closed, that was all I got—even trying to read her. Another worry about the date in a few days, sadness, a man's face.

I waited for her to explain herself, but nothing happened.

After a long moment, her hands tensed on the steering wheel. And her mind opened just enough to let me see her discomfort. She didn't want me in her house while she was sleeping. She didn't want me in her space at all, but we were buddies, and during the day, if I stayed in the living room, it was okay. Not great but okay. But sleeping . . . especially now . . .

I tried to figure out what the right thing to say was. "Look, Cherabino, I—"

"Shut up." She opened the door and got out of the car. Then she got my bag out of the backseat, shoved it at me, and gestured to the door. "Don't make me regret this."

CHAPTER 13

Cherabino's little redbrick house with its tiny yard and a small back patio was only maybe twice the size of my apartment—and probably cost three times or more every month in cash to keep, from location alone. It was in a no-fly zone—not even police cars cut through the airspace above this neighborhood except in real emergencies—and the sounds on the street were children and birdsongs, not shouting and aircars.

Night would fall in a couple hours; the days were long in summer, but it was getting late and no day lasted forever. I cut through the drought-resistant green grass and walked into the house. Cherabino shut the door behind me.

Without another word, she led the way into the house and to the kitchen. She pointed to the small, light-wood square kitchen table. "Sit. I'm cooking."

I pulled out a beat-up chair and sat. My position would be more than close enough to keep her in sight. Hopefully the extra space would make her more comfortable with my being here. I didn't know what she thought I was going to do. I don't know that *she* did—she was just wary. Wary, for no reason I could see, except the obvious. I offered to help cook.

She shook her head hurriedly. "No. When you're done 'cooking,' it isn't food anymore."

"If you say so." I sat back. It was true, when I cooked, sometimes things ended up a little overdone, but that was why you bought extras. Second time a charm, right? Third was less charming, but it happened.

So I watched her move around the kitchen, opening cabinets and moving things around, chopping vegetables and boiling pasta. I watched the tension slowly dissipate off her. But mostly I just watched her, Cherabino, herself. The way she moved, the way she held herself, the shape of her body and the tilt of her head. She was very beautiful, was Cherabino. Very beautiful. And I would do anything to keep her safe. Even stick it out in the house where she didn't want me. Even pull out rusty skills and get in a mind-fight, if I had to. Even go toe-to-toe with a serial killer or two. Maybe.

The bowl of pasta she set in front of me a few minutes later looked pretty, with little bits of brightly colored vegetables and sausage in a white sauce. When I dug in, it was warm and had taste to it too.

"This is good," I told her. You had to be sure to compliment someone who cooked for you. You wanted the person to do it again, right?

"My grandmother would be turning over in her grave to hear you say that." Cherabino turned off the stove and brought her own bowl over. "If I'd tried to serve this to family, she would have hit me with her spoon. It's passable, but not great."

"*I* think it's good."

Cherabino rolled her eyes and started eating. After she'd had a few bites, she paused. "Unless there's a break in the case, I'll be off work Thursday."

I nodded, finishing up the last of my bowl.

"I assume you're still planning on dogging my every move, then, right?"

I nodded again, wondering if I could get away with licking the bowl. Microwaved rehydrated dehydrated food—my steady diet these days—just wasn't the same.

She sat back. "Okay. What would it take to get you to go away on my day off?" Her mind flashed the man's face again, a feeling of loss, and a bouquet of lilies.

I ignored the images and put my fork all the way down. "I am *not* going to leave you. Not now. Not tomorrow, not the day after. Not at all, not until this is over."

She looked at me, annoyed, but very close. There. So *there*. And suddenly I wanted to kiss her. . . .

She looked away and stood up. She grabbed the bowls—hers still half eaten—and started loading the washer-box.

The evening was spent in work. She went over her case notes, spreading out the paper on her dining room table. Not wanting to get very far away, I sat at the opposite end and tried to be productive.

I wrote down the vision, word for word, as detailed as I could get it. I got caught up on my interview notes from the last few days. I spent about a half hour familiarizing myself with the local Mindspace, putting out markers so I'd be able to scan it quickly later. And finally, when there was nothing else to do, I got myself some vitamin-C juice from the fridge and sat down next to Cherabino.

"Have you heard from Kara?"

She looked up. "Who's Kara?"

I paused. "The Guild attaché. The one I left a message with. Was supposed to call me back? Main liaison for the Guild?"

She set down her pen on the stack of papers in front of her and gave me her full attention. "So how come you're on a first-name basis?"

"Um, let's just say we go way back."

She lifted an eyebrow, but when I didn't say anything, only offered, "Can we trust her?" Considering what was going on in her head, the question was heavily ironic. But if she wasn't going to say anything, neither was I.

Instead, I sipped my juice and thought about it seriously. Could I trust Kara? "There was a time when I would have said yes right away. A lot of shit has happened since then, and, really, her family's always been political." I wanted to trust her. I wanted to believe she was still the same person I'd shared a bed—and my mind—with years ago. But when she'd stood up against me on the day the Guild had thrown me out, when she'd cast me to the wolves . . . "I don't know. Depends on what we're talking about."

She shook her head. "Should we go looking for another ally or not?"

I sighed. "No, Kara . . . Kara isn't a killer. That I can tell you. And she wouldn't stand for a killer hiding out in the ranks of the Guild. It's bad PR, for one thing, and she was always going on about purity of purpose and internal government. I'd rather stick with her." I took a breath. "Certainly rather than Enforcement. Those guys have a bad habit of riding in and taking anything not nailed down—including your memories."

Cherabino put the pen down. "I asked because the assistant to the Guild attaché called today and left a message on my phone. Apparently she—this Kara person—wants to meet tomorrow. I need to know, can we trust her not to take this case away? How is she as a person?"

"She's a professional," I said. "She'll do her job."

But Cherabino was looking at me skeptically. "What was your job at the Guild? This construction thing."

"Construct, Deconstruction, Structure, they're all fine. No one says Construction."

"Fine. Structure. Explain to me what you did for Structure." She was annoyed, but she wasn't uncomfortable. At least not at this moment.

Where to start? "You know I wasn't always an addict, right?"

She gestured for me to continue. Stole a sip of my juice. I moved the glass in front of her. If she wanted the half that was left, she could have it.

"Ten years ago I was a professor," I said.

"A professor?" she asked, surprised. She ran a few numbers in her head.

"I was young," I confirmed. "But brilliant. And I had a talent nobody else had had in two generations—I could teach a whole class of students the same lesson at the same time."

She huffawed. "Really? A teacher that could teach a whole classroom? Awesome talent, that!"

"No, really," I came back. "Telepathy isn't like literature. You can't read a book and understand something immediately. There's a process. You learn by seeing, by doing, by having someone guide you until you can pick it up on your own. You learn by experience, yours or someone else's and—"

"You realize I don't have any idea what you're talking about, right?" Her mouth quirked.

I blew out a long line of air. "Okay. I didn't teach the basic classes—by the time the students got to me, they were too far into the Guild to ever see a college or want to, but let's call it PhD-level work. Or, better analogy, the neurosurgery stuff you only get to see three years after you leave medical school."

I frowned and looked at my hands. "Actually, brain surgery's a good way to think about deconstruction, only you're working with the brain's software, not the physical stuff. Deconstructionist training is practical. You learn to take apart a mind piece by piece, to remove the sane and healthy bits—or to replace them—at will. Mistakes happen—there've been personalities changing drastically after a 'construct'—but there are plenty of coma victims who've regained their lives. It's a worthwhile profession."

Cherabino shifted in her chair. "Sounds like a double-edged sword to me. If you can bring them out of a coma, I'll bet you can put them in one."

I nodded. "There is that. The Guild—heartless, self-interested bastards that they are—" She gave me an ironic look; I ignored it and kept going. "They don't strictly care how you use the skills. Good, evil, whatever, so long as the evil you practice is affiliated with a major governmental organization and you don't step on the Guild's toes in the process. Or else they get involved. And trust me, it is *not* a good thing when the Guild gets involved."

She frowned, finished the juice. "You taught the coma stuff?"

"That and other things, the capstone deconstruction training. They only got to take it after they passed about eight rounds of screening and had a strong shot at a job; the Guild doesn't believe in flooding the market. Depending on the job market in black ops and major metropolitan hospitals, some years I had thirty students, some two. There were a couple of other organizations that hired deconstructionists, but those were the main two, and since I was teaching the class, they could actually fill the jobs as fast as they had openings."

"Because you were so darn special."

I shrugged. "They'd been looking for a systematic deconstructionist professor for at least sixty years, since John Xavier got shot in broad daylight in the middle of the Tech Wars. Without a guy like me, you have to apprentice under another structure person for ten years or more, pick things up slowly with a lot of work—that's how I did it, finishing the work early at twenty-three. They found me when a teacher caught me tutoring two other students at the same time—I was short of sleep, and it seemed more efficient than doing it twice. My whole life changed that night.

"I'm kinda rare, or was. Teaching deconstruction is *much* harder than it sounds. Maybe five percent of all Guild members can even *see* the finer structures of the mind, and only a third of that have the control to manipulate them. And then, imagine letting thirty people piggyback on your thoughts as you pluck at the invisible spiderweb strings . . . keeping the plate in your left hand spinning while your right hand performs delicate brain surgery. Only a lot more so. The brain is forgiving of screwups; the mind not so much. Kill a few cells in a clump somewhere, mostly your brain learns to adapt. Kill a processing router in the back of the software of your mind and you might never think in color again. Or worse, lose the ability to learn new names. Or faces. Or much, much worse. That stuff, you kinda notice—and those are easy mistakes for a deconstructionist to make.

"But it's worth doing. You could help a person who'd just had a head injury to reroute that processor to another part of the mind. You could help a man see movement for the first time ever or recognize his wife's face for the first time in years. That's the cool stuff, the stuff you'd pay anything for, the stuff the Guild charges the sun and the moon for. *That* is what I could teach a man (or a woman, or a monkey, so long as he was Abled) to do—in four years or less compared to the fifteen years to get one guy trained. I made the Guild unthinkable amounts of money."

"Not that you're confident or anything."

"Not at all."

"So why aren't you still doing it?"

I looked away. "I couldn't. After I got hooked on Satin, the numbers worked in the beginning. But I couldn't teach anymore—I couldn't do two impossible things at once, not even after they locked me in a box for two weeks to make me dry out."

Her eyes went blank as she processed that, but I went on, unable to stop.

"The only thing worse than not having a deconstructionist teacher is having one who's worthless to you. The Guild let me know I wasn't welcome in no uncertain terms."

I studied the old wooden dining table where we were sitting, her case notes spread out. It had been that final rejection by the Guild that had made me turn to the poison even worse, that made me fall off the wagon so badly, it took a team of cops and a truly traumatic memory to begin to find me again. The Guild did not want me anymore—and no one treats you worse than the best friend you've betrayed.

I went outside for a cigarette—or three. I wasn't sure why I'd told her all of that. It had been a long, long time since I'd talked about that. I wondered if it changed anything, if she'd trust me any better now. I stood there, smoking, trying to decide. Probably not, I settled on. It wouldn't change freaking anything.

I walked in the house and shut the door. She threw me a blanket with excessive force. I caught it, but the top still hit me in the face. I forced the fabric down. Pylar. What?

"What's this?"

She gave me a *look*. "You're on the couch."

I looked at the short, gray, overstuffed couch four feet to my right, then back at her. "There's no way I'm going to fit on that." For one thing, it was almost long enough for a short sixth grader to lie down on lengthwise. Almost. For another thing, I was a long time out of sixth grade. I reined in my temper.

"I can get you a pillow," Cherabino said, with no expression. "Or you can take the floor. Your choice."

I rearranged my grip on the blanket, trying to gather up the part that was falling. I had one shot at this, if I really meant to protect her. "Look, Cherabino, the couch—not that I'm criticizing it—is too short. I'll never fit. And *more importantly*," I said over the top of her protest, "it's way too far from you. The whole point of me being here is to make sure nothing happens to you. There's no way I can do that if you're all the way in the bedroom with the door closed. No way."

She crossed her arms and set her face. "If you think I'm letting you in my bedroom, you're crazy." But in the back of her head she paused, remembering we faced a telepath and teleporter. And that maybe, if all of the talk was true, I had a few skills to fight him. She still didn't trust me.

"I'm *not leaving you*. If that means I sleep on your

floor, that's what it means. I've slept on far worse than that, trust me. Even I can't control the Inverse Square Law."

Her eyebrows drew together. "The what?"

I sighed, dropped the blanket, and pulled my hands through my hair in exasperation. It had been a stressful night, damn it; I didn't want to have to explain every little thing. "Telepathy obeys the laws of physics like everything else—unless something funky is going on, the farther away you are, the weaker the connection gets. That goes double if you're not paying attention—and I'd like to get some sleep tonight if I can."

"You'll get plenty of sleep on the couch." She was being stubborn on purpose. Whatever had made her wary before was still here now. I wished mind reading could help more at the moment, but she wasn't really thinking, just reacting to whatever her latest deal was. I didn't have time for this.

"Sure. I could sleep on the couch. But that would defeat the purpose of being here at all. Minding— mental bodyguarding—is not my specialty. It never was. The little bit of practice I do have is over a decade old. Honestly, I can't sleep *and* watch *and* wake up immediately for anybody but me, not for sure. You get attacked thirty feet away—for real this time, through the window of your bedroom, say—I might sleep through it. If the back of my head doesn't feel personally threatened.

"On the other hand, five feet away, three feet away, your presence is going to overlap me enough in Mindspace I'll wake up automatically in self-defense. Fighting. If anything happens, we're going to need my instincts working for us."

She did *not* look happy; her wariness was overcoming her good sense. And her face said, bullshit, as she twisted her hair back with a pink rubber band. That was usually a move she did right before a physical fight. Or when she felt like fighting. It had been a long night with too much tension, and we were both on edge. Even so, I couldn't afford to give in.

I met her eyes and took a wild guess. "I'm not trying to take advantage of you. I can do the floor, as long as it's right next to the bed. I'll do the floor, no problem. I'm just trying to keep you safe."

I felt the comment register. She shook her head and finally told me the truth. "I don't want you that close to me, not while I'm sleeping. You don't have the self-control."

I answered the unspoken question. "Maybe not about the drug. Maybe not about a lot of things. But this, this I've got. You don't have to worry about *that*. Not today. Not any day. Not if you don't want it."

She opened her mouth to say something, and I could see this could take forever. And like it or not, I really did want to get some sleep tonight.

I reached out and inserted a thought, *my* thought flavored with the sound of *my* voice so she couldn't possibly mistake it. *If I wanted to take advantage, I don't need you to be asleep.* Then, slowly, I trailed soft points of pleasure down her spine.

She shivered and looked away.

"I'll be on the floor," I said firmly.

"Fine," she said, and turned on her heel, every line of her body angry. "But stay out of my head."

Her bedroom carpet was pink. Well, peach. And it didn't match the rest of the room, which was brown and beige, down to the checkered comforter and brown curtains. It didn't match Cherabino.

It was soft, and reasonable to sleep on—which was good, since I was lying on it now and had to sleep—but it was pink. I was vaguely offended.

Cherabino was tucked away two feet above me, trying to sleep and failing, dressed in full-length pajama pants and a ridiculously large T-shirt. I don't know why she'd put up such a fight. This wasn't exactly glamorous. No man woke up in the morning thinking, I'll sleep on my coworker's pink carpet today. Not remotely.

Now, if she would only go to sleep, I could try to do the same. I sighed. If she'd stop jumping every time there was a noise . . .

"You still there?" I heard faintly through the darkness.

"Yes. Go to sleep!"

I stayed up a long time, torturing myself with my last few days at the Guild, with Kara's betrayal, with the head of training stripping off my patch and literally throwing me out of the meeting room. I would do anything not to face that again—and I wanted my drug. Of course I wanted my drug right now, with things falling apart. But I wasn't going to get it. Paulsen's rough disbelief, the contempt of the other interviewers, Swartz's disappointment, all played over and over in my head. I knew it would be worse if I'd actually shot up, a lot worse. But it was plenty bad enough.

Like fate or a capricious Higher Power flexed its muscles, in that moment I saw my vision again: Cherabino abused and beaten on the floor; myself dying. Bradley yelling *at me*, specifically, like he knew me. The old woman's scarf in my hands. This was personal,

and as much as I wanted to run away—into Satin—
into somewhere else, I knew that if I did, I'd never forgive myself.

I had to fix this. I had enough crap to look through
when I stared at the mirror. I didn't need any more.

CHAPTER 14

In the morning, a horrible ringing woke me up far too early.

Cherabino was up, gun trained in less than two seconds on the phone on her nightstand. I blinked at her very nice butt, outlined through the pajamas.

"Sorry," she said, sheepishly. "It's new." She put the gun down on the nightstand and picked up the handset.

She frowned. I felt her decision to lie, to make it seem less suspicious that I was there. She didn't want Paulsen getting the wrong idea. "He's on my couch. Want me to wake him up?"

Huh?

"Just a second." She held the phone against her shoulder, fidgeted for a long moment. "Okay, he's here." She held out the phone to me.

I stood and took it, watching Cherabino carefully. She grabbed the gun and moved away a bit.

"Yes?" I said into the phone.

There was a long pause at the other end.

"Hello?"

Paulsen's voice was testy. "You and Cherabino have been called into Fulton County. Atlanta PD thinks it's another of our murders. They want you there five minutes ago."

"I thought we weren't supposed to do fieldwork for a while?"

"Who told you that?"

"The captain."

"What in *hell* you were doing going to the captain with that vision of yours I'll never know. I'm your boss. You should have come to me!"

"You were busy," I said.

She growled into the phone. "Out of leash, I told you. Twice. If you didn't have the best close rate of any of the interrogators, I swear this would be the very . . ." A pause. "Get up and get to that scene, ASAP. Don't give me any more grief. I'll handle the captain."

"Yes, ma'am," I said. "Um, ma'am?"

"What??!?"

"Where are we going?"

"Oh. Hold on." Clattering sounds came over the line. After a moment, she found what she needed and read me the address, on Ponce de Leon.

"How far down is that?" I asked.

"Near the old City Hall East."

I frowned. "That's almost in Midtown!"

"Thank you, Captain Obvious," Paulsen said. "Now get there. I'm not going to have detectives from another zone waiting around on our clock."

"Yes, ma'am," I said, hanging up.

I looked up at Cherabino. Her hair was sticking straight up on one side, pillow marks on her cheek. Her pajama pants were imprinted with teddy bears, an interesting contrast with the oversized police department shirt. I could see she didn't have on a bra, and I had to look away before I embarrassed myself.

"Another case?" she asked.

"Yeah." I grabbed my bag from the floor. "Atlanta city

cops think they've found another one of our murders down by old City Hall East. We're supposed to be there ASAP. Can I borrow your bathroom?"

She pointed me to the one in the hall, her brain waves slow, tired.

I threw my bag on the counter and closed the door. If we were going to somebody else's territory, I needed to shave.

While I waited for Cherabino to finish her shower— and so I wouldn't picture the process—I sat down by the phone in her dining room. My stomach roiled, unhappy with the fruit-and-nuts oatmeal. I'm sure stress had nothing to do with it.

Cherabino had left the number on a scrap of torn paper on the dining room table. I stared at it for a long moment, called Swartz for courage.

He'd been up for hours, of course, and was just about ready to go to school. "What are you waiting for?" he said pointedly. "Call her. You have to face the fear, or it gets power over you. More every day."

He let me chitchat a little longer before he told me, "Now call her," and hung up.

I stared at the piece of paper for a long time before I dialed.

The phone rang, and I answered Kara's hello with who it was and the fact that this wasn't social. "I'm working with the DeKalb County police. I was the one who called you yesterday to report the abuse and"—I gritted my teeth—"ask for your help."

On the other end of the phone, there was a long, long silence. Then I heard a funny clicking, Kara tapping her teeth with her tongue the way she did when she was thinking. It was like a stab to the heart, and it made me angry all over again. "What do you need exactly?" she asked me.

Kara was Guild to the core; her whole family was Guild, and while she only rated a heavy four on the telepath scale (and only with touch), her Jumping marks were off the charts. She was trained, she was smart, and as she'd proven by me, slavishly devoted to the Guild and to its whole ethical and political system. She had all the right background and connections—and the Ability—to be a good political courier. I'd known, we'd discussed, from there it was a short step to big-city politics, and then to the international stage. So it made sense she would be the city attaché. It also made sense she'd be the one handling the call from DeKalb; as much as metro Atlanta cared about jurisdiction and breaking up the city, the Guild didn't give a damn. But that didn't mean I had to like it. It didn't mean I had to like it at all.

I made a fist. Let it go. Looked down. I could do this. I would do this. "Can you meet this afternoon?"

"Where?"

"The AT&T plaza, by the ice cream place. Do you remember?" We'd stopped for dessert on a date there once. It gave me heartburn to suggest it, but there was a very good reason to meet there in particular, so I'd suck it up.

"I remember," she said, her voice trailing off. "You doing okay?"

"I'll see you at two," I said, and hung up.

Getting called in by another police force was a big step, since somebody had to put jurisdiction and pride aside enough to admit they couldn't get the job done alone. We found out from Branen's messages they'd actually called me to consult on the crime scene—for once, without arguing about budget—instead of Cherabino. I was the telepathic expert, after all. She still came with me.

We were in the north part of DeKalb County. Our destination was the old East City Hall near Freedom Parkway, maybe eight miles as the crow flies south-west. The direct route took us through one of the oldest parts of the city, around Emory University, the ancient trees telling stories of centuries before us, their trunks twisted from the fallout from the Tech Wars, but still standing. The area around the university was a strict no-fly zone with twisty roads, and those eight miles took a good twenty minutes even on a good day. Now, in morning rush hour, it took us more like forty. Paulsen would not be pleased, I thought. I wondered if I could blame it on Cherabino.

She was sad this morning, a sense of loss riding her like a second skin. She kept thinking about tomorrow, worrying about me somehow, then shying away from both thoughts, so that I couldn't follow, and it was only giving me a headache to try.

She also drove sedately for her, not making me grab the handrail even once. Somehow I did not think that was a good sign.

We took a turn onto Ponce de Leon, the new old Peachtree, as commuters clogged the old road and the space just above it. On the sides of the roads, ancient rotting mansions shared space with old churches and debris-filled parks. The street deteriorated further as we went. On the edge of the trendy, dirty city blocks, right by the old City Hall East—now cheap lofts by the same name—we turned into a huge parking lot meant to service the few megastores still left in the area.

We parked in front of the hardware store, intending

to walk around the building to the back alley where the murder scene was. Cherabino led the way. The day was cloudy and dim, the humidity in the air sticking to my skin like the steam in a sauna.

Our shoes crunched on bits of unnamed debris as we stepped into the alley. We walked past a line of dirty recycling bins, including a huge dumpster that smelled of old, rotting wood. Then past a cop car, its red and white lights turning the alley into a flashing red and blue carnival show. Two male detectives in plain clothes stood just beyond the car.

The first was thin, red-haired, and freckled, and he looked far too young to be a detective, his face far too innocent. Atlanta PD—especially in the heart of the center (and inner) city—wasn't a police force that exactly bred innocence, so either he was so new to the job he squeaked, or he was a damn good actor. I marked him as someone to watch either way. When Cherabino stepped forward to introduce us, I stepped closer than was strictly necessary and got the faint impression of a very wily mind. He was McMartin, and he'd been the one to suggest they call me.

The second detective was a big, burly Latino. He looked to be in his late forties, at the top of his game professionally, and clearly in charge. Despite the fact that Cherabino had introduced me as the ex-Guild telepath, Sanchez offered me his hand.

I looked at him just long enough to make sure he knew what he was doing—his eyes were steady enough—and then took the hand. His grasp was firm but not overwhelming. "Sanchez," he introduced himself.

I nodded in turn, releasing his hand as I tried hard to pretend he wasn't at least a Level Three empath. I didn't know whether his coworkers knew, but there was no hiding it with the handshake. He probably had some preliminary training, nothing major, not with the feel of him crawling up my arm like a strong cloud of cologne. So either he didn't think I'd notice—unlikely—or he wanted it out on the table between us immediately. Guessing that I could crush him with a thought, use his Ability against him, and deliberately sticking out his hand anyway.

With those kind of guts, he got my respect immediately.

Cherabino finished the pleasantries, and they all nodded to one another. I echoed, feeling a little out of place, still trying to hide what I knew about Sanchez. The other cop led the way to the end of the alley. A medical examiner in full crime-scene coveralls crouched over what looked at a distance to be a pile of rags.

"Call came in this morning about five thirty," Sanchez summarized as we walked. "One of the store employees taking out the recyclables found the body at the end of the alley. He checked for a pulse, and when he found none, reported it to his supervisor. The supervisor called us."

"Where's the employee now?" Cherabino asked, her hands in her pockets.

The other detective shrugged. "We took his statement and sent him home. He seemed pretty shaken and didn't know anything useful. You missed him by just a couple minutes."

I looked around. "Where's the crime scene analysts?" I asked.

"We called them ten minutes before McMartin suggested talking to you," Sanchez replied. "They're running late. Very late."

We stopped a few feet away from the medical

examiner. Sanchez kept walking a few more steps. "Rogers," he said, "can you give us a few minutes?"

"One moment," Rogers replied in a quiet baritone. He wrote one last thing in his notebook and retrieved his equipment. When he had everything tucked away neatly in his case, he set the lock and stood up.

Way up. The medical examiner was at least six foot five, and his dark complexion matched his baritone. "You the teep?"

"That's right." I *hated* the common slang word for telepath, but I didn't really want to risk the argument right now. If I was here to look at the Mindspace residue around the body, I wanted as few strong emotions from these guys as possible. Ideally, I wanted them to back up about nine feet.

"Could you wait over by the wall?" Sanchez asked Rogers. "Clear the space here." I wondered if I'd accidentally let the thought slip into Mindspace for Sanchez to pick up, or whether he was just that smart.

The examiner nodded, walking the six feet to the back wall of the store. The other cops went with him without being prompted, and only then did I look down. Wedged into the corner of the old wooden fence ending the alley and the concrete wall to our right was a pile of rags. Or so it looked. Finally my eyes resolved the body. On top of a pile of ancient shag carpet lay an old lady. She was painfully thin, her light skin sitting on her face like wrinkled paper. She was also very dirty, her gray hair hanging in strings. What ratted clothes she had on were patchworked with age, until even on her body they looked like piled rags.

"The supervisor says she sleeps here sometimes," Sanchez said. "They bring her food when they can. McMartin claims it's one of your serials. I'm thinking no. It's probably not an exposure death—not in the middle of the night in the summer—so I'm willing to explore possibilities. Even if it's old age that killed her. Worth seeing what you had to say."

"I appreciate that." I nodded, pausing just long enough for politeness. Then, "First, I'll need some space; you'll have to go over to the wall with the others. This will take about fifteen minutes, maybe a little more." I met his eyes. "I probably don't have to say this, but don't touch me while I'm under. It could be bad."

"I have no intention of touching you." His mouth quirked before he joined the others.

Cherabino shifted. "You need me to stay or to go?"

I studied the distance to the back wall. "Could you be about halfway between me and them?" I asked.

She started walking and settled at the spot I'd indicated. The Atlanta detectives started talking among themselves, a running commentary on what I was doing, I'm sure. They'd be surprised when there was nothing to see. Or maybe Sanchez wouldn't—he might be able to spot me in Mindspace if I had to do something big. I wasn't planning on it, but who knew.

The alley seemed very empty, to all my senses, but sometimes if I sank all the way into Mindspace, an area opened up to me.

With my mind I reached across to Cherabino. "You ready?" I asked her, meeting her eyes. She nodded. *Knock, knock* on her mind, and then she let me in—just enough to provide a real-world focus if I should need one. She was picturing a hand, her hand holding mine. She was also carefully thinking about nothing, more sad and wary than I had ever felt her.

I looked back down at the old lady then and took a deep breath. I dropped fully into Mindspace, all at once, hoping to catch a piece of what had killed the woman.

It was too early in the morning; I was too groggy, my mind wanting to drop down into sleep rather than Mindspace. So it took me a little longer than normal to "open my eyes" enough to get a good look. And even then, it took a long moment to understand what I was seeing.

It was clear. Mindspace was clear, as clean and full of light as a freshly scrubbed bathtub full of clean water. Which was impossible. A hundred ways, impossible.

There were small whirls where the people around me were walking through, making little ripples in the shallows, like small boats on a pond. Sanchez was a heavier boat than the rest, but still a shallow-dweller. So I went deeper.

Underneath was still clear, too clear, as if impossibly someone had come through and cleaned it up. As if a vacuum or a broom had whisked the whole thing clean.

I sank down into Mindspace as deep as I could go—my metaphorical ears popping under the strain—and looked. Carefully. Tasting the area as much as looking. Spending a good, long time trying to figure out what had happened.

There, in the area of the body in front of me—almost too faint to notice—were the traces of the second man I'd seen earlier, at the other crime scene. But his presence was obscured, covered, as if someone had chalked it over with raw Mindspace.

I was disturbed. As I surfaced, I was more disturbed. The only thing I'd ever heard of doing this was a small machine at the Guild headquarters here in Atlanta, stored under lock and key and physical barrier, impossible to retrieve. And rumor had it that the machine was broken, had been for twenty years, and it was illegal then.

We were dealing with a telepath/teleporter, yes, but one with access to some of the Guild's secrets and to a good mechanic. And, I suspected, a man who had walked out of here on his own power.

Because, although the whole area was cloaked in thick clear nothing, the nothing was solid and uniform. Without a single pucker in the whole area. Even one. And the second guy noticeably absent.

My stomach cramped. The Guild was letting a lot more than murders out now—if the killer had the machines. . . . It was bad. It was very bad.

By treaty, the Guild got absolute power. But in exchange, they were forbidden several things. Government and political control. Private investments. And most of all, technology. They'd negotiated over the years—they could have low-level basic silicon computers, now, to process their internal data. A government technology auditor came by every month to ensure the data and the computers never touched a network, never touched the WorldNet, and were never altered in any way. If one seal on one hard drive was broken, one circuit breaker changed, the government would bring all hell to bear. Because the big scary thought, the one that kept political analysts up at night, was that the Guild, who'd saved the world from the Tech madmen, might turn to Tech themselves. With no one left to stop them.

But the Guild was run by crazy arrogant bastards, worse thirty years ago, men who didn't care who they screwed so long as it didn't get out. They broke every law, every treaty ever given, and locked the results in a secret vault no one had touched in twenty years. The Guild leaders now wouldn't destroy the machines; they couldn't—but they didn't bring them out either.

But if the contents of that vault at the Guild were to become public ... the street would run with blood before the authorities would allow the Guild to go on. They'd send in every standing army, every reserve force they could find. And the soldiers who worked for the Guild, the Guild black ops, the minders, even the deconstructionists ... well, they wouldn't roll over. Ireland might escape; they'd never agreed to the Guild. India and Brazil might get off lightly—the Guild was weaker there, and its members more integrated into society. But the Western World ... we'd see a war such as the world had never known, something that made the Tech Wars look like a child playing with a machine gun.

I took my time disengaging from Mindspace. I'd lost track of real time, but it had been long enough that Cherabino was getting impatient. Very impatient.

I let go of my link with her. The old lady in front of me still lay quietly, her sad form left sprawled like a child's manikin without its boning.

I turned; behind me was the forensics team I'd felt arrive while I was under. They were impatient, ready to be working, unsure why I was standing staring in the middle of the crime scene. The Atlanta cops had them well controlled, though. I walked forward to meet Cherabino.

"Please look for footprints," I told them all. "Very carefully."

I tried to figure out what to say, how to explain what I'd found without giving away any more Guild secrets than I had to. The best line of defense for this sort of thing was ignorance—even past the locks. As much as I hated the Guild, I hated even more the thought of their secrets getting out. Mass panic was *not* an option. War . . . No.

I needed to talk to Kara. Yesterday.

"Spit it out," Cherabino commanded. They'd been waiting twenty minutes, and she was cranky and hungry and wanted information.

I started on the part I could tell her. "It's empty. The Mindspace around here is empty, much emptier than it should be, and it's not filling up. It's not holding on to anything at all. For all I can tell from Mindspace—and trust me, I looked—the old lady was never here. The clerk you talked to—never here. The supervisor—also, completely missing. And your signatures are fading as fast as you walk away."

"What does that mean?" Sanchez waved the forensics team onto the scene behind me. Then he folded his arms and set his jaw. He wasn't thrilled to have waited. But since it looked like I was done, the rest of the team—waiting for his approval—could go ahead and get started.

I paused for a long moment, figuring out what to say, controlling my face so it didn't show. I settled for saying, "Our killer has Guild training."

He looked at me, frowning; he'd read my decision to lie, but wasn't quite confident enough in his empathy to say anything in front of the others.

I took a deep breath, careful not to have any tells. "You were right. This is the same guy. His signature— his taste, if you will—is exactly the same." I was lying through my teeth, but I thought probably it was the same guy. Though why he would dump a body so far from his stomping ground in East Atlanta—fifteen miles or more to our south and in a different jurisdiction—meant something had changed. I was thinking the profiler lady might have something to her theories.

McMartin shifted. "It did seem a lot like your other cases. No mark on her, scared expression."

The examiner moved a bit closer then, making no secret of the fact that he was listening. "A couple defensive bruises, but no obvious cause of death. Could be exposure, but . . ."

"Not likely in August at night," Cherabino agreed. "Not at a balmy seventy-five degrees."

"Heatstroke can hit anytime, yes, but it seems more likely during the day."

Cherabino nodded. "You should be able to identify them by brain damage if it's one of ours. Talk to the DeKalb coroner—I'm sure she can fax you over the info. Do keep it quiet, though, okay? We're not releasing the brain damage to the press."

The examiner nodded.

I'd been hesitating to add anything else, but I thought they should know. "You've got to realize, I don't feel her death here. It's like she never existed."

"No emotions? No feeling of death at all?" Cherabino asked.

"Very strange," I agreed.

The other detective shrugged, shifted his feet. "Not our primary crime scene, then."

"No way of telling," I returned. "It's just a little too blank around here. But if he was here—he definitely didn't teleport out. I told the guys to check for footprints. Maybe we'll get a good one."

"Twenty minutes of staring into space like a moron—and you've got nothing," the examiner said, his voice more curious than hostile.

"Guild training and a confirmation it's our killer is hardly nothing," Cherabino protested.

"It's okay," I forced myself to say. "I don't have much."

"The problem is, none of us do," Cherabino echoed. Then, to Sanchez she said, "I don't have any problem with you guys forgetting to invoice the department for this one. We didn't help much."

Behind me, one of the Forensics guys was waving to Sanchez with some minor physical clue. Sanchez nodded and went over, and we took our leave of the Atlanta PD cops.

The day was starting to warm up already, well on its way to the usual punishing heat, and something about the taste of the air made me think a storm was coming.

CHAPTER 15

"**What aren't you telling me?**" Cherabino demanded in the car, on the way back to the station.

"This is our guy, and he's had Guild training," I repeated, but my voice wasn't as steady as it could have been. Cherabino was driving recklessly again, and my knuckles were turning white as I gripped the door handle.

She repeated, "What aren't you telling me?"

"This guy has his hands on some serious Guild secrets. Stuff that can't get out, that shouldn't have gotten out even this far. Bad enough he's killing. To do this . . ." I took a deep breath. "If my suspicions are true, we're sitting on a powder keg. I need to talk to Kara. Away from the department. No recordings."

She was frowning. "What kind of powder keg?"

I made a fist, released it. "The bad kind. I don't know, Cherabino! I am not good at political stuff. I'm hoping I'm wrong. But I can tell you—regardless—we don't want to go there. We just . . . we just don't. We need to shut this down now."

She was angry now. "What do you think I've been trying to do the last month! He's not leaving any clues! There's nothing to go on. What powder keg are you talking about anyway?"

I shook my head. "Trust me, there are some things

you're better off not knowing. *I'm* better off not knowing. The Guild should keep its secrets, believe me. This case isn't easy—but we need to do whatever it takes to solve it."

Cherabino shook her head, irritated at me. "I'm already doing everything I can. What more do you want?"

I sighed. "Can you drive me to Midtown for a two o'clock meeting?"

"We're already in Midtown," she said.

"Next to the Fox Theatre," I said. It was maybe a mile and a half due west.

"I have to be at the . . . You've already set up a meeting with Kara?" she barked. "What did you do, send a psychic message by pigeon?"

"Something like that." Most people called it the phone, but if I got social capital from the mystery, so be it.

Cherabino was fighting a hint of fear from what I'd just told her. She was grumpy as a result, still sad about something she wouldn't face, and there were deep, deep circles under her eyes.

"I guess I hadn't realized you were still keeping Guild secrets," she said. "And for the record, I have a right to know why my life is in danger."

"That's a long shot," I said. "I hope it doesn't come to that."

"You're not telling me, are you?" She was highly annoyed.

I tried to explain. "That was a vision. For all we know, the two aren't even related. Some of this Guild stuff I only know about through rumors."

"Rumors?" Cherabino frowned. And decided anything I was this squirrely about she probably shouldn't push. She didn't want to be responsible for Guild secrets—if there were such things—but she resented the fact that I wouldn't tell her. Very, very much resented. "Branen's not going to like it," she said.

"Branen and Paulsen are going to have to deal with it," I told her. "They told me I could pull in other resources, I'm doing just that." The truth was, I just didn't care. This was suddenly about a lot more than just my job.

"I'll drive you," she said reluctantly. "I have to be out here at twelve to talk to the widow again anyway."

"Thank you." Suddenly it hit me again like a knife in the flesh—I was going to have to talk to Kara. To *Kara*, about this.

Two o'clock and we were still ten minutes out. Cherabino had taken too long talking to the widow—her sadness somehow greater then, even though I was two rooms away from their conversation.

"Can we stop for food? I didn't get lunch." I was hungry, and the thought of irritating Kara by being late was suddenly appealing.

"Neither did I," Cherabino said distractedly as she weaved her way through the skyscrapers in the air lanes. "And I'm not complaining. Let's get this done, and we'll see what we can do." She had no intention of getting me lunch, just a handful of nuts or a bar or something; she thought she had something in her desk.

I slouched down in my seat, stomach gnawing on my backbone as she circled the National Bell complex one more time than necessary and pulled into the sky-level parking deck entrance. Waiting impatiently for her turn, she drummed her fingers on the steering wheel before handing the security guard some coins.

He made her sign a waiver that he wasn't responsible for anything in particular, and waved her through.

Great. We were going to do this, weren't we? I reminded myself of the stakes as she parked and we got out of the car.

Downstairs we walked through the lobby, right in the middle of the hundred-year-old speckled marble floor, underneath the faux glass ceiling. I stopped in the middle of the floor. Cherabino frowned at me, paying too much attention to the people passing on either side.

"What?" she asked.

"Just bracing myself." Then I walked much too quickly through the huge rotating door and out to the courtyard. Cherabino rushed to keep up, yelling at me about something or other.

I'd known it was coming, but the impact of the magnetic field was still overwhelming, like nails on a chalkboard overlaid with a hundred angry bees. I took a breath and pulled into myself, lessening it as much as I could.

In front of me, Cherabino paused. "Oh, it's cool out here!" She turned around, looking at the bright green grass, the spring flowers, the people enjoying the outdoors—the sun overhead no longer an adversary but a close friend. To normals, anyway.

"Yeah, they refrigerate the courtyard with a magnetic field cooler," I said, gritting my teeth. After a few moments I'd stop noticing it, I told myself. I'd chosen this place on purpose for this reason—because no one would be able to get a clear picture of anything we said telepathically; the field was just too disruptive.

Her eyes narrowed. "Must take a lot of power." She was wondering about grid consumption and if they had a permit.

I sighed. "See how every third window or so is darker than the others, on both sides?" The skyscrapers had interesting patterns because of it. "The darker windows are modified solar cells, mostly clear. The technology is old, just expensive." You could do anything if you were rich enough, even these days.

She huffed, and asked, "Where are we meeting Kara?"

I looked across the fifty-foot green space toward the ice cream shop, finally able to concentrate on my surroundings rather than the low-level disquiet of the oscillating field. Kara was there all right, her blond head and navy blue business suit standing out even in this crowd. She had a way of doing that.

I turned back to Cherabino. "Would you mind waiting over here? I'm not—"

"Waiting?"

"You made me wait at the widow's," I said. "That was your expertise; this is mine." I met her eyes square on. Was she really going to challenge me? "You can watch from across the way to make sure there's nothing funny going on. I told you most of this you're better off not knowing."

"What about the 'danger' you keep telling me about?" she said. "Won't the perp jump in and spirit me away if I'm not next to you? I mean, that is why you're following me around."

Great, trust Cherabino to make the situation work to her advantage. I ran my hand through my hair, frustrated. "You're perfectly safe if you stay inside the courtyard. Nobody's going to be able to Jump in through the magnetic field dissonance, and if he can focus enough to do anything in this mess, he's better than I am."

An idea hit her like lightning. "Can we install one of these in the department? You know, keep the telepaths under control while you interrogate them?"

If we installed one of these in the basement, I was

quitting. "The field generator's as big as a house and way more expensive. Now, are you going to stay over here or not? Kara doesn't like it when people are late."

"Just how well do you know this woman?"

I clenched my jaw and gestured to the bench. Then moved away quickly. What was going on with Cherabino today? Hopefully she'd get the hint. If not, probably Kara would be over here in a minute anyway, and it would all fall apart. As I walked, there was a noticeable lack of footsteps behind me. Finally.

Now I just had to convince my ex-fiancée to listen. Swallow my pride. I set my jaw and started walking.

A few gray hairs dotted her blond hair, a few more wrinkles marred her face, but Kara was otherwise just as beautiful, just as poised as she'd ever been. Her heart-shaped face was currently pinched in an overly professional facade, but that I could take. The fact that she'd not gained an ounce and kept her impeccable fashion sense was a little harder. I knew I didn't look nearly as good.

She stood and held out her hand. I ignored it. Telepaths didn't normally touch unless they were very good friends, and we weren't that, not anymore. She dropped the hand.

"You said you needed my help? I assume it's an important matter since you wanted to meet here. Unless you just don't want me to be able to read you." Her eyes narrowed. "You didn't used to be a coward."

I slouched onto the bench. Considered defending myself but left it. She'd been notified at the first two trips to rehab and had chosen not to show up. She'd betrayed me to the Guild, the last domino in a chain that tore my old life apart. I didn't owe her anything,

Swartz's claims of apologies aside. I didn't owe her a thing.

Might as well get to it. "The DeKalb police are tracking a killer who's a teleporter and I believe also a telepath. Up until this morning I believed he was killing with his mind, a standard kill at that."

Kara sat down next to me. Her body language relaxed a little. "And you don't want to make an abuse claim through Enforcement, not with your history."

I shrugged. "The police don't want them taking over the case, and the stakes are high enough, I think they're right. We have potential Guild secrets on the line here, yeah, but civilians are dying and you guys aren't doing a thing. Somebody needs to get justice for these families."

She blew out a long line of air. "What's really going on? I don't see you all that upset about justice."

"Yeah, well, you don't know me anymore."

"Maybe I don't." She waited for a long moment. "You called me."

I looked around, made sure none of the business types were close enough to overhear. "The Mindspace in the crime scene this morning was scrubbed clean—cleaner than I've ever seen it," I said. "The only thing I can think—well, it seems like something from the vault. Something from those rumors that never would die out. You know anything about those?"

"The machines?" I could see the shock on her face, then she got pensive. "The vault hasn't been touched in years."

"Well, someone's touched it," I said. "You have a big problem here."

"*If* you're right. You don't have the most credibility in certain circles anymore. You have to know that."

"That's probably true." I looked straight ahead. "But it doesn't matter. Tell me about the machines."

She was quiet for a long time. "This can't get out. You understand?"

I nodded.

"Can't get out, at all."

I nodded again.

She sighed. "There's one. Something that can do what you're saying. Another, bigger one—well, killing normals was a leading topic of research after the wars. Neither machine works, so far as I know. But I wouldn't know." She paused. "You asking isn't going to be taken well."

"I'm not asking; you're asking," I said. "There are people dead, Kara. The killer is likely Guild. It's time for you to help me catch him. Ask to see the vault, ask to have it opened. You know they'll listen. You can make them listen. You play the politics well. You always have."

She looked down. "How many dead?"

I paused, not wanting to repeat my screwup with Joey and the numbers. "More than six, less than a dozen," I finally said. "The profiler thinks there's more coming."

Kara sighed. "Let's say I do this. What is it you want exactly?"

"I get your help with the murder case. We shut down the killings, you, the police, everybody. No fighting. You treat me with respect."

She nodded. "I'll do my best. Do you have any leads?"

I told myself I was getting what I wanted and not to screw it up now. I filled her in about the vision and my identification of Bradley, with Cherabino attacked and myself killed by Bradley in that indefinite future time. "I don't go around making enemies of teleporters," I said. At her frown, I added, "At least not anymore." Kara was a teleporter, and while I hoped we weren't enemies—as angry as I still was, that would hurt far, far too much—I knew we also were not friends. We could not be friends, not after all that had happened.

I shifted on the hard bench. "But in the vision he acted like it was personal, and he went after Cherabino, specifically. I don't see any reason for Bradley to do that unless he's at least half of the team killing these guys, and from what he said in the vision, I think it's all him. I think he's the mastermind of this—whatever it is—and it's starting to feel like he has some agenda I can't see. Some gain, past just the thrill of killing those people."

"Like what?"

"I don't know," I said. "I don't want to know."

"You aren't a member anymore." Kara held up a finger at my protest and barreled on. "I'm not saying it to be cruel, just to let you know you're an unknown factor for the leadership right now. You haven't been tested in years, and we don't know whether your visions are calibrated enough anymore to be relied on. Unless you have evidence against Bradley that would corroborate . . ." She looked at me questioningly.

I shook my head. "We have some physical stuff, but nothing specific to him right now—at least, not without searching his home. You could always let us search his home. It wouldn't take long."

"You won't get that, I can tell you. I don't remember who this guy is you're talking about, but I can crosscheck and find him if he's in the city. But what you're talking about is a privacy issue. Nobody searches

Guild property—or the property of our members—except Guild Enforcement. If you don't have hard evidence, there are limits to what I can do for you. Your credibility issue is a major stumbling block." She sat back, the lines on her forehead getting more pronounced as she thought. "You're sure he's a teleporter?"

"At least a Level Three," I said. "He carried two guys through with him, one mostly dead—I saw the pucker, and I saw the results."

She nodded. "Telepath too?"

"There was a telepath there, somebody who felt vaguely familiar. He was strong, right at the edge of compulsory. Our profiler thinks since the pattern of the killings is changing, there's a second guy too. But I still think it's the first who's the strong telepath. Bradley is both and in the public records; that's how I found him to compare with the face in the vision."

"How much more information can you give me about the killings?"

"Not much more than I have, unfortunately. But it's in the papers, and they mostly have it right—what they have, anyway. You can do your research; the mayor wants this thing solved, so I doubt anybody's going to stand in the way of questions." I frowned. "Try not to get me in trouble if you can help it. I like this job, and I'd like to keep it if I can."

She shook her head, her expression almost . . . amazed. "Never would have pegged you for the detective type," she said. "It suits you, though."

"Consultant," I corrected, "but thanks."

Kara glanced at me. "How are you . . . otherwise?"

"I'm okay. You?"

"I'm good," she said. "Very good. I did tell you that—"

I cut her off with a gesture, not wanting to know. Too angry to care. At least in this place, I didn't have to know—the one upside of the nauseating fields that made me head-blind. Some things I didn't want to know. "Kara, I need to put this guy away. These killings can't go on—they can't. If I have to start talking about some of this to the cops to put him away—if I have to leak the Guild's secrets, I will."

She sat straight up. "There's no need to threaten me. You asked for my help and I intend to give it to you—whether or not you're being civil. One of our people abusing civilians is unacceptable. Period."

"Good," I said, and held up a finger so Cherabino would pause just a moment longer before she came barreling over. "Then we understand each other."

I stood up and walked away. Some part of me was dying inside to see her like this, but most of me was very, very glad. I was walking away with the upper hand, and with Kara, that was a hard, hard thing to get. If I could put her in her place a few times . . . but, no, I told myself. This was about the case. It had to be about the case. And I'd trust her exactly that far.

Cherabino sat on the bench, arms crossed. When I approached, she asked, "Did you get what you needed?"

"Yeah." I fished out my sunglasses to have something to do with my hands. "She's going to help us."

"Good."

"You ready?" I asked, trying to keep my voice casual. I really, really wanted out of here. I wanted away from Kara, away from anything that smelled like Guild. Away from this place where we'd had our date, so long ago.

Cherabino stood. "The department had better

reimburse for parking." As she walked, she said, "I still think we need one of these for the police station."

I ignored the comment, secure in the ongoing budget crisis. Something that expensive just wouldn't happen. "*I think we need to get me some food.*"

CHAPTER 16

On the way into the station, I noticed two other interviewers from downstairs talking with the secretaries at the front desk. One of them, Clark, looked at me suspiciously.

I stopped by to say hello. "I'm working a case," I told him. "Anything interesting come through?"

"A couple murder charges, a robbery. All easy targets," he said. "Paulsen says we've got a clump of arrests coming through late afternoon."

"I'll be there," I said, and followed Cherabino, who was waving impatiently.

An hour later, upstairs in the smaller Holmes conference room, papers from the case—and the murder book—were spread out all over the tables. The boards with their pictures took up half the wall, and Cherabino was on and off the phone coordinating the techs to go and take pictures of the scenes. I was sitting in front of the case notes. I couldn't forget the soap residue, or the fact there was vomit in a corner of the first scene, the killer having dumped his lunch along with the bodies. Somewhere here there was a clue, something that would let us catch this guy.

A knock came on the door frame. Cherabino looked up.

"Michael," she said. "Come in."

It was the junior cop from the earlier meeting. "I just thought you should know the older kid remembered the man with the garbage bag very well. The sketch artist was pleased." He put a page in front of Cherabino, then stood there awkwardly.

I reached over to get a better look. The sketch was of a fifty-something man with regular features and a thinning hairline. The face looked familiar, somehow; I knew I'd seen it before, but I didn't know where.

"Good work," Cherabino said. "This'll give us a place to start."

"Is there something else I can do to help you, ma'am?"

She looked around. "Looks like we're getting out of order, and there's a meeting in here second shift. Could you see if you can match up the right papers to the right victims? Get the murder book squared away? We'll need to be out of here by four thirty." She met my eyes, a clear implication I was supposed to help him since the mess was my fault.

I sighed and got up, paging through pictures and case notes, sorting through them by victim since Cherabino thought it was so important. Attaching papers to the correct pages in the battered gray book, flipping back and forth to make sure I had the timeline in order. Michael got the stack with the coroner's reports first and—well, he was taking too long to hand me stuff.

I went back to his side of the table, my hands full of the book and loose papers.

He was frowning. "What does Ultrate mean?"

"It's an artificial glands company," I said. "Why?"

The cop flipped through the papers, putting his finger on one line of text on each. "Is there a reason why all of the reports have that name?"

Cherabino stood up. "Let me see."

She ripped the paper out of his hands. Turned the pages. Then dropped them on the table and cursed a blue streak.

Michael had shrunk back. "Um, are you okay, ma'am?"

Leaning on the table, she looked up. "I'm an idiot, is what I am. We all looked at that, how many times?"

I'd just looked at it this afternoon; I hadn't thought anything of the brand name. They were the biggest market share. I was an idiot. All that work, and I hadn't even seen the important clue.

Cherabino put out a hand, stopping the junior cop from leaving the room. "No, you did good. Come back here."

Michael came.

"You want to work in Homicide?" she asked him. "It's a lot of stupid details, dead bodies, and no glory whatsoever. You'll work harder than you've ever worked in your life. Interested?"

He smiled. "I'd like that more than anything, ma'am."

She straightened. "There's a hiring freeze from outside the department, and transfers take for-fucking-ever. It could be a couple weeks. But that kind of eye deserves a shot. I'll talk to Branen myself."

"I would appreciate that." Externally, Michael was calm, but inside he was jumping up and down, doing a rather amusing happy dance all over the room. He and Cherabino talked details for a couple seconds, and he left the room with the express intention of doing his happy dance out of sight.

"I thought you couldn't get the money for another detective," I said, worried she was promising something she couldn't deliver. That guy was not going to do well with disappointment.

She started gathering up papers aggressively. "Transfers come out of a different pot. Now"—she looked at
the clock on the wall—"I doubt we can make it across
the city in rush hour before the people in charge leave
for the day, but we can set up an appointment for
tomorrow."

I hesitated to ask, considering. But I did need to
keep her safe. "Can I come?"

"You'll probably need to." She slung her bag over
her shoulder. "Help me get the boards out of the room.
We're running late as it is."

While Cherabino called Ultrate Bioproducts, I called
Kara.

"Any news?" I demanded.

She sighed, and I heard her chair creak as she
leaned back. "You know you're calling me at"—she
paused—"six o'clock after you saw me at two thirty?"

"So?"

"It's a little fast for results, and I *do* have other things
to do with my day."

I waited for it.

As expected, she sighed. "It doesn't look good for
you right now. You're an unknown, like I said. You
didn't leave on good terms. And this accusation of
yours—well, it seems awfully convenient."

"Convenient?" I said. "I felt him choke me to death!
How in hell is that convenient?"

Kara sighed. "Bradley is Dane's replacement. I
thought you knew."

I stared out the window next to Cherabino's cubicle.
How long had my friend been dead before they'd
replaced him? I was furious.

I did vaguely remember some punk nerdy assistant
in Research—had that been Bradley? If so, I hadn't

respected the guy at all. My stomach burned with the thought that this weenie, if that was him, had taken over Dane's position. Maybe this *was* personal.

"Are you there?"

"Yeah. I hadn't realized."

"Well, combined with the circumstances of your leaving, the higher-ups aren't exactly eager to jump on this train. It looks bad."

"It's the truth."

"Maybe, but you need credibility too." She sighed. "Bradley's been complaining to the higher-ups for a year that no one respects him as department head. Considering the circumstances, they're understandably cautious about confronting him over something like this. I promise you, I'm working on it. I've got some balls in motion, and if it can be done quietly, I'll do it. But some of this is out of my hands. I believe you, if it makes any difference. I've never known you to lie about something like this."

I didn't comment. She was blowing me off. I wasn't going to make it easier for her by saying it was okay. It wasn't.

She did the clicking thing with her teeth again. "I've got an appointment set up to open the vault tomorrow midday. I'll get the maintenance team to help me. If anything's missing, we'll find out."

"And then what?"

"If something's missing, they'll turn over whatever rocks it takes to find it. From a credibility standpoint, that's exactly what we need. I hope you'll forgive me when I say I'd rather nothing was missing."

"Yeah," I said. "I understand." If something was missing, the consequences could be unthinkable. But part of me already knew it was gone. Now I just had to wait for them to catch up.

"Look, I'll call you tomorrow," Kara said.

"Fine."

By the time I made it back to the interview rooms, it was too late to help with the scheduled afternoon arrests. I'd broken a promise, even if it was for the multiples case, a good cause. But the other interviewers stopped talking to me. Literally, stopped. And my docket for the next day was suddenly full of drug pushers.

I made a face and told the coordinator for the schedule that it was fine. I hoped to God I made it in tomorrow in enough time to do what I had to. We had the Ultrate meeting tomorrow morning, and I didn't know what was going to happen with Kara. Her distrust, like the other interviewers' distrust, burned like fire in my guts.

Cherabino drove me home without comment, her mind quiet and sad, thoughts drifting through her mind like leaves on a stream. But I was too focused on my own worries to follow any of hers.

That evening we watched television. Cherabino's television, with one silly comedy after another, and she held the remote. It was a small couch; we weren't sitting on top of each other, but we weren't worlds apart either. We were both exhausted, raw from the emotional whiplash of the day.

She started yawning by the third show, and her thoughts spilled contently into the room. I wasn't really trying to listen. Not then. But my headache from earlier was mostly gone, and she and I—we—the connection I'd discovered earlier, was coming through. The soft sad tone of her mind was so beautiful, beautiful in a whole different way than I'd ever seen from her, that I couldn't help but listen. I found myself relaxing as she did.

As she got more tired, she stretched out a bit more, rearranging herself on the couch in what was obviously habit. She went for a pillow to put under her head—and her hand ran into my leg instead. She tensed and started to scoot away on the couch again.

I put my hand on her shoulder to stop her. "I don't mind," I said very softly.

She frowned and yawned again. I could feel how slowly her mind was processing. But on some level—on this level—she wasn't viewing me as a threat. I pulled her a little closer, softly, in the direction her body was already going, until she ended up cuddled half on my shoulder, half on my chest. I expected her to fight, but she didn't.

As her body lost all tension, relaxing into me, her brain fuzzily suggested this was a bad idea, that I probably meant something by it she'd have to deal with later. But it felt so nice, was so comforting. . . .

"It doesn't have to mean anything," I said, very softly. "You can hate me again tomorrow."

She was reassured; her mind muttered softly to itself about unrelated matters until finally she slept. I stayed up, watching her sleep, while I monitored Mindspace.

CHAPTER 17

The old north Atlanta Buckhead business center had been one of the hardest hit during the Tech Wars, both in electronic terms and with, well, actual physical bombs. In the sixty or so years since the end of the war, businesses had seen reclaiming the area as a matter of pride. Most of the craters had been filled in, the streets and skyscrapers rebuilt better than new by now, but the memory of uncontrolled technology lingered like the smell of ozone in the air.

The largest crater in the area was different, though. Shifting earth and fused metal made a lousy foundation. After a few crumbled buildings, they decided the bowl-shaped depression would make an acceptable place to put a park. Ultrate Bioproducts' headquarters was right on the edge of that park, all fifty-seven stories of their glass-and-chrome skyscraper having a very nice view of the drought-resistant grass and sun-resistant flowers. That it used to be a crater didn't seem to bother them. It bothered me.

Cherabino found us a parking spot across the street, and we hiked on foot the hundred yards to the gleaming glass entrance. It was already too hot to think, and sweat dripped down my collar. I tried to ignore both facts.

"I hate mornings," she muttered as we climbed the building steps like supplicants.

"It's nine thirty," I pointed out. "The crime scene was earlier than this."

"That's not the point."

We crossed the ultramodern atrium dotted with senseless sculptures intended to dwarf the visitors. Ahead, a copper reception desk dominated the space. On either side were security guards.

"DeKalb PD," Cherabino barked as she flashed her badge up at the receptionist. "I'm going to need to speak to somebody in charge of your artificial gland program."

We were shown to the office of Jonathon Evans, executive head of gland production—or, more accurately, to the seating area outside his office. The faux leather slab of a couch made me feel unwieldy, as if I didn't belong, while the old receptionist looked at me with beady eyes. I couldn't read her, which made me uncomfortable.

After a half hour, Cherabino put down her magazine with a sigh. "Is Evans even here?" she asked the receptionist too loudly. Clearly, she wasn't interested in getting up for something as minor as a rude question.

"Mr. Evans is finishing up a conference call from London," she said reluctantly. "He'll be another minute or two. Did you require refreshments?" I noticed she didn't make any suggestions as to what kind of refreshments there were.

"That would be nice," I said, just to be difficult. "Do you have any ice cream? Preferably chocolate with rainbow sprinkles?"

"I'm afraid we don't have anything like that. I can

make you some simcoffee if that's something you're
interested in."

"Please," I said. I hated simcoffee—and rather
thought anybody this rich would have the real stuff—
but the thought of her having to get up to make it made
me oddly happy.

Sadly, just then the oak-paneled door opened and a
man of about forty entered the room and Rude Receptionist was off the hook for the coffee. Evans's understated pin-striped suit screamed money, but his smile
was genuine. "Sorry to keep you waiting," he said.

He shook hands with Cherabino but only nodded to
me. Huh. I hadn't been introduced as a telepath yet.
Either he was very, very used to protocol or he had
enough sensitivity to spot one from a few feet away.
Either way I was going to shield hard against him.

I followed him and Cherabino to the office, an open-
floor-plan wood-paneled place with a view of the city.
The chair I took in front of his obscenely large desk
was surprisingly comfortable.

"What can I do for the police?" Evans asked, his
hands folded in front of him politely. "I trust Delaney
offered you refreshments?"

"She offered," I said.

Cherabino quelled me with a look. "We're here to
talk to you about Ultrate artificial glands." She offered
him a piece of paper. "Specifically, the glands in these
eight people."

He took a look at the list before setting it down.
"While this is very interesting to me—particularly as
I've taken time out of my day to meet with you—I'm
afraid I can't discuss specific glands without their
owners' consents. Besides," he said, and laughed sin-
cerely, "I hardly keep those kinds of names in my head.

We sell two thousand thyroid glands a quarter, for example, and that's just through our US affiliates."

I shrugged. "Their owners are dead. I hardly think they'll mind you giving out information that may lead us to their killer."

"And we think those eight glands were sold directly through this office," Cherabino told him. "We'd like the records. Now."

Evans picked up the phone. "Delaney, would you get on the phone and set up a meeting with the records department for this afternoon? Also, please check out the credentials of"—he looked at us, and repeated our names and Cherabino's serial number—"with the DeKalb police, please. Feel free to go up the chain of command. Thank you." He hung up.

I shifted in my chair. I respected him more for being suspicious, but we couldn't wait forever.

"I'm very sorry to hear that some of our customers are dead," Evans replied to us directly, "but I fail to see how our records can possibly be of use to you."

"Didn't you just talk to your records department?" I asked.

"I like to know what's going on in my unit," Evans replied. "That doesn't mean I'm going to give up proprietary information without a warrant, particularly before I'm certain that you are who you say you are."

Cherabino nodded. "Fair enough. While your associate is confirming our credentials, let's talk about the glands. All eight people on that list have glands from your company—who would have access to your customer lists?"

"I hope you're not implying some kind of wrongdoing on our part," Evans said. "Naturally we're as upset as you are to find out about these deaths, but our product is tested and approved, much safer than a comparable natural transplant in every case. We've been independently—"

"Calm down," I said, amused. "We're not here to talk about product safety. We mentioned it earlier. These people were murdered."

He sat back. "Murdered? I'm very sorry to hear that. It's . . . oh, I take it we're discussing the Mystery Death Killer? The one all over the papers?"

I nodded.

"Who would have access to your customer records?" Cherabino repeated. "We're looking at common threads between the victims as a routine part of the investigation."

He exhaled sharply. "Yes, of course. That kind of information isn't easy to get. Our records system is highly secure. Our matching protocols are fastidious, and in any case they are handled by several teams of people. The odds of any one having all of those customers are very slight, though I promise you I will look into it."

"What about your Tuners?" I asked.

"Tuners?" Cherabino frowned.

Evans ran his hand through his hair. "Our Tuners are highly trained, calibrated, recommended highly by the Guild, and extremely professional. In fifty years we've never had a problem."

"Um, what's a Tuner?" she repeated, annoyed.

I glanced at Evans. It was his job; he could explain it.

He leaned forward, the very picture of interesting professionalism. "You know that your heart contains small numbers of brain cells on the organ itself? They're there to help your system regulate how fast it beats, the proper opening and closing of valves, and so forth. Like the mechanical pacemakers they used to implant. Well, artificial organs have similar nerve cells built in, preset with the correct dosage, interactions, and so forth with the rest of the body. But the organ can't go 'live,' so to speak, without the nervous system accepting those cells as part of the grid. A trained telepath is needed to tune the cells to the body's neural net and turn the organ on, so to speak. If it turns out your dosage needs an adjustment later—and your body doesn't take care of the change on its own—we'll bring a Tuner back to make the adjustment painlessly. It's faster and more consistent than external medication in almost every case."

"Who's in charge of your matching protocol?" I asked him. "Is there any way that someone is earmarking certain glands to specific kinds of people?"

"The kind of access they would need would limit—"

"Wait." Cherabino held up a hand. "Let's go back to these Tuner characters. They're Guild, right?" When I nodded, she continued. "Well, you keep saying our killer is Guild. Would a Tuner have the kind of training he'd need to do what we talked about?"

I thought about it. Other than the fact that Bradley was definitely *not* a Tuner—he was in Research, as I recalled from the articles—there wasn't a good reason to say a Tuner couldn't have done it. I hadn't spent a lot of time with those guys, but anyone who interacted with the nervous system every day could probably figure out anything he needed to know. The machine I'd mentioned to Kara would be an easy shortcut.

"Well, yes. But—"

"How many Tuners do you employ on a regular basis?" Cherabino asked Evans.

"Maybe six, perhaps eight in a good quarter. We like

to use the same professionals quarter by quarter if we can—provides a sense of continuity to surgeons and the patients."

"How many of them have you met personally?" she pushed.

"Cherabino, he couldn't possibly—"

Evans cut me off. "Most of them, actually. I oversaw the implantation department until my promotion last year." He smiled at my disconcertment. "You didn't think Delaney was my choice for assistant, did you?"

I didn't know what to say to that—obviously I had. "Where are you going with this, Cherabino?"

She fished out another piece of paper and offered it to Evans—I saw a glimpse of our sketch. "You may not have—"

"Neil Henderson," Evans said decisively. He looked back at her. "It's a good likeness."

Like a key turning in a lock, the name linked to the feelings from the crime scene and the scarf. "Neil Henderson, used to work in Research?" I'd met him maybe five times ten years ago, but it all clicked. I still wasn't sure about the punk nerdy guy who may or may not be Bradley, the guy who'd supposedly taken over Dane's office, the bastard, but old Neil was always barging in on Dane and me on our way to lunch, trying to get himself invited. If he hadn't been so crazy into practical jokes, we might have brought him along, but a joker is a dangerous friend. There was one time he brought in this live chicken. . . . "You're talking about crazy Neil?" I repeated.

The corner of Evans's mouth quirked up. "I haven't heard that nickname in a long time. He's a good Tuner, steady, responsible. Good with the patients. Is he in any danger?" He looked at the two of us.

"I don't imagine so," Cherabino said smoothly as

she put the sketch away. "Just a few more routine questions, if you don't mind."

Evans shrugged. "I have another few minutes."

The phone rang next to him—he picked it up and spoke. "Wonderful. That's what I expected. Yes, go ahead and set up the conference room for the meeting with Telecorp. Yes, thank you."

He turned back to the two of us. "What else can I do for DeKalb's Finest?"

We walked down the street, me a little worried about making it into the station on time for interviews. "You realize that he didn't give us anything useful?" I asked Cherabino.

"He identified the picture. That's more than we had."

"But the records . . . He said all the right things and gave us shit."

She shrugged. "Corporate guys are like that."

"Hold on," I said, seeing a pay phone. "I need to call Kara."

Cherabino shrugged and put her hands in her pockets, clearly willing to wait.

I fished out change and dialed Kara. We needed to talk to Henderson, which meant she would need to set it up.

"You realize it's less than halfway through the workday," Kara said. "You don't have to call me twice a day, I will get back to you, you know."

"We have a lead."

Her tone brightened. "Oh, good. Hard evidence would really help."

"Um, it's not super hard," I said, then realized what that sounded like. "I mean, it's just that we have a couple of witnesses who can identify one of your guys in the area where he shouldn't be, carrying something suspiciously like a body in a trash bag. We got someone to identify the picture. It's Neil Henderson."

"I thought you were going after Bradley?" Kara asked, after a moment to process.

"I'm going where the evidence leads me."

Next to me, Cherabino snorted. It was one of her catchphrases, so what?

"That's still not definitive," Kara noted. "But it's better than what we had. Who identified Henderson?"

"Jonathon Evans, head of the gland unit of Ultrate Bioproducts. He's respectable."

"A friend of yours?"

I was insulted. "The first time I've ever met him is today. What the crap, Kara? I'm not a liar and I resent being called one."

"I'm not calling you a liar. I'm just making sure I have the information to defend you if it comes up."

"Oh." Well, maybe she wasn't blowing me off after all.

"They'll open the vault for me this afternoon, and I'll put in an official request to talk to Henderson as soon as we get off the phone. I'll still talk to him regardless, but having it on the books will help us later if there's really something going on. That kind of identification looks suspicious. That much I think we can all agree on."

"What about Bradley?"

"I'll see if I can link him to Henderson somehow. If I can't, there's nothing I can do unless there's a theft. Get me something else to go on for Bradley—some hard evidence, even circumstantial at this point—and I'll move. But if I go too early, there's nothing I can do for you later."

"What if there's a substantiating vision?" I asked,

and told her about the phone call the captain had taken from Jamie Skelton, head of the Guild precog facility.

"Did she see Bradley specifically?" Kara asked, always practical.

"I don't know—this is thirdhand at least."

"I'll ask her myself," she said. "Watch your back, though. With two visions, I'd say it's a given you're in danger."

"I'll be careful."

As soon as I hung up, Cherabino made me reprise every word of the conversation with Kara. "Do you really think she's going to get us what we need?" she asked.

"Actually, at this point, yes. She's got her teeth in this one, it looks like, and she's actually treating me seriously. If we can get her the lever to move the world, she will," I said. "But she says there's only one shot at this, and she doesn't want to move too soon." Actually, surprisingly, I think I trusted Kara's instincts on this, assuming there wasn't another agenda in play. She always had a good sense of the best time to move.

But something inside me insisted this was taking too long. Henderson, Bradley, or both needed to be off the street, now. We walked back to the car, quiet, while I worried about what would happen if I screwed up. I couldn't screw up, was all. Or someone else would die.

I got to the interview room a little late and found Bellury reading a magazine. He looked up when I rushed in. "Perp waiting for you," he said in that understated way of his. "And Clark wanted to know where you were."

"He's not my boss," I said, then sighed. At this rate the other interviewers might never talk to me. Some days that might be restful, I supposed, if they didn't mutter in their thoughts too much. Guilt stabbed at me anyway. I asked, "What's the perp accused of?"

Bellury gave me the rundown of the case. "You going to be here awhile?" he asked, quietly.

Great, now he was doubting me too. "I was with Cherabino all morning on the case," I told him. "I'm supposed to check in with her this afternoon. Paulsen said the multiples case is high priority."

Bellury nodded, but I could feel him decide to check the story.

I took the case file. I was here to work, I told myself.

At Cherabino's cubicle that afternoon, she fanned out the new pictures from the original crime scenes. In every one except the last, in some corner there was a crushed-earth circle from a bad anti-grav generator. The kid whose father was a mechanic had been right on; our white guy with the garbage bag had an aircar with one bad generator. Cherabino seemed pleased and had even loosened up a bit around me.

Before long, though, we had to go back to our respective corners, she to other cases, me to the interview rooms.

Late that evening, after everyone on day shift had already gone home, I was slouched in the single chair in the coffee closet, scrunched up between the counter and the wall. My head hurt like a mother from the last suspect, and the coffee wasn't helping. He'd been certifiable, and I'd gladly testify in favor of an insane plea if it would get him locked up and away from me forever. People that crazy were a telepath's worst nightmare. He believed himself so intensely that if reality didn't match up, well, that was its problem. All too easy for a telepath to give in to that intensity and believe too.

I'd escaped this time—thank you, Guild training—but it had hurt me and scared me and put me in a really rotten mood. The pounding pain in my head was just making things worse. What I wanted more than anything else in the world was to find a stash of my poison somewhere and fall off the face of the planet for a while.

I indulged in that fantasy for about ten seconds, just long enough to realize it was already past quitting time, a very dangerous time to be fantasizing about my poison. I would have to go all the way to my apartment—or Cherabino's house while she worked and bitched—and sit there, telling myself no for hours on end. Vials or no, Swartz or no, I was maybe sane enough to know I couldn't handle that, not today. And I had a drug test tomorrow I had to pass.

I leaned my head back on the wall and tried to think. Work the problem as best I could around the headache. Finally I grabbed the phone outside the coffee closet, pulling the handset in with me and closing the door. I dialed Swartz's number.

When the message started, I hung up. Then I called back. Still no response.

"Swartz. I . . . It's a bad time. Call me back, man." I hung up and waited. Then I checked my watch. He should call me back in less than five minutes. Then I looked again. My watch was cheap, but not cheap enough to be wrong. It was Wednesday. Wednesdays Swartz took his wife to the movies. It might be hours before he called me back.

For a long minute I stared at the phone while my headache worsened.

I had another number for Wednesdays, somebody Swartz knew. I'd met him only once, an old geezer at the Fourteenth Street meetings. I had called him just the one time, two days before my last fall, when things were so bad I hadn't even gone to work. God only knew what he thought of me.

The door rattled as somebody else came in the coffee closet.

Frances the file clerk was humming loudly as she pushed in. She stopped when she saw me. "You look like shit," she said, cheerfully enough. Apparently she didn't keep up with rumors; she wasn't even slightly mistrustful.

"I feel worse," I said.

"Hmm. Anything I can do?" she asked. She poured herself coffee and doctored it, scooting around me companionably in the small space.

"Your choice: shoot me now or get me an aspirin."

She smiled. "Any particular kind?"

"Aspirin. The simple stuff. No bells and whistles." I put the phone on the counter; I'd return it to the cradle in a minute.

I had to be pretty desperate to even think of painkillers at all, but my head was pounding in time with my pulse, and it wasn't getting better. If I couldn't have my drug, maybe I could at least feel a little less like dying.

"Well, you are in luck. I think I have one." Frances plopped her purse on the countertop and started rummaging. Finally, she came up with a bubble pack, which she handed me. "Here you go, sweetie. Feel better." Then she packed up her purse and her coffee and left the closet, toeing the door closed behind her.

I examined the purported aspirin. The foil and the bubble seemed intact, even at angles to the light; I couldn't detect any tears or holes. The paper on the foil was clearly stamped with a manufacturer's seal—a manufacturer that did, indeed, produce aspirin. Even the lot number seemed reasonable. I was halfway through opening the package for the first taste-test before it hit me that this wasn't normal behavior.

Normal be damned, I thought, as I carefully stuck my tongue on the pressed pill. The last thing I needed was to get hooked on something new. When the sharp-bitter aspirin taste came back, I spat and reached for the coffee. I swallowed the pills, both of them, without further tests. Either a personal triumph or the stupidest thing I'd done all week.

The medicine hit me as I was in the accountant's office, in the last stage of getting a double shift approved. My headache went from excruciating to tolerable in about five minutes, and nothing else happened. I was grateful.

Late second shift, I called Kara, expecting to leave a message. She picked up.

"Aren't you there a little late?" I asked her.

"Aren't you?" she responded automatically. "City liaison is more than a full-time job, as I'm sure you understand. I wish you would stop calling me every few hours, though. I've got the higher-ups breathing down my neck, and I don't need you doing it too."

I was twitchy at the moment, and I had to know. "Any news on the boxes?" I couldn't call them machines, not over an open phone line, but I had to know.

"That's what I've been trying to tell you. They're gone. But not the two you mentioned—the space scrubber, yeah, nothing but scuff marks where it used to be. The imploder's still there, though. What's missing are the *boxes* from Stewart's tests ten years ago. Do you know anything about those?"

The man who introduced me to my drug? Yeah, I

knew about his tests. "It's not boxes, plural. He had one and a couple of hospital things to monitor responses, you know, medical stuff. It was very early stage, very experimental at that point. I can tell you what I was there for, but my understanding is he kept working a long time after that, with different drugs and procedures. He could have added another box; I don't know. Dane had been working on charting the shape of the mind in Mindspace. Last I heard, Stewart was talking about incorporating that research somehow, but I don't know what happened with that."

"Didn't Stewart pioneer the work on boosting drugs?" she asked, distracted.

"What's a boosting drug?"

"Pills they're giving some of the midlevel telepaths to improve their numbers. They don't seem to work for everybody, and you can't use them for long. The Guild likes them for special ops, though."

"You supposed to talk about that kind of stuff on a phone line?"

"Probably not." She sighed. "The shape of the mind in Mindspace? What possible good could that do? And why the scrubber?"

"I have no idea, but I'm worried. If this gets out—"

She paused. "I know. The Guild knows too—we'll turn over every rock, knock on every door. We'll find who took them. We'll get them back. Just give us a couple of days."

"I'm still pretty sure we're looking for the same guy," I told her. "Don't capture somebody and not let us know—we need our case solved too."

"I'll do my best," she promised. "I've got an order out on Bradley. With this confirmation, the higher-ups are a lot more willing to count your vision as cause."

"So it's convenient for them now?"

"There's no need to be snippy," she returned. "I'll get back to you tomorrow when I can."

"It's midnight, Cherabino," I told her tiredly. "Double shift is over."

She looked back, sadness crushing her like a vise, and stretched. She turned the computer off and turned back to me. "Is it really?"

"It is." I shielded hard, having enough of my own problems without adding her sadness to the mix. "Let's get going. Tomorrow's your day off, right?"

"Yeah." She grabbed her jacket, yawned.

"Paulsen said I could have the day too, if I thought it would help." I'd also called Swartz, just in case I couldn't make the usual Thursday-night Narcotics Anonymous meeting. Whatever was going on with Cherabino seemed to be focused on tomorrow.

"You're still following me around, then?" She didn't look happy about it.

"I am. I need to make sure the vision doesn't happen. I'll stay out of your way." If I could.

"You do that."

CHAPTER 18

Late the next morning, Cherabino cut the car off in the grocery store parking lot. "I'm not going to get you to go away, am I?" Her face said she was angry, but the waves of her emotions carried far more sadness and fear.

"Um, no." I was confused. Wasn't that what I had been saying for three days, fifty times a day? Was this a trick question?

"Fine," she said, too sharp, and got out of the car.

Inside the store, instead of heading for the vegetables—Cherabino always went straight for the rabbit food in any grocery store—we turned left. Past the checkers, busy on a Thursday late morning, and through a long aisle of cereal. Cherabino didn't even look at the cereal boxes and hardly noticed when I dropped back for one. When she failed to comment on the sugar content when I caught up to her, I knew something was very wrong.

We turned into the flowers section. She slowed, browsed through the hundreds of flowers, and carefully hand-selected three bouquets of white lilies—real lilies, the old-fashioned kind, pure white from being grown in a greenhouse, sheltered from all pollution. She spent almost twenty minutes—and far, far too much money—on the purchase. In the end, she shoved two flower bunches at me. "Make yourself useful." She kept the third, larger, bouquet in her hands.

In the car, she laid that third bouquet gently across the backseat, putting the others not too far away while she eased into the front.

She looked at the wheel for a long, long moment while the inside of an August-hot car baked my skin.

I cleared my throat. "Are you—?"

"Shut up."

"Okay."

She turned the key and started the car. Hot air blew from the vents, and we pulled out into traffic.

It didn't seem right to be so quiet. But there was something boiling up on the inside of her, some strong thoughts and stronger emotions. The sadness was so strong I could *feel* it, but whatever else was there she was fighting. I got shapes, and shadows, but no definites. And past all of it, pain, mental, emotional. Just pain. I didn't dare speak.

Twenty minutes later, the car pulled up a long, wooded hill, and Mindspace stopped. Well, not stopped, but the constant low-level presence of city minds faded and faded until we were all alone. Until there was no Mindspace at all but Cherabino and me, completely alone. It was then we rounded the corner and saw the sign: WOODED OAKS CEMETERY. And a chill ran up the back of my spine.

Her sadness intensified like a cloak falling on me as we passed through the open gate. She pulled into a tiny parking lot, turned off the car, and stared ahead.

"Shut up," she said out of nowhere, and got out of the car.

"I didn't—," I protested as the car door slammed.

She opened the rear door and carefully lifted the

third bouquet. "Hand me the others," she demanded. I handed them over. Then she said, "You're waiting in the car."

"It's August," I said, trying for matter-of-fact. "It'll be an oven in here."

She didn't meet my eyes. "Fine. Just don't follow me."

I watched her walk up a long grassy hill, toward the first row of tombstones, the strength of her sadness diminishing with distance. Only, I thought as the temperature in the car started to ease upward, her presence didn't get weak enough, not nearly weak enough. That bond she didn't know about yet was getting stronger. And I wasn't sure how to tell her, or even if I should.

At the top of the hill—still well within sight—she stopped, and knelt before a grave. I looked away, trying to give her what privacy I could. As completely dead as this space was, I'd know a mind-attack well before she'd realize it was happening. And dead was the right word—despite all tales to the contrary, cemeteries rarely had even the trace of a ghost. No one died in a cemetery; it was a place for relatives and mourners, not the shock of Mindspace memories left behind.

When her shoulders started shaking—she was crying!—I had to get all the way out of the car, torn between wanting to run toward her and wanting to run away. With neither an option, I felt pulled in too many directions, and I wanted my poison. I wanted it badly. I wanted Cherabino to stop crying, and I wanted the world to disappear in that shimmering rush and *go away*—I just *wanted*. I wanted!

I opened up the car door, sat down, and breathed, in and out, over and over. I had to call Swartz. I was starting down the slippery slope where I couldn't talk myself down. But where was I going to find a pay phone here in the middle of nowhere? Before I could figure it out, the radio buzzed with our car number.

With shaking hands, I picked up the receiver. "Yes?"

"Is this Cherabino?" the dispatcher asked, amid static.

"I can take a message."

A frustrated sound and more static. "Let her know her sister called, said she's here if she needs anything." After a pause: "We all are."

I took a breath and replied, "I will tell her."

I looked to my left, through the car window at Cherabino. Her shoulders weren't shaking anymore, but her body language still looked defeated, crumpled in on herself like an old paper doll.

More than an hour later, with the sun at its hottest point of the day, I walked up quietly, dreading seeing her with tears but not able to wait any longer. Cherabino wasn't the kind of person who cried. The grave she was kneeling by was small, with a modest tombstone and a small central vase for flowers.

I stopped about three steps behind Cherabino's back. "Your sister called the station, says she's here for you. Dispatcher too."

Cherabino didn't turn around, running her fingers over the lilies in the central vase instead. When she had arranged the last petal to the exact place she wanted it, she pulled her hands back and pressed a small push button in the base of the vase. A bubble formed around the lilies. I recognized the gadget by the hum in Mindspace, like a deep buzzing that set my teeth on edge. It was a miniature stasis field, rare, pricey, but it would keep the flowers in perfect freshness for months.

Cherabino arranged the other two bunches of flowers on either side, less gently, and sat back on her heels. The text on the tombstone popped out then: Peter Russell Alexander, only thirty years old when he died. The date of death was six years ago today. Why hadn't I known about this before? I mean, we didn't work together *all* the time, but you would have thought . . . Maybe I hadn't wanted to know. Maybe she'd shied away from thinking it. She couldn't shy away now.

"Isabella?" I said softly.

She stood up, slowly. Tear tracks ran down her cheeks, and she wouldn't meet my eyes. She did, however, start walking to the car. I followed, grateful to get away from that Mindspace hum—and her tears.

When we got back down the hill, I opened my car door first, getting inside to try to set the trend. She followed, folding herself into the car. The door shut hard. And there we were. Her face was completely blank, disturbing shapes moving like eels under the surface of her mind. We sat there several minutes, as she gripped the steering wheel and stared ahead.

A heartbeat before I would have spoken, she exhaled in a rush.

"He was assistant DA to the city, just promoted. We'd decided to keep my maiden name on purpose, to keep anyone from connecting us, back when it was my work that was too dangerous. But it wasn't me that day—it was him. His work. They gunned him down in a shopping mall, right in front of me—and I didn't have my gun. He hated my gun. He'd made me leave it at home that day. Just that day. And there they were, some punk kids he'd put up on drug charges—with automatic weapons. He threw me down—me!—and took three bullets to the chest. In one damn second, just a second and it was over. It was a shopping mall, and I didn't have my gun. The kids were gone because I wouldn't leave him. I wouldn't leave him. He bled out before the paramedics arrived—he died telling me he loved me." She looked up, her eyes empty. "We were trying to get pregnant. It took me ten months to find them. Ten months!"

She started the car abruptly and moved us out of the lot.

So that was why she was so driven, why every case was so personal. For the next twenty minutes, as we drove back to her house, what was not said filled the car until I could barely breathe.

Halfway back to her place, Branen called. Cherabino shut down her emotions like throwing a light switch, pulled over on the side of the road, and answered. Whatever her boss said—and I couldn't quite hear—it was serious. I was shielding my nuts off, trying to get away from the sadness at any cost, so I couldn't overhear that way.

When she hung up, I asked, "What's going on?"

"There's been an incident at the station."

I blinked. "Um, what kind of incident?" It had to be bad if they were calling her back on her day off. On this day—if everyone else had known what I somehow hadn't. Did they?

She looked up. "They won't tell me."

"What?"

"They want you there, unbiased, apparently—and they think you'll read it off my mind." She looked at me critically. "I hope that's not true."

I dodged the question and suggested we turn around.

Sun blazing, the station still somehow managed to look dark. And ominous. The front windows, always dingy, had somehow been taken over completely by the dirt, and the long crack in the cement on the front stoop gaped like a missing tooth. As Cherabino pulled the car into the empty front space, I half registered a few guys on the roof—they had been working on the top air conditioner all summer, and I assumed this was more of the same. They seemed quiet, but at a hundred and ten degrees in the shade I wasn't criticizing.

There was Grateful Thing Number Three this week for Swartz—not having to work on the rooftops for a living under the hot sun. One was Cherabino falling asleep in my arms, and Two was her cooking me dinner. Awesome. I had my three things for the week a whole day early. I shielded harder against Cherabino and tried to concentrate on those.

"You coming?" Cherabino's voice snapped. She was all the way out of the car, her head stuck back in, staring at me. I was frozen halfway through unbuckling my seat belt.

"Sure, yeah, I'm coming." I finished the seat belt and opened the door. By the time I'd gotten out, she was all the way to the station door. She didn't hold it open for me; I had to catch it just shy of pinching my fingers.

"For a man who won't leave, you do a crappy job of keeping up," she said. It was the tone of voice that said she was having a bad day, it was my fault, and I should take it personally.

I ignored her and pushed ahead.

The foyer was dominated by a long counter behind which should have sat Nemo, the chronically bored booking officer on Thursday day shift. Instead, leaning against the counter were three guys who normally worked witness protection, big guys with martial arts belts and marksman ribbons practically tattooed across their foreheads. They looked distracted, and a little angry, but not at me.

The one in the lead—Grant, I think—stood up from the counter. "You're the teep, right?"

"I'm the *telepathic expert*, yes," I said, with emphasis.

He ignored the reference. "Well, they want you on the roof."

Well, crap—that ruined Grateful Thing Number Three.

"The roof?" Cherabino said behind me. "What the hell is going on? No one would tell me."

Grant just stared at her.

"Um, guys," I started tentatively, not wanting to get involved in a pissing contest. Cherabino did those on her own. But I needed to know. "Where is the roof exactly?" Then I realized how stupid that sounded and added: "How do you get there from here, I mean."

We got directions; there was a small ladder right on the other side of the back door. Cherabino, curious and sad and furious by turns, pushed through first, and I was treated to a nice view of her backside climbing the ladder on the side of the sagging gray building. I did follow, more slowly, taking my time.

The wind changed, and as I stood on the top—as Cherabino left the ladder—the smell hit me, the faint smell of corpse. I swallowed hurriedly to kill the gag reflex.

Then I swallowed again—we were on the *department's* roof. Some perp had done it here, over our heads. I pictured blood seeping through the leaks in the roof, blood instead of water going *drip, drip* on the old station carpet below. I turned around carefully, pulling myself over the lip of the building while my feet found the roof.

I stood, and wiped my hands off on my jeans. The ladder had been filthy, covered with things better left unnamed. This had the happy side effect of insulating my hands from the hot metal. It was easily a hundred degrees on the roof—probably far over—and the sun beat down hard enough that the air shimmered and danced, making interesting patterns in pollution. Already I could feel the beads of sweat congealing on my forehead.

I looked over to Cherabino, who was talking to the captain. Next to him, covered in sweat, irritable and uncomfortable, Lieutenant Paulsen appeared almost human. When she saw me, she gestured angrily.

I went.

Four feet away from the lieutenant's left shoe was a body, partially obscured by the medical tech kneeling above it. When he moved, I finally could get a good look.

"Crap," I said.

"That's Henderson," Cherabino said, her voice absolutely dead.

It was Crazy Neil all right, ten years older and matching the sketch perfectly. There was no blood around the body—but the throat was crushed too deep to have been done by hands.

"Who is Henderson?" Lieutenant Paulsen folded her arms. I was still shielding heavily, but by her look, she was brittle with anger.

"Henderson is—was—our best suspect for the multiples case," I put in when Cherabino didn't. "We had an associate identify a sketch of the man—he was outside a crime scene with a lumpy garbage bag big enough to hide a body. Kara was supposed to talk to him this morning."

"Kara is the Guild attaché," Cherabino put in.

The lieutenant pinched the bridge of her nose. "Confirm that didn't happen, please. Do we have any other suspects?"

"Bradley—," I started.

Cherabino cut me off. "None with any evidence behind them," she said.

Paulsen blew out a long line of air. "Obviously you'll need to talk to Branen when he gets back from the courthouse. In the meantime, I need to know everything there is to know about this case."

She pulled Cherabino to the side. When I followed, she held up a hand. "Not you. You need to scan this roof. Now."

I thought about protesting I wasn't some tricorder she could just point and shoot—but thought better of it when I saw her face. If I was standing at the mouth of hell, the sergeant was clearly one of the hellhounds ready to drag me in. She was *not* happy. This was a high-stakes, nasty situation—a messy territorial kill, left to leave a message to the police. I was betting it was Bradley, done to warn us off just as we were getting close, but proof—well, we had still to get that.

So I stopped, braced my legs farther apart, and did something very stupid. I dropped totally into Mindspace, from a cold start, with no one's mind to ground me outside. Cherabino was too upset and too far away to add stability right now, and there was no one else on the roof I trusted enough to even try.

The ghost hit me like a physical blow, like a tidal wave of crushing power that stuck to my lungs and suffocated. My lungs were crushing, and my throat was *stuck*, it was gone, there was no—*stop*. Stop, I said. I'm fine. Breathe—or, well, no air in Mindspace but same idea. Grit your teeth, breathe, and don't let it take you over. You're not going to suffocate on a rooftop surrounded by cops, it's just not a possibility. It's not an option.

I fought the overwhelming tidal wave three times, insisting I could *breathe*, thank you very much, and three times in a row I won. I held on, and on, and I won. Again. Then the ghost retreated into itself, panicking quietly without further struggle. And I took a deep breath. Henderson's last moments had *not* been pleasant—and the Mindspace in this area was thick, and receptive, and eager to learn.

My senses stabilized, and I had a moment when the whole rooftop snapped into place. Thirteen cops, most sick at heart, each a faint and compact presence in Mindspace. I filtered them out and sorted through the rest. There was a screwdriver in the corner, cast off—what had once been a workman's favorite tool, worn to his hand over and over for years on end. Now forgotten, rusting. A long line of bird memories on the far ledge, layer upon layer of jittery hopping pigeons who'd rested for a night before moving on. The ledge was empty now, but it remembered.

And in the center of the roof, like a pool of wasted blood, lay what once had been a man I'd avoided for his practical jokes—and now was only a fading memory of what might have been. Over him, starting already to wear away with the force of the cop's thoughts around it, over the body like a chalk drawing hung a Pattern—organized shapes like a mathematical mural—shapes built like a child's game to initiate Guild trainees. But this was no game.

For behind the strangely uniform, oddly strong Pattern was a thought. A nasty, focused thought. *Too weak,* the killer sneered. *Both of you.*

Too weak for what? And why—why—did I think he was talking to me?

CHAPTER 19

I gritted my teeth and decided Cherabino was probably okay inside the department walls. Whoever this was (Bradley?) had already made his point today, and she was surrounded by cops. Even so, I made her promise not to leave the group—or the building—without telling me. She was pissed, but she promised, and Cherabino kept her promises.

I ducked into the men's room to wash my hands free of whatever was coating the ladder. A man had to have standards.

After turning off the water, I looked at myself in the mirror for a long time. It had been really, really stupid to just drop into Mindspace like that. Even for me. Really stupid. I'd known it was a crime scene; any idiot could see the guy had been killed right there.

Any idiot could have seen there would have been a ghost, and probably a nasty ghost. Guys had been killed doing much less stupid things in Mindspace, and I had used up as much luck as any guy got in a lifetime already. Swartz would be furious. If he understood. (Swartz was bright, but not a telepath. Sometimes he got it, sometimes he didn't. That didn't mean he wouldn't kick my ass for it anyway.)

I washed my hands again, even though the gunk was mostly off already. I needed time to think. I needed . . . something. The stakes were getting higher by the minute. Cherabino in danger, a body on the roof—talk about personal—and now this message, this message that kept playing in my head like a stuck record.

What did Bradley have against me? If he was that nerdy guy from the Guild, we hadn't even really worked together. I certainly hadn't talked to him. I squinted at the mirror, trying to remember. Was there something about him applying to the deconstruction department? Maybe an assistant professor position or some such. It was very vague; this was in the middle of my addiction at the Guild before I got kicked out, I thought. A long time ago, and I was on some heavy doses of my drug.

I tried to think. He'd applied to the department. I think I turned him down. Dane had said something . . . but for the life of me, I couldn't remember what. I hardly remembered this guy. Why was he leaving me messages? Assuming that one was even for me. Why was he going after Cherabino, after the police?

I'd lost a lot of credibility this week, and the stakes were higher than ever. I had to produce that rabbit; I had to get this guy off the street. And I had to do it before something happened to Cherabino, me, or anybody on the force. Without much trust from anyone.

Most of the time I was happy to be a contractor, not a cop. Cherabino was right; I'd never pass the physical—my lungs were trashed from the smoking, and I had no real interest in running five miles a day. Even under duress or for a million ROC money units or whatever the saying was. Just, no.

I didn't really want to carry a gun. You had a weapon, you used it. And I had enough crap on my soul already without adding killing people to the list.

I'd never actually killed someone—probably the only one of the Thou Shalts I hadn't trashed all to hell—and I wasn't interested in starting in on my last holdout. Thank you.

I'd never be a cop, never fit into the inner circle. Never really understand why it hurt something inside them to find a body on the roof, why most everyone in the building was literally killing angry right now. Why it was personal now—it had always been personal for me, since they'd first mentioned the Guild. Since I'd first realized the bastards were letting innocent people die.

I wasn't a cop. I *couldn't* be trusted—hell, I didn't trust myself right now—but the stakes weren't going away. So I had to be twice as useful as annoying. Get the job done.

The useful thing to do right now—the thing I needed to do—was to call Kara. I needed to know where Bradley was.

"There you are." Paulsen caught me on the way out of the bathroom, not that that was uncomfortable or anything. She grabbed my arm and I blocked, hard, to keep from reading her.

I disengaged politely. You shouldn't touch a telepath, damn it. "Look, Paulsen—"

"On the roof, you thought there might be another suspect?"

I paused. "Cherabino said—"

"I asked you the question, not Cherabino."

"My vision had Bradley trying to kill us, and my gut says this is him too. That this is personal to him somehow. But even if you think my gut is full of crap, he's the next logical suspect. He's exactly the kind of teleporter-telepath we're looking for, though by the book his telepathy numbers are a lot weaker than what I saw. Still, with any luck, Kara already—"

"Who?"

"The Guild attaché. Cherabino told you on the roof, remember?"

"Why are you on a first-name basis?"

I coughed. "We knew each other at the Guild. I contacted her Tuesday like you said."

"I haven't seen a report," she said.

"I haven't written one."

Her look could have melted lead. "You want to be treated like everybody else, you want me to listen to you, you want me to keep you, you have to do what everybody else does. Especially now. I told you no leash, and I meant it. The report needs to be on my desk same day. It's Thursday."

"We were a little busy."

"I saw Cherabino's report yesterday." She paused significantly. "Don't let it slide again. The artificial organs seem like our first real connection here. Now you're talking Guild involvement. What's going on?"

Suddenly all my suspicions started pouring out. "Kara put in an official request to talk to Henderson two days ago and hasn't gotten a response back yet. The truth is, the requests are notoriously unsecure— they're almost public knowledge. I think the killer, I think Bradley saw the request and knew we were onto him. He killed Henderson before we could talk to him, left him on the roof like a personal message. My gut says it's for me. It's my fault, for starting this. Otherwise Henderson wouldn't be dead."

Her eyes softened. "If that's what happened—and we don't know that it was—then this Henderson was much too close to the killer, or was the killer himself and made someone else angry. Even if it's true, you can't blame yourself."

"But—"

"How sure are you about this Bradley connection?" she asked. "Did they know each other at the Guild?"

"I think so, but it was a very long time ago," I told her. "My memories aren't all that clear. I was about to call Kara and find out for certain. She was supposed to put Bradley in custody last night. If that's the case, we're at a dead end. But I don't think that's what happened."

Paulsen took a deep breath. "This is our case. You can't just hand it to the Guild—Koshna Accords or no."

I shook my head. I couldn't believe I was arguing this, but . . . "We don't have enough evidence to get him through our system. The Guild considers a vision as reasonable suspicion. But if he's already in custody—"

"Here," she said, and pushed me down the corridor toward her office. "You're going to give me Kara's number, and then I'm going to talk to her boss. This is moving too quickly."

I followed reluctantly and dialed from Paulsen's office phone as told.

"Is Bradley in lockup?" I asked Kara with no introduction.

She sounded annoyed. "No, he's missing, as is Henderson."

I met Paulsen's eyes across her desk. "We have Henderson," I told Kara, "But you're not going to like it."

"Why?"

"He's dead on the police station roof. My boss wants to talk to your boss about why."

Kara made an angry sound, and then I passed the phone. I was handing her a load of political trouble, and honestly I didn't care. She'd let Bradley get away, let him kill Henderson. Let him leave me that message. She could deal with the politics.

I made to sit down in the chair across from Paulsen, but she shooed me away. Reluctance in every move, I did what I was told. This was my case and my connection to the Guild. Shutting me out was stupid and disrespectful—very, very disrespectful. She hadn't forgiven me the slipup yet, had she? Not even a little. I was pissed.

With all the emotions flying around—and the intense, deep-seated *anger* of every cop in the station, with my own anger and my realization of Cherabino's emotions still skittering across my consciousness, I desperately needed *something*. Since the interview rooms were empty and I couldn't have Satin, since Paulsen had dismissed me and Cherabino was already in the workout room, since everybody and his brother was watching me like a hawk, it was time to run.

It was time to run, to make my body work so hard my mind would finally empty completely. Hitting that point took coming to the place where I almost had to stop or I'd faint. So it was a crapshoot, painful, and not guaranteed, while I turned bright red and puffed and the cops looked at me pityingly. But today, now, I had to try. I'd pick up the case and the interviews when I could think, when my brain settled.

I ran my hand down the locker door, trying to get it settled closed securely, since it had no lock. It was prefab metal, the same locker design they'd been making for a couple centuries, the door slightly warped, worn, and metal-cold. I took my hand away, carefully, and it didn't shift. Good. At least one thing was working right today.

I passed through the doorway into the main workout area. On the right, the weight machines and free weights shared space with ancient powered treadmills and a couple of dusty stair steppers that hadn't been used in years. To the left, punching bags and manikins stood with the faces half compressed by years of heavy impacts with someone's fists.

In the center, right in front of the door, was an open space currently filled with mats, where Cherabino was beating up some poor guy, excuse me, girl—it was hard to see—and pinning her to the floor. The position had Cherabino's body weight holding the girl down, her thighs locking in the girl's head. Apparently they'd kicked her off the roof too, and she was working off her anger and overflowing sadness on the mats—probably the best place for her now.

I put off my painful time on the treadmill to watch Cherabino, to make sure she was really okay, and to check out her form. Her sensei thought she was good enough at judo to teach. That is, if she could ever get her anger issues under control.

Cherabino let the girl up and stood, waiting patiently. She critiqued her on some point I didn't really understand, bowed in respect, and looked around for another taker. Her shoulders were tense, too tense; she was still worked up.

Unfortunately, the next taker was Ethan Ricks, brand-new transfer into the department and a real hothead. Heavyset, with a beer belly that never quite went away, Ricks was one of those guys who'd played football once upon a time and had never gotten over it.

Cherabino bowed, and Ricks stepped onto the mat. He was four inches taller and outweighed her by at least eighty pounds.

"I didn't know you had training," she said politely. Even the tone of voice was civil, and that was hard with Ricks.

"In Phoenix *everybody* fought." Ricks took a ready position, sloppy even to my eye, but I wasn't going to be the one to tell him.

By this point, most of the gym had gathered around; Ricks had made an ass of himself in less than six weeks, and everybody was more than ready to see him get what was coming to him.

Cherabino gracefully assumed a fighting stance. Ricks echoed her awkwardly.

Then, suddenly, Ricks rushed her—he was fast, but a fast linebacker, not a warrior. Cherabino moved out of the way easily. She waited. He came around again and grabbed her arm.

Quick as a flash, she had flipped him face-first onto the mat.

He managed to chip her legs out from under her, and she fell. He rolled over and was on her faster than a snake.

For about five seconds I thought he had her; he had all the leverage and that huge weight advantage. She tried two times to buck him off and he held. The third, she locked a leg around him and managed to roll, ending up with her elbow on his throat and her legs immobilizing his.

He punched her in the face. Full force—the sickening *crunch* echoed through the gym as he slammed her head back. Then he tried to roll her over again.

She let him, somehow using his momentum against him. He went flying across the gym, landing outside the mat with a loud, harsh *crack*. She stood, chest heaving with anger, in the center of the mat. An angry red circle on her face marked the beginning of a nasty, nasty bruise. God willing, it was only a bruise.

When Ricks lifted his head, he shook it, sending a few droplets of blood from his lip flying. He looked pissed, but so did she.

She bowed, eyes tracking Ricks carefully.

He wiped his mouth and looked at the blood on his fingers. Then his eyes went back to her. "They were right. You are a frigid bitch."

I was at the right angle to see her face change to rage. She moved so quickly I could barely see her, four steps forward. His attempts at a block didn't faze her—she plowed her knee, full force, directly into his groin.

He went down and I winced, hunching in sympathy.

Then she kicked him, hard, right in the kidney, and spat. When she went to kick him again, the closest two cops—one a rookie, James—moved in to stop her.

It should have ended there, but Cherabino wasn't in a mood to take interference—she fought them, struggled out of their hold, and punched the rookie directly on the jaw.

The rookie went down, and the room held its breath.

Her eyes started leaking angry tears. And behind her, Sergeant Branen spoke.

"Cherabino. My office. Now."

She rushed out of the room, avoiding her boss, but in the right direction. He followed more slowly, but the look on his face and the line of his shoulders were deadly.

On the floor, the older cop was over the rookie, trying to see how badly he was hurt. And suddenly the whole room burst out in furious speculation about what had happened, about what Branen was going to do.

Some of them were defending her, loudly; some were not. But they all thought she was going to get suspended. Or worse.

I dropped my stuff where I stood and found the coffee closet, immediately. I had to know—I had to find out what was happening. And while I'd detached myself from the fight on purpose (I did *not* want to experience another fist in the gut, thanks), right now I wanted back in Cherabino's head. I *had* to know what was happening. I had to make sure she was okay. Especially today. Especially now.

I found the coffee closet—the pleasant smell of half-burned coffee enveloping me like a cloud—and tucked myself into the one tiny chair. I shut the door behind me but left the light on.

I got comfortable, stable, as quickly as possible, and then reached out to Cherabino. I found her, connected with her along that link I had with her. The one I couldn't admit to having.

And *click* I was inside her head. She was a maelstrom of emotion—out of control—wide open. Furious, upset, torn in half, scared it was true, angry if it wasn't—why couldn't they leave her some dignity? Peter was dead, her world was crushed. Why couldn't they leave her the fuck alone?

All of it overlaid by *control*, the need to be professional. . . . *Don't cry, don't cry, don't cry.* Her cheek hurt, throbbing in time to her heartbeat, and she deserved it all.

She was standing in front of the Homicide chair's desk, at attention. She deserved everything Sergeant Branen was saying, her cheek hurt, she deserved every fucking moment.

". . . . *the* most unprofessional stunt I have *ever* seen in twenty years on the force! What in *hell* were you thinking? I should feed you your—"

Cherabino met his eyes, which stopped him cold. Her mind was a firestorm of grief and anger and a hundred other things, and it was leaking out her eyes; she couldn't stop it. "Ricks was an asshole. You don't say that to another cop, not a six weeks' transfer. You just don't. He sure as *hell* shouldn't have been allowed to get away with it, not today. Not any day. I was justified."

Branen stood up, slowly, and walked toward Cherabino. He got all the way into her face. "That's what you think this is all about, Cherabino?"

"It isn't?"

"This is about you *hitting* the rookie. James. Remember? Who was trying to save you from going over the line. Save you from *yourself*. And you decked him."

It was strange—I could actually feel her cheeks heating as she blushed. She looked down. Stupid, stupid, stupid. "Of course, sir. That was uncalled for."

"It is *your* responsibility to be professional. But, no. *You* had to fly off the rocker and punch out a man two grades below you. Who was trying to save you! In defense of your so-called honor. Which half the department would have defended *ourselves* if you had let us! But now, look at you! I can't lift a finger to say anything against Ricks because *I can't support what you did.* Not to a junior grade—not like this. You gave Ricks exactly what he wanted, Cherabino, and now he's going to say it again and again, and my hands are tied. What kind of *shit* situation does that put me in?"

Cherabino's mind churned as she grappled with the fact that he was right. Was it true? "I—"

"Get out of my sight. Right now I don't even want to look at you." And he turned his back to Cherabino.

She felt like someone had stabbed her in the gut. Here it was, the man who'd stood by her in the funeral and *all that happened after,* and he was turning his back on her. Turning away because he couldn't even look at her! Like she'd betrayed *him.*

She turned around and moved to leave the office. When her hand was on the door, her boss stopped her.

"I've docked you two weeks' pay. Publicly. Taken away another week of your vacation. Signed you up for anger management. And—I swear to you, Cherabino—if you pull one more stunt like this, Isabella, just one, if you even look at somebody crossways, you're on suspension. I don't care what day it is." A warning.

"Understood," Cherabino told the door handle, and got out of the office as quickly as her legs could carry her. Was it true? It couldn't be true, could it? She walked like the demons of hell were on her back, away, away. When she passed another cop (who reacted too strongly to her face, she must be crying, he would hate her and think she was weak, she had to stop, she had to stop now), she wiped her eyes on her sleeve and slammed the door closed on her emotions.

Slamming me out in the process.

I "woke up" in the coffee closet, my own face wet with tears that didn't belong to me. I could barely catch my breath. Her devastation was overwhelming, total, heartbreaking.

I staggered up and out, wiping at my eyes. She was heading for the closet—trying to get away from prying eyes, just like I had—and I didn't have the piece of mind to fake it right now. I had to get out. Get out *now*, before she found out. Because as shitty as she felt right now, she'd feel even worse if she knew I'd been witness to her humiliation.

And I didn't want that for her.

I made it outside, on the smoking porch, without noting the steps in between. It took three cigarettes and a hundred breaths for the hot August sun to bake me back into completely *me* again. Which was too long; there was something going on between us I didn't have words for, and it worried me. It worried me a lot. But there wasn't exactly anyone I could call anymore, not without them reporting me ten ways to Tuesday, not without her knowing. And as much as I couldn't afford another strike on my record, even more I couldn't afford for her to know what I'd seen.

I craved my poison, and suddenly that was a good thing, something dependable, something just *mine*. Even if I did have to stand there saying no for another cigarette and a half. But this time it was easier, somehow, as if being in her head helped me in mine.

The sun beat on me all alone, while I heard a few cops above me still on the roof; the sun beat on me while my sweat poured down and I tried to think about what had happened.

Then I went back in the building. I found the showers, cleaned off, and got dressed in my spare almost-uniform white shirt and black pants. I couldn't leave food in my broken locker, but none of the cops would stoop to stealing clothes, so I had a couple changes stored here.

Finally calm, and me again, I asked the detectives' pool for more busywork. I wasn't in any shape to do interviews. I wasn't—and Paulsen shooed me away again, saying we'd talk in the morning about the Guild. She was disappointed in me, that much was clear. I wasn't too happy with her in return.

An hour of busywork later, Bellury found me and said it was time for the drug test. I was so wrapped up in other things, I just got it done. Didn't think about it, didn't stress about it, caught up too much in all the other stresses, all the other thoughts. I knew I would pass, this time.

I called Swartz, to let him know for sure I wouldn't be at the meeting. Cherabino would need me when she finally surfaced from work. She'd need me—or something—worse than I needed my poison. She was having a hell of a day. And I wasn't about to let her go home alone.

"How are you doing?" I asked from the cubicle entrance.

She grunted and continued keying through line after line of computer text. She didn't turn around, but sadness and shame leaked out of her in a steady stream.

"I packed enough for a week, so I don't need to get anything else after work," I said, probably too casually. "Don't leave without me, okay?"

Her fingers paused on the keys for a long moment. "Still not leaving me?" Even her voice sounded like the weight of the world was sitting on her chest.

"That's right," I said.

After another long moment, her fingers started up again. "I'll be working late tonight."

"Okay." I took a long, deep breath of relief. "That's fine."

I spent the next few hours back in the interview rooms, my head finally in the game. Perp after stupid predictable perp, all convinced they were smart enough to fool the system, none of them succeeding. When the last one was done and I had a moment to look up, it was nine thirty.

I put things away, grabbed some stuff, and went to find Cherabino. She was typing away furiously, disturbing images flashing on the screen one after another. I announced myself, but she didn't look up.

I stood behind her and put my hands on her shoulders. "Cherabino."

She looked up. "What?"

I pretended not to see the dried tear tracks on her face. "It's half past nine and time to go."

She shook her head. "No, I've got to do this."

I reached over her and hit the **save** button. Then I hit the **power** button, turning the whole complexity completely off.

She glared at me as the screen cut off. "What the hell are you doing?"

"It's not going to get done tonight, and you'll do better with some rest." I tried to be firm without giving away the fact she looked like shit.

For one long moment she looked up at me, the anger turning vulnerable, and not about anger at all.

I broke the moment by handing her her favorite jacket. "It's time to go."

CHAPTER 20

She handed me the keys. After a moment, I took them, not saying anything, and started the drive to her house. It had been a long time since anyone had trusted me behind the wheel; I drove carefully and stuck to ground-level roads, determined not to mess this up. Next to me in the passenger seat, Cherabino was more and more quiet as her mind screamed louder and louder. I was trying hard to stay in my own head, thank you very much, so I couldn't see any of her thoughts exactly, just the wake they made as they swam around her head.

She flashed angry and sad, angry, shameful, and sad over and over again, to the point where sitting in the same car with her—and having her mind so loud to me without any good reason—was turning torturous.

I cut the car off and got out as quickly as I could. Then, steeling myself, I turned back and opened her door for her. She got out and went into the house, putting one step in front of the other while she wrestled with something I couldn't see.

She did stop to pick up the newspaper from her front doorstep, which I took as a good sign. Inside, she paused as I closed the door. The sadness—now pure sadness—intensified.

"Why don't you take a shower? You might feel

better," I suggested, as much to get her out of the immediate area as anything else. I'd talk to Paulsen in the morning, call Kara, make a fuss. Tonight I needed to calm down. Cherabino was upset enough for both of us.

"I can put a couple TV dinners in to cook," I offered. That was about the limit of my domesticity, but I'd do it, and gladly, if she'd take the damn sadness away from me. I was starting to want to cry again, and damn it, men don't cry. We just don't.

She nodded, and I could *feel* the decision solidify through the pain. And she walked away, away to the back of the house, and the sadness faded until I could think again.

I heated up two dinners from the freezer—both bought at my insistence, since she apparently wasn't raised to use the microwave at all—and brought them back into the living room. I was proud of myself; I even remembered the place mat things so her fancy coffee table wouldn't get scratched. And forks. And water— ice water—because she said it was healthier. I figured we'd do a proper TV dinner night, veg out in front of stupid television and eat, and later maybe she would fall asleep in my arms again.

I was seated and all ready to go when she emerged from the bedroom. Wearing a thin black robe. Which didn't hide much. I was brought back to myself only by the desperate, determined pain coming off her in waves.

I pulled my eyes back to the coffee table by force of will alone. "Um, I don't—"

"Shut up," she said, moving forward all at once. Somehow she ended up straddling my lap, her nose to mine. Then she kissed me. She *kissed* me, aggressively, forcefully, desperately—and suddenly I was right there with her; I wound my hands through her hair and kissed her back with years of repressed desire. With every contact of skin to skin, my mind overlapped a little more with hers, and I could *feel* her desperation. And I was swept away with it, with how good she felt, the silky texture of the robe, the soft firmness of her skin under it.

I tumbled her back on the couch, changing positions to me on top, and her desire skyrocketed. I could *feel* it, and as I kissed a long trail down her neck . . . I let go of the last of my barriers, intending to make this sweeter for both of us—and stopped cold. It wasn't my face she saw in her mind. It was some blond man's. *Peter,* she thought.

"Hold on." I stopped completely and forced her face to tilt up to look at me, trying to make her see *me.*

But she used some judo move to flip me over onto the floor, just missing the coffee table—it was unexpected and hurt, bad—only she ended up on top of me. In exactly the right places, groin to groin; okay, I could work with this, the back of my head said. I could *definitely* work with this, with her hips moving exactly like that. . . .

I moved my hands up to bracket her arms, and the skin-to-skin contact put me back in her mind. I hadn't pulled away. I hadn't closed down.

Her shame from the station today clawed at her, and the shame mixed with her fear, her very real fear that she would be alone *forever*, that Peter was gone and she'd never find anyone else like him, that this sex would be the only sex she'd get for years, that she *needed* (she needed Peter, but he wasn't here; he'd never be here) and I felt so *good*, and the shame (how could he say that? how in hell could he say that? it wasn't true, it wasn't true!) and (didn't Peter love her anymore? God, she missed him, she missed him!) the feel of my body under hers, and some very explicit images. . . .

She leaned in for a very hot kiss, flavored with the images, and then her shame and the desperation rode her again, and I pulled away. I looked into her eyes, seeing the very face of my fantasy, and cursed myself for a fool. Because I couldn't do this. I couldn't let her do this, not like this, not out of shame and guilt and desperation. Not when it wasn't, wasn't anything to do with me. When she'd regret it with every ounce of her later. I—I just, too much, couldn't do that to her. *Wouldn't.* Not to her.

And I wouldn't do it to me, not again, not fuse myself even short term to somebody who didn't want me, who'd cry and scream and vomit and try to get away, get me out of her head at any cost—I wouldn't do it. It wasn't worth it.

I pushed Cherabino off, not gentle, because I couldn't be gentle, not then, and her elbow hit the coffee table with a *crack*. I could *feel* the pain racket up my own arm like an ice bath, and I saw myself reflected in her eyes.

"What in the hell?"

I scooted back from beneath her and set her aside. I put at least three feet between us, and tried to breathe.

She just stared at me, like she didn't understand, as something lacy peered out over the top of the half-undone robe. I cursed myself as a fool a hundred times, but my resolve didn't change. I shook my head, and tried to find a sitting position on the floor that approached comfort.

"No," I said. "Not like this."

I could feel the blow as my rejection hit her like a slap in the face. Her jaw set then, and she stood up. Her anger swelled as she walked past me into the bedroom until it was louder than the slamming door. And for the next hour, I listened to her mind as the rage cooled, and solidified, as her tears dried and she decided she would hate me until the sun exploded.

When she made that decision, I got up from the floor, pieced together my mental walls, and made a phone call. Then I walked out the front door.

I was halfway down the road to the bus stop before Bellury caught up with me. I cursed him for showing up so quickly, I cursed myself for calling him, and then I cursed some more, for the drug I couldn't have. But, finally, I got in the car.

"Bad night, huh?" he asked.

I didn't answer. Finally he turned on the radio, quiet sad music filling the car.

It was a long, long ride.

CHAPTER 21

Swartz was early, with a pot of coffee already set out in front of him, two cups prepared. Mine would be two degrees shy of cold by now, which would make it taste as good as it was going to. Bellury had called him late last night, despite my protests, and somehow Swartz had talked me into coffee and the early-morning meeting at the Y. I was here. *Far* too early. And so was he. But I wasn't happy about it.

I slid into the booth across from him and grabbed for the coffee. My shoulders slumped, as if the weight of the world were crushing me down. Cherabino *hated* me. She *hated* me. I had no idea where to go from here. No idea where to start.

Swartz let me sit for about thirty seconds before grilling me. "So, what are you grateful for this week?"

"Puppies. Sunshine. Rainbows." I gulped down the remainder of the cup of licorice coffee and set it down like a shot glass. I wiped my mouth with the back of my hand and settled back in the booth. "It's not been a good week."

Swartz looked at me with the same expression as an entomologist with a new variety of creepy-crawly—interested, fascinated, but also disgusted. Finally he said, "You've already used puppies. You'll have to come up with something else."

I put my head in my hands and thought. The kiss with Cherabino flashed into my head with the force of a freight train. It was hot. But I couldn't. . . . I actually wasn't grateful at all, because now she hated me, I couldn't even get my drug, and my life *sucked*. "Gummi worms," I finally spat out. I don't think I'd used gummi worms yet.

"Gummi worms?" Swartz said, condemnation flooding his voice.

I looked up. "Yes, gummi worms. They jiggle. They're sticky, and they're fun to eat. I like gummi worms. I guess I'm grateful for gummi worms." I paused. "Good enough?"

Swartz sipped from his cup. "It will have to be. You don't have a grateful bone in your body today, boy, do you?"

I leaned forward to pour more awful coffee for myself, trying to decide how offended I could really afford to be. About the time I'd decided, not really, he moved on to the question I'd been hoping he wouldn't ask.

"How are you?"

I knew if I gave him an obvious answer he'd be pissed. I leaned back in the booth, my arms going to both sides in an effort not to look any more defensive than I could help. "I'm crappy. How are you?"

"Doing better. Only one craving this week, hardly a hiccup. Even giving up smoking hasn't been that big of a thing. Now, you."

I snorted. "I'll never give up smoking. Not in a hundred thousand years."

Swartz gave me a *look*.

I gave up and crossed my arms. "Cherabino and I are fighting. There's a trail of dead bodies all over the city that may or may not belong to some guy who's going to attack us in a warehouse in a week or so—a guy we *can't find*—and Paulsen has cut me out of the conversation with the Guild. Me! When I was the only reason they'd talk to the police in the first place. I choked through talking to Kara . . . for what? Nobody's listening to me!"

"We'll get back to Paulsen. Why are you fighting with Cherabino?" Swartz took another sip of the coffee.

"She's fighting with me!"

"What did you do?"

I picked the cup up and put it down several times. He kept looking at me, calmly, until I had to tell him the truth, the whole truth, just to get that patient, knowing look out of his eyes.

"She threw herself at me last night," I admitted to the cup. "Very forcefully. And imbecile that I am, I turned her down. Flat. What an idiot, right—Cherabino, stacked up to here—" Swartz cut me off with a gesture. I took a deep breath and finally looked up. "It wasn't *me*. She didn't even *want* just me. She wanted the anger to stop, for her husband not to be dead, she wanted a hundred things, and, fucking a', not a single one of those was *me* and you can't lie to a telepath. Not like that." I glared at him. "Frankly it's a real wilter."

Swartz sat back, for all the world looking like a proud papa trying not to smile.

"It's not funny, okay?" I said, about ready to hit him or attack him with an imaginary spider or *something*, anything, to get the smirk off his face.

The owner of the coffee bar arrived just then, with another huge ugly pot of the nasty licorice. He set it down in front of us without commenting on anything he'd overheard; we'd been meeting here too long for him to blink at anything I had to say. "Enjoy," he commanded, then left, heading back to the empty bar.

I took a deep breath and looked up, meeting Swartz's

eyes directly. "Look. You're going to say something, right? So say it."

He leaned forward, putting his hand on top of mine. "I'm proud of you."

I yanked my hand back like it was on fire. *"What? What in the hell right do you have to say that to me?"*

"You had integrity," Swartz said. "You didn't let a woman you respect turn you into an object. You made *her* respect you. Even though your balls were screaming at you to do a horizontal limbo. You said no. That makes you a man."

"But—"

Swartz looked me in the eye. "I'm not saying in different circumstances you should do the same thing. I'm just saying, you did good. Here. Now, you drink your coffee. It's getting cold."

And, in the next half hour, as we talked about the deal with Paulsen and how I could fight for my respect back, I slowly felt something inside me relax a little. Swartz said I did good. And he sounded like he'd meant it.

I wondered how I could get him to keep meaning it. And I wondered how in hell I was going to keep Cherabino safe from Bradley with her hating me so badly I couldn't get near her.

That morning I sat at the bus stop for an endless time, the bus late and getting later. I used the pay phone to call the department and let them know I was going to be late.

"There's a Kara on the other line," Bellury said. "Claims she needs to talk to you."

I made a disgusted sound and the defeated commuters around me looked up, going back to their magazines when I shot them a look. I didn't think they knew I was a telepath, or they would have been a lot more hostile.

"Go ahead and connect us," I told Bellury. A couple clicks came over the line.

"Hello?" I asked.

"It's Kara."

"Oh," I said eloquently.

A long, awkward pause.

Kara spoke first, with a brash tone that grated on my nerves. "I'm calling for two reasons. One, to let you know we still haven't found Bradley. We will tear this city apart on our end, but any help you can give us is appreciated. I've gotten permission to do whatever it takes, which includes waving jurisdiction. If you need something . . ."

I tightened my grip on the metal pay phone divider. Finally. "I need the full list of teleporters/telepaths. Also the list of telepaths who might also have any talent—any talent at all—for telekinesis," I told her.

The old man sitting on the hard bus stop gave me a look and moved to the opposite end. I smiled at him broadly. Nothing here to see but us telepaths. Now he was watching me like he thought I was going to steal his wallet. Great. I turned my back.

On the phone, Kara paused. "Why?"

"Do I have to explain everything? There's no hard proof against Bradley for anything right now, up to possibly an assault on me if they allow the vision as evidence—unlikely. I need to be able to exclude the other possibilities by hand if we're going to get any traction. Him running looks suspicious—but I want him going down for murder, not evasion, when he's caught. I want to be able to prove it, Kara. Work with me here."

"Why telekinesis?"

"Somebody held me down in the vision using it. Bradley was right in front of me, but there's no guarantee it was him actually using it, I suppose. Neil's throat was crushed. Maybe it was a heavy brick, but I don't think so. If we can find another associate who'll talk, another connection, maybe we can find Bradley. Maybe we can put the son of a bitch away for good."

She sighed. "If you swear to me the list will stay in your department and not go anywhere else—even to the water cooler—I'll courier it to DeKalb police headquarters this morning." Hell of a lot of politics to get that released to an ex-Guild guy; Kara must be more of a heavyweight than I'd realized. And she was actually throwing that weight around for me.

"Thank you," I said. "It will stay quiet—Homicide and my boss only."

"You don't work for Homicide?"

"Long story. You said there was something else?"

She was quiet for a long moment. "Yes. I thought you would want to know I set the wheels in motion long before your lieutenant made the call to my boss. She's started a great deal of political pressure on the higher-ups, and I'm getting caught in the middle. I would *appreciate* it if you would actually trust me going forward—I can take care of it my own—"

"Look, Kara, not my—"

"And the *least* your lieutenant could have done is talk to me herself before she started going up the line. I could have done a lot more good for you, but you had to go and—"

"Go and *what*, Kara? What—"

She blew out a hard stream of air into the phone. "I've got to go."

"What are you—"

"You're an idiot," she summed up, and disconnected.

I stared at the phone, seriously considering pounding it against the booth in front of me until it broke into a hundred thousand pieces. And I stopped. Cold.

It had started raining, fat merciless raindrops in a steady stream. The whole air suddenly smelled of wet dirty trees, mildew, and overly humidified humanity. The old man had pulled out a sheet of battered plastic, was huddled under it, still staring at me suspiciously.

Droplets hitting me in the head despite the dubious protection of the booth, I put the public pay phone back. Carefully. Kara sounded like she was wading through some pretty deep politics over there. That could be good for me, or bad—hard to know. No one had told me anything about the politics directly; I hadn't cared. Now maybe it was time to snoop around in people's heads. I huddled deeper under the awning, trying to avoid as much of the pollution-soaked rain as possible.

Finally the bus arrived, and wet and in a foul mood, I climbed on board with the other passengers. The old man sat across the aisle and stared, his mind thinking I might do anything. No one else sat anywhere near me either. I looked away.

As the bus pulled away from the curb with a lurch, I braced myself a little better in the uncomfortable seat. The rain intensified, deep, wet, torrential rainfall hitting the top of the bus stop like a waterfall. We were on West Ponce heading toward Decatur, and the tiny, shifty lanes were too small for the bus in the best of weather. After a block or two of wobbling, the driver slowed down and grounded fully, counting on the mass of the bus on the asphalt to get us through the puddles better than the gravity-assist.

The trees directly on the right side of the bus—most

were directly next to the lanes and historic, having survived the Tech Wars and a couple hundred years—were right up against the lanes and ruined any chance at decent drainage. Within minutes, the small, Southern road—no business being in the big city, but no one had asked—was flooding. The bus slowed further, a hippo in a white-water river, making slow, unhappy progress.

Just then I realized I hadn't brought an umbrella. And the bus stop was two blocks from the station.

I arrived at the station soaked to the skin, like I'd stepped under a waterfall by accident and narrowly avoided getting swept over. I was pissed, tired, worried—and, in the first half hour of the storm, I'd probably been exposed to every kind of foul pollution, the raindrops full to bursting with cancer-causing pollution and worse. I needed a shower. Bad.

Bellury went to get me some of his clothes while I was trying to scrub off whatever nastiness had come in contact with my skin. The scientists said we were getting better, that it was more in the dirt and the concrete than in the air these days, but I didn't trust them. Rainwater shouldn't *smell* like that.

I dried off and got dressed in Bellury's clothes. He was past retirement age but hadn't gone too badly to fat, and we were the same height. If I belted the pants pretty heavily and tucked the shirt all the way in, I could make it work. It was summer, though, so his button-down shirt was short-sleeved, showing the tracks on my arms. I stood in front of the mirror in the empty locker room and looked for a long moment, feeling naked, trying to decide if I would go out like that. Finally I went to get my jacket. Better to sweat endlessly and die from the heat than advertise my weakness to the cops, to the suspects, whoever. I just didn't like strangers staring at my arms. Whatever they were actually thinking at the time, the back of my head was still convinced they were judging me.

Bellury had left the sports jacket in my locker but taken everything else. Again. He'd just tested me, but maybe they thought they'd find something in the clothes that wasn't in the urine. He was welcome to it. The Old-People Conspiracy was keeping me far away from my poison, the bastards. Probably it would stay that way, and I would pass this time, next time, even the next. Swartz said nobody could stay clean forever, but you could do it today, just today, over and over again until you crossed the finish line. Right now that seemed maybe doable, at least for the moment.

Bellury was nice enough to take the clothes to the washer-box while he was at it, though. I would have clean, fresh clothes in my locker at the department again tomorrow. Clothes that smelled good. Not bad.

I wondered how Cherabino was, what had happened last . . . I happened to glance at the clock. Oh, crap.

I grabbed the jacket, slammed the locker door shut, and hustled out. I was late for my first interview, and I needed to make sure Bellury looked out for Kara's courier.

After three rounds of interviews I had a break, and Kara's courier had arrived. I borrowed a viewing tablet from Paulsen. Barely powerful enough to view the data, it would still scream like a banshee if I took it out of the area. But I wasn't going to take it out of the area.

"Can I take a chair and a corner for an hour?" I asked Andrew. "I need to go through some data."

He looked up from a stack of numbered sheets. "Oh

yes." He looked around distractedly, cleared off his guest chair, looked at the little sliver of cubicle counter it sat against. "Um . . ."

"That's fine," I told him, holding up the tablet. "I appreciate it."

I sat on the chair in the little sliver of counter and waited for the tablet to unpack Kara's information. Cherabino was away from her desk for the moment, but I was sure she would be back soon. No need to get in her face about what had happened.

I spent a half hour going through lists, endless lists of data. My eye stopped on the tablet screen, slowly paging through a list from Kara's file—and caught. Gretel Sandsburg. The name of our fourth victim.

I frowned at the file. How could our fourth victim be a telepath? Her family didn't . . . Oh. Kara had sent me more than one list. This one was the fourth-grade testing results from the last twenty years, all the people the Guild had identified with Ability but hadn't thought worth recruiting.

My fingers danced on the tablet. This had to be a— no. Three names. Four. Five.

All of our victims had low-level Ability. All of them. And all of them were listed as available for Atlanta Research.

That was the research department where Bradley worked. The same department that would have every name on this list—and worse—hundreds of other names. All the names of every Good Samaritan willing to be a test subject to advance the Guild's knowledge. The names of these people in particular—all of whom lived in Atlanta.

I had found the connection.

Cherabino was back at her desk right now, her mood like an angry storm cloud over the vicinity. She should probably know about the connection I'd found. Any other day I'd have marched right over there and told her. Maybe brought coffee.

Not today, though. Today she hated me, and I was too much of a coward to see it in her face right now. To have my nose rubbed in it. But I had to know. Did she really hate me? She was close enough to read, link or no link, and if I was careful, she'd never know I was there. I had to know if she could forgive me.

If Mindspace was a long meadow, Cherabino and Andrew and all the other cops were little hills dotting the landscape, and Cherabino's hill was crawling with angry thoughts like ants. As I got closer, I tasted the beginnings of a migraine, and her anger and shame about the night before along with thoughts of the case. She was angry at Bradley for continuing to evade their patrols. No one could find him; no one could even pinpoint where he might have gone. No credit cards, no traces. She was furious.

Worse, Neil had owned an aircar with a defective anti-grav engine—the list had just come through this morning from the metro-area mechanics—and his name was on it. Had she dropped the ball? Could she have found him sooner if she'd worked harder?

I pulled at the thought, trying to get more information, more detail on how she'd found out about Neil, what we knew about Bradley. But as subtle as I was, Cherabino noticed—and turned her attention inward.

She should not have been able to feel me there. She didn't have either the training or the mental ability—but she did it. I felt the knowledge come across her mind like a string of Christmas lights turning on. I was reading her mind.

Her anger swelled, and she pushed me out—hard. I

could have fought, some part of me wanted to fight. With the link between us, I could stay if I wanted; she couldn't stop me.

And I felt her register the thought—that we were linked—before she pushed again and I let it push me out. Her anger like a tidal wave swept over me, and I fought bile. She knew.

Just a cubicle away, Cherabino slammed papers into a bag and threatened to kill me—or worse. Like a coward, I let her go. I let her walk right past the five-foot-high gray fabric-covered cubicle wall. And I didn't say anything. Her wrath faded as she stalked away, down the hall, with the intent of talking to Paulsen. She couldn't work with me now. She wouldn't.

Andrew's cubicle smelled like old coffee and ledgers, ozone, and metal. It smelled like cowardice, my cowardice.

Beside me, he shifted in his chair, stretched. His mind extended with the stretch, and I instinctually shielded for a moment. I was worried about Cherabino, I thought as I looked at the blank walls with faded motivational posters. I was worried about me.

She'd found out at the worst possible time, in the worst possible way. This was like the cut of a betrayal to her, and she was right, I should have told her. But to find out after last night . . . my regret and anger burned like bitter gall.

But I couldn't let it go, as much as I wanted to with every fiber of my being. My mind kept flashing back to the vision, and the picture of her lying on the floor with all her hope extinguished. Nothing I could do— or not do—could ever be worth that. Nothing. But with her scrubbing me off the case, out of her life . . .

Was there any chance in hell I was going to be able

to protect her? And if I couldn't, how in hell would I be able to look myself in the mirror? That couldn't happen. It couldn't.

Paulsen intercepted me in the elevator, getting on at the second floor as the ancient machine stopped. She pushed the faded floor one button even though I'd already lit it up. The doors closed slowly, and the mechanism started with a soft whirr.

"Hello," I told Paulsen, my mind craving Satin, craving an escape at any cost. An escape I couldn't have.

She hit the stop button on the elevator, and the thing stopped with a *clang* I could feel in my bones. My stomach took a moment to settle.

"What is going on with you and Cherabino?" she asked. "The woman just told Branen she wouldn't work with you anymore. I don't need more drama with you right now, not with Clark lobbying for you to be gone. Now Cherabino?"

"I made a mistake." I kept it simple, an admission without specifics.

"And what is that?"

"A mistake. A bad one that I will fix if I can. I found the connection between the victims. They're all volunteers for Guild research."

The overhead light flickered. I had Paulsen's attention now. "Guild research? Why didn't this come up in their files? Or did you just forget to put it in the report?"

"My report's complete," I told her. "This is new. And volunteering for Guild research is like giving blood, it doesn't happen often, and it's confidential. Nobody but the Guild will have that list—and Kara just sent it over this morning."

"So the artificial organ thing is a dead end? We're going on Guild information now?"

"It dovetails, actually. Bradley and Neil were work-ing together, the Tuner with the Research guy. It makes perfect sense. The victims would have to be people both of them had access to, people they knew they had good resonance with. Bradley would have all the Guild research records—the full list of people with Ability who weren't part of the Guild. Neil could find these people and Bradley confirm—"

"You're saying they're telepaths? The victims?" She pushed off the wall where she'd been leaning and moved forward.

"I'm saying they have some kind of Ability. Some-thing." And the way the mind had felt in that first crime scene . . . I'd never felt that before. It was like an absence, almost, like something taken away. . . . Could Bradley have converted the machine to . . . take their minds from them somehow? If so, Kara had to know about it. I'd rub her face in it myself. That thing had to be broken down; it was essentially, ethically wrong. . . .

Paulsen tapped me on the shoulder, and I blinked. Looked at her hand accusingly. You didn't touch a tele-path, not even through clothes so I couldn't feel you. It was rude. It was worse than rude.

"What's going on in that head of yours?" Paulsen asked.

"I'll patch it up with Cherabino," I told her, hoping it was true. "Trust me at least that far. We need to solve this case now, and she needs the information. This guy has to be shut down."

Finally, Paulsen nodded.

When I found Cherabino, she pulled me into the smaller, green conference room and shut the door. The only witnesses were two whiteboards, a large table, and several faded chairs.

I reminded myself I was the one looking for her. That meant I had to speak first. Apologize if necessary. Grovel. "Look, I need to talk to you about—"

"What in hell were you doing in my head?" Her eyes were narrow and dangerous.

"I wasn't quite in your head, per se. I didn't quite—"

"So you were in my head? Really? After the *shit*—"

With no warning, she reared back and punched me on the jaw. The world went gray, lightening just in time for me to get kicked in the side. Pain flashed through my body. I lay with my cheek on the sour-smelling industrial carpet.

As I listened to the door opening and closing behind me, I thought, Okay. She is not going to let me protect her. Not at all. Not even a little.

I'd have to do this another way. Solve the case and protect her another way somehow. Get Bradley off the street.

A half hour later I was at an empty desk in the secretaries' pool downstairs, working like a man driven. The noisy background, the people moving around from every direction, the anger, the sadness, the minds of criminals, didn't matter. I was too focused on my goal.

I went through all the data, cross-checked. Made phone call after phone call as I turned over every rock I could think of. I didn't call Kara, not yet—but others, other former coworkers, other friends, whatever it took to get the information I needed. Bradley had to be stopped.

I was leaned over the desk, staring at the list, at my notes on the Guild research department personnel, when the desk phone rang. I'd told the receptionist to forward calls to this number, but I hadn't expected it to actually ring. I stared at it suspiciously.

The precog decided to work for no good reason; it was Kara again, and she was going to scream at me for stupid power politics I had nothing to do with. And she was going to offer to let our department come along on their search of Bradley's apartment she'd just set up if it was all so damn important we wouldn't stop calling her boss.

I picked up the phone, hit the **answer** button. "Is it cleared with the upper echelons?" I asked Kara. "I'm not all that interested in getting pounded by Security at the Guild apartment building."

Six full seconds passed while she figured out what in the hell I was talking about.

"There's no call to yell at me," I told the desk. "It's been a crappy few days, and you don't need to add to it."

Kara made a disgusted noise. "I hate it when you do that. I really do. And no, it's not. But it's a hell of a ripple you're making, and I want it to stop. Now. It's not Koshna if you're only looking at the apartment. With us there. Probably. If it makes the phone calls stop, I'll swing the heat with the Guild somehow."

I took a breath and decided to risk it. "Kara?"

"So help me God, if you do the trick again, I am going to Jump in there just long enough to get you in trouble. *Bad* trouble," she said.

The precog obligingly provided an image: her arriving in the middle of the busy sea of desks, every cop around reacting with drawn weapons; her popping out again; me getting almost shot and then thrown into an interview room for a while. I winced. "There's no need to do that," I said. "Really." I decided not to ask her what was going on at the Guild after all. "Not that I have anything to do with it either way—low man on the totem pole and all that—but you know the department isn't going to stop the phone calls as long as Bradley's free. *I'm* not going to stop the phone calls. There's a woman's life at stake. Maybe more. He didn't hesitate in killing his partner, he's not going to stop now."

"I understand that. But I've been straight with you, and I want the same courtesy," she said, snippy tone hiding concern over something involved with her job. Her own politics. "Get them to stop calling my boss. I'll get your guys cleared for the search. Okay?"

"When and where am I showing up?" I asked her.

"Not you," she said pointedly. "We want nontelepaths. As deaf as possible, and good at their jobs— crime-scene techs, maybe? I don't want to run the chance he might overhear what we're doing from their minds."

"He can do that?"

She paused. "I don't know. Some of the Research guys are tricky. I don't want to take the chance."

"Fine," I said, trying not to be angry I wasn't wanted. Trying to see the sense of it. "But the department will want to send a couple of cops at minimum. You'll need to call the lieutenant. Do you have her number?"

"If you could handle the politics over there, I'd appreciate it," Kara said in a rude tone—apparently a lot of the pressure was coming directly at *her*. "When you figure it out, though, I'll need you to get back to me—do you have a pencil?"

I fished one out and wrote down what she told me.

"I'd also *appreciate* it if you'd stay out of Guild business in the meantime. I've gotten five calls in the last fifteen minutes from people wanting to know if you're cleared to know things—you can't just call the whole directory and try to get information out of them."

"I don't see why I can't," I said. "If you can't find Bradley, I don't see any reason why I need to sit by and let the vision happen."

"I'm not saying sit by. I'm just saying, these are Guild people, and calling them makes me look like I'm not doing my job."

"That's not my problem," I said. Not anymore. "I'm working the problem the best way I know how—and you know what? I'm making progress."

"Thanks a lot," Kara said, and hung up.

I felt like I should care, that I ought to want to make things easier for her. We'd been engaged for a good while. But that was so long ago now, and she'd been ruled by Guild politics even then. Let her deal with it. I couldn't even be angry anymore, or upset, or really anything. Kara would just have to deal with it.

I went to find Paulsen and set this up.

Cherabino avoided me the rest of the day, but as she went past me, I could feel the anger coming off her in waves. She was picturing great bodily damage to both me and Bradley by turns, and fighting the increasingly bad headache in order to go to the search.

"Why is Cherabino going on the search of Bradley's apartment?" I asked Paulsen. "She's not doing well today. And Kara's worried about what mental tricks he has up his sleeve. Kara asked us to send ignorant folks specifically, mind-deaf. We don't want her upset. And sending Cherabino into a Guild full of telepaths with a migraine is asking for trouble."

Paulsen shrugged. "It's her case. If she says she's okay to go, I'm not going to fight her—Branen's not going to fight her either. Maybe it's just you."

"It's not—"

"What kind of mistake did you make? I've never seen her this angry, much less at you."

I avoided the question.

That night, I called Cherabino four times, but it always rolled into voice mail. I didn't leave a message. I didn't know what to say.

CHAPTER 22

"Hello," Branen greeted me politely. He was slouched back in his chair, more tired than I'd seen him in weeks, his desk covered in unsorted papers. It was late afternoon, after a hard day in the interview room, and I'd hardly slept the night before.

"Hey," I returned, and sat. "You wanted to see me?"

"Yes. I'm afraid the team got back a little while ago. Searching Bradley's apartment didn't come up with anything definite."

"Really?" I said, feeling one last hope shrivel up and die. At least he hadn't jumped out at Cherabino at his apartment. At least there was that. "No leads on where Bradley might be?"

"You're welcome to the report, but my understanding is, no." He paged through the pile of papers on his desk and offered me one, which I took.

It felt odd to be talking to Branen directly. "Where's Cherabino? I haven't seen her around the office." And I was freaking out, having her out of my sight for this long.

Branen sat back and rubbed his neck. "Gone home with a migraine. She asked me to talk to you about the case and get you moving forward on leads. Is there a reason I need to talk to you? She seemed unhappy."

"Not exactly."

He looked at me for a long moment. "Since I'm not in the mediation business, I'd suggest you handle it. Cherabino was the biggest advocate for your job, you know, and there are a lot of people arguing the opposite right now. If she's not there to stick up for you, it's not a good thing."

I shifted in my chair. "Did you need something? Or is my job on the line here?"

He shook his head. "I'm just saying, handle it. Paulsen's still on your side, for the moment. Now, we got back a match on the fingerprints from that anonymous note—the one Paulsen had you interview the guy from?"

"Joey the Fish?"

"I believe that was the interview, yes. The fingerprints belong to Neil Henderson, the body on our roof. Piccanonni thinks he was trying to cry for help, perhaps lead us in the direction of capturing him and Bradley both."

I thought about that for a moment. "Why put us talking to Joey?"

"We got good descriptions from the interview and a confirmation there were two men, at least one wearing a Guild patch. It was a good lead, and a well-executed interview," Branen said sternly. "Have you had a chance to talk to the guy again?"

"I've been making phone calls all afternoon to anybody who might give me useful information," I said. "All day. I had to leave a message with Joey's hangers-on, but I called."

"How likely is that to go through?"

I shrugged. "Hard to know." With any luck the son of a bitch would call me back, but I was just a bit too close to the cops to have any faith in that happening.

A knock on the door interrupted me.

"Branen?" Paulsen stuck her head in the door without further pleasantries. "Sorry to interrupt, but I need boy genius for a bit."

"Now?"

"Now." Paulsen's tone was polite but firm. "We have Joey the Fish on the line, wanting to talk. And he sounds skittish."

Branen's mouth quirked up. "Looks like your message went through. By all means, talk to the man."

Lieutenant Paulsen pulled me into her office, the closest semiprivate area to be had, and gave me a stern look. "We're recording this," she said, and paused suggestively.

Confused, I peeked. She thought I was working the case; probably I was working the case, but I needed to stay clean, and there was always the possibility I was making a deal with the pusher. Joey the Fish had connections to drugs, but he also looked to be connected to Cherabino's multiples case. She was giving me the benefit of the doubt but wanted to be there.

I nodded seriously, showing I understood everything she hadn't said, and held out my hand. She handed me her phone. I gripped the handset carefully and brought it to my ear while Paulsen watched.

"Hello?" I said, half hoping he'd hung up already.

"Tell me who I'm speaking to," an unfamiliar voice came back. I gave him my name, and he promised to connect me to Joey.

After a few seconds, and the popping sound that always indicated the call had suddenly become encrypted, Joey's voice was on the line.

"Hello?" I repeated.

"You still looking for the Frankies?" he asked, straight to the point.

"I'm looking for the guy who killed all those people dumped in your neighborhood."

"Then you're looking for the Frankies," Joey said. "You want 'em, I'll give 'em to you."

"And what do you get out of it?"

"I don't like Frankies. Who says I need somethin' else? You want to talk or what?"

I looked at Paulsen. "Sure." If Branen was right and Neil had sent us to Joey in the first place, the man had to know something we didn't. "You want to come into the station?"

"No," he replied, too quickly. "You meet me or you got nothing. No recorders, no cops. No records. You want this, it happens my way. You come alone."

I flexed my neck. "Let me see if I get this straight. You want me to meet you somewhere—you choose where, I take it?—alone, without any backup. How do I know you won't just shoot me?" I did watch movies. Going off alone is how all the cops in the movies got killed. Had he remembered who I was?

"You're taking backup," Paulsen said very quietly. Behind her eyes was her doubt of my intentions, and the vague feeling if this was on the up-and-up, we'd be more likely to get good intel away from the station. She'd go with me—her reports could wait awhile.

On the phone, Joey spoke up after a pause: "I ain't doing no recorders. No mics, no records, no nothing. I choose the place."

"And I bring a woman cop with me," I replied, in that same certain tone of voice he'd used. "I need the backup."

Paulsen sat back down on her desk, decided not to comment on me jumping ahead.

"Okay," Joey said, after a minute. "Decatur Square,

ifteen minutes. Better be just the two of you." He hung
up.

I looked up and told Paulsen where he wanted to
meet.

"Decatur Square?" she asked, unbelieving. "As in,
center of the capitol buildings of the county government? That Decatur Square?"

"Yep."

She shook her head and got up from the desk, as if
to ask what the world was coming to.

Remind me why I'm here again," I complained,
squinting in the sunlight. It was a hundred degrees in
the shade, and the ugly metal statue in the center of the
square was reflecting the sun in my eyes.

We were in the middle of Decatur Square, with the
public transit MARTA bus station maybe five hundred
feet away in front of us, past a second ugly sculpture;
this one, supposedly centuries old, what once had been
a multicolored cow, now peeling and beaten up. The
train station was behind us, the library across the
street, with shops and restaurants to our left and right.
In front of us and to the right was a park bench; beyond,
the DeKalb courthouse, just a stone's throw away.

The square was crawling with people this time of
day: office workers out for early lunch, people travel-
ing from place to place, students from the local college.
And us, waiting, trying to spot Joey in all the chaos.

"You're here to be patient," Paulsen replied, "and do
your job."

I nodded and suppressed a sigh. The minds of the
crowd surrounding us pressed at me like a crushing
weight; me Atlas, them the heavy iron world. I tried
not to hunch from the perceived pressure, and yawned

to pop my ears, which sometimes helped but didn
now.

I would have sat down, but the benches were all ful
with lunch-goers. We'd been here ten minutes already
and I was wondering if Joey was going to show up a
all. It was too hot to stand around, just too hot, period

A boy about nine ran up from behind us, from th
train station. Short for his age, he was dark skinned
and well dressed. He was also out of breath and carry
ing a folded-up, gray piece of paper. "You the cops?"
he asked, gasping for air.

"Um . . . yes," Paulsen replied. "Why?"

"Here you go!" the boy said, and pushed the pape
at me. I grasped it without thinking, and he was run
ning away again before Paulsen could stop him.

I looked at her.

"Well, don't just stand there, open it," she said.

I opened. The gray paper was soft and too textured
as if overly recycled, and on it was a blurry pen-and
ink rough map of the immediate surroundings, with
diagram sending us several streets and about a mile t
the south to what was labeled, simply, tunnel. "Wha
is this, a spy movie?" I complained.

Paulsen grabbed it out of my hands. I let go just i
time. We were ruining the paper for prints, but I didn
see arguing with her about it. Besides, if it was reall
that many times recycled, it would be hard to get print
from it anyway. I stood there in the heat for nearly
minute while she figured it out. With all the menta
noise around me, I almost missed the moment she did

She frowned at the paper, finally folding it up, an
led the way back to the car. She'd checked out a
unmarked vehicle, a beat-up, tan, classic hydrogen
burning sedan that made me nervous every time

rode in it—didn't she remember how flammable hydrogen was? The little fusion engines were so much more stable, and they only needed one little circuit chip, less powerful than an oven timer, to keep them stable. It wasn't all that much Tech. Really, it wasn't. The power was the physics, the fields. But apparently Paulsen had trust issues. She'd gotten one with the anti-grav generator, though; an old, hydrogen-mechanical model, but one that worked. We wouldn't be confined to ground level.

Paulsen piled us into the car before answering any of my questions. She'd grown up in this area, she said, and negotiated the aircar-filled streets with alacrity. The tunnel we wanted was ancient. Having been there for centuries and rebuilt twice, it was a simple walking connector from the old college to the sidewalks leading to the square. Students still walked it every day—and every year, one or more of them was attacked there at night, no matter what measures the local police took. Usually they found the perps, but not always.

Paulsen shrugged to herself, thinking they couldn't be everywhere. Weird that Joey wanted to meet outside his territory, though.

She made a few turns, waiting on the lights, and finally pulled into the parking lot of a small bar on the corner, Twain's. The sign advertised pool—as in, billiards—and the building looked like it had been standing two weeks past forever.

Paulsen put the car in park and turned off the engine. I wasn't sure where we were exactly and was secretly glad she'd chosen to come along. I didn't want to admit it, but all of this secrecy and spy-novel crap was making me nervous.

I felt her make a decision, and saw her turn to face

me. "I'm here to observe," she told me, turning to look me in the eye. "This guy called you. That means—unless you really, really screw this up—you talk. don't." She opened her door. I could feel her nerves, but also her determination to let me find my rhythm if could. Joey had called me.

She locked the car, then led the way—"easier to walk it," she said—down the sidewalk past crumbling ancient houses with signs for day cares and law firms on their porches. Despite the shade of the old oaks, the air was still oppressively hot; I was sweating freely especially under my long sleeves, and caught myself wishing for a nice glass of ice water. Tried not to think about the confrontation we were walking into. Telling myself again that Cherabino would be fine without me; she just needed time to cool off. My bad feeling was guilt and nothing else.

The road dead-ended, and there Joey was, his ridiculous fan-denim jacket tossed on the ground, a sweating sycophant standing next to him. Behind them there was indeed an entrance to a walking tunnel In the dead end of the street, there were no trees—and the sun was at the wrong angle for the cracked-concrete wall in front of us to provide any shade. I heard the whistle of a train, far off, lonely.

Joey's man provided a folding chair, and Joey sat The man then walked around us—nothing on his mind but being sure we were alone. Paulsen still turned all the way around to watch him until he circled back to us. He pulled out a small handheld radio-frequency detector—slowly, showing us what it was—and systematically scanned us for electronics, which we didn't have. The man, satisfied, returned to Joey.

Droplets of sweat had formed on Joey's forehead but they didn't seem to bother him. If anything, he seemed cleaner than the last time I'd met him, streaks of dirt largely gone. He looked at me appraisingly.

I moved slowly toward him, confidently, even though I felt anything but—I had to show no fear, deal with these guys on the level they understood. I was a comfortable conversation's distance away before I stopped, Paulsen right behind me.

Joey's backup smelled sour, a smell strong enough to permeate the air even as heat-scorched as it was—or perhaps that was the tunnel behind him, dank and slimy and graffiti-filled.

"Joey," I greeted him politely. "You wanted to talk to me?"

"Yeah," he replied, his expression almost . . . wistful. "You look good. Not like before. Didn't recognize you the first time, you look so different, you know?"

He did recognize me. "I know." As crappy as the last few years had been, they made the years on the street look like paradise—except for the fact I couldn't have my poison, there was always that—and the regular sleep, exercise, and meals had done a heck of a lot to turn at least my body around. My mind, well . . . that was a whole different story. I was off balance now, wondering what he'd do, what he'd say where Paulsen could hear him.

Joey crossed his legs, emphasizing his seated position, his comfort with the situation. "Nice gig you landed. Yell at people, get paid regular. I bet you even pay taxes."

I shifted, wanting to get out of the sun. I guess I could have chased that one down and gotten him on tax evasion, but it seemed a little too Al Capone for Joey. The IRS could do its own work.

"Seriously. What do you want to talk about, Joey?"

He looked directly at me. "The bosses up the line

says my boss is dead by now, says I have to step up, be the new boss. Says I have to work with the Frankies now, says whole world works with the Frankies, I can't be any different. And the truth is, I don't like me no Frankies, not any of 'em. Spoiled rich white boys from the north side, think they can come in our territory tell us what to do."

I did not point out that Joey was also white. It didn't seem like a polite thing to say. But Joey was up to his ears with Them, right? The Darkness, L'Obscurité. "What the big bosses say goes, right, Joey?" Paulsen was getting antsy, her back hurting from all the standing.

"We're out of your territory now," I pointed out.

He shrugged. "Not too far. People here still know me. Still know what happened to Marge." He looked directly at me then, a tap from a boxer's glove, a light tap, just to get my attention. Yes, he knew who I was. "The big bosses, they got the suppliers. They got the power t' say whatever they want, whatever they want to happen. But I don't like Frankies."

"You've said that already. Several times."

He cracked his knuckles, slowly, significantly, showing off his meaty hands and the scars from one too many fistfights. I was glad Paulsen was here. Somebody to jump in if things got too bad. Somebody who wasn't Cherabino.

"I'm impressed already," I blustered. "Now get to the point."

He turned his neck and cracked it, then turned back to me, suddenly *more* dangerous for his lack of education. "Here's what we're gonna do. You and me going to work out a deal. I give you the Frankies' warehouse—good intel, the kind you need to wipe 'em out, worse than Marge—and you do it. You take 'em off my blocks."

"A warehouse?" That was tripping alarm bells in my head, if not Paulsen's. "Is the younger one there now?" In other words, "Do you know where he is?"

He nodded. "He's there."

"Then what?"

He looked me straight in the eye, did Joey. "You don't tell nobody where you got the intel. Not one paper, get it? And not me nor anybody else workin' for me ever sells you shit again. And you go someplace else with your vendetta."

"Vendetta?" It seemed like an awfully big word for him.

"The revenge thing you got going," he explained, patiently. "I ain't got no part in it."

Paulsen spoke up. "The department doesn't deal."

"I ain't askin' the department," Joey returned evenly. "I ain't got no beef with you. We got this game all on our own. I'm asking the Avenger over here." He stood up and regarded me. "Marge is out, man. Marge and Harry both. Ain't nobody left who brought you down in those days."

With the sun beating down on me like I was the bug under somebody's magnifying glass, I swallowed a laugh. Not only was Joey going to give us Bradley's location—with any luck, his actual location—but he was offering something the sane me couldn't possibly turn down. A guarantee—guarantee—that the supply for my poison would dry up. That I wouldn't ever get another shot at it. And as much as I hated myself even now for even thinking how to box myself in, part of me was ready to twist the knife. And I wanted this information. I wanted Bradley to go down. I leaned forward and held out my hand.

He folded my hand carefully in his, and shook. I got

an impression of a quick and wily mind; then the contact was over.

"Start talking," I said.

"Anybody asks, this conversation never happened. I never told you nothing."

"I understand."

About the middle of April, the Darkness leaders had approached Joey's boss, Maloy, about helping a third party—the Frankies—make people disappear. People from a list, addresses given. Maloy was supposed to help them end up at a warehouse in an industrial section of College Park. Then, a few days later, he was told to show up again and help some "stiffs" end up properly buried. (Joey was cynical, and here he would only talk about hypotheticals and only about Maloy.)

In the beginning, it was maybe one a month and easy pickings—good money, and nobody anyone would miss, good victims with no real family, no close friends.

But the schedule moved up—one a week, people going in and out of the warehouse. Now the Frankies wanted introductions to other crime groups, and Maloy raised his fees. He raised them three separate times, as the names from the list got more and more connected to people who would mind them missing. It was getting dangerous. Maloy finally said he wouldn't do business. But a few weeks later, the Southeast Darkness Council called.

Maloy went to the council, arguments in hand, intending to shut down the trade for good. "It's bad business," Maloy was going to argue. "It attracts too much attention. They ain't paying us nearly enough for this."

But Maloy never came back. And now the big bosses

were telling Joey he had to play; the Frankies were selling something far too valuable to stop over a little body disposal. "But they won't tell me what," Joey explained to me, dead serious. "And then these bodies show up dumped in my territory, dumped without even the courtesy of a burial at all. Unhygienic. Terrible. Left where any kid can see. But Maloy says I can't do nothing while he's gone, and the big bosses don't want me to touch 'em."

I blinked, searched for something to say. "That must have bothered you."

"Damn right it bothered me. I don't like them Frankies, not at all. I want them out." Joey leaned forward.

He told me everything he knew about the operation, the central warehouse where they'd set up shop. The strange technical supplies they'd asked for. The escalating numbers of orders of missing persons. Then the older guy who didn't show up anymore.

"When did he stop showing up?" I asked.

Joey shrugged. "I've got a guy on the warehouse says maybe a couple days? They had a big fight earlier in the week. Didn't look good."

I watched as Jason Bradley's image floated to the top of Joey's brain along with Neil's.

Wow. I pulled out of his head—and kept asking questions. Kept things out loud where Paulsen could hear them. I think we'd just hit the mother lode.

Joey cracked his knuckles, and I pushed him to say more.

Frankie Junior always seemed off. But he got worse and worse with time. *Felt* different, you know? And the people they—and the other guys—disappeared right out of their beds, the people turned up dead. Got sloppy. Left 'em where they'd be found in my territory.

Then the police were onto it. Then the papers were onto it. It's bad for business, I say it again and again. The big bosses don't listen. And Frankie Junior gets worse.

And Joey looked at me and said point-blank, "It's time to talk to you. And when you don't catch 'em, well, it's maybe time to give you a push."

I digested that for a second. "Paulsen, do you have a piece of paper?"

She found one in a pocket and handed it to me along with a pen.

"Draw me a picture of the warehouse layout, front, back doors, that sort of thing," I said to Joey, handing him the paper and pen. "I swear it won't ever be linked back to you."

Joey shrugged, took the pen and paper, sat down on the folding chair, and started drawing.

Maybe a half hour later, I'd gotten as much information out of Joey as I knew how to get. Paulsen was smug, smiling like a cat presented with a bowl of fresh cream milk, and I could feel that Joey was getting impatient.

He yawned and stretched. "We done yet?"

Lieutenant Paulsen and I looked at each other.

"Let me put that different. We're done now. It's hot out here, and I got someplace to be tonight." He stood up and retrieved his jacket from the ground. His lackey got his chair—with the flair one usually reserves for serving a foreign prince—and followed Joey as he started walking away.

Paulsen shrugged and waved me forward, to catch up with Joey.

I tried, huffing; cigarettes were crap on the lungs. And I caught up just before they entered the tunnel.

Joey stopped, turning back to me. He stood there, threateningly, mind blank for a long moment.

"You look good," he said, meeting my eyes with his, "But it don't have to stay that way. You keep the bargain, I got no problem with you. You break it, well . . ." He trailed off, looking at his fingernails. His words were mild, but the determination coming off him in Mindspace was certain, confident, and as dangerous as a cornered possum.

"Okay," I said, caught between fear, respect, and a sense of ridiculousness that just wouldn't leave. "Understood."

I let him go, halfway through the tunnel and more. I yelled after him, "You did a good thing."

He turned all the way around and snorted. "I hope the hell not." Then he hit the side of the tunnel—hard—and went off about his way, his lackey following with the chair, for all the world like he was the king of some unknown world.

I watched him go, still not sure exactly what had happened. Not sure what had made this ridiculous, dirty, influential street man come in to break our case—other than the obvious. Was that really it? He just didn't like Jason and whoever the other guy was? Or was there more to it? Did he actually object to what those guys were doing? Could Joey have *morals*, however weak?

As he walked out of the tunnel on the other side, ridiculous, faux-fur fan-denim jacket on in a-hundred-degree heat, I frowned.

CHAPTER 23

On the way back to the car, Paulsen's portable radio made a steady stream of noise. She picked it up and held it to her ear. I was lagging back—cigarettes, remember?—and so missed most of the conversation.

"Bad news," she said, turning the volume down with her thumb. Her voice was uncharacteristically grim, even for her.

"What?" I huffed.

"There's a Hailey Caplin found dead about twenty minutes ago in East Atlanta. She works for the Guild. And a second woman, a Tina Novachavich, is missing."

It took a long moment—while my brain processed—before I could even understand what she had said. "Dead?" What the hell? "They're secretaries in Research, practically mind-deaf. There's no reason for them to be—oh."

"What?"

"Bradley leads the research department. Who wants to guess he's tying up loose ends before he teleports out of here?"

Paulsen unlocked the car, looking at me over the top of it. "You think he's going to run?"

"If he hasn't already, yeah. We're onto him, and he has an easy way out. Why wouldn't he run?" I asked as

Tina's face flashed back at me. She'd been a mousy quiet woman who liked her coffee black and her pencils sharpened. I hadn't known Hailey well, but . . . "Where was she found? How long ago?"

"In a dumpster. On the east side. Not a mark on her—as near as we can tell, just like the others. Not long."

"A dumpster. She was thrown away," I said.

After a moment she replied, "Yes."

That didn't bode well for Tina's chances. "Are we going to look for the missing girl?"

"There's a case file open and an investigator assigned as of twenty minutes ago," Paulsen returned. "I'll share what info we have with him, but it doesn't look good."

With a frown, she folded into the car. She started up the hydrogen engine, me holding my breath, and when we didn't die I put on my seat belt. I wondered how angry Cherabino still was at me.

I looked at Paulsen. "Cherabino talk to you today?"

Paulsen shrugged. "She's working from home today. Said something about checking out a lead this morning. She's not mine, so I don't know details."

"She's not taking my phone calls. We need to make sure she's okay."

"We don't need to do anything of the sort." She gave me a dumb-shit look. "You do know she's pissed at you. We need to verify the information and put in the paperwork to raid that warehouse, quickly, and try to catch Bradley while he's still here. If you're right and he's planning to leave town, we can't afford to wait. This information won't be good forever, assuming it's even good in the first place."

"We need to go to her house," I put in stubbornly, "It's a half hour tops. And Joey was telling the truth; I could read it off his mind. Maybe not the whole truth, but he was. We can do the detour to Cherabino's, move on the information at the same time."

She shook her head. "Informants lie. Especially where he is, if he has half the social capital Narcs thinks he does. If he's using us to take out the competition, doesn't matter too much to him whether it solves our case or not. This is a case cracker here."

"I have a bad feeling," I said, the back of my head urging me to push it harder, despite a replay of Tina's face, of Hailey's, of the bodies in the alley, on the roof, behind the Thai restaurant. "Can you at least call her yourself when we get back?"

Paulsen sighed. "It is her case. If it's coming to a head, she deserves to know." She pulled the car out, air conditioning blasting. "I'll call when we get back to the station."

For no reason, my heart sped up and every goose bump on my body engaged. My bad feeling got very, very intense. I breathed through it. "As soon as you get back?" I asked Paulsen.

"I'll call her. Get on the radio, if you want. But we've got a first-priority case here with an emerging SWAT situation—realistically, with only hours before our information gets cold. It's her case; she has a right to be there as much as she did on searching Bradley's apartment. But I am not going to waste our information—or have to tell the captain we lost Bradley—because you and she had a fight, or because she's chasing another lead without a radio. We need to move *now*."

"What if—"

Her disapproval of my protests leaked through and I shut up. I'd been worrying about protecting Cherabino for almost a week, frantic since she'd refused to let me follow her any longer. Could this just be a more extreme version? Shutting down Bradley would protect her just as effectively as me being there—and we were doing that, right?

As we shifted into one of the sky lanes, Paulsen handed me her radio. "Could you switch this to the private channel? Setting five." While I was figuring it out, she added, "Obviously, you can't talk about anything you overhear."

"I know," I said. For crying out loud, I could keep a secret. You couldn't be a telepath without being able to keep a secret—well, not and not end up with a lynch mob after you. I decided Cherabino would probably be okay, at least for a little. I could get Bellury to drive me to her house this afternoon. Hopefully.

I worked the switch while Paulsen drove. She found Sergeant Branen and filled him in on what had happened. "Certainly SWAT. We're pulling a double tonight, easily. This is your department—did you want point? It's Cherabino's case."

"I have to be at court in an hour," Branen said, and made a frustrated sound. "Then a press conference and the senior detective interviews. She's supposed to be sweeping the neighborhood this morning, but no one's heard from her. There's no way I can get away. If you could run with all of this I would appreciate it. I'll be in and out of touch, but ducking out of the press conference will make us look even worse than we already do. Call the courthouse if there's a hiccup; somebody will find me, and I'll do what I can on my end."

"You got it," Paulsen said, and asked to talk to his assistant. She made the poor man walk up and down the senior bigwigs hall with the radio, one conversation after another, all the way back to the station. By the time we arrived, my hand hurt from repeatedly hitting the switch. And she'd gotten an impressive amount of work done in a short drive.

Two hours later, Lieutenant Paulsen frog-marched me to the hallway outside the captain's office. She knocked on the door.

"Come in."

Paulsen strode in. "We need a SWAT team, sir." She stood at parade rest in front of the captain's desk; I did my best to copy her.

Captain Harris looked up. "And why is this?"

"We have a SWAT situation." Paulsen backed up and explained our talk with Joey ("an anonymous informant") and our suspicions about it tying in with the Guild serial case. Then she caught him up on the events of the day, and the excellent map we were now convinced was of the Frankies' (Jason Bradley's) base of operations. She went into enough detail to show him we had done our homework. Then she said, "I say we take a SWAT team in tonight."

Davis uncrossed his arms and went back to the desk. He flipped through a few files. Then he looked up. "As it happens, SWAT is free tonight. And tomorrow. But don't rush it—I want this done right." He looked pleased, actually, like he'd been looking for an excuse to move full-tilt at this case. The paper this morning, which featured the police force as ineffectual fools on the serial case, probably had something to do with it.

"Yes, sir." Paulsen turned to me. "I'm putting you on alert. We may need you at the end of this, to help us sort through the suspects."

I stared at her. All of this and I didn't even get to go?

Apparently I said that out loud, because the captain responded. "You should be glad we're taking you seriously at all. You're the one who said nobody should go into warehouses alone."

"I'd be with the SWAT team!" I protested. I was a damn battle-trained telepath, for crying out loud. It wasn't like I'd be a burden.

Paulsen frowned at me. "They'll be plenty of work to do afterward."

"Okay," I said, moving on to my plans to get Bellury to drive me over to Cherabino's house. That would probably be easier if I didn't go on the SWAT mission anyway. "Has anybody called the Guild yet? They're going to want to send a couple of guys to take custody of Bradley and/or their missing supplies if they're there."

"They have missing supplies?" Paulsen asked.

"Custody?" the captain asked sternly. "We're not giving up custody of this guy to the Guild."

Paulsen made a gesture. "We probably can't hold the guy anyway. I've brokered a deal with their external relations department—they'll hold him, we'll try him in the courts publicly. Saves on jail costs on our side."

This was news to me, but I played along. "The murders are too public for them to get away with an internal sentence anyway. They'll want as much good publicity as they can wring out of it, the same as we do."

The captain sighed. "If that's the way it goes, that's the way it goes. Get this guy off the streets, Paulsen."

"Yes, sir!" she said, grabbed my sleeve-covered arm, and dragged me away.

"I can walk," I protested, two-stepping behind her.

"Can you?"

"Tell me again why I have to take you all the way out here," Bellury demanded grumpily as he drove through a particularly nasty snarl of traffic in the air lanes.

"Cherabino's not picking up her phone. She's not at work. She's not answering the radio. The case is cracking open, and she deserves to be there."

"She probably got one of those migraines. Hurts too bad to listen to the radio—it wouldn't be the first time, kid." He shifted his hands on the wheel and tapped his fingers, waiting for the red light to turn green.

"I just want to make sure," I said. I was stuck in guilt—I'd had a vision, and had still let her out of my sight—and a strong feeling something wasn't right. She was probably fine, sitting in her kitchen, crying over a migraine with her phone unplugged.

"You're being dumb. Really dumb. But at least we'll be there soon." Bellury sighed, slowing as we entered the residential area. Suddenly, old oak trees and century-old small brick houses lined both sides of the street. Small children played with a genetically engineered dog in the front yard while their mother talked animatedly on the front steps of the porch, the phone cord stretching behind her inside the house. The old-fashioned middle-class American pipe dream, and here it was, different in daylight. I hated it, all the more because I'd almost had it once.

Two more turns and we'd be at Cherabino's.

"Thanks for driving me," I told Bellury.

He brought the car to a complete stop at the sign. "Couldn't exactly let you take a cop car out by yourself." He looked at me. "'Sides, I didn't have anything better to do this afternoon anyway. Good day for an errand. You good for clothes? We need to go out again?"

I was looking out the window, trying to see Cherabino's house. Huh? Um, there was . . . "I could probably use another couple of undershirts."

"Maybe we'll pick those up on the way back, then."

For the next few minutes, Bellury started humming an out-of-tune country song as he drove. He kept humming it all the way up Cherabino's street and as he parked on the right side of the street in front of her house, a little bit down from her parked car. He kept humming as we got out and started walking up the driveway.

About halfway up the driveway, he stopped humming.

Cherabino's driver's-side car door—opposite side from the street—was open. Just standing open.

I ran around the car, quickly, Bellury following. The car door was gaping like an open wound. There were a few small spots of red on the ground and the car window—blood?—and a couple of dents in the side of the car, like there'd been a struggle.

Worst of all, her purse lay half open, abandoned, on the ground.

My legs gave out. I crab-walked back, back, until my hands hit the grass of the next yard over. I kept looking at that scene, at the evidence left behind by my failure— at what I'd done at abandoning her, and worse, talking myself out of that feeling, letting it go this long—and fought dry heaves.

Bellury went over and checked her door, still locked. He rang the doorbell, waited. Nothing. He didn't seem surprised.

Then he trotted back to the car. He opened the door while I sat there, unmoving, gave me an odd look, and then pulled out the radio. His presence in Mindspace was worried, worried and strangely calm, as if all his years of experience as a cop, a beat cop, an interviewer, and briefly a detective—as if all of them combined all at once into heavy, steadying weight.

I couldn't hear the conversation, not with my ears, but in my mind I could hear him reporting the scene: It looked like an officer had been taken, probably alive. A few blood spots. Evidence of foul play.

The dispatcher started asking questions, and Bellury gave what answers he could. He looked at me when he ran out of details. I took a deep breath, looked back at the scene, and started feeding the answers he needed back into his mind.

He finally put the radio down and closed the door. Walked back to me.

Bellury thought about mentioning the pictures that had appeared in his head—the pictures that felt like me, somehow—but decided against it. It got the job done, and there was a hell of a job to do. "You're going to have to pull yourself together, kid."

Forensics was crawling all over the scene.

Paulsen took me aside, to a corner of the front porch. "You didn't tell me you had a feeling."

I had my arms crossed, doing my best to look annoyed instead of cold, too cold. "I told everybody about the vision. Didn't seem to matter before—nobody did anything. Not for weeks. Just got obsessed with the aircar tracks and getting interview permission from the Guild."

She pursed her lips. "There's process. And you did have an incident."

"That's exactly it. You didn't look like you were going to listen."

She grabbed my face and turned my head toward her, very unexpectedly. For a long painful moment, our minds half merged. I saw how lonely she was, how badly she wanted a hug—a real hug—from somebody friendly, and her overriding sense of Responsibility. I saw her immediate, pressing need to find Cherabino; to catch Bradley; and her Duty, her greater Duty to the department and the city. After a second of adjustment, she looked me straight in the eye without letting go. I wasn't getting off that easy.

Next time you make *me listen, genius,* she thought, knowing I would overhear it. And I could feel how much she meant it. *Whatever it takes.*

And then she let my chin go, her eyes narrowing.

I was too much of a trained telepath; I couldn't just let it go. I opened my arms, small invitation to a hug.

She snorted and turned away, walking off the porch.

I put my arms down, awkwardly, feeling dumb. And responsible. We had to get Cherabino back. And she was right; I should have told her.

I should have made Cherabino stay. I should have made her listen, whatever the cost. This thing Bradley had out for me—well, it had to be personal, now. It had to be. Otherwise, why kidnap a cop? I had a bad feeling that this was a message to me, that this was my fault.

I wanted Satin. I wanted it all to go away. But it wouldn't, and now I'd have to fix it or die trying. Perhaps literally.

I found a quiet corner in the back of Bellury's car and tried to think. To calm down. But my mind kept unfocusing, like I was being pushed into a dense fuzzy cloud.

The second time I got wise and fought my way out. I sat, blinking at the light, trying to figure out what had happened. The link? It must have been the link.

"I think she's drugged," I finally told Bellury.

"Tell the lieutenant," Bellury said.

The entire department moved into action as suddenly and completely as a kicked anthill.

Every cop in the force gathered in the main room, sitting on desks, standing around them, three and four deep. The pressure of all those buzzing, angry minds was giving me double vision and the beginnings of a pressure headache. But I had to fix this.

Branen was standing near the door, knowing he'd have to leave at any second for the press conference, but still wanting to show support. The head of Electronic Crimes was next to him.

Lieutenant Paulsen was standing at the front of the room. Or should I say, Paulsen was standing *on top of* the receptionist's desk at the front, giving herself an extra three feet of height so everybody could see her.

Paulsen held up a finger on each hand and brought them together. "Focus, people. We've got an officer to find and a case to solve, in that order. And we all know that every hour here hurts our chances of getting our girl back. So, let's move."

She started handing out assignments, pointing to sections of the crowd as she came to them. "We all think this is related to the multiples case, but just in case it's not . . ." She put about fifteen people on tracking down likely suspects from Cherabino's other open cases. Then another five on various old grudges—Cherabino had been a cop for a while, and a good one; she'd made enemies. Paulsen put one mean, hulking ex-military cop on the issues around Cherabino's husband's death. Then she portioned up the rest of the room on following up Cherabino's movements over the last few days, her electronic work, and every conceivable angle of the serial case.

"If you have an assignment, go ahead and get started," she said. "The rest of you, come up a little closer."

People scattered; I stayed back, trying to take advantage of the momentary clear space in the room.

As the room tightened up around her, Paulsen accepted Brown's help down from the desk. Then she addressed the remaining dozen or so officers. "The fastest way to find Cherabino may be to find our perps. As of this morning, the multiples case is our highest priority—now, just behind getting our officer back. The captain is on the phone right now getting help from additional zones to search door to door if necessary. What we need to do," she said. "What *we* need to do is get these guys off the street and hope they lead us to Cherabino. The profiler thinks it's likely they've taken her as retaliation for the bad press lately, or for her searching the killer's apartment. Maybe she got too close."

She fielded a few questions and then portioned up a hell of a lot of investigative work between the right four detectives. Then she said, "You, you, and you," pointing to the three department lawyer-types. "Find me a way around this Guild jurisdictional crap so we can talk to his coworkers. *Invent* something." She overruled an objection. "We have an officer's *life* on the line. Find me a way."

Lieutenant Paulsen then identified four of the remaining five. "You all are ex-military, ex-tactical, that sort of thing. I'm asking you to come back and give us some additional support for today's raid. It's not mandatory, but we could be facing Guild training on the other end with only a couple Guild telepaths as support in kind." After a few questions, all four buzz-cut military types agreed.

She dismissed them, then turned to the last guy and me, waving us forward. My head was spinning from all the decisions made so quickly.

I realized suddenly that the other guy was Andrew, Cherabino's cubicle neighbor, and that he had a slight Ability. I didn't understand how I hadn't realized that before. Was I not paying enough attention?

"Andrew, I need you to do your finance thing and find the money moving here. This is our primary interviewer—I'm sure you've heard of him—for the interview transcript I already gave you. He's also ex-Guild. So if you run into any trouble, or want to get subtext, this is the guy to talk to. He also has access to the case files."

"We've met," Andrew said.

I nodded. "Most of the information is at Cherabino's cubicle. I have the codes to her computer."

Neither Andrew nor Paulsen asked me where I got them, and I didn't volunteer.

"I'll meet you there, then," Andrew returned.

He reached over, touched Paulsen on the shoulder—probably not even realizing why, just knowing on some level that she needed it—and headed in that direction.

Paulsen had actually just treated me like a real person, no accusations, no mistrust, no warnings. Suddenly I was nervous. "What exactly did you see in my head?" I asked her.

She laughed out loud. Hard. "That self-obsessed, are we?" Then she laughed some more, calming slowly. She shrugged. "Get out of your head for the next few hours. We've got an officer missing. I've already got people covering every angle I can think of. It's your job to cover the ones I can't. Pull strings at the Guild, read minds, do hocus-pocus crap in the conference room for all I care. But *find her.* Get her back in one piece. Preferably, before any of us have a chance to finish the to-do's I just handed out."

I shifted uncomfortably, feeling like I had to say something. "I—"

"Question?"

"Well, no . . ."

"Then get to work. The SWAT team leaves in less than an hour, and we need to be ready."

CHAPTER 24

I talked to Andrew, went over my notes and the files, called Kara. I even called Sanchez, the detective from the scene behind the hardware store—the warehouse was on the south end of his territory.

After that, I was out of things to do.

So, I locked myself in the coffee closet, turned off all the lights, made sure there was a sign posted outside to keep people away. I sat in the darkness and took a breath. I was going to try to find Cherabino the creepy way. I was going to do what I'd promised her in the beginning I'd never do—use our interactions, our connection, against her. The exact opposite of "keep your hands and mind to yourself."

Our link—that slow-growing link I'd been worrying about for weeks—was a blessing now. I could find her mind no matter where she was. I didn't know if she would trust me enough, now, to let me rummage around in her mind, to get the physical location. But I had to try.

I thought of Cherabino. Beautiful Cherabino, strong, angry, quiet, sad Cherabino. The woman who'd brought greenhouse-grown lilies to her husband's grave. The one who'd taught me that being beaten up wasn't the end, and how to fight back. The woman who'd dragged me kicking and screaming into a healthy life, again and again, with no regard for the consequences to herself. The woman who'd called me a failure and meant it. Cherabino in the living room with the silky robe, her hair loose and beautiful, her body . . . I moved that one aside. Cherabino.

And I found her. *Her.* Still half drugged. Her mind was fuzzy, slow, and her cheek hurt. Her ribs hurt. And the duct tape around her wrists was pulling at the tiny hairs on her arm, which ached. But the pain was good; the pain was slowly bringing her back into herself.

The whole world smelled sickeningly sweet; if she hadn't been so fuzzy, she would have thrown up. She'd been trying to put a name to the smell, for an interminable time, trying to put a name to it. She thought . . . chloroform.

She'd been drugged with chloroform, and she couldn't quite open her eyes.

Where are you? I asked.

Where am I? she echoed, fuzzily, fuzzily.

The hard surface under her cheek had little bits of something on it—gravel? I suggested—maybe gravel— one of which was pushing right into the bruise on her cheek. Her hip had something else digging into it, and the sprawl of her legs was starting to make her back ache. Getting old, she thought fuzzily.

Her mouth was a little open, and when she breathed in, she breathed in dust. It tasted of chloroform and fine chalky dirt, the gray stuff. It tasted metallic, too, like there was something else in the dirt. She couldn't tell what past the taste of the chloroform.

Oh, hello. She realized there was someone else here—she knew it was me before she even registered telepath. *Hi. Can't get up right now. Have to carry me.*

I'm not really there, I told her.

Don't really hate you.

I paused on that one. I tried to figure out whether that was her or the drugs talking, and decided it didn't matter. Not right now. *Where are you?* If she knew where she was, this would be so much easier.

Not Georgia dirt, not red. Tastes bad. Don't know.

How did they take you?

Suddenly, a flash of a furious struggle. Hatred. Embarrassed. She hadn't seen them; so angry. Dropped her purse on the driveway—they ran in. Furious struggle, judo, elbows, teeth, anything—them slamming her against the car. Hurt. Fight, fight!—but they had the drug. She had to breathe, and the fuzzy air rushed over and over and she was gone.

Embarrassed. Her cheek hurt.

I found you with the link, I said, feeling obligated to say it. *I'm going to need you to cooperate—let me find your location from your mind.*

The link? Anger. Too close. Out of my head!

I can't, I'm sorry. We need to find you—you need to let me find you. I'm not going to hurt you, not like this. Is it Bradley who took you? Did he take you to the Guild? To the warehouse? Somewhere else?

Just woke up. You can't . . . You can't . . .

Above the fuzzy chloroform thoughts, beyond the pain of the rock digging into her hip, she heard a sound. A voice, two voices. I paused to listen, hoping they'd give me the information I needed.

"You kidnapped a cop? How could you—"

"She knows too much. Bitch was sniffing around the warehouse this morning. Same bitch at the apartment—they're taunting me. *He's* taunting me. She was thinking about him the whole time, pretending to be angry with him. I couldn't just let her snoop around,

could I? And Golden Boy needs to be taught a lesson."
A man's voice, annoyed, sharp. Vaguely familiar.

A shuffle as the woman took a step forward. "A lesson? What, you kill her, just to get back at him? This is stupid. She's a cop. They're not going to stop until they find her."

"So what? We just need a couple of days, then we're out of town. Doesn't matter what they know. The Darkness has teeth. We'll be fine."

"This is stupid, Jason. We need to get rid of her—alive—and get the hell out of town. On our own."

So it was Bradley. Good, where were they?

"And turn down the money? I'm not walking away. Not going to let you walk away. Remember what happened to Neil, Tina. Remember. Two days and we'll be scot-free."

The woman's voice lowered in volume and took on a soothing tone. "I'm not fighting. I'm not walking away; I'm in this just as much as you are. I just want to know what we're going to do if they find us. Just a plan. That's all I'm asking for."

His voice was angry. "I'm tired of talking to you. They won't find us. Our guy at the Guild won't let them. Two days, we load up the trucks. That's what we're going to do. And you can either go along with it, or . . ."

"I understand," the woman said in a very small tone. "Can we at least move the cop somewhere else?"

Bradley made a frustrated noise, and footsteps sounded, closer and closer. A boot crunched gravel right by Cherabino's ear. I shivered, feeling her fear increase through the link.

Cherabino was lifted by two blocks of fuzzy force. She was confused—it didn't feel like hands, like feet, like arms. She was panicking. *Telekinesis*, I told her, recognizing the feeling from too many student pranks. *Calm down. The more you struggle, the worse it gets. Calm down. Let me in. We have to find where you are!*

Hauled up against a body—thin, a man—Cherabino gasped with rage as he grabbed her breast. She struck out; still weak from the drug, still blind, but improving. Bastard!

Let me in, I repeated. Should I force it?

"Stop that," the man said, and struck her—pain!—across the cheek. The same cheek from before. Tears rolled. The voice was Bradley's.

I decided to pull at the information. . . .

Meanwhile the man got a better grip on her, and suddenly . . .

The whole world turned inside out like an Escher staircase. Immense, unthinkable pressure. Cherabino gone. My mind ripping, pulled a hundred directions at once, pressure, pulling, Möbius strip turning inside out and crushed—until . . .

I dropped forward out of the chair and vomited on the clean linoleum floor.

I breathed, on my hands and knees, tasting sour bile, back in the "real world," while Mindspace wobbled and settled around me. Then, all at once, the headache hit me like a gale-force hurricane.

My hands gave out, and I hit headfirst on the linoleum, right in the middle of my own mess.

I cried, fat girly tears. Begged God to kill me. I slipped, over and over, on my own vomit, before my hand reached the light switch, eyes streaming.

The light hit my optic nerve like a hundred knives into my brain. Guilt rode me with spurs as my whole body reacted to the severed link. I'd failed. I didn't know her location, and she was in terrible danger.

I limped, slowly, to the showers, ignoring the looks

from the few cops I passed. My eyes were still streaming. The light still felt like a drill in my skull. And all I could think about—other than my poison—was aspirin, crackers, and a cold shower. So cold it would shock my system out of reaction-pain and let me think. I had to save her.

Ten minutes later, as I shivered my ass off from a cold locker-room shower, the headache was manageable.

I found a spare desk in the main room. The department had ordered pizza, which only happened when *everyone* worked a first-priority. I got a slice and forced myself to choke down some of it, though my stomach was roiling. I'd need fuel for later, I told myself, forcing down another bite. No throwing it up.

I think that had been a Jump. I think someone had teleported Cherabino across some significant physical distance through Mindspace. Kara had teleported out once while still holding on to my mind. It had only taken once. I'd thrown up for two days. At least this time wasn't quite so bad, I told myself, and forced down one more bite.

Bellury came and found me, a portable radio in his hand.

"Hello?" I asked.

A burst of static answered me. "Warehouse is clear," Paulsen's voice approximated. "Grab a ride with Forensics. We need you here."

I fought down bile. I had lost a *huge* chunk of time if the warehouse raid had already gone down. I gave Bellury the radio, and looked back down at the half-eaten pizza slice. Probably enough. It would have to be. I needed to be there—to save Cherabino—now.

CHAPTER 25

The ride down in the crime-scene van was not pleasant, all the smells making me want to puke again, but we endured. The pizza was staying down, my head was starting to clear, and everybody in the van was holding on to calm, thinking, professional calm.

I was starting to center again, work through the pain.

We grounded next to the SWAT van, police cars staggering the rest of the lot. The warehouse was a beige-colored industrial box dotted with square openings on the side and top, docks for ground cars and air trucks to make deliveries. One of them was open. The others looked dirty, soot covered, as if they hadn't been used in months.

I piled out of the van along with the crime techs, their minds anticipating what they'd find in long skittery strands of thought heavy on procedure. In front of me, despite the blinding headache, I could feel two strong presences in the warehouse. Like I'd told Cherabino so long ago, strong telepaths made a hell of a big wave in the world. There was no hiding, not with the way I felt now.

Friend or foe? one of the telepaths sent to me; it registered in my mind like lemon juice on a paper cut. The guy was a forty-something man at the peak of his training and career. He was Guild from the top of his head to the tip of his toes. I wanted to hate him on sight but couldn't quite muster up the energy.

Friend, or close enough, I told him, pushing through the pain. *Is Bradley unconscious?*

No, gone when we got here. We've asked for Jumper backup, but it could take a couple of hours. What happened to you?

Severed Link, I spat out. *I'll be there in a minute.*

I made my way up the stained concrete steps and through the loading dock into the cavernous warehouse, an endless space of dirt-splotched concrete under high glaring lights. A hundred feet in front of me, an island of large shapes and figures moving around like ants.

As I got closer to the group, I made out Lieutenant Paulsen by her posture of authority and the dark shade of her skin. She was facing off against what looked like the two "big fish" telepaths, both thin as whipcord, one dark and Indian, one blond and ugly, both overly confident.

"I don't care what you have to do, you're going after them," Paulsen insisted. "The perps were here just a minute ago—see the cigarette still burning on the table? Not even all the way into the ashtray yet. They were here. I want to know where they went." The table she pointed to was in a grouping with two sofas. She was right; a Marlboro cigarette still burned in the tray, letting off a steady stream of smoke and a smell I'd know anywhere. Swartz smoked Marlboros, or had.

Michael, the junior cop, ran up. He reached Paulsen, panting. "They . . . didn't go out the back . . . ma'am. The dust is clean on the back step."

She set her mouth. "Not out the back, then, and we would have seen them out the front. Michael, you and the others start banging on floors and walls—if there's a trapdoor, I want to know about it. Otherwise . . ." She gestured to the two hostile Guild members. "Right now you're going to tell me how they left."

The telepath on the right frowned. "There's nothing we can—"

"Probably teleported, Lieutenant," I said as I walked up.

She glanced at me, and the blond telepath frowned—hostile.

I ignored him, and the banging sound that came from Michael and the other cops following Paulsen's orders. "Bradley's a teleporter, remember? He's been pulling enough other people along with him, I wouldn't be surprised if he 'ported out of here himself."

The telepath on the left, the dark one, shook his head at me. Apparently he didn't think I should be telling the normals anything. "We don't know that's how they escaped," he said, to Paulsen. And, to me, mind to mind, *Without a Jumper, we can't follow him. There's no point in making promises.*

"She's my lieutenant," I said pointedly, out loud. "If she asks me, she gets the truth." *Either deal with it or shun me,* I told him privately, accepting the pain the sending caused me. I was running out of telepathic juice quickly, but this guy was being an asshole. Probably learned it in a Guild class, "How to Be an Asshole to Outsiders."

"If you'll excuse us?" Paulsen asked the guys. When they didn't move, she said, "I'd like you to stand on the other side of the room. Now."

They reluctantly moved—but closer to the furniture, to the machines I could see on the other side of the grouping. The machines were the only thing in the warehouse I could see that didn't look brand-new. I was hoping these were the Guild's, though I couldn't see Bradley abandoning something so valuable without a fight.

Those what you looking for? I sent them, trying not to give away the effort. *If we need to be looking for something else, I need to know about it.*

There was a long pause, and the blond telepath sent a wave of distaste.

Look, I don't want these things out there any more than you do.

Another pause, and his fellow finally spoke. *These are it. Everything that's missing.*

I closed my eyes in relief. Then I noticed the low-level projections they were sending out. *You're messing with their minds, keeping them from seeing the machines,* I observed.

So?

So, don't. Put a sheet over it. Stand there. Do what you have to do. But leave these people alone. I let him see the ruckus I'd make with his bosses, and mine, if he didn't. My head was pounding, and if he got a taste of it, tough for him.

He turned away, the other guy with him, with tense body language. But, slowly, subtly, the projection backed off, until it was a shadow of its former strength. I'd made my point. They stood facing each other, talking to each other mind to mind, probably about me. I didn't care; I couldn't hear them, and the body language of a conversation without words didn't bother me. Still, they were pretty blatant—some of the techs sidled away. Normal people didn't really like telepaths, especially when they didn't bother to blend; I'd learned that the hard way.

"The truth, huh?" Paulsen brought my attention

back to her. "There's something going on with those guys, and I'm expecting you to keep me apprised. Now. Can you do the fish-tank thing?"

"The what?"

"The fish tank. With the honey. Where you can see where someone teleported—what do you call it?"

Ah, she was referring to the metaphor from earlier. "The pucker. Yeah, I can do that. I think. I'm not exactly . . . at full capacity. The other—"

"*Be* at full capacity. If there's even a chance in hell Bradley will lead us to Cherabino, we're going to hunt him down." Her determination had a hard edge, an edge I didn't really want to test. "You need to do your thing now."

Of course she chose now to trust me. Could I do this? Physically, could I? "I need a clear warehouse at minimum," I said, my tone very flat. "No techs—and sure as hell not those two."

"I can do clear." She put two fingers to her lips and whistled—piercingly.

I winced. And every person in the warehouse—maybe twenty officers and techs—turned around.

"Everybody out!" Paulsen yelled. "The teep needs space to work!"

"Telepathic expert," I corrected.

"You can call yourself the Grand Vizier of Tokyo, for all I care, *after* you find my officer."

Completely ignoring protocol, Paulsen traipsed over, grabbed the sleeves of both of the self-important Guild guys, and frog-marched them to the door a hundred feet away. They pulled away and leaned on the wall next to the door, staring at her. Paulsen settled in, arms crossed, and waited.

Now I had to deliver.

Beyond the ashtray and table were other groupings of furniture, some of which looked like a scene from a hospital, some like rooms in a house. All far too new, as if they'd been bought and transported here recently.

I walked around them, slowly. I was working up the courage to go back down, deep into Mindspace, deeper than I'd gone in a while, to face up to the real possibly I might not be able to do it. I had to conquer the fear in my head before I tried it in Mindspace, or I might ruin any chance I had to succeed. I couldn't shake the idea that I could have done this, easily, in the old days. But now . . . I had to believe I could do this. I had to. Cherabino couldn't afford for me to fail.

My steps on the concrete floor echoed against the steel-barred roof. The air was hot and stale, as if central air conditioning was an afterthought, and a bad one at that.

I passed rows and rows of medical supplies, like props for a bad soap opera. A low gurney marked with someone's death. And finally, a grouping that smelled of death and pain.

A tall machine dominated, its empty flat green screen like a terrible eye. Racks of parts were arranged in a long circle on either side, hundreds of electronic things that gave me the willies. And in the center, a chair, like a dentist's chair with straps, sat in front of the machine, lead wires trailing out of it like a scene from a bad horror movie. Two lines of blood stained the fabric of the head of the chair where someone's ears would have been. I shuddered, and hurried to the next grouping, and the next.

Finally, in the far corner—next to a pile of old boards—was a particularly dirty patch of floor that felt familiar. I knelt down, and bent even farther down to smell the ground directly. Chalky gray dusty dirt, with the incredibly faint tinge of chloroform.

I eased into Mindspace. Sure enough, the space was covered in her presence, like fine perfume. Cherabino had been here—and *I* had been here. Not very long ago.

And behind me, less than two feet from the back of my head, was a hole, a little hole, rapidly turning into a Mindspace pucker. The Cherabino-feeling was slowly draining into that hole.

"You want to *what*?" Paulsen looked as confused as if she'd just found a squirrel with an old-fashioned nut-cracker.

"Getting Cherabino back is the priority, right? Not the politics?"

"Okay, sorry, back up. Not the politics," Paulsen said. "That's what the captain's for. And if you can get Cherabino back in one piece, neither one of us cares who we have to screw. But"—she opened her mouth and held up a hand—"you want to *what*?"

"Look, we don't have a lot of time. They Jumped Cherabino out with at least one really strong teleporter—probably Bradley. Maybe more. And the Guild's not sending anybody. Kara can follow some-one else's Jump—usually—and she let Bradley get away. I have to call her *now*, if this has any chance. But she is Guild, Lieutenant, and officially they're not sending anybody for a couple hours. The politics could—"

"Screw the politics! Call your ex," Paulsen inter-rupted. "*I'll* ask her if that's what we need. Hell, we'll take up a collection."

I walked back out, past the two telepaths, while Paulsen kept the techs away from the area.

I sat on the scratched loading dock, feet hanging off the cold concrete side, and called the Guild main phone line on the warehouse's beat-up handset.

The phone rang for forever before the operator picked up. I asked him to connect me to Kara's private number—something they never, never did. I explained why I needed it.

"Hello?" Kara's voice answered. She sounded tired.

I caught her up. "We have a matter of minutes before the pucker runs out. There's nobody else who can be here fast enough. The Battle Ops guys say nobody's coming on their end."

"What does that have to do with me?" Kara asked.

I took a breath. "Look, I need you to help me here. Cherabino's life is on the line. I can't . . . She can't die, Kara. I have to save her. I have to come through this time. I have to."

After a pause, Kara blew out a long line of air. "Give me two minutes to call Logan, and then let me do a 'grab'—be *open* this time, okay?"

Who was Logan? I fought not to respond with a biting comment; that time had been her fault. But she didn't have to come at all. I could deal with her, with whatever she said, if she'd come. Finally I settled for saying, "I'll be here," and hung up. One of the cops carried the phone back inside the dock.

I took a deep breath, queasy. That link with Cherabino? Well, it was nothing to what I'd once had with Kara; nothing at all. I thought I would marry Kara—I thought we would literally be bound together *forever*. As much as had happened since then, some of that was permanent—nothing ever quite went away in Mindspace. Repressed, blocked off as it was, that link was the only reason this would work—she could find me anywhere in the world and Jump there. But the process

was much less dangerous for everyone if I was open—
if I helped.

I carefully ignored the telepaths just a few yards
behind me and spent a few moments remembering.
Visualizing all of the happy/painful memories of
when we were together, when we were truly together
at the height of our happiness; the memories twisted
like a serrated knife. I followed the feeling of *Kara* to
stand directly in front of the mental door I'd walled off
years ago. I pulled down about a third of the bricks—
painfully, breaking metaphorical fingernails—and
then suddenly, recklessly, dropped every shield I had.

I was open.

I was open, damn it! I was standing open and vulnerable to the world—now would be a good time,
Kara.

She rushed through the door, over the bricks, and
grabbed my mind, my position. *Not* gently. My vision
doubled as I staggered under the pain.

Then she appeared with the sound of *crashing* air—
pop!—right next to me on the open loading dock.
"Sorry I'm late," she said. Her tone—if not her mind
itself—made it more than clear she wasn't. Her husband wasn't exactly thrilled her ex-boyfriend was calling her to go on random adventures. *If you get me in
trouble, I swear to you—!—*

She was married? It hit me like a blow.

You never asked, she replied, bitingly. *Woman's life at
stake here, remember?*

Fine.

She stalked past me into the painfully bright warehouse, taking the position of the pucker directly from
my mind.

I took the time to rebuild my defenses from the

ground up—every last layer—and put most of those
bricks back in place. I wanted *some* layers between us,
link or no link. We weren't the people we were all
those years ago, and I did *not* want her in my head one
iota more than necessary.

When I caught up, Kara was arguing with the dark-
haired telepath.

"Look, Rashim—I can only carry one. If I'm going
in, I need professional backup."

A pause while Rashim said something mind to
mind. Paulsen stood to the side, uncomfortable and
rapidly approaching anger.

Kara shook her head and made a point of speaking
out loud where Paulsen could hear her. "Bradley is a
public menace. He almost certainly has an entire team
waiting for us. Surely you can spare *one* of you away
from the machines. I can have another telepath here in
a half hour. Ten guys, if you like."

"Machines?" Paulsen asked. She wasn't happy and
showed it. "Look, my officers—"

Rashim cut her off. "The *equipment* is our priority
right now. Recovering the Guild's property is our primary responsibility. Bradley won't get far."

Paulsen bristled. "How do you—"

"He's a Jumper!" I said. Come on. "A strong one. For
all we know he could Jump to the space station and
leave even the Guild's jurisdiction. We need to follow
him. Now." And as much as I was pained to admit it, in
my current state one of them was worth two of me.
But. "Are you going? We need to move now. Not in five
minutes. Now."

I looked at the blond guy eye to eye and sent painfully: *That's my partner out there, we're not leaving her.*

Like a cut from a dull knife, his thought returned: *Do what you have to do. We have to get these machines out of here.*

"Fine," Paulsen said. She waved Michael over and handed me a small wrapped bundle from his pack. "You two get going. Cherabino is your priority, understand? My officer's life and then the perp. Bring me back both."

"Yes, ma'am."

When I caught up to Kara, she was kneeling in the dust, looking at a spot of empty air very intently, for all the world like a house cat with a dust bunny. The dirty gray spot she was staring at held the pucker, just a few feet over the dirty ground.

Kara knocked politely on my shields.

I opened up just enough. *What?*

Need to borrow your link.

I glared at her but allowed her to take what she needed. I thought of Cherabino, the way she smelled. . . .

And there we were, the tail end of a connection through the disappearing spot in Mindspace—like a yellow rope to nowhere.

Kara warned me mentally, then grabbed me in a bear hug. She smelled like flowers.

The world blinked out, *twisted*, collapsed; between one blink and the next, we arrived.

CHAPTER 26

Kara let me go.

We were in a midsized college lecture hall, musty and old. Endless rows of seats rose up a hill to my right, while an ancient chalkboard took up the whole left wall. I had an overwhelming impression of abandoned space—and then I felt Cherabino.

I felt her take a punch—pain, broken rib, pain! And another.

I turned. She was ten feet away on the other side of the lectern. One brawny black guy held her while two more bruisers with shaved heads peppered her with blows.

"Stop that!" I yelled.

I ran toward them, after Kara, who was already moving fast in front of the chalkboard.

Cherabino kneed one of her attackers in the balls, but he twisted away and hit her across the face. He hit her again, so hard *I* saw stars.

Kara weaved around the old wooden lectern and reached the first of the bruisers. She ducked under his guard and grabbed him around the waist, hard. Blink, and the air *whooshed* as it filled in the hole. They were gone.

The second bruiser glared while the third struggled

with a now-wildcat Cherabino. He pushed her against the chalkboard, harshly.

Then the other one rushed me, the scars on his face distorting.

I reached out and found a painful, impossible hold on his mind. I saw what he wanted to do to Cherabino—what he would have done, was about to do. Rape and worse. Much worse. In the moment, I had all the time in the world.

I could burn out a few spots on his brain, just a few little spots. Make it impossible for him to ever think about rape—or sex—again. Cripple his brain. It would be unethical as hell, illegal, dangerous. But I could do it. I should do it.

The world swam with wavy pain lines as Kara *grabbed*. She popped back into the room with a crack of displaced air.

I swallowed bile, the hold on the guy broken in the middle of pain. He rushed me—and I grabbed onto his mind again, freezing him in place.

No! Kara sent. *No.*

In front of me, Cherabino hit the other guy again, struggling.

Whatever I was going to do, I had to do now. Maybe Kara was right.

I adjusted my mental grip and wrenched—sending the guy to sleep. He'd wake up with the mother of all hangovers, since I wasn't gentle, but no damage.

I stood swaying, green around the gills, in severe pain myself. But I stood up under it and turned my attention to the last guy. Maybe I could bluff this one.

He took one look at me, at his now-unconscious friend, and threw Cherabino at me, running away.

I caught her, barely kept us both from hitting the floor.

The last tough made it to the Exit door. He was projecting loudly. He was going to keep running until he ended up back at his dad's junkyard fifty miles away. He'd ended up in the wrong crowd just like his dad had said, and he was going home. These freaks could take care of their own.

Kara and I looked at each other and let him go.

I stood over the pervert and regretted the decision intensely. He'd get away scot-free.

He'll rape someone else, I told Kara.

She pulled away.

Cherabino moaned then, and I set her down on the old gray carpet. Half of her face was swollen with one bruise on top of another. She looked pitiful, and felt worse. I reached out to touch her cheek, carefully.

"Son of a bitch!" She jerked away. "Hurts."

I smiled in relief. It was still *her.*

"Where are we, do you think?" Kara asked. She let me see she didn't regret the decision. The ethics—our ethics—were more important than the decisions one man might make in the future. His decisions were his.

Oblivious to the side conversation, Cherabino pushed up to a sitting position—carefully. "That prick Jason Bradley popped everybody here. He kept screaming about getting the machines. That nurse kept telling him they couldn't."

"We got the machines already," I said, and Kara gave me a quelling look.

"That's—" Cherabino coughed hard, and I could *feel* the broken rib object. Kara and I both winced. But Cherabino waited a few seconds, and decided she really did want to stand up again. She tried, with painful results, and I couldn't take it. I pulled her the rest of the way up, her leaning on the chalkboard, panting shallowly.

"Bradley teleported everybody?" Kara asked. "By himself?"

Cherabino coughed. "Yeah, everybody. In two trips—it was unreal."

Kara frowned. She wasn't sure that was possible, not with eight people or more. Or if it was—Bradley wasn't rated high enough to do it. Not nearly; he was at her level.

I waved my hand to get her attention. "Where did you take that first bruiser?" I asked Kara.

"Maximum-security prison."

I stared at her.

She shrugged. "No, really. It seemed appropriate."

Cherabino laughed, hard. And stopped abruptly, both hands on the chalkboard as the broken ribs put fire through her side. "Don't do that right now," she told Kara.

"Do what?"

"Make me laugh."

Cherabino was upright, but I couldn't quite bring myself to take my hands from her shoulders. Half her face was swollen and her lip was split—her wrist wrenched badly, and her foot dangerously bruised so that it hurt even to stand—but she wasn't complaining. Instead, she looked over at Kara, and I could *feel* her intention.

"Bradley said they're only going to stay here a few hours. If we're going to shut them down, we need to go ahead and do it. Do you think you could find your way back here with the teep stuff?"

Kara frowned. "Once, if at all. He's not going to be able to give me more than one more good grab. He's exhausted."

I opened my mouth to protest.

I know, Kara interrupted. And added I probably

wanted to shore up my shields. *It's cute and all, with your mooning over the lady cop, but it's just luck Bradley hasn't spotted us yet. Smarter not to be a target.*

Cute? What the . . .

"If you can only make it once, go get a tracker and bring it back here," Cherabino said. "That way we get the cavalry on its way." She turned to me, a little too slowly. Her foot was holding her weight only with difficulty. "We need to find Bradley."

"We don't need a tracker." I reached into my pocket and pulled out a thick black disk, the little light on top blinking lazily. "We have one already. Paulsen made me take it."

She closed her eyes, in relief. "Oh, good. Kara, you go tell them there's a landing field to the northwest of the complex. They're planning to fly an aircar out of here and into Canada. They've got a deal going with the Darkness, some kind of tech sell, and the deal is going down in Toronto. The department needs to know that in case we don't make it. Make sure the local cops know."

Kara paused. "Do you want me to take you—"

"*No.*" Cherabino took a deep breath. "No, you need to be able to ferry other people around if you can. Save your strength."

"But—"

"*Go*, Kara. Now. We need backup."

Kara stared for a long moment, then *whooshed* out.

Cherabino straightened as much as she could. "Now. Are you going to tell me about what this Link is? Or am I going to have to hurt you?"

Behind her, the rows of lecture hall seats looked on.

CHAPTER 27

My head throbbed, her broken rib hurt with every exhalation, and I didn't know what to say. Instead, on Kara's advice, I gritted my teeth and strengthened my shields, hoping we wouldn't attract any attention for a little while at least.

I also turned away so I couldn't see the empty student desks staring at me.

"Well? The link?" Cherabino prompted. "I'd suggest you start talking, because we don't have much time here."

"We have enough," I said. "The men thought they would have a little while undisturbed."

She winced at that. Bruised face, eyes dull with pain, her uniform torn and her hair hopelessly messed up. She was still so beautiful, so *her*, it took my breath away, even leaning on a battered college lectern.

The Link went both ways; I saw her pick up on my thoughts and not understand. She got angry, pushed off, and limped into my personal space. "Now would be a good time."

"I'm sorry," I said, but I wasn't. "I didn't mean for this to happen."

She took a breath, her chest rising. "What happened exactly?"

"I don't know. I'm thinking I used you as my anchor

one too many times. Maybe leaned on you too much at the station, to block out the others. I find you . . . calming."

Cherabino laughed, a short huffaw, and then regretted it on her ribs. She found a desk on the first row and sat down. "Calming? Really? You find me calming? So you start a link with me?"

"I didn't do it on purpose," I said.

She fought down instinctive nausea. "What exactly am I dealing with here?"

I took a breath. "I can find your mind anywhere in the world. In the Solar System, maybe. We can communicate over long distances. Share thoughts. In fact, it's going to be hard *not* to share thoughts." At her frightened look, I said, "It goes both ways, Cherabino."

"How long will this go on?" she asked, feeling dirty. She ran her good hand over the lectern, the feel of the old wood solid under her hands.

"I don't know. That's honest. As much as we know about the mind, about telepathy, there's limits. It could wear off in a couple weeks. It could take a year. I don't know."

I could feel her abhorrence. "You're telling me I have to have you *in my head* for a year? Maybe more?" She'd leave the city. She'd move to Mars.

"I'm sorry," I said. "Moving won't help. If we can get through today, I can teach you how to block me out better. Rummage through *my* head if it will make it feel more equal. I'm not a bad guy. I'm not trying to— I'm not going to hurt you, Cherabino. I'm not. But we have to get through today."

Cherabino hobbled painfully forward, and I forced myself not to help her. "How bad are the odds?" she asked me.

She deserved the truth, no matter how painful, how

awful, how humiliating. With the link, it was her danger too. "With just Bradley, I'd say it's fifty-fifty. He's powerful, and I'm out of it, but I used to be very, very good at this. With my life on the line, I'll be good again. But with backup on his side? I don't know. It's your mind too. We can still wait, stay here until our own backup arrives. It's your decision."

"And let him get away?" Her eyes flashed. "Not a chance in hell. But don't think you're off the hook. This isn't over."

"I know."

On the other side of the room's door, there was a musty hallway, maybe ten feet long and floored in fake white tile. The air smelled of mold and damp concrete. A flickering red Exit sign pointed the way out.

When I pushed down on the cold metal bar that would open the heavy door, I held it open for Cherabino. She limped into the landing, looked up to endless flights of worn stairs, and made a small, disgusted sound.

"Great," Cherabino said. She started climbing. She did *not* complain. In fact, she made a point of not complaining.

About the third step, I literally couldn't stand it anymore.

"I'll carry you."

She paused, weighing her pain against the insult.

"Why else have I been lifting all these weights?" I asked reasonably. "Besides, if I have to feel your ankle bones grinding together one more time, I'm going to yell. Loud."

She paused, halfway up a stair. "You can feel that?"

"Yes. Don't freak out. I can't shield from you right now. If you pay attention, you can probably feel how exhausted I am."

She thought about that, and I could feel her testing out the link like someone feeling her way in a dark, unfamiliar room.

Hi, I said, tiredly.

She retreated. "I don't like this."

"Like it or not, it saved your life once already today."

She closed her mouth and stood, undecided. "You're exhausted—and I'm not light."

Success. "It's mental, not physical; my muscles are fine."

She paused, looking up the long array of endless stairs and landings. "No taking liberties," she said. Firmly.

"Hands and mind to myself?" I asked. "I'll try, but I can't promise. I'm too tired to guarantee anything."

My muscles were fine, and she wasn't all *that* heavy. But—damn cigarettes—I was huffing and puffing after the tenth stair. She complained about this loudly, and without meaning to, I bitched back over the link. I didn't have the breath to respond *and* climb the stairs.

It took her a while to catch on that I wasn't actually talking. And then she shut up.

We reached the landing, the door to the hallway closed. I stopped cold. The sign, that orange-gold sign on the door, faded but distinctive—I'd have known it anywhere. "We're at Toppenguild," I said, with shock.

"Where?"

I stepped past the heavy door, into the hallway. "Toppenguild. The Guild Institute Campus in north Tennessee. We're two hours from Atlanta by aircar. No wonder Bradley came here—the campus is closed this time of year. *Great* place to be an evil scientist—lots of supplies and research files. Why didn't somebody think of this earlier?"

"Everything seems obvious in retrospect," Cherabino said, "but you were the only one in the department with the information." She squirmed. "Are you
going to put me down?"

"Did your ankle mysteriously heal in the last few
minutes?" I asked.

"Did the bad guys suddenly start caring?" she
returned. "There's at least two more toughs out here,
plus a nurse type, the woman Bradley kept arguing
with, and the guy to load the aircar. I don't imagine
they'll just let us wander around blindly—I need to be
able to get to my gun."

"You don't have a gun," I pointed out. "And I'm not
putting you down just yet. We're up against telepaths
here, and your ankle pain is distracting."

"Well, I have a knife," she said, annoyed. "They
never found it in my boot. It's not a small knife. Do you
really want me waving it around so close to your face?"

"If you had a knife, why didn't you use it on those
guys?"

"You try getting a concealed knife out of a tight boot
in the middle of a fistfight. Go ahead, try. Then come
back and criticize my decisions. Go ahead."

"You're getting cranky," I told her. "Give me five
minutes." I showed her my old memory of this place,
more than fifteen years old, from when I'd been a student trying to specialize in tuning. That hadn't worked
out so well—I'd hated the teachers, and the subject
matter wasn't nearly as interesting as it sounded—but
I'd been here, at Toppenguild, for over a year. There
should be labs on this floor, and one of them had a cut-
through to the pyro training room.

The training room was two feet thick of concrete on
all sides, with a door that could barricade from either

inside or out. The pyros were terrifying while training; that room was reinforced enough to hold a rampaging elephant. From either side. It was exactly what we needed now.

"We'll get you to that room," I said, shifting her for a better hold. "You could hold it against an army in the physical world while I go after Bradley in Mindspace."

Her head came up. "Do you hear that?"

"Hear what?"

"Someone's coming," she hissed. "Put me down."

I ignored her and dropped into Mindspace. And pulled out just as quick, trying to cover my tracks, trying to minimize my own presence, shore up my own shields. There was a telepath coming, one frighteningly strong, and I'd bet anything it was Bradley. He made ripples in the very fabric of Mindspace just by moving—I wasn't looking forward to facing him, not on terms we couldn't control. We needed that practice room, and the gadgets they kept inside. Did they still use flamethrowers?

"Hang on," I told Cherabino. I ran toward the lab I remembered, her weight nearly overbalancing me. She made little pain sounds every time my stride hit the floor, hard. I didn't have time to be gentle, and I wasn't very good at the running-while-carrying-the-girl thing yet. She hung on as best she could and complained in a steady, quiet stream.

I came to a stop at the beginning of the blue-painted science hall. A framed picture of Space Station Freedom shared space with a blueprint of a genetically engineered ferret from Thailand. We didn't have far to go, maybe two hundred feet down the hall of doors. I kept the image of that flamethrower in my mind.

I set Cherabino down, settling her on the good foot.

"You think you can climb up on my back? The balance would be better. If we can just get to the practice room . . ."

"I'm not an invalid." She strode forward, every step a shooting pain. She'd taken the location of the lab from my mind.

I made a disgusted sound and hurried to catch up. Behind us, the huge presence that was Bradley came slowly closer. Even through my shields, I could feel the disturbance in Mindspace, like a huge ship's prow pushing the water aside. I'd never felt anything like it.

Then it disappeared, and a chill ran up my back. Carefully, carefully I thinned my shields. He was still there, still huge, but he had stopped, cold, right next to a much smaller presence. Maybe he was talking. Closer to me, a few rooms away to my left, something felt wrong, disturbed, but I didn't dare thin my shields any more to see what it was. Bradley was the threat. I don't think he'd seen me. But I was out of time; the waves of his movement hit the edges of my shields.

I pulled back into myself with a painful lurch, shoring up my shields again with an effort that almost made me bleed. I couldn't do that again, or he would see me.

I opened my eyes and fought double vision. Finally I resolved Cherabino standing ten yards in front of me. She was in front of the door to the lab, gesturing impatiently. Her eyes widened. Behind me I heard a gasp, a clatter.

I turned. A nurse and a hulking bodyguard had just rounded the corner. The redheaded nurse, in full scrubs, was pale, her mouth open in shock, her hands out. A metal tray was on the floor, instruments strewn. The bodyguard went for a gun at his hip.

There was no way I could run to Cherabino in time

No choice. I reached out—shields straining nearly to breaking. The barrel of the gun came up. My mind slowly enveloped his unshielded thoughts. The gun paused halfway.

Our wills battled, him to pull the gun up, to pull the trigger, me to stop him cold. He was strong for a normal, strong-willed. Probably why he got hired in the first place.

The nurse ran, gasping, down the hall in the other direction, and I couldn't stop her. Finally my grip on the guard was strong enough—I found the right place in his brain and pushed. He fell over.

The sound of shuffling footsteps came to my right.

"Did you kill him?" Cherabino's voice strained.

I weaved a little on my feet, head pounding, pain hitting in waves. I would get this under control. I had to.

"Are you okay?" Cherabino asked, getting the edge of it.

I shook, and held, and held. I finally was stable, but there was Bradley, coming down the hallway, still around the corner, still a hundred feet away, but closing far too fast.

"We need to go," I told her.

I lurched down the hallway, grabbing Cherabino's jacket and pulling her along. I was disoriented, under pressure, and I knew if we didn't make it to the room to regroup I might fall apart. I might die, unable to fight back. Taking her with me.

She doubled her steps, trying to keep up, and the *stab, stab, stab* of the pain of her foot echoed in my head like a bad rock song on stadium speakers. "Did you kill him?" she repeated in a small voice.

"No," I said. I didn't kill people with my mind. "He's asleep. Hurry up."

I could feel Bradley's wake behind me getting closer and closer. I had his attention now.

Fifteen feet from the lab door. Ten. Five.

"Stop!" a man's voice called out in booming tones.

Bradley had arrived.

CHAPTER 28

Cherabino's hand touched the doorknob.

"Go," I told her, and turned around. I heard the door open and backed up, slowly, toward it. At least she'd get away, even if I didn't.

Bradley looked just like he did in the picture, just like he did in the vision, a skinny, pasty geek with tortoiseshell glasses and a small sneer.

"You! You weren't supposed to get here until later," he told me, in the tone you'd use on an old friend who had just kicked your dog. "Always ruining everything. The girl was supposed to keep you busy." In Mindspace, he was huge, far larger than I'd thought him to be, a dark blimp with rough edges. In the real world, the fluorescent lights glinted off his glasses ominously.

"You know she's a cop," I said, taking a small step back. "You have to know it's dumb to kidnap a cop."

"She was yours. You hit me where it hurt, I did the same. It's only fair." He moved forward, measured paces, seemingly in no hurry. I inched back, counting on my peripheral vision to tell me when I'd gone far enough. His harmless-looking body just made his looming presence in Mindspace that much more terrible.

The next logical question was, how in hell had I hurt him, but that seemed like the kind of thing that would get the bad guy mad, and I was a big proponent of talk now, fight later. Especially when fighting later would give me more weapons. My mind kept going back to the flamethrower—maybe they'd left it in the training room again. They'd done that all the time when I was here.

I took another small step back. "Why is this so damn personal?" Oops, probably not the right tone to keep him from getting angry.

He frowned, hard, then laughed with a bitter edge. "You don't remember."

I thought about using the strong-drugs excuse, but took the higher road. "No. I'm sorry."

He made a disgusted sound. "All the girls. All the money. All the accolades. And Golden Boy doesn't even remember the research fellow who's going to kill him. Tragic."

"I heard you made head of the department," I said. "Congratulations. Really. Is that where you found the machines?" I backed up faster.

His glasses glinted like the carapace of a bug. "Think you're so clever, just because you're a professor. I left the machines. You made me, you and the cops. Think it will stop me. But you don't know everything. I have the blueprints, and they'll make me better ones."

"Who will make you better ones?" I asked.

His eyes narrowed, and he held up a hand, palm out. "I'm done talking now."

Overwhelming force threw me back, past the doorway. I landed on the floor, seeing stars.

In front of me the door opened and a glass container flew through the air. Bradley ducked as glass broke in front of him. He hissed in pain, cradled his eye, screamed out names. Reinforcements—he was calling reinforcements.

"Take that, teep!" Cherabino yelled. She grabbed my ankle, pulled. What?

She pulled again. "Help me out."

I pushed with my hands, my body halfway into the door. Another push, my vision still blurry. I sat up, got to my hands and knees.

Down the hallway, Bradley rubbed at his eye while another big guy came up behind him. Much farther down the hall, the first guard slept on, oblivious. He'd be out for at least another hour.

I was not so lucky. Pulling myself up, I grappled with the heavy steel door until it closed, locking it with the one small deadbolt I had available. My eyes finally focused, but the back of my head was throbbing in time with my heartbeat.

"What was in the beaker?" I asked Cherabino.

"Baking soda and water. Everything else is locked up. Unless we can figure out a way to throw lit propane, all that's here is glass, baking soda, and water. Maybe some salt."

I looked around, panting. We were in the middle of a chemistry lab full of low black tables, tables covered in beakers, tubing, gas burners, and jars. The smell of chemicals, glass, and burnt wood permeated the room. I saw a couple boxes of that baking soda, some salt, sand, even a few pipettes. But she was right, no chemicals were out, not even a plain acid.

At the end of the room was the solid wooden door I wanted, less than twenty feet away. Bad design to make it wood, but maybe there was another steel door on the inside. Regardless, we needed to get out of here and into the pyro practice room, now. I did not want to be in a room full of glass and propane lines with a telekinetic on the loose.

On the floor, Cherabino held her ankle. "Damn foot."

"We're out of time. I'm carrying you."

"No you're not." Her expression was firm as she reached up to grab a table.

"Fine." I stood up myself. "At least pull out that knife of yours. The door won't hold him for long." I paused. "This is the part where the nasty stuff starts flying around. The real world, yeah, but also Mind-space. Hide under a table if you have to, do the same in your mind. Distract him in the real world if you can."

"Got it," she said, leaning against the table with a determined expression. "Get going."

A *thud* came from the door.

I limped to the next student table, turned it over quickly, violently. Glass beakers crashed against the floor on the other side, metal tinkling, rubber thudding. I got my hands under the side of the table and lifted, using every muscle in my back to keep the bulky table moving.

"You might want to move," I told Cherabino. Then I yanked the table over in front of the door, bracing it against a vibration I could feel in my bones. That should buy us a few seconds at least.

"You okay?" I asked her. She looked pained and was already limping to the center aisle, knife in one hand.

"I'm fine. Get that door open."

I staggered past her, through eight rows of chemistry tables, all the way to the front teacher's station. The chalkboard at the front of the room was emblazoned with the words *Safety First*. My equilibrium was going, but I got my hand on the doorknob to the door next to it. Another crash came from the hallway.

Cherabino was almost halfway down the aisles, a

steady stream of pain and cursing accompanying
every step.

I turned the knob. It was locked. "Damn it."

Another crash, and a low, tortured hum from the
hallway. The table bracing the door started to shake
visibly. I looked around, heart pounding. There on the
teacher's desk. A couple of very long thin pieces of
metal—sharp flat thermometers. The top edge of them
would work nicely. I'd learned a few things on the
streets; I could pick an easy lock if my life depended
on it. It might now.

There was a long silence from the door, while I felt
ripples in Mindspace. I grabbed the thin metal thermometers and fed them carefully into the lock, hoping
they'd fit. Yes. I moved them around with shaking
hands. . . . I had to do this; I had to. . . .

A click. The steel door from the hallway made an
awful sound. The table was splintering, the hard steel
of the hallway door was stretching, straining like a
bubble inward, cracking the table. It wouldn't be much
longer. I turned the knob—

Only to come face-to-face with five shelves of bottles
and a tangle of beakers. I stared, adrenaline pumping,
not able to understand what I was seeing. Shelves? Sul-
furic acid? Beakers? Magnesium? Sodium? A bag of
sand? This couldn't be right. I reached out a hand
through the bottles—the back wall was solid. A closet.
A chemistry supply closet.

Damn it, damn it, damn it.

"What's wrong?" Cherabino said in a pained voice.
"Why aren't you going through?"

"It's not the cut-through," I said. "We're in the
wrong room."

There was no way out. None but the door to the
hallway that was even now about to break. We would

be stuck in a chem lab with a telekinetic who could throw all the nice sharp glass objects directly at our heads. I hit my head on the shelf.

While Cherabino cursed, I tried to think, tried to make my brain work while a truly nasty scraping sound came from the door. My eyes ran over the bottles, clear glass the length of my arm with black stoppers and handwritten labels. My eye went back to the magnesium, the little jar with the dull gray metal strips.

One of the professors at the Guild liked to do demos with that stuff—it burned. Hot. With a really bright light that was dangerous to look at. I grabbed the bottle, shut the door. I didn't want anyone else to see the chemicals and use them against us.

I needed fire. Something hot. My eyes ran over the teacher's station, the gas line already set up, a snaking line leading to a simple Bunsen burner. I hustled over there. Now I just needed a spark—something to light it with.

"Do you see any matches?" I asked Cherabino, who was taking a pained rest stop halfway up the room. She was sweating and pale, but the knife was still in her hand.

She took a breath, looked up at me. "What's wrong with your lighter?"

Oh. I felt like an idiot. I fished the lighter out of my pocket and—

The outside door flew with impossible force, hitting the opposite wall with a *clang*.

I gulped. Two men, one tall and beefy, the other Bradley in all his skinny geekiness, entered the room. Bradley's left eye was bright red, leaking fluid. He looked pissed.

Knife in hand, Cherabino stepped toward them, one lurching step at a time. "You're under arrest," she said.

Bradley raised one hand and threw her back with solid force.

Cherabino's face lit up with surprise as she flew through the air. Her knees struck one of the student desks with painful force, her head slamming into the tabletop. She slid off the table, landing on the hard tile floor with a *crunch*. Then came the lighter sound of the knife hitting tile.

She tried to rise, her vision swimming, before collapsing into a puddle, her consciousness sliding away. I caught myself at the edge of that same abyss, fought back with my vision turning into a tunnel—and stayed standing.

My hands flew, hitting the gas valve, opening the air, bringing the lighter up. It caught—

And Bradley threw me back, hard, against the chalkboard. I hit with an impact that jarred my teeth, the lighter flying across the room. I blinked, disoriented, while he paced forward, grabbing beaker after beaker with his mind. A bottle of water next to me started to rise in midair, the changing air currents making the flame on the Bunsen burner flicker.

I lurched ahead—surprised to find I could. No pressure held me to the board. Before he could change that, I grabbed for the magnesium, threw it at the fire, and turned my head.

Blinding light flashed out with a popping sound, and I threw myself forward, under the first row of student desks. The water bottle dropped onto the floor with a *thud*. I dropped into Mindspace, quickly, knowing I'd have one chance at this.

Bradley's shields were down, his mind full of the

painful flash of light. I darted in like a fish into the mouth of a whale—fast, quick, no apologies, swimming as hard as my mind would let me. While my mind cracked and bled, I kept going, kept pushing, holding the course no matter what it took.

He started to react—but he was too slow. I reached the right spot, grabbing with my whole mind and clamping down. He froze, literally unable to make a decision.

I took a breath. With painful double vision, I opened an eye. There was still another bad guy out there. If my concentration slipped for a moment, Bradley would be free, but I couldn't just let the bruiser hit me over the head.

I looked around, holding, holding on to impossible pressure. Cherabino's body sprawled three feet to my left. The shadow of the bright magnesium started turning red, and the high hiss it made started to crackle, to crackle like a wood fire. I was betting the teacher's desk was starting to catch; I hadn't been all that careful with the magnesium.

I grabbed at Bradley again when he struggled. Where was the second bad guy? Cherabino's knife was maybe two feet to my left. Could I get it in time?

The bruiser ran straight down the aisle, ignoring me in favor of the fire. His thick legs darted back and forth, dashing forward to the wall to turn the gas off at the source. The fire got quieter, suddenly, and the bruiser hurried forward to get the red fire extinguisher under the teacher's desk. The wrong one—the red carbon dioxide, not the black chemical extinguisher. Crap.

I heard the safety pin tinkle on the floor, closed my eyes, and braced.

The *boom* of an explosion, a flash of light visible

hrough my eyelids. I'd been expecting it; my mind slipped, but I recovered, holding, holding, keeping Bradley immobile by my will alone. Had it spread beyond the desk?

The bruiser cried out, hit the floor with a *thud*. I opened my eyes; he was scrabbling back, on his back like a crab, cursing up a storm, his face splotched with burns.

On the board, the erasers caught fire, but the tray was metal. We had a few seconds at least.

"Fire!" the bruiser yelled at Bradley, and Bradley struggled, trying to react.

"Fire!" the man screamed in Bradley's face, shaking Bradley, hard, and my mind stretched like taffy to keep his will—and held. I felt warmth trickle down my lips as my nose started to bleed. But I had to hold this. I had to. I grabbed control of Bradley's body—

I made his leg kick at the bruiser's knees. Connect. The bruiser's arms windmilled, and he hit the side of a table—hit it hard. He didn't get up. For ten seconds and more, he didn't get up; he didn't move.

I breathed. I'd gotten lucky. But I could feel the heat of the fire, hear the crackle of the flames. It was spreading.

I stood up, holding my grip on Bradley's mind through sheer will and concentration. Sweat rolled down my face, and blood ran in a steady stream down my face as I held him, carefully, taking one concentrated step at a time. I was walking the high wire with no net, one step from death.

The center of the teacher's table *cracked*, and the hot flames grew higher. Fingers of flame ran all the way under the desk, a few feet—and a minute—from lighting the whole room on fire. The chemical extinguisher was no longer an option.

I couldn't do water, I thought, in careful small thoughts as I took step after tiny step down that tight rope. I couldn't smother it with another table, not with it about to fall apart. A fire-retardant blanket? Or sand? Sand. There was a fifteen-pound bag of sand in the closet.

Ten careful steps later, the fire roaring, I pulled the rip cord to the sandbag. I shoveled out handful after handful of sand with my hands, throwing it on the fire with slow, careful moves.

My concentration split, Bradley strained against my hold like a giant moth in a small glass jar. Blood ran down my face faster, sweat pooling, as my head pounded like the beat of a gong. Handful after handful of sand hit the burning table. The last handful of sand went on the last flame, which sputtered and died. I breathed.

The smell was acrid, deadly, the table turned into so much splinter and ash. For a long moment, I stood swaying, in so much mental pain I could hardly think. I put a hand on one of the student tables to support me. I was out of juice—and Bradley was struggling harder.

I had to do something, had to know what he knew, so I forced a partial merge. It might kill us both—

Just you, Bradley spat at me. *You deserve to die.*

My brain pushed farther than it had ever been, I actually held on. Tears streaming, nose bleeding, arm throbbing, I actually held on.

I saw myself from his point of view, the handsome guy, the Golden Boy at the Guild, the head of the department Bradley wanted more than anything to work in. He'd screwed up his courage, put the application in, and two days later saw it come back in a red envelope with two words scrawled on it: *Too Weak.* The words were in my handwriting, Golden Boy's hand-writing. His jealousy surged. I'd gotten everything he'd ever wanted, ignored him at every turn, and now I dared to sneer at him? It was like a kick to the ribs, a kick from an angry horse. He still felt the impact.

He'd decided he would never be weak again. He'd find a way to be stronger than me, to do more than me, to take what I had. Years of research—and more of testing—to get to the point where he could steal the Ability he deserved, years where I was gone from the Guild and he was in control again. But he wasn't surprised to see me here. It was right. I was the enemy, I was fighting him, of course I was fighting him. I always had. But he would win.

Nameless, faceless test subjects stretched out before me in a line. Dozens. Over years. People who were dead, people with no family, no one to report them missing. Subjects who'd finally given him what he deserved. But Neil was a fool; he washed the bodies and told the cops. No matter, Neil was dead now. Like I would be. Like the cop woman would be. And then Bradley could make it to New Orleans and his meeting with Garrett Fiske, the criminal boss, head of the Darkness in the Southeast. With blueprints in hand, Bradley would get everything he needed from Fiske—money, supplies, new machines, mechanics to build them. Give him a year—just a year—and Bradley would be back in business, only this time with buyers. Fiske said there were a lot of people willing to buy Ability, no questions asked. Bradley would finally get the recognition he deserved.

Go back to the victims. What were their names? I pushed. *How many? Where in New Orleans?*

Something *popped* inside my brain, and I lost the hold.

I woke up next to a student desk, with no memory o
how I'd gotten there. Worse, Bradley was levitating m
up and across the room like a bad student prank bu
much more ominous. I couldn't move. Bands of forc
locked around my hands and feet, heavier thar
hundred-pound weights. I struggled against them. . .

"I said no," Bradley barked, and threw me agains
the chalkboard.

I hit and saw stars, the impact so hard it broke the
chalkboard. I screamed, pain radiating down my spin
from the knot on my head. The area smelled of sulfuri
acid reaction from the bubbling tile and ash, over
whelming ash.

I reached for Mindspace—and lost it. The pain wa
too great, and Bradley, like a huge suffocating pillow
overlaid everything; he blocked my every movement
my every struggle. I was going to die, I realized, pinnec
to a chalkboard like a bug on a collector's card.

Too late, I thought to call Kara. He blocked me, pin
ning me down harder. Blood rushed down my face
and I struck out at his mind. I bounced off his shield.
scrabbled around the edges, but I had no power, no
control.

He looked at me, head tilted to the side, and I had ar
overwhelming sense of déjà vu. We were in my vision

Bradley held up a hand. He was so average, pasty
skin, light brown hair, average height. Skinny. Harm
less. This was the face of the man who was going to kil
me, I thought with despair. A man I couldn't ever
remember.

Behind him Cherabino sprawled unconscious, jus
like in the vision. She hadn't been assaulted, not thi
time, but it seemed like that didn't matter in the end

Overcome with despair, I tried to pull my hand off the board—and got slapped down.

Bradley started pressing down; impossible pressure inside and out—my mind, my body crushing. I felt the chalkboard crack again behind me.

He sneered. "Thought you were so smart, didn't you? Thought you knew everything. Well, Golden Boy, who's the smart one now? All the sniffing cops around my apartment, all the taunts and Guild guys crawling around, you didn't find a shred of evidence. Not a shred, and the girl, thinking about you like a billboard. You think I would just let that one go? I grabbed her right from under your nose, and you couldn't stop me. You can't stop me, Golden Boy, not anymore. Now who's too weak?"

I threw pain at him, and he shrugged it off like the buzzing of a fly.

"I'm sorry," I said. "I really am." With nowhere to run, it was time to try something else. I knew I was an idiot back then—rejecting his application with two words was cruel. That much was true. I could be sorry for that, truly sorry. If it would save my life, and Cherabino's life, I could be sorry.

"No you're not," Bradley said, and his eyes flashed hurt all of a sudden. "You know what? I'm tired of listening to your lies." He pushed down, my bones grinding against the board, the eraser tray at the bottom of the board cutting painfully into my thighs.

And then the real pain started.

A hundred knives pierced my skull while light and dark changed places and danced on my neurons with vicious glee. White-hot pain radiated from my entire body. I forced myself to open my eyes, to look, to think of something, anything but the pain.

Bradley was focused, angry, watching me like a boy pulling the wings off a bug. Behind him, Cherabino's body started to twitch. Her arms and legs jumped like a seizure, over and over, as my pain echoed through the link. I felt her mind, dark with the red pain of a concussion sharing space with my sharper torture—she was struggling up.

It occurred to me like a silent movie that Bradley was talking again. And déjà vu descended like a cloud of pain-touched perfume.

Bradley's anger built, and he clamped down with all the force he was capable of, closing my airway until I literally couldn't breathe. Until not one iota of air could come down the pipeway.

I told myself not to panic, don't panic, panicking just used up the oxygen faster.

Bradley watched my face, hard, waiting for me to pass out and then to die, with all of his anger filling the room. "I told Neil at the beginning this was a messy business, but he couldn't take it. They couldn't take it. So I found someone who can. Who'll pay me what I'm worth. And you—you wanted me to stop. Well, I won't. And you'll be rotting garbage while I'm rich. Respected. While I have whatever I want. I want you to know that, as you die. I want you to remember. I want you to know this is your fault."

My vision was graying quickly. Don't panic, don't panic! My heart ignored me and doubled its beating. I tried to move, tried to move—but I couldn't. I couldn't, and my vision was graying out. Suddenly I smelled chalk dust, strongly, and felt dark red-lined pain, my ankle bones rasping against one another.

Cherabino's knife plunged down into Bradley's shoulder.

His mental hold released, all at once. I fell to the ground, jarring impact. I gasped, the air rushing into my lungs. And the pain stopped. I looked up.

Bradley turned to kill Cherabino, his decision so strong, I could taste it—and for one precious second he was distracted. Shields totally down. Adrenaline was running through my system so strongly, I shook with it—I had one, final, rush of energy.

I took my moment. Pushed into his mind, knowing exactly what I was looking for. Before he could react, I made my mind a blade, and cut. Sliced the central processor, destroyed the quantum gating array. And, right *there*, and *there*, I ripped, as hard as I possibly could, stars appearing in my vision as I strained.

It was enough, barely enough.

His arm halfway out, the knife sticking out behind him, Bradley collapsed.

I stared at his lax face, two feet away on the floor, and watched the hill that was his mind flatten and lose most of its mass, like a balloon leaking helium. Blood seeped slowly from the knife still in his collarbone. His back rose, slightly, with a small, shallow breath.

I gasped, breathing hard, almost hyperventilating. My body shook uncontrollably. I had killed his mind. I had destroyed him—the one thing I said I'd never do, not to anyone. I huddled against the white-tiled floor and shook. Mindspace started to flash in and out, wobbly like the worst Satin high with no payoff.

Across the room, Cherabino sat down on the floor, the pain of her foot echoing dimly through our link. "Stop breathing like that," she said tiredly. "You'll only make yourself pass out."

I pushed up carefully, past the shaking, putting my knees in front of my chest and my forehead on them. I concentrated on slowing down my breathing. I did that for maybe five minutes, while the adrenaline settled and I adjusted to the fact that I was going to live. Tried with all my might not to throw up on the already nasty tile.

I had killed him.

CHAPTER 29

The precog flashed, but too late. Kara *grabbed*. Hurricane force rippled at my mind from every direction.

With an explosion of air, Kara appeared. She said something to Cherabino, but the words turned into useless mush, and darkness overtook me.

My head hurt. The bump on my head hurt like a son of a bitch; the throbbing pain was forcing me slowly into consciousness. My ears rang, my mind struggled to put together thoughts, and my head felt like a gong someone was hitting, over and over.

I raised my head. The tile under my hands was warm.

"Hold on, I'm coming," Cherabino's voice came from close by. "Are you okay?" I heard the sound of shuffling, and a pain sound. Then her scuffed boots appeared. "You passed out when Kara showed up. She looked pretty worried, said there was something seriously wrong. She left again quickly."

I looked over, down the line of student desks. Bradley, closer, was still down, his chest rising and falling slowly while the knife still stuck out of his back. Legally, he wasn't dead, but ethically, morally—I'd killed him. I pushed myself up to sitting position, the world swimming. "What happened? Why did she come back?"

With a pained expression and a hand on her ribs, Cherabino slowly lowered herself down to my level.

"You okay?" I asked.

"I think a rib's broken," she said, her tone very matter-of-fact. "Our guys will be here in an hour, plus the Tennessee state troopers are on their way and are going to come in shooting. Kara wanted to make sure we kept our heads down, inside this wing, out of the fight. I told her we weren't going anywhere any time soon. She went to coordinate details."

I tried to reach out in Mindspace—and nearly fell over. Mind pounding, I swallowed bile, and swore.

"What's wrong with you?" Cherabino asked.

"I can't find Mindspace, that's what's wrong with me!" I barked, and had to hold my head. "I'm broken. Kara broke me."

Cherabino was silent, and it tortured me that I didn't know what she was thinking. That I *couldn't* know what she was thinking.

Was it going to come back? Let it come back, I prayed, as I found a way to lean against the table leg, huddling over my knees like a child. Let it come back.

I shook, unable to imagine a world without Mindspace, without telepathy, without the very things that made me *me*.

"Where are they?" I barked at Cherabino for about the tenth time.

"They'll get here when they get here," she said. She wasn't looking good, the circles under her eyes getting even darker. And she was coughing, a lot, far more than I thought was good for her.

She coughed again, stopped, made a choked sound.

"Anything I can do?" I offered. "Help you stand up maybe?"

She paused for a long time before talking. Finally she said, "If it's all the same to you, I'd rather not move. I think one of the ribs is broken pretty bad." She didn't say she'd like to keep her lung, but I knew her well enough to know that was what was on her mind. Even if I couldn't read it—and the thought pierced me like a knife in the gut.

I paused. "You sure they're coming?" I asked.

She half laughed and then stopped. Immediately. After a deep breath, she said, "You really think Branen's going to sit on his ass while we have all the fun? *Clearly* you don't know him that well. Screw the Tennessee cops. Our guys will be here."

I subsided, then went back to panicking about Mindspace. I pushed at it over and over, like poking at the empty place a tooth had been with my tongue, painful as hell but I couldn't stop. I couldn't. I had to get the telepathy back. I had to. My head hurt so bad, on so many levels. . . .

"I'd kill for an aspirin right about now," Cherabino said.

I looked up then. "An aspirin? You want an aspirin?"

"Why? You have one in your back pocket?" she asked.

"No. But this is damn Toppenguild. I know where everything is—infirmary, everything. It's even in the wing, so we won't get shot or anything."

"You didn't know where the fireproof room was." She shifted her head, turning it more toward me. "For all we know, that nurse is still wandering around. Plus that Tina lady—she has a gun, and I don't think she's going to hesitate."

"So what?" I said, not quite able to get the desperation out of my tone. "I need to walk. Aspirin's as good an excuse as any. If I get lost, I get lost. You still have that knife?"

"No." She was quiet, looking down. "Get me some water too, okay? A decent brand of bottled."

"You got it." I hesitated, then finally went for it, stroking her hair back from her face. I felt a glimmer of shadow-pain; maybe it was coming back. Maybe I was fooling myself. I held her face a little longer, and like a dim light far away, I saw annoyance.

"Stop fondling my cheek," she said. "You promised me aspirin; you'd better deliver."

I dropped my hand. Inside, though, I had a glimmer of hope.

Ding, the elevator said as it arrived. I felt like I had been through a war. My head was still pounding, my clothes torn and dirty and smelling of smoke. I was limping, exhausted, and running on empty.

So of course, when I opened the infirmary door, there stood Tina Novachavich, a forty-something Guild secretary from the research department and Bradley's accomplice. She had liked lemon meringue cookies, my brain informed me, and would flirt with Dane if she was in a good mood. She looked about twenty pounds thinner than she had, infinitely older, with a gun holstered at her hip.

She looked up at my entrance, dropping half the papers in her hands, a mishmash of loose papers, files, and a few long tubes that looked like blueprints. She cursed, her hand going to the gun.

I was out of juice, likely with a concussion, with no weapons. "Let's not do this," I said, holding my hands up.

She eased her hand away, looking me in the eye as she slowly knelt. She grabbed most of the papers, paused over one file. After a second, she tossed it to me. "You deserve to know," she said. "But don't follow me, or I will kill you."

Then, between one breath and the next, she was gone. Air *whooshed* into the gap.

"Great," I mumbled. I hadn't realized she was a teleporter, damn it. Was she enhanced with the machine, or was I that out of touch?

I limped forward, finally getting my first good look at the room. White cabinets lined the back wall, chairs sat close to me, and through a door on the back wall I could see an exam table. A long metal countertop sat on the back wall, and another, a movable one like an island on wheels, took up the center of the room. It was covered in boxes and boxes of syringes, two small glass bottles out on the table with a sheaf of papers.

The file she'd thrown sat on the tile floor a foot in front of me.

I looked around, listened. As near as I could tell, I was alone. I reached down to pick up the file—and found it labeled with my name.

I set it down on the metal countertop in the center of the room, paged through with a sense of apprehension. This wasn't my Guild file, the account of my education or my classes or even the reasons I'd been thrown out.

No, this was *Stewart's* file, the file of the crazy son of a bitch whose research had introduced me to my drug. It was an account of the effects of Satin on the brain— my brain—and how it loosened the hold of the mind on the body. Stewart's typewritten comments had the drug as therefore useless, at least to him. But it wasn't useless to someone else; in the margins of the file, careful handwritten notes said this, *this* was what was needed for the machine. To separate the Ability from a subject. This was the key.

I felt sick. My drug, my addiction, had played a part in this. I had helped Bradley kill all those people.

I leaned over the table, my hand hitting the closest box. My eyes focused on it, on the chemical formula handwritten on the side of the box in a larger, blocky scrawl. I knew that formula. I'd have known that formula anywhere.

Three boxes of syringes, two more of small glass bottles—I was surrounded by Satin, by pure, high-grade Satin.

I sat down on the short lab stool and stared. My fuzzy mind just looked at them, at the bounty, all the highs, just sitting there. Just sitting there.

I could do it. I could pick up a syringe, and shoot up, and fall into the cloud-coated rush—no one would ever have to know. Ever.

Cherabino wasn't here. Swartz wasn't here.

But the file in front of me stared, the careful writing like a brand. This wasn't for me, wasn't for fun or need or anything else. It was made, kept, used to steal Ability. To let Bradley take what wasn't his. These containers of helpfully labeled drugs were here to let him mind-rape—and then kill—probably hundreds of people. All in pretty little bottles. All because of me.

The boxes around me suddenly seemed like poison, like the poison Swartz said it was.

Did I really want to throw away the last two years and seven months of fighting my poison for a two-hour rush? Start over from scratch? Realistically, sooner or later Bellury or Cherabino or Paulsen—or worse, Swartz—would find the bottles and drag me back to rehab. I hated rehab.

And there was always the chance they wouldn't forgive me this time. That everything I'd worked to build—that Cherabino had worked to build—would go away if I gave in. My life sucked, but it was a lot better than it had been. And it couldn't exist with Satin in it. That much *everybody* had made clear.

If I went back on Satin, I'd probably never have Cherabino falling asleep on my shoulder again. Never again have Paulsen's respect. And I would have to wait years—years more—to hear Swartz say, "Good job." Assuming he was still in this. Which could not be taken for granted forever. He was getting old, and testy. And tired of newbies; he'd said it several times.

I caressed the side of the bottle again, almost tasting the salt of my poison. It would feel so good. . . .

But I saw the death in it this time. Saw the results of that path.

And I realized something, something huge—and something I'd known quietly, obviously, for weeks.

I wanted to be clean. Not just not shooting up at the moment; not just not taking my drug today, but to truly not be a junkie. I wanted to be a real person; I wanted the life I was building. I wanted to be clean.

I put my hand down, away from the bottle, cursed myself for a fool—who knew when I'd get another chance at this?—and searched through the white-laminated wooden cabinets and drawers until I found a packet of aspirin. I also found a pile of quarters, which I took. Then I hauled ass out of there, away from temptation, as far away as I could.

The vending machine was down the hall, next floor down, and if I remembered right, it had good, cold water for sale.

But with every step I took away from the mother lode, I paused. Then I made myself take the next one. I was going to regret this for weeks, like bitter gall. Weeks. Years, maybe.

And maybe, just maybe, not at all.

Despite all the promises of backup, the return trip to the lab was uneventful. I announced myself before walking in the door.

"What took you so long?" she complained, her voice rough and testy.

I knelt down next to her and offered my spoils.

The aspirin was easy. But half of the water ended up on the tiled floor—she wasn't good at drinking lying down, probably not enough hangovers—but in the end she got it down.

I settled down next to her, leaning on the leg of the lab table, watching Bradley's chest go up and down. The blood from his shoulder slowly stopped. And I waited.

I wanted to offer to fix her headache, to use the shape of my mind in Mindspace to reset her mental polarity, reboot her brain waves—I used to be really good at that. It wasn't exactly a low-stakes procedure—one of my students had made a migraine permanent; another put a guy in a coma I'd had the hardest time getting him out of. But I used to be really good at it. Good enough to stop the migraines completely for a couple of months.

I wanted to offer; I wanted to ride in and be the hero, to fix everything. Make her grateful, make her proud. Maybe with the link she could have read my confidence, maybe she would even have let me do it. And maybe pigs would fly outside of an aircar. But I wanted to offer.

I couldn't, though, not now. More burned out than I'd been since I was a teenager, I could feel literally nothing but the inside of my own thoughts. I've sprained something, I thought, in my head. Who knew what I'd have to do to fix it. Who knew if I even could. I held on to the annoyance I'd felt from her earlier, a thin, faint feeling; I held on to that feeling like a lifeline.

Exhaustion swept over me like waves on a seashore. And by the time Branen, Paulsen, and another set of SWAT showed up, I was out cold.

They couldn't wake me up by screaming at me—so Paulsen shook me awake, her hand on my neck. She was pissed—pissed and relieved; I could see it on her face. But I couldn't feel it.

I let her help me up and push us to the ambulance-flyer.

CHAPTER 30

Cherabino's side was so taped, she could barely walk. She'd made me go with her to buy a black button-down shirt. Carry everything for her. Hold the keys. Because, she said, we were *going* to the funeral.

We stood in the back of the tiny group of mourners, squinting at the bright sunlight. The department and the Guild had competed to see who could send the largest—and most ornate—set of flowers.

People got up to say quiet, awkward things about a man no one quite seemed to know. Neil had gotten himself into unimaginable trouble but then had somehow decided to end it. Tipping off the police to Joey's involvement had been at considerable personal risk. It boggled the mind.

I regretted deeply not arguing more with Paulsen, not acting on the vision sooner. Not pulling strings with Kara. Not sticking it out with Cherabino. Maybe if I'd done more, said more . . .

But then I looked over at Cherabino, battered and bruised but still very much herself. And I could feel her tiredness, just a little, through the link. If I could feel no one else, I could feel her. And maybe that was enough.

Pay attention to the preacher, she snapped at me mentally.

So I put my eyes back on the little man talking about ashes to ashes, and a life ending. No one was crying, and no matter how much I tried, I couldn't either. I couldn't even manage sadness—just guilt, inexplicable, unreasonable guilt, and it ate at me stronger than a supercancer.

The funeral home started the machine that would lower the flower-covered coffin. It squeaked horribly, and we all tried to pretend it didn't.

Cherabino accidentally met my gaze and looked away. She was learning to lock me out more and more, but had chosen not to today. She was starting to understand I panicked without *some* kind of mental connection with the world. I'd tried to tough it out one too many times, and she'd caught on. But, with respect, I kept it light and let her control the connection. I was in no position to push for anything.

Bradley was still in a coma at the hospital, and there was talk about bringing in a Guild expert to fix whatever was wrong with him before he stood trial. Kara wanted me to be there, to talk the expert through what I'd done. I wanted more than anything to leave the Guild to it—to rub their noses in their part of this. But if there was any hope, any hope at all that we could reverse what I'd done to Bradley . . . I'd call her.

The department was still putting together details, still trying to figure out what had happened. As political as this case was, as many unanswered questions as it had, I thought we would be at it for a while. The Guild was making a full inquiry into the events of the last month, and I would have to testify in front of a full panel of telepaths, probably mind-deaf while I did it. I was going to tell the whole truth, mind-deaf or not. Let them face up to what they'd done. Make sure this never happened again. The old idealist in me demanded that much.

Here, at the funeral, the first shovelfuls of dirt hit the coffin, and the group started to disband. Cherabino and I stood there a long time, out of her sense of respect for the dead, and especially respect for an informant. Good or bad, Neil had broken the case at considerable personal cost.

Finally it was over. I walked toward the car, trying to be sedate so Cherabino could keep up without straining herself. She minced behind me, struggling to keep her feet in the high heels and not hurt her taped ribs—at the same time. She'd insisted she'd had to wear heels to the funeral but cursed herself in a constant litany at the back of her mind. The sound of that cursing was the best thought I'd ever heard.

In the parking lot, with us standing in the marginally cooler shadow of an old pine tree next to the car, Cherabino's radio spat static. She turned it up, listened. "Understood," she said into the mike, and put it back on her hip.

She looked at me. "They have a new high-level interview for you."

I sighed. "Do I have time for a cigarette?" It might help me ignore the craving for Satin. I might try praying again, too, maybe. Swartz said I should get more serious about the God part of the Twelve Steps.

"Probably, if it's quick."

I could do quick. I fished the pack out and lit up. She sat on the side of the car—wincing at the heat, even at ten o'clock in the morning.

"Want me to change out your shoes?" I asked her.

"In a minute," she said. The whole right side of her face was covered in splotchy colors. She held out her hand; I handed over the pack.

"Branen going to let you get back to work soon?"

She looked at me, annoyed I'd brought it up. "Couple weeks, if I heal up right."

Rumor had it Branen had told her getting herself kidnapped was against department policy. An amateur mistake. So now she was on administrative leave—could only work twenty-hour weeks, desk work only—until she did her time and healed properly.

She was getting full pay. Some people would have just sat back and enjoyed the sick leave. Instead, Cherabino sat there on the hood of the car and plotted how to get around it. Like I said, everyone has a poison.

That evening, after another long day of difficult, nasty interviews, Swartz took me to an NA meeting a little outside my usual stomping ground, one that met in Midtown.

He turned on the radio in the car to listen to the news. They were broadcasting the big press conference from this morning—Kara and the mayor of Decatur both taking credit for catching the serial killer due to the "amazing joint effort" of a bunch of people who weren't the cops who'd actually made the arrest. Neither Cherabino nor Paulsen was mentioned—I snorted and changed the channel. At least Kara was getting something out of this.

We parked in a grungy pay lot, feeding paper bills into the slot to pay for the parking outside the church where the meeting would be held. Swartz walked beside me companionably. The soot-covered arches of the church stood like sentinels against the night.

The meeting was held in the church basement, a badly lit twenty-by-thirty space covered in Sunday school drawings. The concrete walls and old carpet smelled like dry mold and hope.

I got a cup of coffee and a slice of real lemon cake from the long, chipped table, and took a seat. I didn't know these eight people—neither did Swartz—but I knew what would happen. We opened with the serenity prayer, and moved on from there.

When the turn came to me, I put my coffee on the floor and stood up.

"My name is Adam, and I'm an addict," I said.

"Hi, Adam," they echoed.

ABOUT THE AUTHOR

Alex Hughes has written since early childhood, and loves great stories in any form, including scifi, fantasy, and mystery. Over the years, Alex has lived in many neighborhoods of the sprawling metro Atlanta area. Decatur, the neighborhood in which *Clean* is centered, was Alex's college home.

DOUBLETAKE

A CAL LEANDROS NOVEL
by
ROB THURMAN

Half-human/half-monster Cal Leandros knows that family is a
pain. But now that pain belongs to his half-brother, Niko.
Niko's shady father is in town, and he needs a big favor.
Even worse is the reunion being held by the devious Puck
race—including the Leandros' friend, Robin—featuring a
lottery that no Puck wants to win.

As Cal tries to keep both Niko and Robin from paying the
ultimate price for their kin, a horrific reminder from Cal's own
past arrives to remind him that blood is thicker than water—
and that's why it's so much more fun to spill.

**"Thurman continues to deliver strong
tales of dark urban fantasy."
—SF Revu**

Available wherever books are sold or at
penguin.com

facebook.com/AceRocBooks

AVAILABLE NOW FROM

SIMON R. GREEN

LIVE AND LET DROOD

The brand-new book in the series following *For Heaven's Eyes Only*.

Eddie Drood's family has been keeping the forces of evil contained in the shadows for as long as Droods have walked the earth. But now Eddie's entire family has been banished to an alternate dimension. And when he finds out who—or what—attacked his clan, there will be hell to pay...

Praise for the Secret Histories novels:

"Another action-packed melding of spy story and fantasy, featuring suave sleuthing, magical powers, and a generous dash of dry wit."
—*Kirkus Reviews*

Available wherever books are sold or at penguin.com

facebook.com/AceRocBooks

ROC

JIM BUTCHER
The Dresden Files

The #1 *New York Times* bestselling series

"Think *Buffy the Vampire Slayer* starring Philip Marlowe." —*Entertainment Weekly*

STORM FRONT

FOOL MOON

GRAVE PERIL

SUMMER KNIGHT

DEATH MASKS

BLOOD RITES

DEAD BEAT

PROVEN GUILTY

WHITE NIGHT

SMALL FAVOR

TURN COAT

CHANGES

SIDE JOBS

GHOST STORY

Available wherever books are sold or at penguin.com

R0037